Baddest
Bad Boys

Baddest
Bad Boys

SHANNON McKENNA
E.C. SHEEDY
CATE NOBLE

KENSINGTON PUBLISHING CORP.
http://www.kensingtonbooks.com

KENSINGTON BOOKS are published by

Kensington Publishing Corp.
119 West 40th Street
New York, NY 10018

All Kensington Titles, Imprints and Distributed Lines are available at special quantity discounts for bulk purchases for sales promotions, premiums, fund-raising, and educational or institutional use. Special book excerpts or customized printings can also be created to fit specific needs. For details, write or phone the office of the Kensington special sales manager: Kensington Publishing Corp., 119 West 40th Street, New York, NY 10018, attn: Special Sales Department, Phone: 1-800-221-2647.

Kensington and the K logo Reg. U.S. Pat. & TM Off.

ISBN-13: 978-1-4967-1100-7
ISBN-10: 1-4967-1100-9
First Kensington Trade Edition: May 2008
First Kensington Mass Market Edition: August 2018

eISBN-13: 978-0-7582-3242-7
eISBN-10: 0-7582-3242-X

10 9 8 7 6 5 4 3 2 1

Printed in the United States of America

CONTENTS

ANYTIME, ANYWHERE

Shannon McKenna

1

The phones had gone nuts, and she was following right behind. Robin MacNamara stabbed the buttons, repeating, "Crowne Royale Group, please hold," in her best cheerful chirp until she'd gotten the whole pesky lot of them distributed onto the switchboard and waiting their own freaking turns. Whew. She cracked a mental whip. Take *that*.

She stared at the row of flashing lights and sighed. A woman needed a cool head, a detail-oriented brain and nerves of steel to work a crazy-busy switchboard. She herself had none of those things. A fact which she repeated constantly to her stubborn brothers, in her ongoing campaign to get herself honestly fired. Which was to say, liberated.

So far, they ignored her, and she hadn't yet worked up the nerve to tell them she was quitting for good. Soon. Danny and Mac were an intimidating pair. Particularly when they ganged up on her, which was always. And worse, agreed with each other, which was relatively rare.

On this point, though, they were as one. They wanted

their little sister to discover a calling for the hotel industry, and they were willing to bully and nag without rest until it happened. Forever, if need be.

They would not accept what she really wanted to do. No, rephrase that. What she had *decided* to do. They thought being a professional clown was a joke. Ha ha. That wacky Robin. What will she think of next.

She had yet to find the nerve to tell them her amazing, stunning, nerve-tingling career news that they *so* would not get. She'd auditioned six months ago in San Francisco, and hooray, she'd been accepted into the Circo della Luna Rossa, a hot, sexy, new circus show from Italy that was getting rave reviews and sold-out crowds the world over. That she was starting the training program in San Francisco in less than a month. That it was a coup, an incredible accomplishment, an amazing opportunity. That they should be proud of her.

Uh-huh. Like they were going to see it that way. But even so. Until she told her brothers, it was not going to seem real. Or be real.

She took a deep breath, stabbed Line 1. "Thanks for holding, how may I direct your call?" Stock phrases singsonged out of her. *"I'm sorry, he's out of the office, would you like his voicemail? I'm sorry, she's in a meeting, may I take a message?"*

She was so not made for this. She would rather wait tables, wash dishes, walk dogs, scoop poop for her day job, until she could make it as a full time clown. Anything but this. Anything at all.

She plodded all the way down to the last one, Line 10, and hit it. "Thanks for holding," she sang out. "How may I direct your call?"

"Danny MacNamara, please. Jon Amendola calling."

She froze, and then her stomach flip-twirled and did

that weird, freefall thing. *Jon.* Oh, God. His deep voice sent pulses of excitement up her body. "One moment, please," she squeaked, and hit Hold again.

Don't be the receptionist from hell. He's already been waiting for five minutes, she told herself, but she was so rattled, she had to hug herself to squeeze that stuttering-fluttering-breathless feeling that any fleeting contact with that guy set off in her body. One . . . two . . . three breaths. OK. Get a grip. She was a big girl. She buzzed Danny's office.

"What is it, Robin?" Danny's voice was crabby, which was normal.

"It's Jon," she told him.

"Put him through," Danny rapped out, as she knew he would.

Danny never kept Jon waiting. They'd been roommates their freshman year in college, and best buddies ever since. Danny had brought Jon home for the Christmas and spring breaks, he being an orphan, just like the MacNamaras. She'd been eleven—and smitten.

Jon was tough, cynical, foul-mouthed, funny, and flat-out, drop dead gorgeous. He'd grown up knocking from foster home to foster home on the mean streets of North Portland, but he was smart and ambitious. He'd wangled himself a scholarship to U-Dub, studying criminal psych, and now he was Detective Amendola of the PPD.

And she'd been in love with him ever since she laid eyes on him.

Hopeless puppy love, impossible to hide. She'd never been able to hide her feelings. She was a blusher. But it didn't matter. They hadn't taken her seriously. She was just wacky little Robin, the clown, to them.

But she wasn't. Not anymore. Even if her brothers couldn't see it.

She was nine years younger than Jon. Twenty-five now, and all grown up, but probably he still thought of her as a gangly adolescent with glasses and orthodontic problems. The adult braces had been a big, fat fashion challenge. She'd been so glad to bid farewell to them forever last year, in exchange for straight, lovely teeth. *So* glad.

And that fluttery, stuttering thing was not abating, not while Line 10 was lit up. Not that she wanted it to. She actively sought out that feeling by sneaking often into Danny's office whenever possible to peek at the photo of Jon, Danny and herself, taken a few years ago, one of the times the guys had climbed Rainier. All of them grinning. Sunlight flashed off her braces. Other than that stupid detail, the picture rocked.

And if she didn't want to walk that far, she could just flip open her wallet and fish out the color photocopy she'd made of that same shot. She'd cut out herself and Danny, and slipped the Jon part into a plastic envelope. Just his face, laughing open-mouthed, head thrown back. Those perfect white teeth flashing, the crinkles around his electric blue eyes creased from laughing. The man was crazy gorgeous.

She could moon over that picture for hours. And sometimes did.

She stared down at the lit-up Line 10. Her finger hovered over it.

Oh, no. Of course she wouldn't. Couldn't. Eavesdropping was unethical, despicable. That she was tempted to do something so dumb, so contemptible, just showed how crushed out she was. Way too old for this silly juvenile crap, and no way was she going to—

Her finger came down, against her volition. Hit the button. *Tap.*

". . . would be great," Jon was saying. "This case I just closed did me in. I've been neck deep in shit. My boss doesn't want to see my face for two weeks, minimum. Gotta park my ass somewhere where I can't get into any trouble. You sure you or Mac won't be needing it?"

"Nah," said Danny. "Mac and Jane have the twins to deal with, and I'm taking up the slack at work. I won't be able to get up there until July at the earliest, so you'd be doing us a favor if you aired the place out, chased off the animals. Otherwise we'll find it full of raccoon shit."

"Good, then." Jon's voice was dull and heavy, not vibrating with its usual brilliant manic energy. "I appreciate it."

"You've still got the keys to my place, right? I'll be in meetings til nine. Keys to the cabin are hanging on the board next to the kitchen door on a red canvas strap. Sure you don't want to crash with me, and drive up tomorrow morning? We could order out. Do some catching up."

"Nah, sorry. I'll pass this time. I'm kind of fucked up right now. I wouldn't be very good company," Jon said. "Maybe on the outswing."

Mary Ann from accounting came bouncing by, and Robin hastily pushed Line 10 and flashed the woman a huge, guilty smile.

Another storm of phone calls came through, and Robin passed them all to the appropriate lines with a flurry of organizational energy that startled her. When she finished, Line 10 was dark and desolate.

But she buzzed with the new info. Her heart thumped. Jon, going up to Danny's cabin on Kerrigan Creek. All alone . . . and defenseless.

The idea that popped into her head was nuts. A recipe for total humiliation and embarrassment. But still, that lonely-cabin-in-the-woods scenario was a whole subcategory of classic Jon fantasies, right along with shipwrecked-with-Jon-on-a-desert-island, or snow-bound-with-Jon-in-the-Himalayas. Jon as the sexy pirate, she as the cheerfully ravished maiden. Jon as the macho Texas Ranger, she as the spunky saloon girl in low-cut black and red ruffles. Always Jon, Jon, Jon. She'd tried to plug Brad Pitt and George Clooney in, just for variety, but Brad and George didn't ring her bells like Jon did. A girl had to go with what worked, when it came to orgasms. And Jon—well, he worked. Bigtime.

And she was going to do a double backflip right out of the reception desk if she didn't move. She buzzed Eliza, the secretary who covered her potty breaks. "Eliza? Would you let me run to the ladies'?" she begged.

"Sure thing, Rob. Be there in a sec," Eliza promised.

Liberated from the monster console, she raced for the bathroom and locked herself into a stall, where she proceeded to rock back and forth and make terrified keening sounds that only dogs could hear. Oh, God, oh, God. This could be her chance. Could she . . . really?

Ever since she'd turned fourteen, Jon had ruffled her hair when he saw her and teased her about boyfriends. Were they behaving, and if not, did she want him to kick their asses. Boyfriends, hah. What a joke.

It was a sore spot. What with late blooming, and un-believably overprotective older brothers, she'd had precious few boyfriends. While she was living at home, the only guys who could get near her were ones that Danny and Mac deemed "safe." Which was to say, total nerds. All the guys with sneak-into-her-pants erotic potential had been duly scared away by dire threats of death and dismemberment.

To be fair, though, she hadn't had much time for guys even when she moved out, what with all the gymnastics competing she'd done in college. She'd been training like a fiend when she wasn't studying, or doing clown gigs. Besides, knuckle-dragging, inarticulate jocks didn't thrill her. Neither did alienated intellectuals with goatees. And the rest of them were gay. Or else madly in love with themselves.

The truth was, her monster crush on Jon had raised the bar impossibly high and made her insanely picky. The end result being a horrible state. Too dreadful to contemplate. Too shameful to confess.

A virgin, at twenty-five. And climbing the flipping walls.

She wasn't sure how it happened. She wasn't the virginal type. Really. It wasn't a moral thing, or a lifestyle choice. She had no hangups that she knew about. She had stacks of sexy romance and erotica books. And she definitely knew how to be her own best friend.

It was more a matter of poor timing, too much athletic training, and some regular, old-fashioned bad luck. She'd swung in close a few times, but always veered away at the last minute, never sure if it was the right moment, the right guy. So she never broke the ice, and the ice kept getting thicker, and . . . well, crapola. A very bad state of affairs.

She strongly suspected that one of the reasons she'd stayed untouched was because she'd dreamed for so long of having that first time be with Jon. She didn't have any illusions about him falling in love with her, or anything dumb-ass like that, but still. It would be great to have the guy she'd fantasized about since before puberty do the honors.

So she'd better get cracking, before he got another

girlfriend. Which would happen in, like, five minutes?
Jon always had a girlfriend. He went through women
like popcorn. Worse yet, he could get married again.
His marriage to Vicki the blond bombshell had shattered Robin's heart. The subsequent ugly, vicious di-
vorce had promptly mended it.

She left the stall, and stared at herself in the mirror.
Danny and Mac went ballistic when she showed off
her navel, so she made a special point of it. Still, she
wasn't glamorous enough in the snug, lime green
blouse and mini, bare midriff or no. She'd have to do
better than this.

And she'd been in too much of a rush this morning
to do anything interesting with her hair that would
bother her brothers, like a towering neo-punk beehive,
or the purple and lime green streaks with matching
eyeshadow, or the space alien checkerboard of knob-
bly buns. It was just pulled up into a fountaining brown
ponytail. But for this, she'd wear it down and loose.
Down was sexiest, or so she'd been told.

She gave her body a critical once-over. She'd been
working out like a freak to get ready for the Circo della
Luna Rossa's training program, so no problems there.
She was lithe and trim. Had the taut tummy and the
boobs happening, thank God. They weren't excessive,
but they were perky and cheerful, and they did their di-
vinely ordained boobly duty of filling out her bra and
dragging mens' eyes away from her face. Jon had never
looked at them yet. So she'd wear something sheer. Put
those boobs to work. About time they stopped bouncing
aimlessly around on her chest and started earning their
keep.

She smiled experimentally as she studied her own
face, trying to see what Jon would see. Hmm. She

knew, objectively at least, that she was relatively cute, particularly with some cosmetic help, but she still saw her awkward younger face superimposed over her actual face, in spite of all the changes. The glasses, now exchanged for contacts. That thick dark mono-brow, now carefully shaped into normal eyebrows. The buck teeth, finally, blessedly, fixed. And of course, her embarrassing emotions. Sprawled out there, for all to see and marvel at.

That was one of the reasons she'd been attracted to clowning in the first place. Facial transparency was an actual asset. Expressions had to be exaggerated and super-readable by necessity. Once she stuck that red nose on her face, something kicked in, and set her free, like a bird in the air. She hit the zone, and people laughed. Beautiful.

But Danny and Mac didn't get it. She wondered if Jon could.

Then again. He was a cop, after all. It was a dark, tough, serious job. Probably clowning would seem silly and frivolous to a guy like him.

But hey. It wasn't like she needed approval for her career choices from Jon Amendola. She needed something very different. Very specific.

She gave herself another smile. It looked tense, false. Scared. She let it fade, and in that naked moment, she saw a flash of something different in the mirror. Her future. Her woman's face. Older, more defined. Vulnerable too, but in a different way. A deeper, realer way.

It occurred to her how different life was going to feel once she abandoned her protective shell. She usually blamed her brothers for it, but she'd done her own part in creating it and maintaining it. It had kept her focused on her goals, sure. And it had also kept her safe.

It was too small for her now. It chafed and pinched. Pressure from the inside, opposing pressure from the outside. Crushing her.

She didn't want to start a difficult, challenging adventure like the Circo della Luna Rossa with this extra inner struggle to cope with.

Then again. Once she broke the spell, once she cast off that shell, that was it. No going back. She'd be out in the cold, where the wind whipped and the wolves howled. Where anything could happen. Brrr.

She shivered, and then blew out a sharp breath and straightened her spine to its proudest height. This was no time to wimp out.

Besides. Jon was a wolf, yeah, but not that kind of wolf. He was exactly, precisely the right kind of wolf for this job. And the chance for a good whack at him might never roll around again. Her, Jon, alone and surrounded by the immense privacy of the Cascade Mountains—mmm.

The shiver that rippled through her then was very different—a toe curling, lip biting, thigh clenching tingle of hopeful anticipation. *Whew.*

Enough already. This potty break had stretched out to unprofessional proportions. She had to get her butt back to the monster console before Eliza got annoyed and sent out a posse to retrieve her.

Danny swept by as she was plugging herself back into the infernal machine, his habitual fierce scowl of concentration on his face. "You coming to Mac and Jane's for dinner tomorrow?" he rapped out.

She blinked. "Uh . . . nope. Sorry. Can't," she lied. "I'm working back to back birthday parties all afternoon, and I've got a Commedia Dell' Arte class in the evening. Til late. Very late."

Danny snorted, and charged off on his important CFO business. Both brothers were like that. Alpha didn't begin to describe it.

She sat in the ergonomic chair and vibrated. Doubts assailed her thick and fast. Jon had said he was bad company. Neck deep in shit. He'd sounded depressed. He'd probably be unthrilled to see her.

Yeah, and that was exactly the kind of chickenshit, cowardly-ass reasoning that produced twenty-five-year-old virgins.

It was now or never. If he blew her off, she'd cope. She might fall into a crack in the ground and be crushed to a fine paste first, of course, but then she would just stick on that red nose and soldier on.

Jon jerked up the emergency brake on his pickup and sat there, feeling blank. The light was almost gone. He should move, so he didn't have to fumble through the dark. He didn't have the goddamn energy.

The Geddes case had gotten to him. He didn't know why. He'd worked plenty of grisly murders over the years, but this one wiped him out. Wallowing inside the twisted mind of this perp had poisoned him.

William Geddes, the "Egg Man." So called for the blue robin's egg he'd place into the mouth of his victims—after he'd killed them, with agonizing slowness, in ways that defied the imagination. Five girls that they knew of, ages eighteen to twenty-two. Just thinking about the guy's frozen face and staring eyes in the courtroom gave him the shudders. Fucking head case. And Jon had seen a lot of bad shit.

He'd finally nailed that pustulant shitbag, but not

until five girls—at least, he hoped to God it was only five—had died, badly. The trial had wrapped up a couple weeks ago, a drawn-out, sprawling media circus, full of press and politics and pontificating bullshit. But he'd seen to it that the prosecution's case had been watertight.

Geddes would be inside forever. Five consecutive life sentences, in a maximum security hellhole where that pumped up prick's blond Viking good looks would not go unappreciated. Jon took a fierce satisfaction in that. Justice had been done, insofar as possible.

Cold comfort for the families of the girls, though.

So? He should be feeling accomplishment. Maybe even pride.

But he felt like shit. Nervous, jagged, on edge. He couldn't sleep. He had nightmares, about blood, birds. He was tormented by details that couldn't be explained. Uneasy about vibes that didn't add up. He couldn't pin down what the problem was. But he felt like it wasn't over.

His boss hadn't liked it, either. She'd kicked his ass out on a mandatory vacation after he'd been caught one too many times poring over the Geddes files after the conviction. That stung. He was a good cop. The one thing he knew he was good at. He may have been a rotten husband, he may be a no-good boyfriend, and God forbid he ever have kids. But when someone dissed him as a cop, it got his back way up.

It was the one thing in his life that he gave a shit about these days, though he knew damn well it was dangerous to care too much about anything. He'd grown up in a series of foster homes, some OK, some less so. He'd seen too many kids get exploited by predators.

Now, when he heard about innocent kids being abused, something revved up inside him that he couldn't control. Sleep wasn't even an option. He started putting in those thirty-six-hour days without even getting tired.

Or maybe that was overstating it. Look at him now. Monumentally fucked up. He got an unwelcome memory flash of how Vicki used to nag and bitch about how emotionally unavailable he was. But how could a guy be available to a woman who constantly whined? He tried briefly to remember if Vicki had whined during their whirlwind courtship. Maybe she had, and he'd been too hypnotized by her big, jiggling tits to notice.

Fuck it. This line of thought was not going to energize him.

He forced his leaden body into action. Shoved open the truck door, grabbed his grip and the bag of groceries. He made his way with heavy feet up the switchback path to the hillside cabin—and froze.

Footsteps around the corner of the cabin. Someone was passing through the foliage. The *shush-shush* of jeans legs, rubbing each other. The *swish-slap* of bushes. He heard every sound like it was miked.

He let the duffel, the groceries drop. His gun materialized in his hand, though he had no memory of drawing it, or flattening his back to the weatherbeaten shingles, creeping towards the corner . . . waiting—

Grab, twist, and he had the fucker bent over in a hammerlock, wrist torqued at an agonizing angle, gun to the nape. It squawked.

Female. Long hair, swishing and tickling over his bare arm. A delicate wrist that felt like it might break in his grip. What the *hell?*

"Jon! Stop this! Let go! It's me!"

Huh? The chick knew him? His body had ascertained that she was no physical threat, so he shoved her away to take a better look.

His jaw dropped when she straightened up, rubbing her twisted wrist. He tried to drag in oxygen, but his lungs were locked. Holy shit. No way had he met this girl before. He would have remembered. *Wow.*

Long hair swung to her waist. Big dark eyes, exotically tilted, flashing with anger. High cheekbones, perfect skin, pointy chin. That full pink mouth, glossed up with lip goo, calculated to make a guy think of one thing only, and suffer the immediate physiological consequences.

And her body, Jesus. Feline grace; long legs, slim waist, round hips. High, suckable, braless tits, the nipples of which poked through a thin cotton blouse. Low-rise jeans that clung desperately to the undercurve of that perfect ass. Who the hell . . . ? This was private property, in the middle of nowhere. His dick twitched, swelled.

She did not look armed. He slipped the Glock back into the shoulder holster. "You scared me," he said. "Who the hell are you?"

Her eyes widened in outrage. "What do you mean, who the hell am I? It's me! Robin!"

Robin? His brain spun its wheels to reconcile the irreconcilable.

Danny's baby sister? He'd practically pissed himself laughing the night she'd juggled flaming torches in Danny's kitchen, although Danny had been unamused when the rib-eye he'd grilled got unexpectedly flambéed. The steak had tasted faintly of petroleum fuel, but what the hell. She hadn't burned down the building.

Robin? Robin of the dorky glasses, the mouthful of metal? Robin who was as cute and funny as a bouncing labrador puppy?

The irreconcilable images slammed together, like a truck hitting his mind. Those big brown eyes, magnified behind Coke bottle lenses.

It *was* Robin. Holy shit. In his mind he'd already been nailing this girl, right and left and center. Danny would kill him if he knew Jon had entertained pornographic thoughts about his baby sister. "Ah, sorry," he muttered lamely. "I didn't recognize you. You look . . . different than I remembered. Do your brothers know you're out dressed like that?"

Her back straightened and her eyes narrowed to gleaming brown slits. "Mac and Danny have nothing to say about my wardrobe."

"Maybe they should." He jerked his chin in the general direction of her taut brown nipples, all too evident in the chill, and averted his eyes.

"Why should they?" Her slender arms folded over her chest, propping the tits up higher for his tormented perusal. "I'm twenty-five, Jon. That's a two, and then a five."

He blinked at her. "No shit."

"Absolutely, shit. Want to see my driver's license? I wear what I please. I answer to no one."

This was surreal. He dragged his eyes away from her gleaming pink lips, and pulled himself together. "Uh, I don't mean to be rude, but what the fuck does your age have to do with anything? And what are you doing up here, anyhow?"

The gleaming lips pursed. "I could ask you the same question."

"You could," he conceded. "But it would be none of your goddamn business. Your brother gave me the keys.

I'm crashing up here for a couple weeks to do some fishing and stare at the wall with my mouth hanging open. And now? Your turn. What did you come up here for?"

Her gaze fell. She started to speak. Pressed her hand to her belly.

"Um . . . you," she said.

2

Jon looked at her. Twilight deepened in visible increments. He cleared his throat. "Could you clarify what the fuck you mean by that?"

Robin threw her head back to look into his eyes. "I don't need to clarify anything. You understand me perfectly well."

"You mean . . ." His mouth stopped moving. He just couldn't say it. It was evidently too horrific an idea to him, too shocking to verbalize.

Mayday. Going down. She resisted the urge to wrap her goose-bumped arms over her braless, much too visible boobs. "Yes," she said.

A scowl furled his brows together. "You have got to be kidding."

Hope soured inside her. "I've never been so serious in my life."

He was starting to look pissed, as if someone were playing an unfunny joke on him. "What put this crazy shit into your head?"

"It's been in my head for over ten years," she announced.

He couldn't stop shaking his head. "I cannot believe it," he muttered. "I cannot fucking believe it. This is all I need. Come on, let's get inside." She followed him arround the side of the cabin. He turned, scowling, when he found the door open. "What the hell?"

"I have a key," she said simply. "I've been here for a while."

His gaze sharpened. "Did Danny tell you I was coming up here?"

She bit her lip, and looked away. "Not exactly."

"Wait. You were the receptionist today, right? Did you listen in?"

She flushed. "Um . . ."

"Bad." He shook his head at her, scowling. "Bad karma."

She lifted her chin. "A girl's gotta do what a girl's gotta do."

"Yeah, well, you're not gonna do me. Get your ass in here. And sit. Down. *Now.*"

His voice snapped like a whipcrack, working on her nerves in some mysterious way that made her body obey before she knew what she was doing. Suddenly she was sitting, ramrod straight in the dim kitchen. On the spot. She regretted having chosen the tight, sheer chemise top. He was so big, vibrating intense man energy at her.

"Don't glare at me," she said sulkily.

"What's going on?" he demanded. "Are you on the rebound? Do you want to make some guy jealous? What's the deal?"

"There's no deal." She tried to lick her lips, and tasted the strawberry-flavored gloss she'd glopped over it. "And there's no boyfriend."

"Then why the *fuck* are you here?"

She flinched at the harsh punch of his voice. The truth popped right out, like it always did when she was put on the spot. "Because I'm tired of waiting for this to happen! And I wanted you to be the first!"

"First?" His eyes went wary. "You mean to say you've never . . . oh, holy fuck. You've never . . ." He sounded afraid to just up and say it.

"Yes! I do mean that! I want you to break the ice for me, OK? That's all! Just . . . do the honors. So I can exhale and get on with it! I won't get clingy on you. I don't expect you to fall in love with me or—"

"That," he said, through gritted teeth, "is fortunate."

His clipped tone chilled her, but the damage was done. She might as well just go for it. "It's just this one little thing. To break the spell."

He looked ferociously offended. "Little thing? You call that little? It's not. And it's flat out against my rules. So you can fucking forget it."

"Rules?" She goggled at him. "You have rules about this?"

"Yeah. I do. Let me get this straight. You want me to just pop your cherry and then walk away, and pretend I didn't just fuck my best friend's baby sister? No, scratch that—my best friend's *virginal* baby sister. What kind of opportunistic asshole do you think I am?"

"I am not a baby!" She leaped to her feet. "Do I look like a baby?"

"You're acting like one. If Danny knew I was having this conversation, he'd rip out my intestines and strangle me with them."

"But he doesn't know!" she protested. "And he won't! Get it?"

"Great. Even better. Now you're asking me to lie to my friend."

"No, I am not!" she flared. "Keeping your private life private is not lying! It's none of Danny's business!"

Jon snorted. "You know, I very much doubt he'd see it that way."

"Danny and Mac are the reason I have this problem in the first place!" she raged. "All through school! It never failed! Any time a guy ever got near me, he got The Talk. If he did anything more than hold my hand, they'd threaten to break every bone in his body with a hammer."

He was trying not to smile, the bastard. "So I get to be the chump asshole who gets the compound fractures? Wow. I'm so honored."

"It's not funny." Robin spat the words out. "I am not laughing."

"I see that. But there's a good reason your brothers try to protect you. Men are filthy dogs. They're men themselves, so they know this. I don't blame them for doing it, and neither should you."

"Well, I'm sick of it! It's going to end, one way or another. I'm out of here. Goodbye, Jon. I'm really sorry I bothered you."

She tried to flounce past him, but he grabbed her arm and swung her back around. She landed in the chair again with a grunt.

"Where do you think you're going?" he asked.

"To lose my virginity." She flung the words at him.

"Oh, yeah?" His eyes narrowed to bright, glittering slits. "To who?"

She shrugged. "I don't know yet. I had what I thought was a workable plan, but it blew up in my face. Time to move on to Plan B."

"And what's Plan B?"

"Oh, the usual techniques. Bars. Clubs. Tight clothes, high heels, too much alcohol. Whatever it takes."

She launched herself out of the chair, and got thumped right back down again. He held her in a vise grip. "You're not going to do that."

"Let go of me." She flailed and wiggled. "You don't like virgins? Fine. The next time you see me, I'll be an ex-virgin. I promise."

He gripped her upper arms and lifted her out of the chair and up off her feet, so she dangled there like a doll. He bumped her up against the wood paneled wall. "No way. I'll be damned if I'll let you go out there and let some random fuckhead wipe his feet on your body."

"Tough shit," she hissed, shoving at his chest. "It's not up to you!"

"It is now." His voice was grim.

Tears of humiliation welled into her eyes. "Get your hands off me."

His grip loosened. She sank down from her tiptoes onto her feet.

He loomed over her, still frowning. "Robin," he said, his voice gentler. "Listen to me. You want your first time to be with a guy who worships you. Who's overcome with the honor. Not with some bar scum who just wants to score. I'm sorry, but I just can't let that happen."

Their gazes locked, and something happened. The air got thick, hot. Hard to breathe, like it had turned to viscous liquid. Jon looked almost scared. He lifted his hand from her face and took two quick steps back.

"I am not that guy," he said warily. "I am a selfish bastard. I've got an ex-wife and a string of ex-girlfriends who all hate my guts. I'm not nice and I'm not gentle, and I don't worship anybody or anything."

"You've always been nice to me," she whispered.

"That was a big mistake. One that I won't be making again." He dug his cell phone out of his pocket and started punching it.

She grabbed his arm, alarmed. "Who are you calling?"

"Danny." He held the phone to his ear.

"No way!" She lunged for the phone. "He and Mac will kill me!"

"Should have thought about that before." He peered at the display. "Shit. He's still in his meeting. Phone's turned off. Lucky you."

"You asshole!" Her voice was fogged with angry tears.

"Thank God, she's starting to face reality."

Robin wheeled away and dove for the door. His arm clamped under her rib cage from behind and lifted her right off her feet. "Uh-huh. You're not going anywhere until one of your brothers is here to escort you. I don't want the responsibility."

"I have my car here," she snapped. "I have to drive it down."

"So I'll tell Danny to bring Mac up. He can drive your car down."

She bucked and flailed. "You cannot do this to me!"

"Watch me." His voice was steely.

"I'm not a minor! My brothers don't have any authority over me!"

"That's their problem, thank God. Not mine. Nod if you're going to be good. If you mess with me, I'll cuff you to the stove. Understand?"

She nodded. He shoved her down into the chair. His footsteps receded. She gauged the distance to the door, got up and tiptoed—

"Don't even try it. Sit your ass back down."

She spun around, nerves jangling. Jon tossed her a tattered gray sweatshirt. "It smells like mold, but it's better than . . . that." He jerked his chin at her chemise top.

Bossy, controlling bastard. He was worse than both her brothers put together. Anger made her bold. She tilted up her rib cage, making her boobs strain against the buttons. "Do my tits scare you, Jon?"

His mouth tightened, as his eyes flicked down to her chest.

An unfamiliar sense of power unfurled inside her. An instinct to push him, and then push him harder, just to see where it went. She reached up, popped the top button of her chemise.

"Don't you dare." His voice was hoarse and menacing.

"What are you going to do?" she taunted, popping a second button. "Turn me over your knee? Spank me?"

He advanced on her, until he was inches from her, staring down into her face. "Don't mess with me, Robin," he warned. "Just . . . don't."

"Why not? You're completely safe, right? You don't want me. You have a rule. I'm off limits. So why not have my slutty fun with you?"

He tilted her chin up. "Look into my eyes. Do you know where you're going when you push me? Are you sure you want to go there?"

She gazed back, and realized that she wasn't. She'd thought she was, but she'd imagined a tender seduction that would make her feel, well, safe. That predatory glow in his eyes was anything but.

Nope. She didn't have the nerve. He was so angry. So big. So . . . hard looking. She broke eye contact. *Chickenshit.* Tears stung her eyes.

He had the gall to look relieved that she'd backed down. Bastard.

"I'm going to fix some dinner while we wait for Danny to call me back," he said. "Put on the goddamn sweatshirt."

Robin sighed, and pulled the chilly, mildewed fabric over her head. When her face emerged from the frayed neck, he held out a plastic bag of tomatoes and cucumbers, a look of challenge on his face.

"Make yourself useful," he said. "Do the salad."

Jon focused on the garlic he was slicing into spikes, which he then stabbed with unnecessary fierceness into the thick steak he was about to grill. Good thing he'd left on that denim shirt. Or she'd take one look at his tent-pole hard-on, and know she had him cold. Millimeters away from falling to his knees. Begging for a piece of that.

He wasn't sure if the sweatshirt helped. The damage was done. The sweatshirt was slipping off one gleaming golden shoulder. Her skin was so soft. His hands itched to touch her again to confirm that sensation. And other sensations, beckoning him. Like the long, sinewy curve of her taut belly. The swell and hollows of her hips. The nipples of those plump cupcake boobs, straining against thin lace. Sweet.

He squeezed his brain, did the math again. She'd been ten, eleven when he met her. He'd been, what, twenty? A smart-ass, swaggering hoodlum. Yeah. It tracked. Twenty-five. Wow. He was thirty-four. That was still a big, eyebrow waggling, wink-wink, nudge-nudge age gap, even if it wasn't out and out cradle robbing. And what the fuck was he thinking, anyway? Was he actually trying to justify . . . ?

Whoa. No way. Down, boy. She was Mac and Danny's precious princess. She would always be a baby to them, and this thing was a fucking train wreck in the making. He could feel it. He valued his friendship with Danny. He wasn't going to screw around with it. Uh-uh.

He shook salt and pepper over the garlic-impaled meat, set the rice to boil on the propane stovetop. A thudding sound made him turn.

She was juggling. Five fat hothouse tomatoes were in the air, whirling in a dizzying circle. "Robin," he complained. "What the hell?"

"I'm tense," she said, her voice distant. "Juggling relaxes me. I can take another one. Give me another. Go on. Toss me one."

"But that's my dinner," he said, plaintively. "Can't you relax yourself juggling something else? How about rolls of toilet paper?"

"Shut up. Throw me another." Her concentration never wavered.

He groaned, grabbed a tomato, intuited her rhythm, and tossed.

Sure enough. She danced back, eyes far away as the sixth tomato flew perilously close to the ceiling. Hair swung, hands flashed, as she maintained perfect equilibrium in constant movement. She was good.

And gorgeous. Out of her skull, maybe, but total eye candy. How could he have missed it for so long? She'd sucker-punched him. He stared at the dick-tingling-spectacle for several awestruck minutes.

"How did you reach twenty-five still a virgin?" he asked.

Splat, a tomato landed at his feet, exploding juice and seeds all over his shoes. Robin caught the others, *thuddity thud thud* in her crooked arm, looking abashed. "How could you ask a question like that to a woman who's got six tomatoes in the air?" She dumped them on the counter, grabbed a paper towel. "Sorry," she said. "Can I—"

"I'll do it." He snatched the towel out of her hands and wiped the mess off himself. No way was he letting her kneel in front of him for a front-row view of his boner. He dropped the towel into the plastic bag designated as garbage, and triple checked that the shirt was closed over his crotch. "You haven't answered my question," he prompted.

Robin's mouth tightened. She sliced a cucumber, tossed it in the bowl. "It just happened," she said quietly. "In high school, it was mostly Max and Danny, and The Talk. And in college, I was super busy, with training, gymnastics competitions, clown gigs. There was never time for it to happen. And then . . . I guess I wanted . . ." Her voice trailed off.

"Yeah?" he prompted, relentless. "What did you want?"

"I didn't want it to be just anyone," she whispered.

"Right. You were hoping for someone special. Who's crazy about you. And so you should," he said vehemently. "So you should."

She hacked a tomato in half. "Don't start in on me again," she said. "Believe me, I heard you. It was bad enough the first time around."

"Hey. You're the one who started this, birdie, and I—"

"Do. Not. Call. Me. That. Ever again, hear?"

He glanced at her, startled. Her face was hot pink, eyes sparkling with anger. "What? Why? Your brothers always used to—"

"Yeah. When I was a fucking *infant* they did. Not anymore. They've learned. The hard way. I've got a name, Jon. Use it."

He was a contrary, smart-ass bastard by nature, and saw no reason at all to downplay that quality, being as how he was not, repeat, *not* getting laid tonight. He gave her a toothy, in-your-face grin. "Don't get your panties in a wad, birdie. I think it's kind of cute."

Thwanngggg. The chef's knife she'd been chopping with quivered in the doorjamb, two feet from his head. He stared at it. His jaw sagged.

"Uh, Robin?" he said faintly. "You just threw a knife. At me."

Robin's hands were on her hips. Her eyes had a hot battle glow. "No, Jon," she said sweetly. "If I had thrown a knife at you, it would be sticking out of you. It's sticking out of the wall. Important distinction."

"It's two feet from my head!" he protested.

"Yes? And? Your point is?"

He took a deep breath, and shoved the words out from behind a wall of gritted teeth. "I don't want you to do that. Ever again."

She shrugged. "I'm sure that you don't," she said lightly.

The nerve of the chick was mind-boggling. He glared at her. "I do not like knives flying at my—"

"Of course you don't. Duh. I grew up with a couple of big lunks like you and I found, by trial and error, that the most successful form of communication with them is non-verbal. Bet you'll think before that nickname comes out of your mouth again, won't you? Admit it."

He yanked the knife out of the doorjamb, shoved her out of the way and proceeded to slice up the abused tomato himself. "Just shut up, Robin," he muttered. "You're bugging me."

He loaded her up with fluffy, buttered rice, salad and

a juicy chunk of seared sirloin, and slapped the plate down in front of her. Then he pulled the beer out of the bag, and gave her a doubtful glance.

She gave him a look. "Yes. In case you were wondering, twenty-five is definitely old enough to drink a beer. Thanks, yes. I'll have one."

He shrugged, popped the top, handed her the long-necked bottle.

"My turn to ask embarrassing provocative questions," she said.

He sawed off a chunk of steak. "What do you want to know?"

"What have you got against virgins?"

He choked on the beer, and coughed. "Virgins are bad news. I don't touch them with a ten-foot pole. I learned the hard way."

"But everybody was a virgin, once," she argued. "Even you!"

"Was I? Really? I barely remember," he said blandly.

"But why?" she persisted. "If it's just a matter of skill—"

"Nah." He waved her words away with his beer bottle. "It's not that. It's that virgins are walking emotional bombs. They fall in love the first time you fuck them, if you do it right. And then it's a bad scene."

She rolled her eyes. "Oh, please. That's ridiculous."

"And furthermore. If you're stupid enough to actually give a shit about a chick that you've de-virginized, she'll tear you to pieces the minute she starts wondering what she's missing with other guys."

"Well." She harrumphed. "That's hardly relevant in our case—"

"They can't help it," he went on. "And I don't blame them for it, either. It's just natural curiosity. Everybody needs a wide range of sexual experience to find out what they like. What works for them. But that's when guy number one gets fucked up the ass. Bummer for him."

Robin left a delicate pause. "I have a feeling you could provide a pretty broad range of experience all by yourself," she murmured.

He shook his head stubbornly. "If a guy is stupid enough to do a virgin, he has to be calculated about it. Cold. Pop 'em and drop 'em."

She let out a snort of startled laughter. "That's so crass."

"You bet it is. See why it's not in your best interests?"

"No, I don't, Jon. That's literally what I was asking you to do!"

"Pop you and drop you? Are you fucking nuts?" He stared into her eyes until her gaze dropped. "You know damn well I can't do that."

She stared down into her plate. "It just seemed so simple to me," she muttered rebelliously.

"It's not simple when sex is mixed into it. Not going to happen."

"You don't have to tell me a tenth time," she snapped. "I heard you the first nine times. You don't want me. Fine. So just let me leave!"

"Uh-uh, Robin." His voice was flat and matter of fact. "The question is not 'do I want to fuck you.' Of course I want to fuck you. Any guy with a pulse would want to fuck you."

She blinked into his intense gaze for a startled moment. She jerked her eyes away and gulped her beer, starting to blush hotly. "Um. Really. That, uh, hasn't really been my experience so far, but thanks."

"The question is whether I want to deal with the cat-astrophe that will crash down on me afterwards," he went on.

She let out a sharp sigh. "Well, then. No wonder I stayed untouched for so long. Men wilt before my cat-astrophic—"

"No," he said. "Wilting is definitely not my prob-lem."

Excitement vibrated inside her. Um, wow. This was clearly the part where she should tease, seduce, or trick him into doing what she wanted. But she was so not a tricky girl. What-you-see-is-what-you-get Robin, that was her. She pushed her empty plate away, and blurted, "Does this mean you're considering it? Or are you just torturing me?"

"Neither," he said blandly. "I'm just telling you how it is. Nothing has changed."

Her heart sank. That was disheartening, but she de-cided to be cautiously optimistic. After all, Danny hadn't called back yet. She had til then to cajole Jon into changing his mind.

"Get enough to eat?" He polished off his steak juice with a hunk of bread, eyeing her emptied plate. "You need some more?"

"No, thanks, I'm good," she said. "You're a good cook."

"If I keep it simple. Want to wash the dishes, or build the fire?"

Hah. No-brainer. She grinned at him. "I'll make the fire."

He looked hurt. "Hey! What the hell? I cooked!"

"I did the salad," she pointed out.

"You juggled the salad," he grumbled. "You man-gled the salad. Before risking my life with the knife. That doesn't count as helping."

Robin ignored that, and lit another kerosene lamp. She carried it into the living room and got busy at the fireplace. The sound of clanking of pots floated in from the kitchen as she assembled kindling.

By the time Jon came in, she had a nice fire crackling in the grate, and he was drying his hands on the legs of his jeans, looking put upon. She stifled a giggle. Just like her brothers. Men and dishes.

"Jon?" she ventured. "What I said, about going to a club to pick up a guy? I just want you to know . . . that I wouldn't. I just said it because I was angry. So there's no need to get Danny and Mac all riled up. Mac's short on sleep anyway, what with the twins. So I'll just—"

"You're not going anywhere. It's pitch dark, on a washboard road with hairpin curves, and you've got a beer in you. You're sleeping here."

She stood, brushing bark dust off her hands. "Don't muscle me around. I get enough from Mac and Danny. I don't need it from you."

"You picked out the wrong guy to throw yourself at, then," he said curtly. "Sit your ass down. You're not going anywhere tonight."

She fell into the couch, twisting handfuls of the mildewed shirt. He sat next to her, bowing the springs into a deep well, hands resting on his thighs. His profile was so stark. Carved cheekbones, that grim, sexy mouth. God, she loved that bump on his nose. Always had.

"There's something I want to know," he said slowly.

"If it's sexual in nature, I don't want to tell you," she said swiftly.

He slanted her a glance. "You're the one who set the tone for the evening when you invited me to pop your cherry," he observed.

"Don't remind me. It's indelicate," she said tartly.

"Besides, you turned me down flat. So you have no right to keep harping on it."

"Exactly how much of a virgin are you?" he asked baldly.

She squinted at him, uncomprehending. "Huh? You mean, there are degrees? It's not quantitative, Jon. You are or you aren't."

"There are always degrees," he said. "How about oral? Done it?"

She pulled her knees to her chest, muscles clenching around the rush of startled arousal that the question had provoked. "Nope."

"You mean, you've never given it, or you've never gotten it?"

"Neither one," she said. "Strange, but true."

He let out a low whistle. "Ever jerked a guy off?"

She covered her pinkening face. "Ah, no."

"Finger fucking?" he went on. "Has any guy ever made you come?"

She thought about it, biting her lip. "Well . . . there was this party in college once. I drank too much, and passed out on a pile of coats. And when I woke up, this guy I barely knew had his hand in my underwear. It was really gross. So I guess that doesn't count."

"I guess not." His face was hard. "What did you do?"

"Screamed," she admitted. "Kicked him."

"Good," he said savagely. "Asshole. I'm glad you woke up when you did. Who was the shit?"

"Who cares?" she asked.

"I do," he said. "Guys who molest unconscious girls deserve to be neutered. To improve the quality of the human gene pool."

"Oh." She peeked at his profile. "I don't remember his name."

The fire crackled. Crazy shadows from the flickering lamp roamed over the walls. She stared at the stark planes and shadows of his face, and wondered if she should read any softening of his position into all these sexually charged questions. She didn't know him that well, in spite of having a crush on him for fourteen years.

But hell with it. He'd had a little time to get used to the shocking idea. And he was asking questions that made her thighs tingle and her face turn pink. What did she have to lose? Why not just . . . try again?

More aggressively, this time. Men were simple physical creatures, or so she'd been told. In thrall to their own bodies. Stimulus equals response. The only problem now was that she was too scared to move.

For God's sake. She wasn't asking him to marry her. She wanted what he gave a different woman every week. No big fucking deal. Really.

She got up, pulled off the sweatshirt, and felt his tension rise.

"Put that right back on," he said softly.

She spun, with a burst of fierce resolve, planted her knee next to him and swung the other over his lap. He made a shocked sound, and tried to wrestle her off. She countered by putting her weight on his crotch. His fingers tightened on her arms. "What the fuck is this?"

"I just want to convince you that it's worth the catastrophe."

He caught his breath as she undulated on his lap. "Oh, God."

"It's not your fault," she assured him. "Don't worry. You're absolved of blame. I jumped you. There was nothing you could do."

"Bullshit! I outweigh you by at least eighty pounds! Get off me!"

She took a deep breath, arched her back, popped open

the buttons on her chemise top. One . . . then two . . . three. It gaped.

He stared down at her, his breathing quickening. "Oh, Jesus."

She shrugged the garment off. "You don't have to go all the way, if you're so anxious," she coaxed. "But could you reduce my virgin status by a few dinky, insignificant percentage points? Is it so much to ask?"

His hands were shaking. "It doesn't work that way."

"No? Why not?" She cuddled closer. "Just touch me. Please, Jon."

She pried his hands off her arms. His fingers had left marks. She dropped soothing kisses on his hands, uncurled the clawed fingers, and pressed them against her breasts. He made a harsh, gasping sound.

She gasped, went motionless. She'd been so focused on getting this far with him, she'd lost sight of her feelings. The fear, the hunger. The electric touch of his hot, callused hands made full awareness come roaring back. And the movements she made against his body were far from calculated now. They were involuntary.

Jon put both hands on her breasts, cupping them. He ran his thumbs around her taut nipples, and made a low, tortured sound.

Then he leaned forward and put his mouth to her.

3

Stop. Just stop it. Put her perfect squirming ass some-where other than right on top of your dick. Then go fall face first into the snowmelt, and cool . . . the fuck . . . *down. Now.*

The orders weren't making it to command central, though, and this crazy thing was picking up momen-tum while the rational, adult choice maker inside him watched, tied and gagged.

Her tits were perfect. The springy softness and those puckered nipples, the sinuous way she moved, oh, Jesus. So sexy. So silky and smooth and gorgeous. Too much. He was on overload.

She cradled his head in her slender arms, whimper-ing, her slender body shivering at each hungry stroke of his tongue, and all he could think was how much he wanted to peel off those jeans, spread her out and show her just how big the trouble she was in really was.

Whoa. She wasn't up for anything wild. Even if he were going to indulge. Which he wasn't. She was a vir-gin. Full of soft focus, pink-tinged, unrealistic expecta-tions. Programmed to go gooey on him. To say nothing of way too small. Turned on as he was, he couldn't be as gentle as he would need to be. That kind of thing required cast-iron self control. Hah. He was in danger of coming in his pants like a kid.

Her naked waist was clamped in his hands, so narrow, his fingers almost touched, but he felt the catlike play of lean, lithe muscle beneath. His hands roved hungrily, exploring that deep curve, that flare, those jeans that barely clung to her hips. The cleft of her ass.

Her hair was silky against his face. Her lips soft against his hot forehead. Her lip gloss smelled sugary, fruity. He was salivating to taste it, to lick and savor those soft, full, shining lips. Find her tongue. Kiss her senseless. She flung her head back, eyes closed, breath quickening.

Oh, man. She was moving in on her first climax, already. He clamped her hips against himself, sucked in air. Hung on for take-off.

Jesus. Like being on the inside of a fountain of light.

She arched, and he caught her, felt every violent pulse wrench through her and slowly fade to a sweet, lingering tremor of pleasure.

Wow. He hadn't done a damn thing to make that happen. She'd done it all herself. And now he was worse off than before. Now he was in a world of hurt. Restless, desperate. Fucking furious, at himself, at her.

Robin lifted her head. Her face glowed with a sheen of sweat. Her lips were red, gleaming. They shook. "Kiss me," she whispered.

His whole body clamored to obey. "No," he said harshly.

She looked startled. "But you—but we—"

"Forget it." Kissing would blow his lid off, even more than fucking would. He couldn't. He felt too shriveled and blackened inside to risk it. Not with the smoke damage, the toxic waste. Fallout from the Egg Man.

"You're still angry," she said.

"Yeah," he said. "I don't like being played with."

Her eyes looked hurt. "Played with? I'm not playing! I offered you everything God gave me! You seemed to like it. So just take it, already!"

He dumped her on her back on the sofa, her leg still sprawled over his, and slid off the couch and onto his knees. He rearranged his boner and his balls in their strangling prison of denim, and stared down at her body, laid out on the couch. She gazed up, apprehensive.

His hand came to rest on the petal-soft curve of her belly. Slid up to touch the undercurve of her breast. Something gave way inside him.

A compromise. It might not preserve his honor or integrity, but it was a measure of damage control. And it was the best he could do.

"OK. You win," he said hoarsely. "Up to a point."

Her eyes widened. She jerked up, half sitting.

"Let me tell you how it's going to be," he said. "I'll get you off, as many times as you want. I'll teach you to give head, because if you don't make me come, I'm going to be in need of medical intervention. But I'm not going to kiss you. And I'm not going to fuck you. No penetration."

Her eyes glowed, golden brown in the flickering firelight. "Wow," she whispered. "Um, why not?"

"Damage control," he said. "I don't have any latex, for one thing—"

"I do!" she offered brightly.

"No. Penetration. And that's. Fucking. Final. Got it?"

Robin rolled her eyes. "You're being silly. The rest

of what you're suggesting is just as compromising and intimate, if not more so—"

"Believe me. You don't want me for your first lover."

She propped herself onto her elbows and studied him, fascinated. "Why on earth not? I've dreamed of it for years. You're gorgeous. So?"

He flushed, like a teenage boy. "Because I'm hung like a horse, that's why. Which is great for some women, if they're built for it. And it sucks for others. Virgins belong in the second category."

Her mouth dangled open, eyes wide. Her gaze flicked down to his crotch. "Let me see," she said, reaching down.

He blocked her hand and pinned it against the sofa cushion. "Uh-uh. Do not let the beast out of its cage," he said, teeth clenched.

"Poor trapped beast won't have any fun unless you let him out."

"You think this is fun?" he snarled.

She struggled up into a sitting position. "I hoped it would be," she said softly. "I didn't mean to torture you. I wish you could lighten up."

His laughter was bitter. Lighten up, his hairy ass. After months of worming through the sewer of Geddes's sick mind?

But he didn't want to lay that tortured crap on Robin.

"I am who I am," he said grimly. "If you don't like me this way, we can just stop. I'll just go lock myself in the bathroom and jerk off."

She gazed at him, looking uncertain. "I don't want to stop," she whispered. "Whatever you want to give me . . . I'll take."

He sagged over her, and pressed his face against her belly, nuzzling the secret cleft of her navel. She shuddered, sliding her fingers into his hair as he slid his hand into her jeans. His searching fingers found a silky swatch of fine pubic hair, smooth and flush to her skin.

Lower, to find the dampness, the plump, cushiony lips of her pussy. The seam was slick and hot. Panties soaked with lube.

She whimpered, and clutched his wrist. She was primed.

He had to see it. Taste it. Feel her come with her clit in his mouth. He pulled his hand out, and sucked his gleaming fingers. Sweet as candy. The roar in his ears got louder. "Get those jeans off," he said.

She was too damn slow. She couldn't get the knots of her sneakers undone, so she pried them off her heels. He wrenched the buttons open, and yanked panties and jeans down together.

It happened so fast. One minute she was arguing, and the next, she was buck naked but for her ankle socks.

"This is like Sexual Fantasy Number 2017B. My ravishing pirate fantasy," she babbled. "Remarkably similar to the medieval knight fantasy. Or the Scottish Laird fantasy. You star in them all."

His grim mouth twitched. "You fantasized about me?"

She made a rude sound. "Dumb question," she murmured.

His hands slid up her thighs. "What did I do in these fantasies?"

Robin's giggles stopped. She was sobered by a stab of longing.

"You, um, you wanted me," she whispered.

Jon's face went hard. "I'm warning you again. Don't get all intense about me." His voice was flinty. "Don't even look at me that way."

She looked away. *Shit.* She was scaring him off already, wrecking this for herself. "Sorry," she whispered. "Can't help it."

He was silent for a moment. "Help it," he said flatly. "Maybe this isn't such a good idea after all. What a fucking surprise."

Oh, no, no, no. She was playing what few cards she had all wrong. "Oh, don't worry." She forced lightness into her voice. "My intentions are completely dishonorable. I'm leaving the Northwest, too."

"You are? Where are you going?"

"San Francisco," she informed him. "I got accepted into the training program of the Circo della Luna Rossa a few months ago. I cannot wait. I am so out of here."

He looked impressed. "Wow. I've heard about that show. That's, uh, pretty amazing. What do Mac and Danny think of it all?"

Her eyes dropped. "They, uh, don't actually know about it yet."

There was an expressive silence. "Ah," he said.

"They're going to be unthrilled," she confessed. "But it's not up to them. Anyhow. Never mind my brothers. The point is, I want no ties. I need to be able to just pick up and go. Travel the world for months at a time. So put your mind at ease. I'm just using you for sex."

"I see," he said, his voice velvety. "If you're such a hardboiled, tough broad using me for sex, why are your legs clamped together?"

In fact, they were. Jon's hands were exerting gentle, constant pressure. Her thighs shook with the effort of resisting. She laughed, which released the tension. Her thighs opened to his coaxing hands.

He stared down at her, rapt. That muscle still pulsed in his jaw.

She felt so exposed. Her pubic hair was just a dark silky swatch that hid nothing of her tender private bits.

Jon looked hypnotized. His eyes glowed with a focused hunger more potent than physical touch. He caressed her pussy with his fingertips. She jerked, like she'd been shocked. He grabbed her hips and scooted them to the edge of the couch. She fought for balance, and lost. Tumbled back, splayed wide. He leaned down and put his mouth to her.

Oh. It felt so good, it was scary. She'd naively thought, with her erotic reading, and being her own enthusiastic best friend and all, that she knew how deliciously nice that would feel. She hadn't had a clue.

She hadn't factored in the trembling, shivering, on-the-edge feeling, the cool air that shivered over the surface of her skin, the flickering from the fire. Those fierce, bright eyes, flicking up to watch her reaction.

She quivered and moaned. Every swirling caress of his mouth, his tongue, was a shock of startled delight. She couldn't stop moving, twitching, but only because it was so . . . damn . . . *good,* oh God—

The explosion was so wrenching, she fell away, lost herself.

He was at her again when she came back to herself, but she tried to push his face away. "Let me rest," she begged. "Give me a sec."

"I'm not leaving you wanting more. I'm going to leave you too tired to move," he said. "If we're gonna do this, I'm gonna make it count."

He went at it slower the next time, building her up, making her wait. She was shivering on the brink of an explosion when he forced his finger inside her. "So tight," he muttered. "I love how you hug me."

She pushed herself against his hand, pleading for deeper, faster. *More.* She needed something so bad and he had it to give. He stroked that spot inside she'd never known about, while his tongue lapped and swirled, and then fastened his lips over the taut bud of her clit, exerting the perfect suckling pressure, fluttering his tongue . . .

The climax took her so violently, she passed out, for a few seconds.

When she opened her eyes again, he was staring into her face, his eyes blazing. The force of his need pulled her. She wrapped her arms around his neck, tugged him closer. "Make love to me," she pleaded.

He shook his head. A muscle in his jaw twitched with tension.

She shoved against his chest. "You are so goddamn stubborn!"

He started getting up. "So they tell me."

She grabbed his belt as she realized he was about to walk away.

"Not so fast," she said. "You said that you'd teach me how to . . . that we'd . . ." She couldn't quite force the bold words out.

"Changed my mind," he said. "I've decided that it's inadvisable."

"You can't change the rules now, after what you just did to me!"

"I can do what I damn well please," he said.

She wrenched his buckle open. "And what about the beast?"

"I'll take care of the beast myself."

"But the poor thing's trapped in there, pleading for release," she said, trying to tease a smile out of him.

Not a chance. His mouth was grim, but still, he was passive as she popped the buttons of his fly. "Don't waste any compassion on the beast," he said. "He gets his rocks off on a regular basis."

That was not what she wanted to hear, but she brushed it off, and wrenched down his jeans. His penis sprang out at her, right in her face.

Holy cow. He hadn't been exaggerating. His penis was way thicker and broader and . . . well, redder and angrier looking than anything she'd expected. A rush of lube moistened her thighs, just looking at it.

She grabbed it, curling her fingers around it tightly so he couldn't change his mind and pull away. The contact made her hand tingle. His skin was so soft, and beneath it, the flesh hard and hot and pulsing. Smooth skin sliding over that stiff shaft, the thick knotwork of empurpled veins. She'd never played with one of these up close. Never imagined how it would feel to be a man and have it all sticking out there on display. Intimidating, but also . . . vulnerable.She could read the vulnerability on his face, even beneath the simmering tension.

"Wow," she commented. "What a truly excellent toy."

He let out a bark of laughter, and that was her cue to just go for it, before he gathered his defense, or she lost her nerve, either one. If he didn't like how she did it, he could give her pointers along the way.

After all, please. Like, how complicated could this be?

Jon threw his head back with a groan of agonized delight. God. What she lacked in experience, she more than made up for with sheer intensity, and what he suspected was incredible innate talent.

So good. He got his cock sucked whenever he wanted it, never lacking for willing female company, and he enjoyed it lustily every time, but this desperate emotional edge he had right now changed it into something almost . . . dangerous.

He must be on the brink like this because he was so fucked up over the Geddes thing. He hadn't had sex in months. Rare, for him. He had tankloads of backed-up mojo to unload. That was all it was.

But that and all other sure things he knew about himself were breaking down because of this girl, those slender hands gripping him, that clever tongue, licking, swirling, sucking. She sucked his glans into her mouth while her tongue circled and fluttered the underside.

He locked his knees, trembling, so he wouldn't fall.

It took a while for her to figure out the choreography, but any woman capable of juggling tomatoes or flaming torches was more than capable of coordinating tongue, lips, hands to drive him out of his skull. She milked his root with her hands, finding that spot under the glans that made him nuts, the suckling outstroke, the perfect rhythm . . .

He had a bad moment imagining what Danny would say if he walked in, but the charge was building. He was going to explode.

The phone in his shirt pocket started to ring.

They froze, eyes locked. He plucked the vibrating thing out of his pocket. Two rings. Three. Sure enough. It was Danny. Aw, fuck. *Fuck.*

Four rings. Robin waited, caressing his slick, throbbing cock with her hands like she couldn't bear to let go, a question in her eyes.

A challenge, too. Guilt made him furious.

Danny waited ten rings before he gave up. Jon flung

the thing onto the couch, disgusted with himself. Hogtied by a woman's mouth. She'd wrangled him so easily. All his bluster, all his resolve, had led him straight to this. Her lube all over his face. His cock in her mouth.

"So?" His voice came out hard. "You won. Finish me off."

She blinked, startled by his harsh tone, but got right to it. Sucked him right back into that vortex of white hot pleasure.

He should have asked if she was OK with him coming in her mouth, but by the time it occurred to him, it was thundering down, pounding him under.

He could hardly believe he was still on his feet. He looked down as she wiped her mouth and pressed a kiss to the tuft of springy dark hair at his groin. He felt like shit. Even if she wasn't his best friend's baby sister, she was a sweet, vulnerable girl. She had no business getting mixed up with him. He could have stopped himself. And should. Right now. Because as he stared at her body, her big, glowing eyes, he knew he was capable of making it worse. Taking it all the way. Oh, yeah.

He pulled himself out of her grip, shoved his still turgid dick back into his pants and fastened them. "Class dismissed," he said.

She looked disillusioned. "But I . . . didn't you like it?"

"Sure, I liked it, and now it stops. Get your damn clothes on."

He walked away. Out the kitchen, out the door, into the rustling moonless night. The wind was tossing the firs, petting them like a big hand. He stumbled out into their midst, watched them bend and sway.

He had to do something about the cold, dead feeling the Geddes case had left him with. It sat there in the middle of his chest like a rock. He'd tried alcohol, but he didn't like getting as drunk as he needed to be to blunt it. He hadn't noticed it when he was wallowing between Robin's thighs, a voice in his head pointed out. Hadn't felt it when she was blowing him, either.

Huh. He'd have to think about that. But it wasn't permanent. The instant the sexual buzz eased off, the feeling crashed down, just like now. Tenfold. He heard the ringing of his cell. The door opened, and Robin appeared in the door, mercifully, clothed. Silhouetted against the kerosene lamplight, staring down at the screen display.

"I don't want to talk to him," he said.

"It's not Danny," she said. "It's someone called Mendez."

Constance Mendez, the colleague who was covering for him. She wouldn't call him without a good reason. He strode to the door, grabbed the phone out of Robin's outstretched hand, and hit Talk. "Yeah?"

"Amendola. Sorry to bug you, but I thought you'd want to know this." Her usually crisp voice sounded subdued. "Geddes is dead."

Of all things to feel at a piece of news like that, a stab of irrational fear was the most inappropriate he could think of. "Huh?"

"He sucked down a bunch of hand gel in the bathroom," she said. "Happened this afternoon. Took him a while to die. I just found out."

His stomach lurched. He tasted bile. "Thanks for letting me know."

"Maybe, uh . . . this will help you relax?"

"Don't hold your breath," he said. "Later, Mendez."

He broke the connection, stared down at the phone for a minute, and thumbed the thing definitively off. No more calls. He was done.

Here it was, another opportunity to feel finality, closure. Geddes was cold meat in the prison morgue. You couldn't get any more final than that. Right? He searched his soul for that finished feeling. He didn't find it.

Robin had put on the sweatshirt again. She crossed her arms over her chest. "Bad news?" she asked.

He opened his mouth to tell her it was none of her business. "The guy I just put in jail," he blurted. "Son of a bitch just committed suicide. He found a way to off himself after just a few days in the joint."

She bit her lip and gazed at him, big-eyed, like she wanted to say something, but was afraid to let it out. "And, ah . . . this is bad?"

"Too easy!" He was breathing hard. "Too fucking easy. The bastard deserved to have his extremities pulled off by tractor trailers! He deserved to be some tattooed Nazi sadist's bitch! Not a half gallon of fucking hand gel, and off he drifts to fucking never-never land! Fuck that!" He punctuated that by punching the closest pine tree.

Shit. The bastard was covered with rough bark. What a dickhead.

Robin grabbed his shaking fist, and looked at it, murmuring softly at his bloody knuckles. She took his wrist and tugged. He followed her into the cabin, feeling docile and thick. And unbelievably stupid.

She led him to the sink and washed his hand, then rummaged in the cupboards for cotton balls, ointment, bandaids. Then she sat him down, spread his hand out on a clean dish towel. Dabbed and tweezed, smeared him with ointment, wrapped bandaids around each lacerated knuckle. When she was done, she lifted his hand, kissed it. Something twisted in his chest, unstable and dangerous. He pulled his hand back.

Robin sighed, and bent over the fridge. She pulled out two more beers, popped them open, set one before him. He took a grateful pull.

The silence was thick. He was intensely embarrassed, about the wild oral sex, his insane rudeness, the flagrant tree abuse. All of it.

"I don't think I've ever heard you keep your mouth shut for this long at one time since I've known you," he said, just to say something.

Robin propped her face in her hand, tracing designs on the fog of condensation on her beer bottle. Her eyes were thoughtful.

"Usually I ham it up, clown around," she said. "My way of dealing with scary stuff is to make a joke of it, make people laugh. But I can't make fun of something like this."

He shook with bitter laughter. "Oh, you'd be surprised what we can make fun of."

"Sure. You're a cop. But it would be inappropriate from me to try it. It's outside my scope. I'm just sorry this happened."

He acknowledged her words with a brusque nod.

"Who was this guy?" she asked. "What did he do?"

"You don't want to know," he said brusquely.

"Um, actually, I do." Her voice was quietly stubborn.

He gulped his beer. "He liked to kill young women. Slowly."

"The Egg Man?"

He looked up at her, startled. "You know about him?"

"I watch the news. You're right. He didn't deserve an easy death."

Robin ventured to lay her hand on top of his battered one, barely touching it. She stared down at it as if she were willing the lacerations to heal. The warmth of her soft fingers felt good. More than good.

He pulled his hand out from under hers. "You should get some sleep," he said gruffly. "It's getting late."

She put her hand back. "The only bed fit to sleep in is the sofa bed in the living room," she said. "I checked the bedrooms. In one room, there was a leak over the bed. The mattress is molded slop. And in the other, some mammal clawed through the wall and had a litter on the mattress. So, ah, I'll just take the sofa cushions and sleep on the floor."

"No," he said promptly. "Don't be ridiculous."

"Hey. Get real. You're the one who's been chasing serial killers," Robin argued. "And I came up here un-invited. Besides—"

"Shut up, Robin. You're taking the bed. Go get the sleeping bags."

She scurried off. He went into the living room and wrestled the couch into position. Robin came back with pillows and sleeping bags. She offered him one of each, without looking at him. He'd stung her into silence.

He should be glad. It was the only way to survive this.

Julia sat on the chair next to the telephone table, immobile as a rock. Stupefied, she stared at the answering machine.

She couldn't take it in. It wasn't possible. Not William. She'd just seen him, talked to him. That very afternoon at the prison. The fateful message had been blinking on the machine when she stumbled in after the long drive back to the luxurious desert lair that she'd shared with William. One of his many residences. William had been very wealthy.

Her hand reached out. It felt numb, an appendage that belonged to another person. This hostile alien insisted on punching the Play button of the machine again, like a self-flagellant wielding the lash.

Click. The message began to play once again, the words pounding at her like rocks, bruising flesh, breaking bones. *"Hello, this is a message for a Ms. Julia Kirkland,"* said a flat, nasal male voice. *"I'm Bob Bruckner, a member of William Geddes's legal team. I have bad news. Mr. Geddes died this afternoon. I'm sorry to say that he took his own life. He drank a container of sterilizing hand gel from the prison bathroom dispenser, and the ethanol depressed his respiratory system. Mr. Geddes left a note asking that you be contacted, which is why I'm calling this number. Uh, I'm very sorry for. your loss, Ms. Kirkland. If you have any questions, feel free to call me at this number."* Bruckner rattled off a number, hesitated, as if feeling the urge to say something more. He let out an embarrassed grunt. *Click.*

Julia pressed her hand against the heavy raw silk of her white Gucci suit jacket, pressing it hard against the raw, screaming empty spot inside her. Gone. Her William was gone. Her fingers closed around the fabric of the jacket, crumpling it in a white, shaking fist. She never would have guessed that he'd do that to her. She'd been so certain that he'd find a way to escape. He was so smart, so indomitable.

She must have looked so strange today in that place, in a white designer suit. Blazing with the jewels William had given her. All done up like a doll to visit a maximum security prison. But it had seemed appropriate. A gesture of respect and love. All she could offer him.

She closed her eyes and saw it all again, every detail. From the moment they led him into the glass-fronted cubicle. He'd been so pale. Hollows under his cheeks, shadows under his eyes. The orange jumper and harsh lights made his skin seem blue. And the bruises! Someone had *beaten* him! It made her so angry, she wanted to vomit.

But his eyes still burned like lasers, transfixing her like always.

He had been so brave and noble, to pay the whole price for what they had done together. He'd forbidden her to turn herself in, or to confess. Insisted that she stay away during the trial. It nearly killed her.

She would have died for him. Anything.

You have to carry on, he'd said. *You fly for both of us now.*

It made her cry to think of it, but William despised tears, so she forced them back. They picked up the phones, but neither spoke. So many things could not be said in words, particularly not in front of listening ears. Others were too obvious to say. How it tore her heart out to see him like this. How she wished she could suffer every blow in his place. The worst pain could be sweet, if it was suffered for love.

William taught her that, in the eight years they'd been together.

She'd been barely seventeen when he'd found her, cheerleading at a high school football game. He'd found her e-mail address, and quickly became the one ray of light in her monumentally shitty life. The one person in the world who understood her. Her true soulmate.

It had taken her months to work up the courage, but she'd finally let him take her away from the insanity of it all. Her cold, uncaring bitch of a mom, the rich, bloated lech of a stepdad with the hot eyes and the wandering hands. The stupidity of panting high school jocks.

William had showed her a new world, a different universe. His inner power electrified her. She'd looked for her picture on milk cartons for a while, but no one ever found her. Not with a genius like William covering her tracks. He'd given her a new name, a new face. A new life.

She'd belonged to him, completely. He was her everything.

"What can I do?" she'd asked him. "My love."

His eyes held hers, full of dark shadows like storm clouds. "One thing, Jule," he had whispered. "All I'll ever ask from you."

"Anything," she promised. "Anything, William."

He lifted his hand, and pressed his palm to the glass.

AMENDOLA was sliced into his flesh, in big, jagged bloody block letters. Blood smeared over the thick layers of glass.

Excitement buzzed through her as she stared at it. All she wanted in the world was to punish the police detective who had gutted their lives. But so far, William had forbidden her to risk exposure.

Jon Amendola of the PPD was the reason she wasn't with William right now, liberating their sixth candidate. They'd chosen the girl so carefully. Blonde, like Julia. Pretty, like Julia. Smart, like Julia. Bouncing from frat party to frat party at a nearby college. No clue she was about to transcend her own body and fly with the angel of death.

She nodded slowly. *Yes.* Gladly. She could hardly wait.

Lightning flashed deep in William's fathomless blue eyes. *Make it slow,* he mouthed. *Make it hurt.*

She nodded, eyes locked with his. One with him. And then their time was up. They'd spent the whole time staring at each other.

Their gazes stayed locked to the last, until they led him away.

So she had a task to accomplish. The huge responsibility had electrified her, kept her awake for the long drive home. But he hadn't told her that he was going to leave her alone forever. That was cruel.

Julia squeezed her eyes shut to block out the blinking answering machine. Those bloody letters were carved into her brain. AMENDOLA.

She went into her bedroom, removed her clothing. Paced into the room that she and William had used for their special, private rituals. She lit the candelabra, and stared at her nude body in the mirror, the intricate beauty of her scars. She was a living work of art. William had sculpted her, with knives and fire. She was his legacy, his masterpiece.

Amendola would pay. Double. She would take his wife, or his girlfriend, and perform the ultimate tribute to William's memory upon her. She would toss the limp, broken body back at him like garbage. And when she finally did kill him, he would already be dead inside.

William's face took form in her mind, giving her a burst of joy. She realized, in a blinding flash of insight, that he was free now. Really free.

Free of the burden of his own body. Free to guide her.

Make it hurt. She'd been tutored by a master in the intricacies of pain. Levels upon levels of agony that transformed the soul.

Make it hurt.

Oh, yes. She would. And inside her head, William smiled at her.

4

Flapping wings, beating. Glaring eyes, hooked beak, a shriek that froze his blood. Rending claws, plummeting like a missile—

And he was looking down at the girl, staked out, her naked body scarcely recognizable as human. Her jaw gaped. In her slack mouth was that telltale gleam of a delicate blue ovoid. The robin's egg.

The girl's eyes snapped open. Horror stopped his heart.

Robin's huge brown eyes. Whites showed all around. They stared out, weeping tears of blood that streaked down her distorted face—

Jon jerked upright, choking off a scream, and stared around, trying to orient himself. The cabin. The kitchen. Robin. Geddes and his hand gel. Jesus. Just a dream. One of the worst.

It wasn't getting better. He didn't get it. He was thick-skinned. He bounced back from whatever plowed into him. Growing up in foster homes had made him tough, resiliant. He knew how to look out for himself. He knew better than to let anyone or anything get too close. He kept the world at bay, by habit. It worked for him. It always had.

That had worked for him as a cop too. He wasn't cold or uncaring. He was just detached. Victims had counselors to be empathetic to them. Empathy wasn't his job, thank God. His job was to hunt those fuckers down and haul them in. To make them stop.

So how was the Egg Man messing with him from beyond the grave? It made him feel violated. Helpless. A feeling he hated intensely.

He forced himself to consider all the possibilities, however unpalatable. Maybe he was having a breakdown. Accumulated job stress. He'd never dreamed it could happen to a cast-iron bastard like himself, but how else would he let himself get snookered into fooling around with Robin? He was losing his mind. It was the only explanation.

His heart still galloped from the dream. He tried to breathe deep, calm down, but it wasn't happening. He twisted around, stared at the bed, dimly visible in the light of the dying fire. The virgin sacrifice.

What the hell. She wouldn't know he was gawking. He padded into the other room and stared at her, curled up in her nest of puffy nylon. Her shoulder had slipped out of the sweatshirt. So soft, and pretty. And sweeter than sweet. That made it so much worse somehow.

He went back to the kitchen and snagged a chair, carried it back with him. He sat down near the bed. Hell, he couldn't sleep anyway.

It made him breathe easier. As long as he was watching, no stinking bird of prey could swoop down on her and start rending.

* * *

The dream was deliciously erotic. Rocking bursts of delight pulsed through her as she twined herself around Jon's body. But she knew it was only a dream. Something was pulling on her from the outside, tugging at her mind. An urgent, anxious feeling. Someone needed her.

She drifted into a near-waking state, smelled mothballs and mold, woodsmoke and pine resin. And that feeling between her legs. Oh, boy.

It flooded back. Her eyes popped open, and the source of that urgent pull at her mind was abruptly revealed.

Jon was sitting next to the bed in a straight-backed chair. He wore only jeans and a small gold medallion that dangled at his throat. His chest was breathtaking. Thick slabs of muscle, dark hair arrowing down towards his groin. His feet were bare, his dark hair spiked out every which way. His eyes bored into hers. A shiver racked her at the fierce intensity of his eyes. No smiles. On the contrary. He looked tense.

Robin sat up. "Jon? Are you OK?"

He shook his head.

Robin studied him. She ached to reach out to him, but she still smarted from all his previous rejections. And yet, he seemed to be coming around. Not in any sort of playful way, that was for sure. But he looked like he needed something. She did too.

Though she had a feeling that what she got wasn't going to be anything like her girlish fantasies. But whatever. She was flexible.

She slid her legs out of the bed, unzipped the bag completely, smoothing so that it covered the entire, red-striped sofabed mattress. Then she padded to the armchair where she'd dumped her tote, and rummaged til she found the bag with the condoms. She pried it open, pulled one out and marched back, waggling it. She was prepared.

He didn't say a word. His expression did not change.

She dragged in as deep a breath as she could manage, and laid it on the bed next to the pillow. She'd just take that flat silence as a resounding yes. God knows, she'd heard what a no sounded like.

She pulled off the sweatshirt. His gaze fastened onto her naked breasts. He didn't tell her to stop. Encouraged, she tugged off jeans, panties and ankle socks. And just stood there. *Come and get me.*

He was not behaving the way her girlfriends had given her to understand that men did. What did she have to do to get him to make a move? Hold a gun to his head? She took a step closer. A muscle twitched in his jaw. His penis poked out of his waistband. There was a smear of precome on the dark hair arrowing to his groin.

She sank to her knees in front of him, and pressed her mouth to his glans, lashing her tongue across it. Licking salty drops on his belly.

He gasped, jerked. "Jesus, Robin." The chair teetered on its legs.

She looked up. "Well? You're just sitting there, like a freaking rock." She ran her finger around the flare of the glans. "What does it take to get you going? Do I have to light a bomb under your chair?"

"Oh, God," he muttered, but he didn't protest when she wrenched his belt open and tugged him to his feet. She pushed his jeans down.

His penis sproinged up, and she gripped it, caressing the broad shaft. Jon seized her beneath the armpits and hauled her to her feet.

"Once I get started, I'm not stopping," he warned.

She snorted. "I should hope not. You've been such a shrinking violet. You'd think you were the one who'd never done it before."

"Shrinking violet? Huh." He laughed, which made her happy, and slid his hand between her legs, which made her gasp.

Oh, he was so good. Better than she was herself. He fluttered his fingers against her labia until her breath was all stuck in her throat, hitching in ineffectual gasps, and then he insinuated his finger inside, slid it tenderly around the slick folds and crevices.

She whimpered and gasped as he found her clit, fondled it.

He thrust deeper. Two fingers, stretching. It hurt, but it felt so achingly good. His body burned her, all that scorching skin. He smelled so good. She clutched his shoulders, hiding her face against his chest.

"Squeeze your pussy around my hand. Come for me again."

She lifted her head, confused. "But I thought we—I thought—"

"I will. But the more times I get you off first, the better it'll be."

The sensations built with every delving stroke, every sliding thrust. The tension built, aching and swelling until something snapped, and wild rapture throbbed through her. Huge, sweet waves of it.

He held her up on wobbling knees when she drifted back. He jerked his chin toward the bed, eyes gleaming with fierce purpose.

She stumbled back, sat down. Scrambled back on the mattress until she lay on her back. She felt so vulnerable, naked with that big man looming over her. To say nothing of that enormous thing of his, bobbing and swaying before him. She grabbed the pillow, propped it behind her head, and watched him open the condom, smooth it on. He stroked his erection with a rough hand as he stared down at her.

"Open up. Show me everything," he said.

She struggled onto her elbows, and parted her legs. Her face was red, her breath quick. She felt weepy and strange. Like she might cry. God forbid. If anything could put him off, it would be that.

"Wider," he said.

She forced her trembling thighs as wide as they would go. Jon climbed onto the bed. The springs bowed under his weight. The breath was zapped out of her body at the contact of his body to hers.

He fitted himself against her. Robin braced her hands against his chest, letting her nails dig in lest he think she was pushing him away. She craved the play of powerful muscles beneath her fingers, the rasp of coarse hair, the tang of sweat. He slid the tip of himself up and down her cleft, then stared into her eyes and began to force his way inside.

She caught her breath, nails digging deeper. Oh. *Whoa.*

He paused, his mouth set in a fierce line. "I told you," he said savagely. "I *warned* you, goddammit."

"Did you hear me complaining?" she snapped back. "Did I tell you to stop? No! So shut up, and do your job!"

He vibrated with amusement, and kept on pushing. The pressure mounted. She reached down, sliding her hands greedily over the contours of his back, the slabbed, bumpy ridges of muscle and bone. She sank her nails into his tight ass and dragged him deeper. *Ouch.*

It was his turn to gasp. "Take it easy, for fuck's sake!"

"Just making sure you don't chicken out on me."

"Not a chance," he promised. "Too late."

She wiggled, seeking relief from that immense, dull pressure. She was immobilized by his huge body. He gasped again at her writhing. "For God's sake," he complained. "Be still. Let me take this slow."

"I thought the whole act was a little more dynamic," she snapped.

"Not yet." He rolled to the side, and that helped. He searched out her clitoris and played with it, barely moving inside her as he swirled his thumb around the taut nub. His lips found her nipple, sucked it deep, and her body slowly began to make sense of the invasion.

Her chest shivered, softened. It still hurt, but it glowed too, pulsing. A strange urgency was building up, and she wiggled madly to explore the throb, the tender strokes. He rolled back on top of her again, and began to move, wedging impossibly deeper.

"Good God, aren't you all the way inside yet?" she asked.

"We're getting there."

"Who knew there was so far to go?" she said testily.

That feral wolf smile appeared on his face, and his hips shoved hard against hers. "You have no idea how far we're going to go."

She stared into his face. His thrusts deepened. The feeling was so strong. She felt helpless, every nerve in thrall. Her heart was about to explode, but he didn't want her to love him, and what the *hell* was she going to do about that?

She wanted to pierce through the armor of his self-command. She wrapped her arms around his neck, jerked his head down and kissed him. His eyes popped open, startled, and after a second, he kissed her back, demanding more. As if she hadn't given him everything.

Even the parts he did not want. *Like her heart.*

She pushed that thought away. This was for pleasure, for opening herself up to all the possibilities in her life. This was a gift to herself, and she would damn well enjoy it without getting all wound up with it.

The kiss opened up nameless depths inside her, a wilderness of unknown, terrifying sensations. She drew him deeper, bathed his phallus with slick warmth to make the glide easier, and it was so good, so sweet, so fine. All pain was forgotten in the swelling surge of bliss.

She almost dragged him along with her, but Jon clenched his teeth and breathed it down, forcing himself to wait while she exploded.

He wanted to feel it. The bright wash of her pleasure shooting up, her pussy clenching hard, pumping him. He could blow his own wad later. This was special. He'd never been with a woman so responsive.

After her orgasm eased down to a shimmer, her eyes opened, heavy-lidded and dazed. Her pink tongue darted out to moisten her lips.

"Sorry," she whispered. "I'm sort of . . . um . . . on a hair trigger."

"You're apologizing?" he asked, incredulous. "There's nothing in the world better than making a woman come with your cock inside her."

The generic statement was not what she wanted to hear, but he was too far gone for self-censorship or delicacy. In fact, he was about to explode from the strain of holding back. "I'm not done," he said.

She arched beneath him, moving her hips in a gesture of sweet, sensual surrender. It made his chest ache. "Do it," she said. "Anything."

He scooped her legs up, draping them over his elbows. Her smile was so sweet, he could hardly bear to look at it. Something swelled inside him, strained, then snapped. He took her at her word, going at her harder than he'd meant to, but once started, he was helpless to stop. No way out but straight through to the pounding finish, and he hoped to God those sounds were wails of pleasure—

His climax thundered down. He spurted out his very soul.

They lay there for a sweat-drenched, panting eternity. He would have been horrified at himself, if it had not so obviously worked for her.

Wild and raw. When he really let go, which was rare, it all came roaring out. Too much for some women. "You OK?"

She hid her face against his shoulder. "OK is not the first word that comes to mind."

"Did you like it?" He felt like an idiot for persisting, but whatever.

She peeked up at him. "You mean, you didn't notice?"

"Oh yeah. You coming like crazy." He grinned. "It was hard to miss."

He rolled onto his side, and eased out of her. Slick and wet as she was, she still tugged him with a tender parting clutch as he withdrew.

He reached down to keep the condom in place, and saw blood on his fingers. It sent a jolt through him. Not a lot, just a pinkish smear, but still. It shook him. She'd been so trusting. He'd been . . . rough.

"Got to get rid of the condom," he said, getting up. He fled to the bathroom, splashed his belly and his dauntless dick, which would not calm down. He washed until the water swirling down the drain was no longer pinkish and stared into the mirror, realizing with wonder that he could breathe. No soured, dead feeling. No cramp. The air went in and it came out. Smooth, natural. Just as it should. Ah.

He met Robin on his way out. Her cheeks were pink, eyes downcast. "My turn," she murmured, disappearing into the bathroom.

She was in there for a long time, and he spent the whole interval staring at the reddish smears on the sleeping bag. He had to buy a new one tomorrow. His chest felt so strange. Hot and soft. Shaky.

He retrieved the other sleeping bag, unzipped it, and tossed it over the bed for a blanket. When she came out, she was startled to see him in the bed. He lifted up the sleeping bag in silent invitation.

Something inside him loosened as her face lit up.

She fitted herself to him. Cool, smooth, silky soft. He rolled her on top of him so the feeling could penetrate his whole body. Hell, who knew? Maybe he could even sleep. If his dick would settle down.

Catastrophe. Doom. Apocalypse, said the frantic chorus in his head.

Fuck you all, he said to them silently. He hadn't felt this good in longer than he could remember. Hell with the chorus, the rules, Danny.

He wanted to breathe, to sleep. To feel that warm, soft feeling, after being clenched like a fist for so long. He wanted this.

It had been freely offered to him, and he was damn well taking it.

* * *

Julia parked down the street from Amendola's duplex, trying hard to calm down. She vibrated with excitement. It was going so smoothly, so quickly. Amendola's colleague had innocently revealed that he was on vacation. She'd ferreted his address out of a public database, and driven all night to get to this shabby North Portland neighborhood.

She didn't have a plan yet, but that didn't worry her. She had William himself, inside her head. Way better than a plan.

It hadn't taken long to prepare. Her suitcase was full of designer clothes, by necessity high-necked and long-sleeved to cover William's body art. She drove one of the vans, in case she had a chance to use the surveillance equipment, which she could install like a professional.

And behind the driver's seat was the special case: the ebony chest filled with implements that they had used for their liberation rituals.

Julia had always had the honor of cleaning and polishing each blade, scissor, drill, hook, pincer and pick to a glowing sheen, lovingly laying each one in its nest of blood red velvet when they were done.

On the seat next to her was the final detail, tucked into a box she had carved herself out of styrofoam. The last of her most recent clutch of robin's eggs. Delicate and beautiful. She pictured putting it into the slack, bloodied mouth of Amendola's woman. A knife to his gut. *Yes*.

She got out, and walked up the cracked sidewalk like she had every right to be there. Fortunately, the door was not parallel to the street, but to the side, facing the other half of the duplex, and shielded by a shaggy, overgrown rhododendron. That slob Amendola was clearly not a talented gardener or landscape artist.

Minutes later, the lock snicked open to her skillful picking. Julia braced herself for the squeal of a burglar alarm. There was none.

As she pushed the door open and entered the modest duplex, she understood why he didn't bother. The place was dull and stark—a sand colored shag rug, a beige couch in front of a large screen plasma TV. Plain black-out shades. No pictures, posters, bookcases. The blandest lamps a person could find, if they were looking hard. Nothing personal. Nothing worth protecting, other than good quality electronic equipment. The bareness of the man's home must reflect the emptiness of his soul.

Unfortunately, it also implied that there was no important woman in his life. No woman could live in a place so featureless.

The kitchen was likewise unremarkable. Unusually clean, for a man living alone, but that could just mean that he ate out, or had a cleaning service come in and wipe up his filthy messes. Cupboards revealed whiskies and bourbons. In the refrigerator were condiments and beer. So. He was a heavy drinker. Big surprise.

She went into the bathroom, searching for feminine products, and found only condoms. If he brought women here, he must throw them out before it occurred to them to need a toothbrush or a panty-liner. He probably bent them over the table, humped for a moment, and then speed dialed a car service to get them the hell out of his way when he came. Empathy clutched her throat for the women he'd maltreated.

Slimy, disgusting user. He should be put down. Like a rabid dog.

On the Internet, she'd found records of a brief marriage. She wondered if he'd beaten the woman. Probably raped and sodomized her.

His bedroom was plain. A king-sized bed, a silver gray corduroy duvet cover. His closet had an unremarkable assortment of shirts, suits and jackets. No designer brands. A handful of inexpensive, unattractive ties were snarled around a wire clothes hanger, abandoned and forgotten. So he was cheap, too.

William had worn only the best. Of course.

Two more bedrooms. One was a catch-all, with a weight lifting set in one corner, a scaffold piled with skiing and climbing equipment in the other. Finally she saw how he spent what money he made. She'd checked his pay grade. His monthly income was less than her monthly clothing budget. Unless he was on the take. Which was probable.

The other bedroom was a studio, with a huge desk, a filing cabinet and a laptop. Here she found a hinged frame boasting two five-by-seven photos. One showed Amendola with a good-looking man more or less his age, and a younger girl, in the mountains. The men were dressed in climbing gear, with sunburned laughing faces. The girl would have been pretty but for the bad glasses and the braces. The girl's face was similar to the other man's. His sister, maybe. Amendola's arm was around her shoulder. Julia's eyes lingered on that point of contact.

The other photograph was taken from a lakeside. The same two men in a boat. Amendola held up a large trout, looking absurdly pleased with himself. A spectacular view of a sunset pink Mt. Rainier was reflected in the lakewater.

Finally, a pinhole window into the man's private life. She closed her eyes. Summoned William's face. He smiled mysteriously. She took this to mean what it had always meant: the answers were before her and she had to use her own brain to ferret them out. William's rigorous attitude comforted her, obscurely. Although they were on different planes, nothing had changed. William was still William.

Amendola's computer was password protected. His filing cabinet had a dull assortment of tax records. She began sorting through the garbage on his desk. Bills, bank statements, junk mail.

And then, on the very bottom of the pile, she found it.

It was an envelope with a newspaper clipping, dated two years back. A local Olympia paper told the story of Jon Amendola and Daniel MacNamara, who had come upon an unfortunate climber on their way up the Disappointment Cleaver route to the summit of Mt. Rainier. The man had been trapped in a rockfall in Cathedral Gap. Amendola and MacNamara had gotten the injured man out and transported him to Camp Muir. A grainy photo verified that Amendola's climbing partner was the same man in the other photos. A Post-It was stuck to the clipping, upon which was scrawled, *You're famous. Hope you're not still undercover, because Robin's laminated this sucker all over her dorm room door.* It was signed simply "Danny."

Julia stared at the green square of paper. She was trembling.

Robin? Was it possible? The name of the girl in that photograph—she assumed she was Daniel MacNamara's sister—had a name that evoked William's avocation? Their whole life's work? Robin. Incredible.

The robin's egg had been Julia's idea. She'd been so honored when William had adopted it. It symbolized the cosmic potential inside each girl. The color invoked both the blue of the sky and William's piercing blue eyes. The ovoid delicacy, the smallness, the femininity, symbolized the care they took with each soul they taught to fly.

Robin. It was a sign. She looked young, too. William had liked them young. They'd done most of their hunting at college campuses.

Julia closed her eyes. William's smile of approval shone. She basked in it. And abruptly, his smile faded, and he made a gesture that said, *And? Enough self-congratulation.* She jolted into action, tucked the photos into her purse. The envelope had a letterhead that read Crowne Royale Group, with a Seattle address. That, too, she put in her purse.

She was closing the front door behind her when the door of the other duplex popped open, emitting a fragrance of vanilla.

It was an old lady, shriveled and bent, dressed in an oversized pink cardigan trimmed with yarn pompom balls. She peered through glasses that grotesquely enlarged her watery, colorless eyes. "Are you Joanna?" she demanded, in the strident tones of the partially deaf.

Julia opened her mouth, but the old lady barged on. "Jonny told me you'd be coming from Social Services to help me sort my medicines. Usually Jonny does it for me, but he's gone off fishing, so he got me a girl to come. So you're the girl? You're this Joanna?"

Julia smiled. "Why, ah, yes. I am Joanna. I'm so sorry, but when Jon told me your name, I forgot to write it down in my notes. Mrs.—?"

"Oh, call me Molly. Come on in, and have some lemon cookies."

Julia followed the wizened crone into her stuffy, crowded lair.

"Thank you. I love lemon cookies," she purred.

* * *

Robin felt so warm. Deliciously warm, curled up in a hot embrace and someone was stroking her hair, too. Slow, featherlight strokes. As she became aware of them, each gentle touch made tender, tickling warmth pulse under the surface of her skin.

Mmm. She didn't want to wake up. She drank it up, like a kitten lapping cream. But she was drifting up to consciousness, bracing herself for that moment when it all melted away, leaving her alone.

Her eyes fluttered open, and met Jon's. Bright blue chips of clear August sky. Shock, followed by a thrill of delight, and then pleasure racing and tingling and throbbing here and there, in strategic points of her body and then all points in between. It was real. *He* was real.

Omigod. This had really, truly, honest-to-God happened.

It had been more intense than she'd imagined. Well worth the effort it had taken to wrangle that guy into submission.

Although one could hardly characterize his exploits last night as submissive. She pressed her thighs together, biting her lip at the glow, the soreness. She remembered it like a crazy fever dream. Like being caught in the heart of a raging storm. Like being possessed by a god.

Jon stared into her face. The look in his eyes was so unguarded, it hurt her heart. Tears welled up. She wiped them away, smiled shakily. The knot in her throat shriveled up all possibility of speech.

Her feelings for him were plastered all over her face, like posters on a billboard. He'd said, *virgins always fall in love with you when you fuck them, if you do it right.* Well, he'd done it right, by God. She would never be the same again. And she thought she had it bad before.

Her girlish imaginings had been pale and thin compared to the lusty reality of his big body against hers, his huge penis, his rampaging sexual style. She was starting to squirm just thinking about it.

Her face was getting hot, but she couldn't look away. He looked like he was silently asking for something, but the plea was locked inside him, behind thick soundproof walls, clamoring to get out.

But she could hear him, loud and clear. From inside her heart.

She snuggled closer to him, until their noses almost touched, and lost herself in those bright eyes, the black curling eyelashes. His beard had grown out to a sexy, stubbly shadow that brought into focus the sculpted planes and angles of his jaw. That mouth, that knew no limits.

So close to hers. It happened slowly, so gradually, with no clear act of volition on anyone's part, a seamless, inevitable melding. One minute they were gazing, the next, they were kissing as if they'd always been kissing, as if they would never be able to stop.

The sweetest, loveliest kiss. She was a flower opening, aching to give him all the nectar she had, with perfect trust. Their lips met, explored, nibbled and plucked and stroked. His tongue touched hers, and molten delight shot down, shimmering in her nipples, blooming between her thighs, making her knees tingle, her toes curl.

He put his hand between her legs, slipping his fingers inside, and his low growl vibrated through her body when he found her wet.

One dizzy, disoriented movement, and he'd rolled heavily on top of her, shoving her legs wide. He lodged himself against her, and started squeezing that big, rock-hard phallus into her body. She was still sore from last night's adventures, yet the whimpers that jerked out of her with each deep shove were cries of pleasure.

He stopped when he was as deep as he could go. She could feel his heartbeat, throbbing inside her at the mouth of her womb, pressing all those lovely areas that just loved to be pressed.

"Am I hurting you?" he asked.

She let out a crack of breathless laughter, and dug her nails into his chest. "Oh, sure. Ask me now, why don't you, when you're so deep inside me, you're practically coming out my mouth."

He swiveled his hips, making her gasp and rock against him.

"You know how it is. Easier to ask for forgiveness than permission. But you didn't answer my question."

"Don't stop." She wiggled madly against him. "I like it."

"Answer my question." He froze into place, his eyes steely.

She let out a sharp sigh. "I didn't answer it because it's a dumb question. Sure, it hurts. I don't care. So stop bothering me."

"I could stop," he said. "If you're too—"

"Shut. Up." She shook him, wiggling her hips to get him going.

"I'll be gentle," he promised.

"Not on my account," she snapped, but the rest of her lecture was lost when he cupped the back of her head and started kissing again.

It was different this time. He was gentler, much gentler. Last night had a desperate, urgent, life-or-death quality. This morning, the movement of his body was playful, voluptuous. A slow thrust and glide, no hurry. A seeking, swirling, skillful pulse that teased and beckoned, that drove her half mad with rising desire with each slick stroke.

She squeezed her eyes shut, clutched his shoulders and raised herself to meet each lunge. The shimmering tension was rising, about to crest, but something tugged at her mind, distracting her.

"Um, Jon? We forgot the condom," she asked shakily.

He looked pleased with himself. "Nope. We didn't. It's on."

"Huh?" she was baffled. "But how did you—when did you—"

"I put it on a while ago," he confessed. "I've been waiting. Forever."

She laughed at him, but the laughter choked off into wails as he churned her up into a wonderful, shining froth of delight. She lost herself in pulsing surges of heat, light, beyond thought.

When she forced her wet eyes to open, he was motionless, poised over her, with a look of wonder in his eyes. "You're amazing," he said.

"Me?" She giggled helplessly. "I'm the one who's amazing? Hah!"

"I have never felt anything like that," he went on.

She licked her dry lips, cleared her throat. "Like, er, what?"

"Like the way you come. Your pussy just grabs my dick and milks it, hard, like a wet fist, with the fireworks going off, and the loud rock music blasting, and strobe lights flashing. Un-fucking-believable."

She blinked at him, at a loss for words. "Gee." Her

voice came out like a dry croak. "That's, ah, cool. I'm, um, glad you like it. But I think you should take a bit more credit for the phenomenon yourself."

She wiggled. He was huge, and stone hard inside her. "Didn't you come?"

He shook his head. "I wanted to feel yours," he said simply. "From beginning to end. No distractions."

"But don't you want to?" she asked, anxiously.

He frowned. "If I let myself come, I'd lose it and be too rough again, like last night. You're sore. It won't kill me not to come inside you. You can get me off some other way if you want."

"No way." She trapped him inside her, twining her thighs around his. "You're not slinking away without giving me mine."

He made a frustrated sound. "I'm not slinking—"

"No way. It's only fair. I show you mine. You show me yours. I want to see fireworks, and hear music and see strobe lights, too."

He stared down at her, eyes narrowed, and lifted his muscular torso up off her body, his penis still inside her. He tossed the sleeping bag back as he rose, so that the chilly air displaced the warmth. Goosebumps popped up, though she was a molten glow around his thick staff. He scooped her legs up, draping her knees over his elbows, stretching her so wide, it made her gasp.

"Fine. You asked for it," he said. "Brace yourself then."

She'd loved the tenderness, but she loved the wild ride too, his body hunched, muscular abdomen clutching and releasing. Sweat stood out on his forehead, and his eyes burned out of his stark face. His hips slammed against hers. He grunted with each jarring stroke.

The medallion around his neck flashed and swung.

Robin slid her fingers into the mat of damp black hair on his hard chest, and gave herself up to it, letting him jolt her closer and closer to another peak.

She tried to hold back, to wait so that she could watch him as he'd done to her, but his skill was too compelling. He dragged her implacably along with him, and pulled her over the brink into chaos.

They lay together after, a damp snarl of limbs. Robin stroked his shoulders, felt the jolting thud of his heart. The sweat cooled. Jon twitched the sleeping bag over them. "You OK?" he asked.

"Stop asking me that," she said lazily. "It's getting ridiculous."

"You make me crazy. I can't believe I did that to you. Again."

"Relax, already. I begged you to," she mumbled.

He reached down, holding the condom in place, and pulled out of her body with a groan. "God, I love how you hug me. Plush and tight."

She was too shy to offer compliments about his male member, though God knows it deserved a few.

He lay, limp. "I have to get rid of this thing," he muttered.

"OK. I can take a hint." She slid the condom carefully off him.

"Hey," he protested. "It's my dick, it's my come. I'll take care of it."

"No, you just lie there like a strand of overcooked linguini," she said. "You've put out quite enough for the moment."

She trotted into the kitchen and took care of it. Then she took the opportunity to answer the call of nature, splash her face, rinse her mouth. When she came back, she gazed down at his sprawled body.

She wasn't the linger-in-bed type. She was up before six, out of the shower and about her business in ten minutes or less. But it wasn't every day she had the man of her dreams in her bed. And it wasn't going to be for long, either. She forced herself to swallow that down.

It went down hard, but she was disposed to be appreciative of what she'd already gotten. Already more than she'd dared to hope for.

She climbed into bed, and snuggled down into the crumpled nylon nest with him. His arms tightened, dragging her into his force field of scorching heat. "So?" he said, his voice almost apprehensive.

She draped her leg over his muscular, hairy thigh. Her skin prickled with delight at the contact. "So what?"

"So what's the verdict? As a first sexual experience, how did this measure up to your fantasies?"

She considered her reply, her face going stupidly pink. "I've been wondering how anybody lucky enough to have a lover ever gets anything done. Why aren't they all boinking like bunnies, day and night?"

He laughed, and for the first time the sound was relaxed and unforced, not a harsh, cynical bark. "It's not always like this."

"It's not?" She studied his somber face.

He shook his head. "Almost never. Sometimes it's hot and sometimes it's fun. But a lot of the time, it's a lot of pounding and sweating, and then just . . . a quick shudder. And afterwards, you look at the woman, and you just don't know what the fuck to say to her."

Robin didn't know how to respond. She sensed that it was the kind of admission he was unused to making. It was so bleak and lonely.

She ran her fingers through his silky hair. Caressed his scratchy jaw. "Do you feel that way now, with me?" she asked.

His eyes widened, in shock. "Fuck, no! Not in the least."

"Good," she whispered, relieved.

"On the contrary. Sex this good . . . it's not normal," he said, in a halting voice. "I don't know if I've ever had sex this hot in my life."

She swatted his shoulder for his extravagant silliness. "Oh, get out of town. With a total beginner? Tell me a better one."

"I swear. It's like we're in each other's heads. The feedback loop is out of control. I thought sex like that only happened when you're in—"

Love. He cut the phrase off before the word sneaked out, but she heard it, hanging between them. She felt his tension rise. "Uh, I—"

"Don't sweat it," she said softly.

He looked miserable. "Robin, I—"

"Shhh." She put her finger to his lips. "I told you yesterday no strings. I meant it. I was prepared to leave first thing this morning."

"Robin, it's not like that—"

"Hear me out," she said. "I'm having an excellent time, and I want to stay, at least till tomorrow afternoon. I have a clown gig tomorrow evening. So let's make a magic bubble. We don't say the L-word, or talk about the future. We just enjoy this, and when it ends, it ends. You've got your life and career, and so do I. What plays in Vegas, and all that."

He looked disgruntled. "You're cool about this, for a virgin."

She blinked. "I'm no longer a virgin. Or didn't you notice?"

"I noticed." His eyes narrowed. "I'm warning you. You let the beast out of its cage. There's no putting it back in. Not without a dart gun and leg shackles. If you stick around, I'll be at you all the time. I'm talking a wild boar in rut."

"I was counting on it," she said demurely.

There was a charged silence, and his eyes took on that hot glow. He reached for her. Robin scooted back, giggling, and slid off the bed.

"Not before you feed me some breakfast. I'm hungry."

He bounded out of bed. "I'm hungry, too, now that you mention it. Cheese, pepper and tomato omelette and some bacon sound good?"

"Fabulous. Have you ever seen a naked woman juggle raw eggs?"

"Oh, Jesus," he said, with feeling. "I am so in for it."

5

Julia nibbled on her third lemon cookie. Normally she would never indulge. William had disapproved of gluttony and required her to stay trim. But she hadn't eaten in thirty-six hours. Until she joined William on a higher plane, she was still a slave to her body's needs.

She'd sorted Molly's medicines according to a complex chart. It had occurred to her to start her mischief by maliciously mixing up the old hag's medicines. The shriveled creature was clearly important to Amendola, if Molly's prattle was to be believed. He did odd jobs for her, took her to the doctor, drove her to the senior center, spent holidays with her, picked up her medicines, et cetera. She, in return, baked him casseroles, cookies and chicken pot pies, and meddled in his life.

But Julia simply wasn't familiar enough with these drugs to ensure a lethal dose of anything. Too many risks, too many unknowns.

"So where did Jon go off fishing to, anyway?" she asked, in a just-making-conversation tone. "Did he go down to Rogue River again?"

"Oh, no," the lady said. "He went up to Danny's place, I expect."

Julia blinked. "Danny's place?" she asked. "Where is that?"

Crumbs clung to the old lady's chin as she waved a gnarled hand. "Some cabin on a lake, up in the mountains. Jonny loves to fish."

"Which mountains?" It was hard, not sounding eager.

"Oh, I don't remember, if I ever knew. I must say, it's about time he got a rest. He ran himself ragged putting away that monster, that awful Egg Man person. Poor Jonny deserves a bit of fun."

Julia abruptly reconsidered the feasibility of killing Molly, but William shook his head in her mind, glancing at his wrist. The old crone was so close to death already, there would hardly be any point in it.

"I'm so sorry, Molly, but I must be running along," she said.

"You'll be back in a couple of days, won't you?" the old lady fussed. "Jonny said you'd check in on me every two days til he got back."

"Of course," Julia soothed. "I look forward to it."

She eased herself out the door. It took strength of will not to crush the old woman's arthritically deformed hand when she shook it.

Monster. The mouthy old bitch. How dare she.

Julia swept by a chubby lady with frizzy hair and a white uniform pantsuit that emphasized the big span of her hips, waddling purposefully up the walk. Her nametag read *Joanna Hirsch*.

She slipped into her van and pulled away. Whew. That was close, but William had helped her. Time to find a hotel, take what bits of straw she had gleaned, and spin them cleverly into gold.

* * *

Amazingly, breakfast happened, despite the naked egg juggling. To say nothing of the death-defying knife toss display, which continued to freak him out of his skull. Robin scoffed at his wimp-ass lily liver as she yanked the carving knife out of the cedar paneling. A guy needed nerves of steel to hang out with this chick.

Although the steel part of the equation was being cheerfully provided by his indefatigable dick. Cooking breakfast naked had been a mistake. Cooking required concentration. Having his prong waving around in front of him, drooling with eagerness, was distracting. And the bouncing tits, and swinging hair did not help matters.

He was so titillated, he was about to explode. And his jaw and his gut both ached from smiling so much. Laughing so hard.

They devoured omelette, toast, fresh OJ, a heap of crisp bacon, and finished their meal both gazing speculatively at the last piece of bacon on the plate. Jon put a martyred look on his face and did the gallant thing. "Go ahead," he sighed. "Take it. It's yours."

"Oh, no," she said demurely. "I couldn't possibly."

"I insist," he said, stoic to the last.

"OK." She popped it into her mouth and crunched, eyes sparkling.

"Hey!" He scowled, betrayed. "You didn't even share!"

She washed it down with orange juice, eyes sparkling. "I grew up with two hungry brothers. I know how to grab food before it vanishes."

Jon grunted. He could forage like a stray dog too. Not in all the foster homes he'd lived in, but many of them, it had been every kid for himself. Though he'd tried to look out for the little ones. When he could.

Robin sensed his shift in mood, and her face went

somber. "Sorry. That was dumb. I guess you must have had it a lot worse than me."

"Aw, I did OK. I was a big, bad-tempered punk," he said shortly. "I didn't get messed with too much. It's the weaker ones that suffer."

Robin reached across the table and touched the tiny medallion at his throat. She stood up and bent over the table, tits dangling before her, squinting to make out the tiny image in relief on the gold surface. Two angels, bending over a baby in a cradle. "What's this?"

He rubbed it between his thumb and forefinger, a nervous habit he had when he was thinking hard. "It's a baptismal medallion."

"Are you Catholic?" She looked fascinated. "I never even thought about your religious bents before. Call me shallow."

"No shallower than me," he said. "I never thought about them, either. I was born Catholic, I guess. And I was baptized, evidently. My mother's name on my birth cert is Maria Grazia Amendola. Father unknown. She must have been Italian Catholic. She died shortly after I was born. This is all I have from her." He fingered it. "I never take it off," he admitted. "Don't know why."

"I know why." Robin circled his chair, leaning against him and nuzzling the top of his head. Her warm weight felt great. "So? If you're not Catholic, are you something else?" she probed.

He shook his head. "I don't bother with that stuff." It was hard to concentrate, while his back was so occupied feeling how the tight little nubs of her nipples rubbed him, in such exquisite, tingling detail. "I don't really believe in anything much. Except justice, maybe."

"Justice?" She sounded puzzled, but curious. "Believe in it how?"

He shook his head. "It's more like I just want to believe in it," he said, in a halting voice. "The possibility of it, anyhow. It's all you can offer people who get hurt by fuckheads who don't care about anything but money or themselves. Or people who run into monsters who enjoy inflicting pain. It never makes up for what's been lost. But it's all there is to give. If there's anything I want to stand for, it's that."

She sat down on his lap, her smooth, perfect buttocks nestling against his erection, slid her arms round his neck and gave him a soft kiss, part holy benediction from a sweet madonna, part pure, red-hot scorching temptation. "Jon Amendola, you are one righteous dude."

He struggled to find his voice. "Don't be fooled," he said. "I'm a heinous dickwad most of the time. Ask my exes."

She tapped his lips, looking stern. "No talking about past lovers. It's not fair, since you've had hordes and I don't have any."

"No past, no future? Sort of limits conversational possibilities," he grumbled. "And I'm not much of a chatterbox to begin with."

"Phooey. You're doing just fine." She kissed him again. "So cope."

It was definitely looking like he was going to get lucky again, but now he had his own questions to ask, before his brain melted down.

"How old were you when your mom died?" he asked.

Her eyes went flat. It unnerved him. "Danny never told you?"

"Told me what?" He was getting apprehensive.

She looked away. "She's not dead," she said. "She walked out on us, after our daddy got himself killed. I was one at the time. I don't remember her at all. I'm surprised Danny never told you."

He cast back, trying to remember. "I thought he said he was an orphan. Or maybe I just made assumptions and he never corrected me."

"Did he tell you about our father?" Robin asked.

"How he was a con man? Yeah, he did tell me that. He said your dad used to use him to run his scams. That he was pretty good at it."

"Yeah, Danny's the sneakiest one of us. Me and Mac are hopeless that way. Not a sneaky bone in our bodies. So both parents were pretty problematic. Maybe we're better off without them. I don't know." Robin's voice was muted. "I tried to pry details out of Mac and Danny when I was littler. They just got angry. Finally I got a clue, and let them be."

"You've never . . ." His voice trailed off as Robin shook her head.

"Never," she said. "She never called, never wrote. My uncle tracked her down about a decade ago. At that point, she was in Texas, married. With another family. My half brothers and sisters." She shrugged. "I guess she liked them better than us."

He was speechless with fury at the selfish bitch. Walking out on her baby, to say nothing of her older sons, and never a fucking word.

God, that was cold. He pulled her closer. Her head dropped against his shoulder, and her satiny hair swirled over his shoulder and chest.

"We have pictures," she said, her voice musing. "I look exactly like her. It's freaky. Like looking at myself, in eighties drag."

He squeezed. She cuddled closer. "When I was little, I fantasized about becoming this amazing person, finding her and flaunting how excellent I was. To make her guilty, I guess. Show her how much she'd missed out. Then I got older. My ideas got a lot less grandiose."

"You *are* excellent and amazing," he found himself saying. "You don't need her to recognize it in order for it to be true."

She pressed her face against his neck. "You're sweet to say that. But I'm OK with it. I guess when your mom runs out on you, there's always a part of you that's thinking, what am I, chopped liver? But most of me knows I'm not. Mac and Danny drive me nuts, but I've never doubted I was important to them. That's more than lots of people have."

She slid her hand up his chest, and touched the medallion again with her fingertip. "Still. You're lucky to have this. Little though it is."

He wanted to do something, say something, but shit. He usually left the touchy-feely stuff to people who knew how to deal with it. He didn't. It rattled him. Made him feel thick, stupid.

He was reminded, uncomfortably, of all his own long-lost-mom-comes-back fantasies. He'd finally rooted them out, replaced them with armor-plated reality. But Robin shouldn't have had to.

No sweet, innocent little kid should have to. And aw, Christ. This was why he left touchy-feely stuff to other people. It got to you. It hurt.

He cupped her face, turned it towards him. "I'm lucky to have *this*," he said roughly.

He put it all into the kiss, everything he was too nervous to say, everything he had no words for. She deserved a mom who gave a shit, who appreciated how special she was. She deserved the best. All of it.

It wasn't anything so coherent as a plan, or even a thought. More just a primeval impulse, but once he made the split second resolve, it was unbreakable. As long as he had this gorgeous, red hot, live wire chick within arm's length, she was going to feel properly appreciated, by God. He would damn well make this adventure worth her time.

He still couldn't believe she'd picked a clueless bozo like himself to deflower her. What a gift. It dazzled him. Dazed him with raw lust.

And lust, at least, was an emotion he knew how to deal with.

He stood up, letting her slip off his lap, and sent plates, glasses, cups sliding back across the battered table with a rattling shove. He scooped her up and perched her on the edge of the table, and scooted his own chair closer between those perfect thighs.

She squeaked, realizing his intentions, but he clamped her knees wide and kissed her belly, flicking his tongue over her navel.

"I'm still hungry," he said. "And you took the last piece of bacon."

"But I haven't—I need to take a shower—"

"And wash away all that yummy lube? What a waste." He pressed his face against her muff, kissing the ringlets clustered over the hood of her clit until the giggles faded into the trembling silence of anticipation.

Only then did he venture to tease his tongue inside. She tasted of latex, but a couple minutes of ravenous licking and her own sweet sea flavor welled up and shone through. He wallowed in the tender pink and crimson folds of her succulent cunt, lavishing her with tenderness. Her nails dug into his shoulders, trying to hold herself steady, and her shivering sharpened, tightening.

Her climax throbbed against his mouth as he sucked

and tongued her clit. She clutched his shoulders. The sting of her nails felt so good.

He groped for the condom he'd left on the table. He rolled it on and pressed himself against her, forcing himself inside.

Robin leaned back on her elbows, an arch in her back worthy of a classical dancer. She opened her legs wider, offering herself. Every detail of her, from her gleaming hair, her shining eyes on down to the gleaming pink folds of her pussy, stretched taut around the shaft of his cock, moved him. He rocked, sinking deeper with each thrust, until his cock shaft gleamed like it was oiled. Hugged by the quivering muscles inside her.

They hit their stride, a deep, pumping thrust-and-glide. He lost all sense of time. Every licking shove into her juicy pussy was a question, every clutching, sighing response she gave was an utterly satisfying answer.

Their eyes locked, a raw, electric contact so intimate it scared him. No jokes, no smiles, just panting breath, soft moans. And a sense that something huge was waking up inside of him, displacing his old, familiar self. Shuffling it off like a scaly husk. Leaving him with a new self that he did not know, and could not predict or control.

Or protect. He was totally exposed. Naked under the floodlights.

You are so in for it. Fear pierced him, like a needle of ice.

She transformed him. Every time he touched her, kissed her, put his cock into her. Even the way he came was different. Usually he let loose at the starting gate and pounded madly to the finish like a racing stallion, but he was melting into a shimmering blur of total one-ness with her, riding long, cresting waves with her, one after the other. A piece of him stood aside and watched, stupefied. Multiple goddamn orgasms, for Christ's sake. Like a woman. This shit was not normal.

But God, it was nice. He followed her slavishly to the end, let her sobbing, clutching orgasm finally milk the come out of him, in violent spurts, like a geyser, and then sagged against her, hiding his wet eyes.

He pulled out, turned away. Covered his face with his hands until it felt more like his own mug, and less like a neon signboard.

The silence scared him. She was waiting for him to make a move, break the spell. Wasn't happening. He was too naked. He couldn't deal.

"Why don't you go take the first shower?" he suggested, gruffly.

She slipped off the table and marched into the bath-room. Back very straight. Pissed at him, for chickening out on her. *Fuck.*

It wasn't like he wasn't used to it. He'd seen that anger radiating off a naked woman's back before. But still. He hated it. He couldn't steel himself against it, like he usually did. His steel was melted down.

The shower started to hiss. He had just that much time to pull himself together. He gathered jumbled plates from the table, dumped them into the sink. His phone lay on the table, still off. He thumbed it on, to see if anything was happening out there.

Six calls. All from Jo Hirsch, his buddy from Social Services whom he'd asked to check on Molly. His chest seized up at the thought of something happening to sweet, dotty old Molly, his honorary grandma. He was pulling up Jo's number when the phone buzzed in his hand. He hit Talk. "Yeah? Jo? What's up with Molly?"

"Thank God you finally turned your phone on," Joanna fussed.

"I know." Impatience roughened his voice. "What's up with Molly? Is she sick? Did she fall? Did something happen?"

"Molly's OK. But something weird happened. I saw this woman come out of your duplex. Young, pretty, blond hair, well dressed. Turns out she was in there with Molly for the last half hour, eating lemon cookies and sorting her meds! She told Molly she was me!"

"No shit," he said slowly. "That is really weird."

"It sure was," Joanna said forcefully. "Particularly since it took me twenty minutes of talking through her door, plus a call to my boss, to persuade Molly that I was not the impostor. And now Molly's all wound up. I stayed with her as long as I could, but I have lots of calls to make."

"Yeah. Thanks for letting me know." His mind buzzed, wondering who he knew who would pull a stunt like that. He came up blank.

"Have you disappointed any of your lady friends recently, Jon?"

Yeah, right. He snorted. Jo enjoyed needling him. "No hot blondes come to mind except for Vicki, and Molly knows Vicki. Hates her too."

"I don't blame her," Joanna commented. "I checked Molly's meds, and they were sorted appropriately, but still. It makes my flesh creep."

"Jo, I know you're busy, but could you check on her tomorrow?"

"Yes, of course. I've already slotted her in. Don't worry."

Good old Jo. He sighed in relief. "I owe you. I'll call tomorrow."

"OK. Till then. Have a good one."

He hit End and stared down at the phone, sick with foreboding.

He punched in Molly's number, waited for the ten rings it took for the arthritic old lady to hobble to the phone. "Hello?" she quavered.

"Hey, Molly, it's me, Jon."

"Jonny! The funniest thing just happened! There were two Joannas this morning!"

"Yeah, I know. Joanna number two was the real one. If you ever see Joanna number one again, lock your door and call 911. Then speed dial the other number I programmed into your phone, OK? That's Mendez, the detective that works with me. Talk to her. Understand?"

It took fifteen solid minutes of stroking and soothing to get the rattled Molly calmed down and coherent. When he finally ended the call, Robin stood behind him. Damp, naked and gorgeous, toweling her long, wet hair. She looked troubled. "Problems?"

He tossed the phone down. "I got a friend to look in on my neighbor while I was gone. Molly's ninety. She can't get around much. And some blonde came to see Molly this morning who said that she was Jo. Sorted her meds. Ate her cookies. What the *fuck* is that about?"

Robin's eyes widened. "Ooh. That's creepy."

"Yeah," he agreed. "Oh, yeah."

"Are you, um . . ." She chewed her lip. "Are you thinking you need to go back early?"

"Yeah, I am," he admitted. "I don't like this. At all."

"I don't blame you," she said. "When will you leave?"

He hesitated. "Not before tomorrow. I don't want to pop our magic bubble yet. Not before we absolutely have to."

Her face lit up, like dawn lighting the sky. "What'll we do today?"

"You mean, aside from . . ." He waggled his eyebrows lasciviously.

She giggled. "Aside from that."

He glanced out the window. "It's a beautiful day," he said. "Let's go out and play in the woods."

Her grin grew dazzling. "That sounds great to me."

"I'll call Molly every couple of hours or so," he said. "If anything else weird happens, I'll have Mendez send someone to check it out."

He was talking out loud, trying to justify a purely selfish, egoistic decision, but God, just look at that woman. Buck naked and smiling at him like that. She fucking glowed. How was a man expected to resist?

The business suite was equipped with Internet access, and Julia made excellent use of it. Crowne Royale Group's corporate website was sleek and professional. As was the flattering photo of Danny MacNamara, CFO. Julia read his bio, dismissed him, and moved on.

She typed "Robin MacNamara" into the engine. After a half hour, she hit the Ace Entertainment Agency site, and got a photo and bio of Wiggles the Clown. Wiggles offered general clowning, face painting, juggling, balloon twisting, humorous magic, stories, games and puppetry. Wiggles claimed to meet all clowning needs, be they birthday parties, corporate events, holiday parties, charity bashes, children's hospitals, daycares, and so on. Wiggles had purportedly been entertaining in the Greater Seattle area and bringing smiles to faces of children and adults for the past six years.

Another paragraph revealed that the clown's alter ego was Robin MacNamara. Julia stared at the big dark eyes and wide smile of the garishly painted creature who sported an enormous green wig and protruding red nose. Wiggles was Robin. Strange, but true.

Entertaining for six years? Either she was older than she looked, or she'd been clowning since she was no more than a child.

She found a contact number. "Ace Entertainment," said a woman.

"Hi. My name's Melinda Sykes, and Robin MacNamara did a birthday party for my nephew a few weeks ago at my house. I just found her handbag," Julia said. "Could you give me her home number? I could just drop it by for her on my way to work."

The woman hesitated. "Um, I could pass your number on to her."

Julia sighed. Sometimes people were stupid and credulous. Sometimes not. She gave the woman a fake number, and hit End.

There was always the passwords William had obtained from the DMV. She entered the Washington system, with "Robin MacNamara," scrolled, she found the girl's face. Wide brown eyes. Born twenty-five years ago. A bit old, but when she closed her eyes, William gave her an assenting nod.

She cross-referenced the address with a reverse directory, found an R. MacNamara on Etruria, and dialed the number.

"Hi, is this Robin?" Julia asked, when a woman responded.

"No, this is Esther. I'm her roommate. Can I take a message?"

"I'm throwing a birthday party for my son, and the clown canceled on me. I'm scrambling for a replacement." Julia feigned the harried tone of a busy mom. "Do you know if she'd be available tonight at six?"

"I'm sorry, but I really doubt it," Esther said regretfully. "She's not even in town. She went up to the mountains for a few days."

The mountains? A shuddering thrill went up Julia's spine.

Of course, Robin might not have gone to the same place . . . but if she had? Oh, wow. It would be so incredibly perfect.

"Very well," she said. "Thanks for your help."

Lake. Cabin. Mountains. Everything pointed to it— the clipping, Molly, Esther, her prickling skin. Amendola and Robin were up there, having a secret rendezvous. A scumbag like Amendola was more than capable of betraying his friend by defiling his innocent little sister. The man's disregard for anything but his own pleasure sickened her.

But where? She pulled the photographs out of her purse. She had no way to be sure this was the same place, but Molly had implied he went there often. And MacNamara was in that photo, too. If he owned his own cabin on a lake in the mountains, why go fishing elsewhere?

There were a thousand reasons why a rich CFO might go fishing elsewhere, but Julia dismissed them all like stinging insects. She had to trust her instincts. The picture was of MacNamara's lake. The lake was the place. There was a symmetry to it. Cosmic perfection. She felt it.

She stared at the photo, studying the mottled face of Mt. Rainier.

She typed "Mt. Rainier climbing routes" into the engine, and hit on a website filled with up-to-the-minute climbing conditions on every approach to the mountain's summit, each of which had its own photo gallery.

Photos of every angle. Detailed topographical maps. Perfect.

She studied each approach, compared them to the lake photograph, and found an almost perfect match in the South Tahoma Glacier pictures. It was off by a few degrees, but she would compensate for that. The geological configurations were identical. Southwest, then.

She spread out her Washington map, and puzzled out the distances. She estimated no less than twenty-five miles, no more than thirty-five. She found the correct angle, calculated a fan of territory. Allowing margin on all sides, she came up with a list of eleven towns.

Well and good. And now? She was exhausted, from lack of food and sleep. Her head pounded. But with every hammer blow of her heart, she saw William's blood-smeared hand, pressed to the glass. Those cruel letters, carved into his flesh.

Think, Julia. Think.

She stared at the two men in the boat. Amendola holding up the fish, like a little boy with a toy. *Fishing.* One needed a license to fish.

A fishing license. Sporting goods stores. Oh, yes. Of course.

She let out a happy sigh, dialed room service, and ordered a turkey on dry whole wheat toast, a fruit cup and black coffee, as a reward to herself. Then she dove right back into the digital soup of state telephone databases to make a list of sporting goods stores in the area.

Hours later found her exhausted and irritated, her euphoria gone. Twenty-seven sporting goods stores, and she had called all but two of them. Perhaps she'd missed one. Miscalculated the angles, the distances. Was this stupid, wasted effort?

William was looking impatient and stern. It made her anxious.

She took a grim swallow of cold, bitter coffee and continued down the list. Kerrigan Creek was next. Chad's Sporting Goods. She dialed.

"Hi, this is Chad's," said a bubbly young female voice.

Julia made her voice young and chirpy. "Hi. My name's Kelly, and I'm calling on behalf of my boss, Daniel MacNamara. He just had a change of address, and he wanted to make sure the info on his fishing license was up to date. Could you check the address for me?"

The girl hesitated. "Uh, I don't think it makes any difference—"

"Could you just check for me?" Julia wheedled, woman-to-woman. "He had problems in the past, and he's a perfectionist. It has to be just so, you know? He's like that. Just check it? As a favor to me?"

"Hold on a sec." The phone clunked and rattled. Julia waited for several minutes. "Hi, you still there, Kelly?" the girl asked.

"Sure am," Julia replied brightly.

"The address listed on this license is on Mercer, in Seattle," the girl said. "Is that his current address?"

Excitement bubbled through Julia's body like fuel. Better than food. "It sure is. You don't have to change a thing. Thanks so much!"

She hung up, hugging herself in delight, and then accessed the phone directory for Kerrigan Creek, and found a number for the tax assessor. The snippy receptionist informed her that the assessor's name was Stan Borg, and put Julia through to him with bad grace.

"Hello?" Borg's voice was that of an older man.

Julia made her voice deep, sugary, mature. "Hello, Mr. Borg. My name's Cassie Kelly, from the Department of Tax and Finance. I was hoping you might check a name for me, for property ownership?"

The old fellow cleared his throat. "Ah, why, yes, I suppose I could. Let me have that name, and a call back number for you, Ms. Kelly."

"Thanks so much," she cooed. "The name is Daniel MacNamara." She gave him a carefully chosen number, the area code and exchange of which were identical to a number of several official Washington State offices, but the final four digits were 9970, which would always ring busy. It was time to get going and drive on up to Kerrigan Creek. By the time she got there, the pleasant, helpful Mr. Borg would be ripe for a call back, and ready to tell her anything she needed to know.

The woods dazed her. Luminous spring flowers, stark white skeletons of long dead trees sticking through the tender pine and spruce that surrounded the lake. Ferns burgeoned, and the perfume of omnipresent water tickled her nose. She'd always loved hiking, but today every nook was a treasure, every clump of flowers a discovery. She'd floated up the slopes, inches off the ground.

They'd skipped rocks along the torrent that fed the lake. Stopped to feast on sandwiches and fruit on a slab of rock in the middle of the stream, to bake in the sun, kiss, fool around. Either he started it, or she did, but someone got the ball rolling, and once it started—wow.

This place was particularly seductive. They were twined together on a warm rock under the sky, with white water foaming and gurgling through tumbled rocks on every side. She was currently on his lap, kissing him madly. Her jeans were unbuttoned, his hand moving inside her panties with a skill that stole her breath. It was a wonder she got enough oxygen to function, he stole so damn much breath. He teased her up to the brink of a climax, and dug a condom out of his pocket. "Last one."

"Oh, God." She giggled, thighs quivering with anticipation. "You are a sex freak. I've created a monster."

"What I want to know is how you got it into your head to seduce me with only four condoms. What the hell were you thinking?"

She twitched the foil packet out of his hands. "I was thinking four was pretty damn ambitious. I brought four in case I got super lucky."

"Lucky. Hah. Four. A drop in the fucking bucket. Literally."

She scrambled out of his lap. "Stop complaining. The savage beast is getting a whole lot of quality time."

He laughed, but the laughter faded into a glittering-eyed mask as she rose, pried off her shoes. Pulled off the sweatshirt. Shucked jeans, panties. She held her arms up, and spun, slowly displaying herself.

"I've never been naked outdoors before," she said. "Feels good."

He stared at her body. "Yeah," he said hoarsely. "Sure does."

She knelt, wrenched his jeans open with a boldness she couldn't have imagined a day ago. She was so comfortable with him, as if they'd been lovers forever. Two souls split in two, longing for completion.

She pushed that thought away as she shoved his jeans down and seized the thick, hot stalk of his penis in her hands.

He made as if to put the condom on, but she batted

his hand away and bent down to have at him with her eager mouth. He'd made her come more times than she could count. Fair was fair. Besides, she seemed to be developing some skill at this. And a definite taste for it.

At least, a taste for Jon. The flavor of him, the pressure of the taut, engorged flesh against her mouth, her tongue, made her shiver and squirm with excitement. As if her mouth was a sexual organ, receiving pleasure, not just giving it. As if he were everywhere, moving inside her, touching her, caressing. Loving her.

Don't. Don't think that way, ditz-brain. Keep it light. Light as air.

He put his hand on her head, stroking her hair. "Wait," he begged. "I don't want to come yet. I wanted to be inside you."

She pulled herself onto her knees obligingly enough as he arranged himself crosslegged on the rocks, and held out his arms.

She straddled him and lowered herself, crouching until he'd prodded himself into position. Then she sank down slowly, her body clasping him. It ached, they were definitely overdoing it, but what the hell. She had the rest of her life to recover. And remember.

This time wasn't like the other times. He barely moved inside her, just the slightest rocking pulse. He let her do it all. Squeezing him. Clasped in his arms, legs hugging his waist. Wound into a loose, undulating knot of everchanging emotion. Lazy and infinite. Timeless.

She couldn't have said how long they made love. Shadows shifted and moved, the sun changed position in the sky. It could have been hours, or centuries of enchanted time, like the tales of people who fell asleep in fairy rings. Or visited the hall of the Mountain King and found that hundreds of years had passed. Sweet, intoxicating magic.

The perfection found its inevitable peak, lifted them high, and laid them down again, as gently as a kiss, but he couldn't seem to loosen his tight, trembling embrace. He couldn't stop kissing her. Like he could never get enough. Like he was storing it up for a drought to come.

Finally, he murmured something about dealing with the condom.

He lifted her off, and she sagged back, boneless. Jon lowered her onto her back, against the warm granite slab. Her legs splayed to either side of him. Her arms flung wide, in an ecstasy of trust to the open sky.

As she opened her eyes, a shadow swooped low. The wingspan of some big raptor, an eagle or hawk. She couldn't tell with the sun in her eyes. It let out a shrill cry. A shudder went through her. She thought of rabbits, mice, voles. Vulnerable things for whom the sky was an enemy.

"Don't." Jon scooped her up, crushing her against his naked chest. She felt his heart thudding.

"Don't what?" she asked, against the skin of his neck.

His arms tightened. "That position you were in," he muttered. "That X-man pose. It reminded me of . . . it has bad associations."

"It's OK," she said, kissing his neck. "Egg Man stuff?"

His body tensed. "I don't want any of that sick filth to touch you."

She nuzzled his jaw. "If it touches you, it touches me."

"Like hell. Leave it." He averted his face. "Get yourself dressed."

She pulled her clothes back on, bewildered. His

mellow, blissed-out energy was gone. And just when she'd gotten all strung out on it.

He punched into his cell phone while she struggled with her shoes. He found no signal, and his explosion of profanity jolted her.

He stared up at the cut made by the torrent of water. "We've got to get out of this gully to get reception. Get your shoes on. Fast."

She did as he commanded and trailed after him in forlorn silence. The spell was broken. The walls were up. He was armor plated again.

Party's over. Everybody out of the pool.

It was extremely silly, but she had to struggle not to cry.

"Mr. Borg? It's Cassie Kelly, from Tax and Finance? I've been waiting for your call." Julia shaded her voice with gentle reproof.

"I'm sorry, Ms. Kelly, but I've been trying to call you all afternoon!" the man blustered. "That number you gave me was busy every time!"

Julia softened her voice. "Well, we've been busy. The phones were really hopping today. Anyway, I have you now. Did you find anything?"

"Yes, indeed. Daniel MacNamara is on file for a hundred and sixty acre plot that fronts on Kerrigan Lake, with a small hunting cabin. The property is currently valued at a hundred and forty thousand."

"Ah. One moment while I jot that down . . . and this is the Yardley Creek Road property, right?" she murmured distractedly.

"No, ma'am, it's on the Horsetail Bluff Mountain Road. Thirteen point six miles from the junction at Route 4."

"Oh! Yes, of course," Julia said, contrite. "Silly me, I was looking at the wrong piece of paper! Thank you so much for your help, Mr. Borg. You've been just a treasure."

"My pleasure, Ms. Kelly. You have a good evening, now."

"Oh, I will," Julia promised him, with utter sincerity.

6

It took the rest of the afternoon and evening to get comfortable with each other again. Robin showered while he fried fish, and tried, with limited success, to chill out. Twilight fishing on the lake had helped a little, as had the four big flopping silver trout. And the sunset was nice, reflected off Robin's face. A nice meal should clinch it.

He was making a big effort to be civil. Robin didn't deserve to get her head bitten off. She'd been nothing but sweet to him. She'd been a freaking wet dream. There was no reason not to be wallowing in bliss.

He knew exactly what it would take to push him into the realm of perfect bliss, but they didn't have any more latex. But hey. They hadn't tried sixty-nining. His dick throbbed at the happy thought.

Robin had gotten sun that afternoon, so her face glowed pink in the big, raggedy white bathrobe. She tucked away fried fish with her usual appetite, but her eyes darted nervously to his. Her blush deepened, her gaze dropped.

They were back to shy silences again.

"There are a few games in the kitchen drawer," she ventured. "Know how to play backgammon? Or poker? Or spit?"

"No," he said. "I had a different game in mind." He loaded butter onto a second baked potato and shook salt and pepper over it.

"Well. Actually," she murmured, eyes downcast. "That gives me an excellent segue for, um, something I've been meaning to mention."

His fork froze halfway to his mouth. "Mention away," he said.

"A couple months ago, when I got the call from the Circo, I, um went to my doctor, and got a contraceptive implant."

Jon abruptly stopped chewing. Or breathing.

"So I'm baby-proof," she rushed on. "For the next few years."

He cleared his throat. "I thought you weren't . . ."

"I wasn't, but I hoped that would change," she said. "I wanted to erase the issue. While, of course, taking all due safe sex precautions."

He couldn't speak. She gave him an encouraging smile. "So? You know every single detail of my sexual history intimately at this point."

"What exactly are you saying?" he asked slowly.

Her brows twitched together in irritation. "Isn't it obvious?"

They stared at each other. Robin looked perplexed. It made him angry, the thought of Robin, baby-proofing herself so she could hook up with some as-yet-to-be-announced asshole in some goddamn circus.

Like *hell*. He wanted to smash his beer bottle. Have at his imaginary rival with the jagged end. "You're inviting me to fuck you with no condom."

She flinched at his crudeness. "No," she said. "I'm

asking you if there's any reason why we shouldn't. Because it would be lovely."

Lovely. Hah. He was sweating at the mere thought. And furious.

Bad combination. He swallowed, put his fork down. His appetite was gone. "I've had safe sex since I was old enough to know better. I was negative for everything on my last physical." His voice felt metallic. "I haven't been with anyone since then. I was too busy with this case."

Her face brightened. "Oh. Great. So, then?"

"What do you mean, so, then?" His voice was getting harder.

She lifted her hands in helpless confusion. "I don't understand. I thought you'd be pleased. I thought guys liked—"

"Of course guys like it," he snarled.

"So why are you angry?"

Good question, and he didn't have an answer, at least not one he could own. Anything he felt that was squirmy or nasty got channeled straight into the anger slot. A handy catch-all for all that inconvenient shit.

His hand slammed the table, making the plates rattle and jump.

Robin recoiled. His hand welcomed the burning sting of contact.

"The fact that guys like it is exactly the problem," he said harshly. "Just what makes you think I'm telling you the truth about not having any STD's? What the fuck makes you think that?"

She bit her trembling lip, and swallowed. "Because I trust you."

"Trust me? On what basis? Twenty-four hours of hot sex?"

She seemed to curl in on herself. "I thought it was more."

"Your mistake." He couldn't stop the ugliness once it started churning out. Part of him was screaming, *stop trashing it, stop hurting her*, but he was powerless to stop. "Sex without latex is something you can offer a guy once he's promised to be faithful for the rest of his life. And that's only after the blood test results and the background check."

"Oh, don't be ridiculous—"

"I'm dead serious!" he bellowed. "It's not something to offer to me!"

Her chin lifted. "Well, call me stupid, but it's mine to offer," she said quietly. "And I'm offering it to you. Nyah nyah. So there."

"I do call you stupid," he flung at her. "Is this the way you're going to be with guys, once you get out into the real world? It's a fucking wasteland out there. A pile of steaming shit. You have to protect yourself. Starting right now. From me. Do you hear?"

She scooted back in her chair, wrapping her arms around her chest. "I don't know what the hell you're talking about—"

"Don't trust me!" he yelled at her. "I could be lying to you. Feeding you a line. Any guy would, if you offered yourself up like you did to me. Oh, pretty please, pop my cherry. Oh, pretty please, let me suck your cock. Oh, pretty please, won't you fuck me with no condom—"

"Just. Shut. *Up*." She leaped to her feet, sending the chair spinning back against the wall. "You *asshole*."

"Do not treat me like your boyfriend. Or your fiancé."

"Don't worry. I won't." Her voice was clipped.

"And you shouldn't criticize my sexual style, Jon. After all, you're my only teacher. So far."

His hands fisted. "What the *fuck* is that supposed to mean?"

She shrugged. "Just being realistic. Would it make you feel better if I solemnly promise to use latex with my next lover? Or next several lovers, I should say. I'll have to do my own experimenting, just as you said. And hunting down a decent boyfriend is a very inexact science."

"You're trying to make me jealous?" His voice vibrated with strain.

"Not at all, Jon. Why on earth should you care? If you'll excuse me, this is my cue to get dressed and leave. Thanks for the professional job of deflowering me. Masterful, really. You set the tone for what promises to be a fabulous future sex life. Wish me luck."

He was on his feet and blocking her before she'd finished speaking. "Do not fuck with my head, Robin," he hissed.

"You drove me to it," she retorted icily. "Here I am, trying to be as nice to you as a woman can be to a man, and you rip my head off for my trouble. So I'll change tactics. I'll be cold. I can be taught. There's hope for me yet. Now get the hell out of my way. I am out of here."

"No." He ducked in front of her in the doorway to the living room.

"Don't you dare." She shoved past him. "I want privacy to dress."

"Tough," the grunting primeval caveman inside him replied.

She made a derisive sound, and tossed the bathrobe off her slender shoulders. "Fine. Gawk if you must. I'm still leaving."

That heart-stopping back view as she bent over the duffel to rummage for her underwear was a blatant provocation. He moved up behind her, making no sound. She sensed him and froze.

"You're not leaving," he said softly. "I'm not done with you yet."

"Of course I'm leaving," she snapped. "You're unbearable."

He slid his arm around her waist, and tension rose, more volatile and dangerous than before."Don't," she whispered. "Don't you dare. You'll lose the family jewels. Snip, snip."

"Thanks for the warning," he said. "I'll be careful."

"No, you'll be dead. Don't muscle me around, you lout. Let me go!" She struggled, but he automatically countered her every move.

Bad move.Very bad. Back off, pig dog. The voice of reason was screaming at him, but he'd been hijacked. In any case, what he had to say to her could only be said with his body. He carried her, clamped against his chest, to the sofabed, bunched a sleeping bag into a fluffy heap and bent her over it. Her thrashing body was strong, but he was stronger. He caught her flailing hands, trapped them. "Shhh."

"Do not shush me, you condescending son of a bitch!"

He held her against the bed, slid down and started kissing her ass. She let out a shriek and shook as he nuzzled his way down her shadowy cleft, down to her furled-up pink pussy lips. He went at her, tongue delving, trilling over her clit at the end of every stroke.

"Oh . . . my . . . *God* . . ." Her voice broke. The muscles in her thighs trembled, convulsed, and she made a bewildered sobbing sound as they yielded, parted. She lifted her ass to give him better access to all that slick, juicy bounty. It gleamed, puffy and soft and ready, her lube flooding out. He jerked his fly open and freed his aching cock.

"Looks like being muscled around by a lout gets you off," he observed. "Who knew. The indomitable Robin likes to be mastered."

Her body jerked beneath his hands. "Like hell," she hissed. "Don't think for one second that you can control me by making me come. When I'm done, I'll still spit in your face and blow you off, you butthead. So if you're trying to make a point about who's boss, don't bother."

He was impressed. "Wow. You never shut up, do you?"

"Never." Her voice was breathless, shaking. "Pig."

He resumed, figuring he'd get in less trouble if he kept his tongue as far up her pussy as it would go. But he wasn't going to last much longer just tongue fucking. He lifted his head. "Do you want my cock?"

"What kind of sick question is that?" she snarled back.

He choked off the burst of laughter that would get him castrated or worse. "Seemed straightforward to me."

"You haven't asked permission so far, so why bother now?"

"Yeah, you'd love it if I just mounted up and rode without asking, right? That would suit your mood perfectly—"

"Fuck you, Jon Amendola," she spat.

"With pleasure," he said. "If you ask nicely."

She let out a sob of laughter. "Oh, God. I do not get you at all."

"You'll get as much of me as you want. Just say the magic word."

"Magic word, my ass. Would that turn you on, to make me beg?"

"No. You can say I jerked you around, seduced you, manipulated you, teased you. But you're never going to say I forced you."

"Word games," she shot back. "Meaningless. Stupid. Dumb."

"Maybe. But they're my games." He slid his tongue down the slick furrow, circled her clit, teased, fluttered, and lapped back up to the overflowing well of sweet girl juice. He pulled away, panting. "Say it."

She wailed with frustration. "Do it," she said savagely.

He waited. "Yeah? And?"

"I'm not going to say please. I'd rather die. Just do it. Or else fuck off and leave me alone."

Aw, what the hell. Being commanded to fuck by the queen of the universe had as salutory an effect on his cock as pleading would have.

He grabbed her waist. She let out a squeak as he lifted her up, pitching her face first onto the bed. He dragged her hips back until she was kneeling with her ass to him, glowing with sweat, shuddering with excitement. His hands shook as he fitted his cockhead to her.

He dragged in a breath as he entered her. Hot, scalding. Bare naked, live wire, screamingly intense. He almost came on the first tight, squeezing shove inside. He flung his head back, gritted his teeth, breathed the climax down, gripped her ass and started in on the slick, swirling pump and grind that would melt her down into mindless pleasure. This would be one ride she would never forget.

No matter how many goddamn lovers she took after him.

* * *

Robin clutched the sleeping bag, trying to stifle the sounds jerking out of her throat. Her whimpers sounded pleading, her body moved of its own volition. She was too crazy in love to shield herself. It made her feel weak, stupid, but still she rocked back, begging for more.

Something huge and muscular was uncoiling inside her. It was happening too soon. She could tell by his urgency that he wasn't going to wait out her climax and start again, as he often did. This was it. *The last time.* The realization burned as all other thought disintegrated.

After this, she had to get as far away from him as she could.

Faster, deeper. She yelled, lost in the twisting frenzy as his climax pumped into her. He collapsed, crushing her to the bed. She struggled to breathe. Crying again. Anger was better, but it was melted down.

When she could move again, she shoved until he rolled onto his back. She fled to the bathroom. His semen trickled down her thigh.

This was so much more dangerous than she'd ever dreamed.

Julia let the field glasses drop. She could hardly believe what she'd just seen. Her hands shook, she was so horrified.

She had to shake herself back into action. She scrambled to her feet and made her way down the hill to Robin's car. The girl hadn't bothered to lock it. How convenient. Easy enough to set something up just in case she did.

Julia took a length of fishing twine from her bag,

tied a noose and slipped the thing around the knob lock on the passenger's side. Then she threaded it through the top of the window, and closed it, leaving a near invisible filament with a knot hanging out the top. She tested it with a gentle tug.

The lock popped open. Brilliant in its low tech simplicity. William would be proud of her. It would be nothing to just lean over the car as if she were unlocking it, give the thread a yank, and voilà.

Headlights sliced through the woods. She scrambled back up to her hiding place, yanked up her hood over the beacon of her fair hair, and peered towards the window through the glasses again. She saw only Amendola this time, sitting on the bed, looking thick and brutish.

She felt as sickened as if she herself had been raped. That poor girl. She must be shattered. But pain had a purpose. Always.

Julia had learned that lesson well. It was her guiding principle.

William had made sure of it.

Jon sat on the bed, head dangling. Exhausted. An apology seemed lame after all that drama. She'd spit in his face anyway.

It made him crazy. Like some shining thing was being held out to him, but there was a sheet of soundproof, bulletproof glass between him and it. And now he'd made her hate him. His chest burned.

He headed towards the bathroom. No idea what he was going to do. What could he say to her? *Don't go. Don't listen to the stupid trash I talk. Don't believe a word I say. Don't disappear into the dark.*

And under it, the hollow suck of fear, pulling at his

insides. He was afraid, as if some evil thing were lurking out there, hungry for her sweet flesh. He was flat-out paranoid. He'd never been this bad before. Just the normal bad attitude of a guy who saw too much violence.

He stood outside the bathroom door for minutes before he mustered the nerve to speak. "Hey. Robin."

"I'm not speaking to you." Her voice floated through the door. She'd latched it, but a smack of his shoulder ripped the latch loose.

Robin stood in the tub, her eyes huge. The detachable shower head was in her hands. She'd been sudsing up her muff. Clumps of shower foam slid down her long, perfect, gleaming thighs.

"Jon! For God's sake!" Her voice was crisp with outrage.

He gulped hard, having entirely forgotten everything he'd had in mind to say. Mesmerized by how beautiful her body was dripping wet.

She rolled her eyes and briskly finished rinsing herself. "Go put that thing of yours away before it gets you in any more trouble than you're already in," she said, with a significant glance at his crotch.

He glanced down at his lengthening dick, and walked in, letting the door swing shut behind him. What needed to be said had to be said right now, this moment. Before he froze up again.

He opened his mouth—and stopped, hearing a sound that congealed his blood. The warped front door made a loud, rasping squeal over the scarred linoleum. "Hey? Jon? You in here?"

Holy screaming *fuck*. It was Danny. He and Robin exchanged glances of naked panic. He stared wildly around the tiny bathroom.

"There's no towels," Robin whispered. "I left the bathrobe outside!"

Great. His balls hanging out, a bullseye painted on them. He took a deep breath. "Yo, Danny," he called out dully. "I'm in the john."

"I see dinner for two," Danny said suspiciously. "You got company in there?"

"We might as well get it over with," Robin said. She flung the door open. Back straight, chin high, tits up, she marched right on out.

One would think being naked as a jaybird in front of a big brother who had changed one's diapers when one was an infant wouldn't be such a big hairy deal. One would be dead wrong. The look on her brother's face morphed from astonishment to fury when he looked past her and saw Jon in the bathroom. "What the fuck is this, Robin?"

She flinched at the punch in his voice. "Trust your instincts, Danny. It's exactly what it looks like."

Jon followed her out, his face taut and unhappy. Danny looked him over, and zapped him with a vicious uppercut that knocked him off his feet and onto the kitchen table. Beers tipped, food slopped, salad scattered, dishes clattered to the ground.

Jon hadn't even tried to block that punch. And she knew that he could. She'd watched them spar since she was a kid. They were well matched. A couple of ninja fiends.

Jon pulled himself to his feet and just stood there, waiting.

"Fight back, you bozo!" she yelled. "Don't just stand there!"

He shook his head without replying.

Danny moved towards him again, winding up for another blow, but Robin grabbed his arm. "Don't touch him!"

Danny shook her off. "Get your clothes on. I'll deal with you later."

"No. You don't understand." She grabbed his arm again. "I overheard you talking. I knew he was up here. He had no idea. I wanted this, so I came up here and got it. End of story."

"Like hell it is," Danny snarled.

"I begged him, you brainless clod!" she yelled. "I literally tore off my clothes and jumped his bones!"

Danny looked at her, then at Jon's big, muscular body. "Oh, yeah. I'm sure he fought like a fucking demon," he said bitterly.

"He did, goddammit! It was my choice!" she hollered.

"It's not anymore. Get your clothes on. I'm taking you home."

She swallowed. "No, Danny," she said quietly. "You're not."

Her brother shot her a steely glance. "That's an order, Robin."

A strange calm had settled over her. "I don't take orders anymore," she replied. "Not from you, not from Mac, not from anyone. And not from you, either." She shot the last remark in Jon's direction, for good measure.

"I'd figured that much out all by myself," Jon said.

"You," Danny snarled. "Keep your goddamn mouth shut."

"And while I'm at it, I might as well let you know it all," she went on. "I'm quitting Crowne Royale Group. I'm not going for a degree in hotel management. I've been accepted into the training program of the Circo della Luna Rossa. I'm leaving in three weeks. So now you know."

Danny made a disgusted sound. "Robin, we've been through this before. Now is not the time to argue about your ridiculous—"

"I'm not arguing," she cut in. "I'm informing you. And now, if you two would excuse me, I've had enough of both of you."

She marched out of the room and started yanking on her clothes.

So. She'd done it. Abandoned her livelihood, alienated her brothers, lost her virginity, smashed her heart into tiny grotty bits, all in one blow. There wasn't much of anything left in her life to demolish.

Jon and Danny avoided each other's eyes for the forty-five seconds it took for Robin to wrench on her jeans and a T-shirt and sling her bag over her shoulder. She looked at Jon as she stalked to the door.

"I guess this is goodbye. Have a nice life, Jon. It was real."

Danny scowled, bewildered. "What the hell?"

"I don't have any designs on him, Danny," she said. "I was just using him for sex. Girls have animal needs too. Deal with it."

Silence followed the slam of the screen door shutting after her. Robin's car coughed, protested, and finally started up and pulled away.

Danny cleared his throat. "Get your clothes on and your shit out of my place," he said. "I do not want to see your face ever again."

Jon turned away without speaking and did as he was told.

He felt oddly numb as he got his stuff together. Hell, he was used to worse case scenarios. He'd grown up right in the middle of one.

And that didn't make it any easier to bear.

Julia peered through the infrared goggles as she coasted slowly down the switchbacks. As soon as she got off Horsetail Bluff, she could drop behind a curve and turn her headlights back on.

Robin signaled at the convenience store and Julia's whole body tingled. Maybe her chance would come sooner than she'd dreamed. She pulled into the parking lot to the side, waited as Robin got out, got gas.

Robin reparked the car outside the store, and went inside. *Yes.* She'd locked it this time.

She had to be quick and decisive. There were people around, but it had been Julia's experience that a pretty woman acting with confidence could get away with just about anything. William had used that trick often. Julia had been the perfect lure. Many times.

She strode over to the passenger's side of Robin's car and pretended to use a key while she yanked the filament that opened the lock. She slid inside, popped the hood. Once she'd ascertained that Robin was still in the bathroom, she lifted the hood, let the clippers slide out into her hand, reached in and severed the battery connection. *Snip.* She let the hood fall, and headed in to buy coffee. No one had blinked an eye.

Julia feigned drinking the nasty brew, using peripheral vision to observe Robin as she emerged from the bathroom. The girl hurried out to her car, eyes puffy. The car, of course, would not start.

Julia drifted to the window, watching obliquely as the girl cursed, yelled, pounded the steering wheel, and finally burst into tears.

Robin got out of the car and poked around under the hood, but she didn't notice the severed battery line hidden under the manifest.

Robin finally came back into the store. "Excuse me," she asked the tight-lipped lady behind the register whose nametag read *Ruby*. "Do you know of a mechanic around here that I could call at this hour?"

Ruby glanced at the clock, and looked dubious. "I don't know. There's Robbie, I guess, but he's usually drunk by now."

"Who's Robbie?" Robin pleaded. "Where could I find him?"

"You could go ask Earl. He runs the bar next door," Ruby said. "Robbie's his half brother. If Robbie's there, you can see for yourself if he's too drunk to be any use. Other than that, hon, I don't know."

"Thanks." Robin walked out, and stared forlornly at her car.

Julia followed the girl out. "Car trouble?" she asked gently.

Robin laughed, a bitter sound. "Hah. Life trouble, more like."

"Do you need a phone? Could I call someone for you?"

"No, thanks," Robin said. "I've got a phone. I could call my brother, but at the moment I think I'd rather stick needles in my eyes."

"Ouch," said Julia. "So you're heading to that bar? Excuse me for butting in, but the place looks rough. You want some company?"

Robin seemed to actually see her for the first time.

"Uh, thanks. That's kind of you, but I don't want to trouble you. I'll be fine."

"Oh, no trouble at all. I insist. My name's Kelly. And yours?"

Julia fell into step beside her, and produced some soothing chitchat. By the time they reached the bar, she'd developed a perfect plan.

7

When Robin's eyes adjusted to the dimness, she was grateful that Kelly had insisted on accompanying her. It was a nice thing to do. In fact, the girl seemed almost too nice. Her niceness was so focused. Something she did, rather than something that she was. If she flipped a switch, that niceness could flip off like a light. Or maybe Robin was reading negativity into a helpful, pleasant girl. Pulling a Jon, in short.

The bar had bowls at intervals, heaped with multi-colored dyed Easter eggs. Robin had forgotten about Easter. Not that she'd ever really noticed it. A person needed a mom to make Easter eggs and bonnets and baskets and bunny hunts happen. Busy older brothers couldn't be bothered with stuff like that. She perched on a stool and tried to catch the eye of the bearded guy with the big belly who was tending bar.

He lumbered over, looking grumpy. "What can I get for ya?"

"Are you Earl?" Robin asked.

"Who wants to know?"

"Ruby at the store told me you might know where

Robbie is," Robin explained. "My car won't start. I need a mechanic."

Earl grunted. "He ain't here."

"Is he likely to drop by? Does he have a phone?"

"Nah. Deadbeat don't pay his bills."

Robin let out a slow, controlled breath. "Could I wait for him?"

"Gotta buy a drink if you want to take up bar space."

"I'll have a diet Coke," Robin said.

Earl rolled his eyes, and looked pointedly at Kelly.

"Mineral water with a twist of lemon," the woman said brightly.

Earl slapped the drinks on the bar and turned his back on them.

"They pride themselves on service, I see," Kelly murmured.

Robin tried to smile, but her face wouldn't work. "Looks like it."

"I should have mentioned this before, but I'm a pretty decent mechanic myself," Kelly said. "On older cars, anyway. My dad was a mechanic. If you like, I'll take a look at it for you."

Robin looked at her, startled. The woman was so pretty, with the bouncing blond ponytail, the delicate features. She didn't look like a mechanic. She looked like a china doll, in forest camo and polar fleece.

Kelly laughed. "Yes, that's one of the reasons I went into sales. No one took me seriously as a mechanic. But I'm good, really. Just one thing."

"Yes? And what's that?"

"My tool chest is in the van," Kelly explained. "And I've got a torn rotator cuff. Could you help me haul my chest over to your car?"

"Oh, sure. What a question," Robin said.

Kelly beamed. "Great. So let's just—"

"What the *fuck* are you doing in a dive like this?"

Robin spun at the harsh voice. It was Jon, glowering down at her.

The impulse to yank Robin off that bar stool, clamp her under his arm and carry her out of that stinking bar was almost overwhelming.

"How did you find me?" Her voice was accusing.

"Saw your car. And the cashier tipped me off. Stalled?"

"Don't worry about it," Robin said crisply. "It's covered."

Damn. What he wanted to say was stuck in his throat. He had to get her someplace private, to pry it out somehow. Make her understand.

"I'm helping her with the car," said the woman next to her.

Jon turned his attention reluctantly to the delicate-looking pale blonde. "You?" he asked. "Helping her how?"

"She's a mechanic," Robin said.

A secretive smile curled the blonde's lips. "Strange, but true."

He could give a flying fuck about the blonde's mechanical ability. He wanted to talk to Robin. But the woman showed no sign of disappearing. She grabbed an egg, cracked it, and peeled it.

"Forget the car, Robin," he pleaded. "Let's just go get a beer somewhere. Not here. We need to talk."

"We've said it all. I think we should stick to the original plan."

He scowled. "We had an original plan?"

"Remember? When it's over, it's over? What plays in Vegas?"

"That wasn't a plan," he barked. "That was a starting point."

"And now it's an end point," Robin said. "We've come full circle."

Desperation clawed from within at the stone wall in his throat.

Robin broke eye contact. "Damn it," she whispered. "Don't, Jon."

"Do you want me to call someone?" the blond chick asked. She shook salt on her egg, took a bite, watched them avidly as she chewed.

Robin shook her head. "I'll just go wait by my car." She glared at Jon. "Do not follow me. Or I will scream, and make a spectacle."

She hurried out. Jon stood there, feeling empty and gutted. The blonde reached over the bar to get herself a slice of lemon. Her sleeve rode up, revealing—what the hell? At first glance, it seemed a crocheted bracelet. Dots and lines, curling spirals . . . cuts and burns.

Decorative scarring. A weird chill shuddered down his back.

She dropped her lemon into her water. The sleeve slipped back down. Surreal. He could see it on a punk rocker, a Goth. But not her.

"She seems special," the woman said, her voice sugary with false sympathy. "I can see why it's hard to let go."

He stared coldly into her fake smile. *None of your business, you nosy bitch.* He let his vibe say it. Professional necessity had put some checks and balances on his natural tendency for bluntness.

"Have a nice evening." She dropped a twenty on the bar, and left.

He stared after her morosely. Every guy in the place ogled the woman's ass, showcased in tight jeans. He turned, stared at the liquor bottles on the wall. Considered that option. Dismissed it. No point in it.

Everything about that fake, snotty blonde just served as a poignant foil for everything that was so intensely special about Robin. She was so natural. Sincere and direct and real. He'd never been with a woman so sweet and funny. Who made him feel so alive. Switched on.

And he never would again.

The realization electrified him, and a wave of cold accompanied it. A premonition of loss, a neck-prickling shudder of naked fear.

Shit. Here he went, with the random freakouts and anxiety attacks again. He needed to eat a pill, maybe. Just chill the fuck out.

He slid off the stool, and his eyes fell on the heap of eggshells the blonde had left on the bar. Blue. Delicate, robin's-egg blue—

Robin's . . . egg . . . oh. Holy. *Fuck.* Fear slammed into him like a hollowpoint bullet. He launched off the bar stool and bolted.

Robin stumbled over the curb, dug for a tissue, honked into it.

She wiped her eyes, and looked for Kelly. It seemed too good to be true that this lady would step out of the woodwork and fix her car.

"My van's parked around to the side," said Kelly's musical voice.

The girl's smile was so bright. As if fiddling with some stranger's car late at night in a convenience store parking lot was just the coolest thing ever. Then again. Maybe Kelly was just an extremely nice person, and she, Robin, needed a swift attitude adjustment, right in the heinie.

"Um, yeah," she said. "Are you sure you want to bother with this? I mean, I can just get a room, or—"

"No bother! Just help carry my chest and it'll be no problem!"

Robin followed. It occurred to her to ask Kelly to park her van by the car, but the suggestion felt snotty and ungrateful, so she let it go.

The parking lot on the side was deserted. Kelly made for a van that was parked there, chattering all the while. The woman wrenched open the side of the van and climbed nimbly into the dark interior.

Robin peered in. It looked like the van was rigged with a bunch of electronic equipment. "What is this stuff? Is this a surveillance van?"

"It's for my boyfriend's work," Kelly explained. "He's in law enforcement. You get ready to grab the handle on the box, OK?"

"You want me to do it? You shouldn't strain your shoulder at all."

"It's fine. Just reach over and grab that side, and pull . . ."

"Sure." Robin reached for the box, saw Kelly's foot take a swift step forward. She looked up, saw the woman's wild, grinning grimace.

Crazy flashed through her mind, and the club whipped down—

Crack, white sparks, disbelief. A long, sinking fall. Then nothing.

* * *

Jon skidded to a stop by Robin's car and looked frantically around. Christ, where was she? It had only been a couple of minutes!

Headlights switched to the side of the store. A van peeled towards the exit. He barely made out the blonde behind the wheel. She saw him.

Tires squealed. He bolted after it, memorizing the plates. The laws of physics decreed that he'd never catch up, but still he pounded along, screaming. He got his big break when the van jerked to a stop to avoid plowing into a logging truck. A final spurt of adrenaline fueled his leap.

He grabbed the luggage rack, groped one-handed for the door handle. Locked. The van weaved, braked, swerved, trying to buck him off. He swung and flopped. Groped for his gun, clawing it out of the shoulder holster. He smashed the window. Blood spattered, flew. A gunshot blasted. Fuck. The crazy bitch was shooting at him.

She was screaming. He hung grimly on, and braced his legs as best he could against the vehicle. "Pull over or I'll shoot!"

"Filthy pig!" she shrieked. "Pig! Pig!"

She yanked the wheel around. They careened off the highway, over the shoulder, juddering down the long, sloping embankment. A wall of brush approached. Terribly fast, slow motion, sure death.

They hit. He flew, smashed into dark and scrub and thorn.

A thread of grim purpose kept him tethered to himself. He clawed his way to consciousness, blinked back the blood in his eyes. Struggled towards air, space. Branches scratched, bit. Light filtered down from the streetlight at the highway junction, just enough to assess the scene.

The van was tipped halfway over. A clump of flexible young firs had held it up. Windshield shattered. The impact had knocked his gun from his hand. He dragged himself towards the van. His leg buckled.

He held the side of the van for balance, leaving a wavering streak of blood on its surface. The side door was unlocked, but the crash had warped it. He wrestled it open. Couldn't make out anything in the dark.

An icy blade of self-doubt sliced deep as the scenario played out: Detective Jon Amendola, charged with fatally attacking an innocent blond bimbette in a parking lot. What a crowning end to his career.

He dug out his car keys, shone the penlight on the keychain inside, and saw Robin crumpled against the back corner of the van.

His heart practically stopped. Her face was streaked with blood. She was cuffed and shackled. Scattered around was a hoard of cutting instruments. Scalpels, picks, cleavers, scissors, picks and tongs.

He climbed in. The van shook, threatening to tip. He crept over to her. Her pulse was strong. He gathered her up as if she were made of blown glass, scooted on lacerated knees over the traveling torture kit, and clambered out the door. The van bounced, swayed.

He cradled her against his chest, using his shoulders to batter his way out of the snarl of conifers. His eyes streamed. He set Robin gently on the ground, and groped for his phone—

Bam. The gunshot knocked him over Robin's body and onto his face. His shoulder was numb, burning, ice cold. *Jesus.* What a brain-dead asshole. Getting himself shot by a bouncy blond psychopath with a fucking ponytail. He was dead meat, but the contrary bastard inside him who never knew when he was beat got up, staggering.

The blonde had a wild light in her eyes. She grinned, her teeth bloody and disarranged. The gun shook in her two-handed grip.

"You Geddes's bitch?" He made his voice hard and taunting. "Were you his little helper? Like a fluffer on a porn set?"

"I wouldn't expect a pig like you to understand." The woman's voice was high-pitched, wobbly. "I was his ultimate work of art. See?"

She yanked up her shirt. Her torso was covered with scars, in a swirling, hypnotic pattern, horribly similar to the bloody welts and cuts on Geddes's other victims. Her nipples had been removed. Shiny flat scars remained. He didn't like to imagine the state of her nether parts.

His gorge rose. He was looking at the Egg Man's first victim. Alive, bugged out of her flipping skull—and holding a gun on him.

"He hurt you too?" he asked. "How long ago did he take you?"

"He didn't hurt me!" she shrieked. "He saved me! He loved me! He was transforming me, like I was going to transform her." She stabbed a bloody finger towards Robin's supine body. The gun's muzzle wavered in her hand. "You can bleed to death while you watch me do it!"

As if she'd heard, Robin shifted and moaned. In the instant that the blonde's eyes flicked towards her, Jon's body was in the air, leg flashing in a whip-swift front kick. *Smack,* the gun flew out of her hands. Her despairing shriek was like the cry of a prehistoric bird.

Grab the wrist, spin, torque and wrench. *Crunch.* She shrieked, her arm dislocated and broken. A punch to the point of the chin finished the job. She thudded to the ground. He swayed on his feet.

So his instincts had some basis after all, he thought numbly. The Egg Man had left the zombie bride behind to carry on his evil deeds.

He couldn't believe he'd missed it. It seemed so obvious now. The last puzzle piece, the fragment that made the whole sick, bloody mess finally make sense. Geddes had an accomplice all along. It was a man-woman serial murder team. A classic scenario, and he'd missed it.

And Robin had almost paid the price for his stupidity. If she hadn't already.

He stumbled back to her, and thudded to his knees. Made his fingers punch in 911, getting the cops, the EMT's.

That done, he cradled her against his chest, and cried like a baby as he waited for the med techs to come and do their thing.

8

Jon peered at his watch. 4:20 A.M. Too late for a beautiful girl to finish her second waitressing shift of the day and head home in her piece of shit car to her piece of shit apartment.

It made him tense. As did contemplating activities in which he did not excel, i.e., apologizing, groveling, expressing tender emotions. Being charming and seductive when he felt like hammered shit.

Finding her had been easy. He'd taken some overdue leave and driven down a few days ago. Familiarized himself with her schedule.

Stalking, he guessed. There really wasn't any other word for it.

A car with a shot muffler pulled into the parking lot. Adrenaline jolted through him. Heels started clicking up the steps. He'd scare her to death if he just waited here with his mouth shut.

"Hey, Robin," he called out. "It's me."

The clicking stopped. He counted the thuds of his heart.

He coughed to clear his throat. "Please. Come up and talk."

He held his breath, and let it out slowly when he heard the heel clicks begin again. She stopped on the landing below, and stared up.

"What are you doing here?" she asked, her voice hushed.

There was so much to say to that, it bottlenecked in his aching throat. "Can I come in?" was all he could manage.

She marched past, swaying to avoid touching him, and unlocked the rattling, antiquated knob lock. She marched in.

He waited for it to slam. It did not. He moved towards the dim slice of light that came out of the crack, and pushed the door open.

She stood with her back to him, radiating tension. She'd switched on a cheap gooseneck desk lamp that illuminated a dim patch on the wall. She looked hot. Black miniskirt, no hose, those great, slim legs that went on forever. A skimpy blouse. Way too sexy for a work uniform.

"Have you started, the, uh, circus training thing yet?" he asked.

"Soon," she said distantly. "Next week is the orientation. I've just been trying to scrape together some extra money until then. What's happening with, ah . . . her?"

"The process is gearing itself up," he said. "It could take years. I'm sure her team will go with an insanity plea, which usually pisses me off, but not this time. The woman was tortured by that psycho prick since she was seventeen years old. She's batshit. She needs to be confined, yeah, but not in a prison."

Robin hugged herself. "That's so horrible," she whispered.

"Don't think about her," he said flatly. "Just turn it off."

She snorted. "Like it's so easy. How's the shoulder?"

"Healed up." He opened his mouth to launch into his rehearsed spiel, and something else popped out. "You didn't come to the hospital."

"Danny kept me updated," she replied stiffly.

"Still. It would have been nice to see you."

She hesitated. "I've been meaning to send a note. To thank you."

"A goddamn *note?*" His voice cracked.

She made a sharp gesture. "I thought if I came in person, it might be, um, awkward. Considering."

He snorted. "Did you now." She hunched her shoulders. They looked like they were vibrating. She was crying. Smooth move, Jon.

"This isn't fair," she said, her low voice shaking. "The last time we were together, you screamed at me, insulted me, told me not to trust you. Then you pinned me to the bed and coerced me into weird sex—"

"I did not coerce—"

"Shut up. Don't play word games. You know exactly what I mean."

He shut his mouth. Now was not the time to contradict her.

"Then I get attacked by a psycho serial killer who's trying to punish you. You rescue me from a horrible fate, which was very nice of you, but God, Jon! Talk about mixed messages! My circuits blew!"

"I'm sorry," he blurted.

She looked over her shoulder, and regarded him with wet, suspicious eyes. "For what?"

He hesitated. "For freaking out," he said heavily. "For saying all that rude, crazy stuff to you. I got scared. I hadn't made the leap yet."

"What leap?" she demanded.

"I hadn't realized . . ." His voice cracked, trailed off. He coughed.

Robin stamped her foot. "Realized *what?*"

Heat followed cold, flushing through his body. The pressure built, the cork finally popped. "That I love you!" he yelled.

Her eyes went wide. Her knees about buckled.

There it was, his heart ripped loose and bleeding out. All he had to do now was grit his teeth and wait for the verdict to come down.

I love you.

The words reverberated, unravelling all she'd done to put her sorry self together after that shattering weekend.

She still felt so fragile, even after all the psychobabble, the pep talks, the chocolate. Not to mention all the disapproval from Mac and Danny. The frantic bustle of packing up, leaving town, finding a place to crash and some waitressing gigs had helped, but still, it all crashed down on her whenever she tried to rest. So she avoided rest. Food, too. She was running on coffee, adrenaline, and self-denial.

That blunt *I love you* was an explosive charge in the depths of her being. And it was bringing her down, down, down.

"Oh, God. You twisted, sadistic bastard," she whispered.

He hesitated. "Huh. That was not the response I was hoping for."

"Don't you be flip with me," she hissed. She covered her shaking face with her hands. "You want to get laid, I presume. You'll be all sweet and nice, fuck me practically senseless, and when I least expect it, you'll put it to me? Make me feel like I'm an inch tall?"

He closed his eyes. His jaw ached. "No," he said. "Never again."

"Then why did you do it in the first place?" she demanded.

"Because I was scared! I was an idiot!" he yelled. "I wasn't used to feeling that way. I wasn't used to giving a shit. I panicked! I'm sorry!"

"You're sorry," she repeated. "He's sorry. So you were scared, huh? Are you scared now? Because you should be, Jon. You should be!"

The truth rasped his throat like cactus spines. "Sure I am. Scared you'll turn me down. That you won't give me another chance. Scared that I killed this thing we have between us stone cold dead."

He'd let that last phrase dangle, almost like a question.

She ground her knuckles into her wet eyes and then remembered the mascara caked on her lashes. Damn. "And when did this epiphany take place?" Her voice sounded both shaky and bratty to her own ears.

"It started when we were making love that last time—"

"No, Jon. Not making love. *Fucking* me. Call it what it is, please."

He shoved doggedly on. "Uh, whatever. Then you walked out the cabin door and took all the oxygen with you. That was my second clue."

Tears spilled over again. She turned away, dabbing and sniffing.

"And when that crazy bitch got to you, I went nuts. I knew I'd die, too. That you are the most important thing that ever happened to me."

"I'm sorry I didn't come to the hospital," she whispered. "I couldn't risk feeling any worse than I did. One more hit, and I was going down."

He made an incredulous sound. "I jumped on a van in motion, crashed into a tree and took a bullet, and you thought I'd blow you off?"

She shook her head. "You'd do that for any stranger you met on the street," she whispered. "I'd be a bubble-head to take it personally."

"Oh, what a crock of steaming shit," he said savagely.

Suddenly his arms were around her. He smelled and felt incredibly delicious and solid and strong. He tipped her mascara-blurred face up. "So what's the deal? Does this mean you've still got some feelings for me after all?" he asked.

She wiped her eyes. "I'm not ready to give one inch yet, so back off."

His expression was cautiously hopeful. "Uh, OK. Meaning that in some as yet undisclosed future time, you will be ready? Maybe?"

She shook her finger at him. "Not one inch," she hissed.

He grinned. "Whatever. My inches are all jazzed up and at the ready, whenever you feel like taking them. Say the word. They're yours."

She shoved at him. "Don't you dare come on to me."

"I'm sorry," he said. "It just slips out. You really turn me on."

"We're not anywhere near there yet," she said primly.

He vibrated with silent laughter. "Exactly how far are we?"

"After that last time at the cabin . . ." Her voice trailed off, and her face went flaming hot. "Pretty damn far."

His grin faded. "I'm sorry what I did made you feel bad."

She sniffed, eyeing him sidewise. "Hmmph."

"I don't apologize for making you come, though," he added baldly.

She shoved, but the circle of his arms just tightened. She glared up into his unrepentant face. "You don't apologize much, do you?"

His eyebrow twitched. "Is it so obvious? I'm just being honest. When I've got you in bed, I don't care about what's polite. I go straight for the prize. Watching you come so hard you pass out—I love that."

His voice rasped across her nerve endings. His erection pressed her belly. "You're rushing me," she whispered. "Ten minutes in the door, and you're rubbing your hard-on against me and talking dirty."

He dropped his arms, and stepped back. Cold air rushed in around her where his delicious heat had been. She missed it.

"I will not force you." The quiet words had ceremonial weight.

She was at a loss, wavering without his sustaining embrace.

Jon looked around the bare apartment, the single folding chair, the narrow cot. "That's one hell of a narrow bed," he commented.

"Is this your sneaky way of asking me if I've entertained a dozen lovers on it since I last saw you?" she flared.

His gaze whipped back to her. Something dangerous flickered in his eyes. "No, actually, it was just a
random observation."

The silence stretched out and sagged under its own
weight.

"So?" His voice was hard. "Have you?"

She swallowed. "What if I had?" she asked quietly.

His jaw clenched. "I'd hate it. And then I'd get the
fuck over it."

"It wouldn't matter to you?"

"I couldn't say that. But it wouldn't put me off. I
love you, Robin."

Her eyes filled up again, to her dismay. "Jon, I—"

"I've never said that to anybody before. Ever, in my
life," he said. "Not even when I got married to Vicki.
But I'm saying it now. And I hope you're listening. I
love you, Robin MacNamara."

"I'm listening. I hear you," she said. "And I, um . . .
haven't."

"Haven't what?" he demanded.

"Had any lovers," she blurted. "No one."

Jon passed his hand over his forehead, and exhaled
slowly. "That's good news," he muttered. "Jesus, Robin.
For a beginner, you know how to put a guy through the
wringer."

I'm sorry. The words quivered on the tip of her
tongue. *I love you too* was right on its heels. But nothing came out. Not yet. This hope was too fresh, too
tender. A pale green shoot, so easily crushed.

"I wish I could be more flowery and eloquent about
it," he offered.

She gestured towards her cluttered desk. "I've got a
thesaurus."

His eyes sparkled. "What is that, a challenge?"

She shrugged. "Just a suggestion," she said primly.

"OK, let's see if I can vamp it up," he mused. "I, um, adore you. Revere you. My body explodes with volcanic passion for you. You are, uh, sweeter than a cupcake with buttercream frosting and sprinkles. Hotter than a Polish kielbasa smeared with wasabi mustard—"

"Stop it!" she cut him off, waving her arms. "That's terrible!"

He blinked. "Aw. Well, verbal skills are highly overrated in men, anyway. I'm much more skilled with body language. Wanna see?"

She covered her mouth to hide the smile. "There you go again."

His arms encircled her. He nuzzled her shoulders, stroking her back. "It's a serious suggestion. Let me worship at your shrine. The beast stays locked up until you let him out yourself. This is all about you. Showing you how much pleasure I can give you. How much I love you, how much I'm going to love you. Forever."

"Oh. Wow," she whispered. Her head dropped back into his hand, and she melted into a kiss that made her forget everything. If she let it.

She pulled away. "I don't want you to keep any part of yourself locked up," she said. "I'm not afraid of it. I want it all. No more games."

He gazed down at her for a long moment. "That works for me."

They stared into each other's eyes. A thousand *I love you's* jostled to get past the lump of emotion in her throat, but the barrier held, and body language was all she had to work with. So she got to it, starting in on the buttons of her blouse. Jon helped, with a clumsy urgency that sent buttons spinning to the floor. He tugged the thing off her shoulders, and fumbled for the zip of her mini while his other hand splayed over the black tank top. "No bra?" He sounded scandalized.

Laughter loosened her throat. "Don't need one."

"The hell you don't." He shoved the mini down over her hips, and gasped when his hands found her bottom bared by a skimpy black lace thong. "A thong, with a miniskirt? What is this place, a strip joint?"

Her laughter redoubled. "So I won't have panty lines, you puritanical lunk. Are you going to get on with it, or what?"

He tugged the flimsy stretch lace down over her bottom. "God, yes. But I think you need to change jobs. I can't handle the uniform."

He pushed her down against the cot, and shoved the tank top up over her breasts. She wore only that and the wildly impractical spike-heeled sandals. Absurd for waitressing, but just right in bed for Jon.

He stared down, hot-eyed, and wrenched off his shirt. He was so beautiful. The need in his eyes almost dazzled her to the angry weal on his shoulder. She reached out and caressed it with her fingertips as he sank to his knees beside the cot. "Does it still hurt?" she asked softly.

"Right now, I don't notice a thing." He bent like he meant to make good on his promise to worship at her shrine with his tongue, but she reached down and yanked at his belt. She wanted head to toe contact, every hard, hot inch of him deep inside her. His mouth on hers, his whisker burn rasping her, his weight shaking the bed frame.

"Get those jeans off," she ordered. "Right now."

"But I wanted to—"

"No back talk," she said. "Didn't you say this was all about me?"

"Yeah, and that's exactly why I want to—"

"I'm telling you what I want. I want those jeans. Off. *Now*."

He shoved his pants down. "But I want you to be ready."

"You can make me wet with your voice alone," she told him.

His eyes flashed. "Oh yeah? Show me."

She opened her legs for him, showing him the flushed, glistening folds. He stared down, mesmerized. "God, you're beautiful," he said.

"I love you." The words rushed out. "I love you, Jon."

He closed his eyes, and sighed. "God, it feels good to hear that."

She curled her fingers around him. His heartbeat throbbed against her hand. He covered her hands with his own and guided them, sliding his erection against the length of her slick furrow.

"I'm still going to do the Circo, you know," she blurted as he settled between her legs. "I want it more than anything."

"Of course. It's who you are. It's what I'm in love with."

"Oh," she said shakily, as he nudged his way inside. "Oh."

"We'll do the long distance thing if we have to, I guess, but I don't know how long I'll survive that. I want to be with you every damn day."

"Me, too." She clutched his shoulders as he sank deeper. "Maybe I'll . . . maybe I'll get lucky, and be able to work one of the fixed shows, in New York, or Chicago. Or even here, in San Francisco."

He kissed her with reverent tenderness. "We'll work it out," he said. "I love it that you juggle eggs naked and wear a red nose and make kids laugh. I love it that you're brave enough to follow your dream. I want to spend the rest of my life enjoying that. Honoring it."

She dragged him closer, taking in every delicious bit of him. "Aw. Jon. How sweet," she said breathlessly. "Who says you're not eloquent?"

"I guess you just inspire me."

"Well, let me just inspire you for the rest of your life, how about?"

A grin of pure joy split his face. "Done deal," he said.

AFTER THE LOVIN'

E.C. Sheedy

1

He seized her upper arms and yanked her hard against him, his grip a vise. Too tight. *Tighter.*

Tommi struggled to escape, pushed at his chest, fear rooting deep behind her rib cage. "Let go of me." She wished the words sounded more demanding, less frantic.

She wished she'd kept her mouth shut.

Reid slid his hands up to encircle her neck, rested his thumbs on the pulse jumping insanely at the base of her throat. He smiled down at her, his brilliant blue eyes shards of ice behind eyelids narrowed in threat.

Again she tried to step back, pull away from his grasp.

"Don't move, baby. I like you exactly where you are." He put pressure on her larynx and lifted her chin with a thumb, forcing her to look up at him. "Let's make sure you've got things straight." There was no smile this time. "You fuck with me, you pay the price. You clear on that?"

"Clear," she choked out. Clearer still was the ugly

fact she'd dug herself into a bottomless, black hole she didn't know how to get out of.

"Here's the drill. We meet at the bank when the doors open. You give me everything from your safety deposit box. From there you go directly to the office, hand in your resignation, and leave the building, and"— he kissed her, a harsh, punishing kiss, wet and open-mouthed—"you keep this luscious mouth of yours shut. You behave yourself, do as you're told, and we forget this ever happened. You don't—" He tightened his grip until her breath clotted under his thumb, thick and aching.

When she clawed at his hands, he squeezed harder, his mouth twisted, his face bloated with grim purpose.

Anger beat at Tommi's panic.

He was enjoying himself. The bastard! The lying, thieving, traitorous bastard!

Abruptly, he shoved her backward into the corner. She stumbled but didn't fall. When she'd wiped the slime of him from her mouth and drawn enough air into her lungs to allow for speech, she said, "You're scum, Reid. And dangerously sure of yourself."

He picked up his jacket, shrugged into it, and walked to where she stood. He grabbed her chin, pinned her against the wall, and ground his body into hers. His handsome face, inches from her own, seethed with malice. "I'm sure of two things. You want to keep this made-for-sex body of yours in one piece, and I don't intend to let a righteous bitch like you ruin me." He twisted her chin painfully, dug his nails into her jaw. "And I'm not the only one with something at stake here." He sneered, let her go. "I'm the gentle one. You might want to think on that."

He walked to the door, looked back, and slid his gaze from her feet to her breasts. "It's been fun, Smith.

If I have any regret, it's that I didn't get between those long legs of yours before you got between me and my money."

He strode out.

She ran to the door, locked it behind him, and leaned against it. Breathing like a crazed thing, she hurried to the window, waited there and struggled to calm herself.

A few minutes later she watched his platinum Jag power through the rain and turn the corner a half block down the street. Cold to the bone, she released the curtain. When it fell straight to shut out the dark November night, she rubbed her tender upper arms, winced.

He'd hurt her.

Tommi Smith was no innocent. She'd dated a lot of men and made more than her quota of mistakes, but Reid McNeil was the worst yet, and the first one who'd touched her in anger. She didn't intend to let it happen again.

He'd said there were *others*. Her nerves spiked and her throat constricted. If there were, she had no idea *who* they were, or how dangerous. She knew about Reid—and Reid was an embezzler. Tommi had the paper trail to prove it.

She sat on the edge of the sofa, hugged herself, and rocked . . . back and forth, back and forth . . . the motion soothing in a useless kind of way. Chilled and trembling, she tried to think, to plan. She'd been a fool and sickeningly naïve to confront Reid about the files—expect him to put the money back.

Stupid, stupid call!

And dating him? Stupider still. Once again she'd let wishful thinking and a man's soft words erode her common sense. She was a savvy, capable, thirty-five-year-old woman, and one of the most successful commercial designers and project managers in Seattle, but when it came to men, she acted as if she were a twelve-year-old girl looking for love in poster city.

God! She'd even let the ever-elusive *love* word skip into her brain. It had skittered away, a rat to its eternally dark hole, when he'd embedded his fingers in her arms and tried to shake her teeth loose, then threatened worse to come.

Disgusted by her own idiocy, she got up and paced her living room, forced her fractured thoughts back to the problem at hand.

She straightened. Maybe she'd been a fool, but she wasn't a coward—and she was *not* going to let Reid get away with stealing from Del Design Inc.

Much as she itched to turn the thieving creep over to the police, she just couldn't. She had to wait for Paul to come back. He was the only one she could trust, and she owed him. But he was out of town for at least a week. Maybe more. Which meant she needed time . . .

Which meant . . . she needed to run; she needed to run tonight, and she needed a place to run to. A safe place.

Thank God Reid believed her story about the files being in her safety deposit box; it gave her precious time.

She stopped pacing and headed for her bedroom. There, she sat on the bed and looked at her bedside clock.

Damn! It was nearly midnight.

Her hand shook when she reached for the phone, slipped off the buttons twice as she keyed the telephone number. When she got it right, she lifted her eyes to heaven, prayed softly, "Please, please—let Hugh, not Veronica, answer the phone." A man's current woman didn't thrill over calls from old girlfriends.

He picked up on the second ring.

"Hugh, it's Tommi. I need to talk." Her voice quavered, but she got control of it. "No, I take that back. I need your help. Can you meet me?"

The all-night coffee shop had a scatter of customers. Tommi took a seat at a back table and hooked her bag over the chair. Hugh Fleming, tall, and even more good-looking today than he was in high school, set two steaming coffees on the table and took the seat opposite her.

"Where's Veronica?" she asked, buying time, not knowing where to start this dreaded conversation.

"Away for the weekend."

"Does she know you're here? With me?"

"No. Should she?" He drank some coffee, grinned. "You planning to seduce me after all these years?"

"No. I'm planning to do what I've done too many times in the past. Take advantage of your friendship."

"Damn!" His smile held.

"You had your chance."

"Did not. You were sixteen, I was seventeen. You only hung around me to get to my buddy, Jake."

She smiled, but it wouldn't hold. "Funny. I don't even remember Jake's last name, but I've never forgotten yours." Tommi had used Hugh to get to Jake, and even knowing she'd come a long way from being that vain, selfish teenager didn't help. She still regretted the hurt she'd caused him. She raised her eyes. "You're a better friend than I deserve, Hugh Fleming. Veronica is a lucky woman." She stopped, rubbed the bowl of her spoon idly across her folded napkin. Unable to find a starting point. Uncertain how much to confide.

"What's the deal, Tommi? Are you in some kind of

trouble?" Hugh studied her, his easy banter gone, his expression serious.

"I need a place to stay." She decided to keep her mouth shut and not drag him any deeper into her mess than she had to. "And I don't want you to ask why."

"Come home with me."

She knew her eyes widened. "You, me, and Veronica. Are you mad?"

"Let me guess. This has something to do with that guy you're seeing." His eyes narrowed. "Did he hurt you?"

Tommi, taken back by his insight, glanced away. She also started to shrug into her coat. "This was a mistake. I shouldn't have called you."

He reached across the table, clasped her wrist. "I can't help if you won't level with me." He released his grip. "I could have told you McNeil was no good from the beginning."

"Why didn't you?"

"Would you have listened?"

She took a breath. "Probably not."

"So spill. What's going on?"

"I *can't* 'spill.' Not yet, anyway." She stopped. "Not until I sort things out myself."

"Not just man trouble then?"

"I wish it were. I'm an expert in that arena." She tapped the rim of her coffee mug. "This is more than that, and because I *don't know* who all is involved, telling you or anyone else about it at this stage would be . . . irresponsible." *Maybe dangerous.* "What I need is to get out of Seattle. And I need to go tonight."

He looked at her for a long time, finally nodded. "Okay. I'll stop asking questions." He rubbed his chin, thought for a minute. "You can go to Mac's place. He's there now. I'll call him, tell him you're coming."

She hadn't expected this. "Where exactly is *there?*"

"His fishing camp on the west coast of Vancouver Island. Three hours to the border, a ferry ride, maybe another three or four hours of driving, and you're there. Damn wilderness, but Mac loves it. You could fly, but at this time of year the weather might get in the way. Better to drive."

"What's Mac going to think about this?" she asked. Mac was Hugh's brother, maybe five years younger than herself, but he'd never looked at her without a sneer of distaste. No matter how much she'd tried to win him over, that sneer stuck. Mac Fleming, unlike his older brother, had disliked her on sight.

The last time she'd seen him he'd been an acne-plagued teenager, hazel-eyed and thin as a stick. Already six feet tall, he'd looked as if his bones were growing too fast for his skin to keep up. His nose was always stuck in a book, and on the occasions he lifted it long enough to acknowledge her, his expression, behind those awful glasses, bordered on obnoxious—or disdainful. He might have been a kid, but he always looked at Tommi as if she were a pane of glass and the view on the other side wasn't pretty. He made her seriously uncomfortable, enough to add, "He might not like the intrusion."

"Don't worry about Mac," Hugh said. "He can use the distraction. My guess is he's up there with a satellite laptop and a hundred business proposals. He's in communications, cable TV, wireless—God knows what-all. The guy has no idea how to relax. Probably ignore you the whole time you're there. But he won't let you down." He drank the last of his coffee. "I'll tell him your ETA, and he'll be waiting. He's there for at least a couple more weeks."

If she could tolerate Mac not tolerating her, it would

be perfect. Still she hesitated. "Actually, when I called you, I was thinking about your cabin on Whidbey Island, Hugh."

"That's where Veronica is—with her mother." He grimaced. "Making 'arrangements.' "

"Ah."

"Don't ask."

"Don't have to." Any other time she'd have chided him about his poor-captured-male expression, because she knew it was an act, knew marrying Veronica was all he ever wanted.

"Besides, if someone starts looking for you, they'll make our connection." He shook his head. "No. Mac's place is best."

He was right. Half the women in her office knew about her special friendship with Hugh. It wouldn't take long for Reid to find out about it—if he hadn't already. "You're right. Okay, if it's okay with Mac, it's okay with me." She ignored her lingering reluctance. "But tell him I promise to stay out of his way." If Mac chose to ignore her, it was fine with her. Better to be ignored than suffer those dark glares of his, his obvious dislike.

She looked at her watch—well after midnight.

"First ferry is 5:15 in the morning," Hugh said.

"I'll make it."

"I'll go back to your apartment with you, wait while you pack." He stood and offered his hand. She took it, and when she was on her feet, she hugged him. "I don't know what I'd do without you, Hugh. I really don't."

"We're friends, Tommi. You won't ever have to."

An hour later, in the gray-lit parking garage under Tommi's apartment building, Hugh loaded her bags into the trunk of her silver Lexus, then opened the driver-side door. He handed her a crude map.

She got in and lowered the window. "You're sure Mac said my coming was okay?" Useless question, because she was sure Hugh wouldn't have taken no for an answer no matter what Mac said. Like it or not, she was about to foist herself on an unwilling man.

"He said he's glad you're coming, and he's looking forward to seeing you again."

Tommi eyed him, nearly smiled. "Liar."

He shrugged, slapped the top of the car above her door. "Just go. Mac will come around."

"I'll have to take your word for that."

"Call me. Let me know you made it okay."

She nodded, locked all her doors, and started the car.

Truth was, she no longer cared if Mac wanted her at his fishing camp or not, and she was more determined than ever to get out of Seattle. Her voice mail and call display told her Reid had called four times; twice while she was out with Hugh, and twice while she was packing. His messages were veiled threats for her to be careful, not to do anything foolish. He'd be furious and suspicious as to why she wasn't in her apartment and hadn't returned his calls.

She intended to be long gone before he decided to arrive in person. She shuddered at the thought.

Her hand slid to the large tote on the passenger seat. She had the means to ruin him, and after what she'd experienced tonight, she had no doubt Reid would do whatever it took to stop her.

She remembered his hands on her throat; it brought a simmer of panic, made her heart thump erratically. She tightened her grip on the wheel and took some deep breaths.

When she pulled up to the parking lot security gate and looked through it to the heavy gusting rain and the blessedly empty street, she relaxed. And even though the night matched her mood, grim and dark, she suddenly looked forward to the long, solitary drive to the ferry.

At the top of the exit lane, she glanced left and right down shadowy, night-lit streets, then cleared the building.

The aging, dark-blue Chrysler gave Tommi a few minutes' lead time before it swerved out of the shadows. Lights off, it positioned itself some distance back in her rain-splashed wake.

The burly man in the car picked up his cell phone from the passenger seat, hit a number on autodial. "McNeil? She's on the road. What do you want me to do?"

"I knew she was lying! That stupid, stupid bitch!"

"Hey man, I'm not interested in your woman troubles, just the job. So what do ya want me to do?"

"Follow her, Borg. And don't let her out of your sight."

"It'll cost you."

"It'll cost me a hell of a lot more if she decides to do what I think she might. Stay on her ass!"

"I *ain't* drivin' across the damn country, McNeil. Not in this old beater."

"You want to pay that bookie of yours, you'll do what I say. Call me . . . on the hour."

When the phone went dead in his hand, Borg cursed violently, punched his radio on, and twisted the dial until country music filled the car.

He swore again, took a swig of black coffee, and settled in for a long night.

2

Mac Fleming put down his book, pinched the bridge of his nose, and looked at his watch. Almost six. By now it was cave-dark out there.

If Smith had left when Hugh said she'd left, she should be here by now. Hugh hadn't told him much—said he couldn't tell him what he didn't know, but Mac had the gist of it.

She was in some kind of trouble, and Mac had no doubt a man was somewhere in the mix. Probably some pissed-off guy she'd cut loose who'd decided to give her a hard time.

Not that he gave a damn. But he still should have warned her about the road. Eight miles of ruts and bumps, barely okay on a good day, but today, given the nonstop rain, there was a good chance it might be washed out. She could be stuck.

Hell!

He got to his feet just as the wind slammed the side of the lodge and whistled down the chimney to send a spray of sparks across the deep slate hearth. The fire sputtered but held. The stone fireplace was gigantic, and he'd already banked it with enough logs to power a fifty-car steam train, but he threw another on for good measure, pulled the mesh curtain to a tight close, and headed for the door.

Outside, the rain was merciless and the wind non-stop, strong, sharp gusts carrying heavy inflows of frigid ocean air, salt-filled and harsh. And this was only the beginning of a storm the weather idiots said wouldn't hit hard until midnight. Hell, if this wasn't hard, Mac didn't know what was. He pulled the hood of his rain slicker over his now dripping hair.

The weather might be miserable, par for the course this time of year on the northwest coast, but what pissed him off most was having Hugh lob Smith his way. He'd come here to get away, catch up on some work, then grab some downtime, not play the caped crusader. He didn't like Tommi Smith, never had—even if she had inspired his first wet dream.

Hell, he'd been twelve—a triple-breasted gargoyle would have done the same thing, as long as the breasts were naked.

When they were kids in Phoenix, she'd played his brother for a fool—along with every other guy she hooked up with—and judging from Hugh's phone call this morning, she still was.

Tommi Smith, Arizona beauty. Take a number, boys, the line forms on the right.

Not a line he planned to join. Ever.

When a sudden blast of wind damn near took him off his feet, he lowered his head and made for his truck, parked a few feet from the bottom of the lodge stairs. He had his hand on the door handle when he heard a car motor. Through sheets of rain, he saw headlights emerge from behind the tall cedars and dense rain forest undergrowth that ringed the camp clearing. The car's windshield wipers were working overtime and a blond head tilted from side to side as if struggling to see through the heavy rain and swirling mist.

He stepped away from his truck and lifted a hand.

When she saw him, she also raised a hand, driving slowly toward where he stood beside his truck.

She was here. Tommi was on his own damn doorstep.

Mac's stomach did a feint and drop. He ignored it and strode toward her mud-spattered car. When she turned off the motor, he heard the drumbeat of rain on its hood.

When he stepped up beside the car, the woman behind the glass looked up at him, those blue-violet eyes wide as plates, her sex-kitten blond hair curling and streaming over her shoulders. The rain, a waterfall on the car window, distorted her features, made her quick smile crazy and lopsided, her skin a pale, shimmering white.

Mac's breathing shallowed, and a familiar tension lodged in his groin. When he was a dumb kid, just looking at her made him hard as a rail spike. Always embarrassed the hell out of him. The Tommi Effect, he'd named it later, a magnetism every male within sniffing distance recognized and responded to. Including his brother.

Always his brother.

He'd seen her twice since then. Once when he'd spotted her in an airport, maybe five years ago, then as recently as last year, when one of his companies hired Del Design to do a renovation. He'd been in one of the glassed-in meeting rooms and looked up to see her stroll by with one of his managers. When she'd smiled up at the guy, he looked as if she'd handed him sex on a stick. Mac made no attempt to reintroduce himself. She was Hugh's business, never his.

But even here, in the middle of nowhere, in a raging November storm, the Tommi Effect hit him full force. And made him mad as hell.

She was the most beautiful, most sensual, most erotic woman he'd ever seen, and on a deeply primitive level, he understood his brother's obsession with her.

And she went through men as if they were sold by the dozen on the shopping channel and her credit card had no limit.

He reminded himself how much he disliked her and yanked open the car door. "Better make a run for it." He gestured with his head toward the front door of the lodge. "Pop the trunk, and I'll bring in your bags."

She nodded, did as he asked, and grabbed the large tote from the passenger seat. Instead of putting her raincoat on, she held it over her head and dashed for the porch.

She packed light, he'd give her that—two small bags and a tote. He took the last of the three stairs to the porch and didn't waste any time opening the door. She quickly stepped in.

"Let me have that." He took the coat she'd started to drape over her arm and hung it on one of the pegs beside the door.

"Thanks." She shifted her gaze, turned slowly to take in the large room with its assortment of pine tables, overstuffed furniture—cabin plaid—and sky-high fireplace. Everything big, solid, simple. The way he liked it. Still looking her fill, she said, "This is nice. Impressive. Not at all what I expected."

"What did you expect?" He took off his wet slicker, hung it beside her coat.

"I'm not sure, but when Hugh said fishing camp, I guess . . . something more rustic?" She turned to look at him, the polite smile fading when her eyes met his.

He ran his hands through his wet hair to get it off his forehead. "It's comfortable," he muttered, and tried to ignore the way her gaze—slightly stunned—traveled his body from stem to stern. He told himself he didn't give a damn whether she liked his place or not. What irritated him was the big lodge had begun to feel like the incredible shrinking house from the moment she set foot in it. "You're later than I expected. Trouble?"

She was still staring at him, but he wasn't sure she saw him. "Pardon?"

What the hell was wrong with her? "I said, did you run into a problem getting here?"

"Exhaustion. I've been up since yesterday morning. I stopped for lunch and fell asleep in the parking lot." Her smile was quick, embarrassed. "I'd probably still be there if the restaurant owner hadn't come to check on me."

She did look tired and pale. "We'll get you settled as soon as you warm up. The bedrooms are upstairs." He gestured toward the mezzanine above them.

"Would you like me to stay there?" She wandered to the blazing fire and toasted her hands over it before turning back to look at him.

"Excuse me?"

"In the bedroom. Out of your way." Her expression was dead serious. "Hugh told me you'd be working."

"Some. Not enough to make you a prisoner on the second floor. Come and go as you like. It won't bother me." *Much.*

"I know you don't want me here, Mac. So as soon as I work things out, I'll be gone. I promise." She ran a hand nervously through her hair, shoved one side of it back. Mac caught a glimpse of an ivory throat, the sparkle of a single diamond on her lobe. "I'm just grateful you took me in." She laughed lightly. "God, I sound like a stray cat—probably look like one, too."

As strays went, this one merited a bowlful of rich cream and a warm place in the master's bed. He deep-sixed the image.

He could see she was working hard to look casual, stay in control. "Hugh said you were in some kind of trouble." Mac waited, watched.

Her hand fluttered from her hair to the deep vee of her top; she tucked her fingers under its trim to massage the space between the shoulder and the top of her breast. Mac followed the play of her hand as she idly stroked herself. The fire made her hair glow to gold, an angel halo atop the body of a Penthouse bunny.

Fuck! She hadn't been in the room five minutes and he wanted her.

"If it's all the same to you, I'd rather not talk about it." Her eyes darted from his. "Not yet, anyway."

"Suit yourself." He strode toward the kitchen area, set apart from the great room by a long counter. The more distance between them, the better. "Hungry?"

"Starved." She gave him a grateful smile, either for not asking any more questions or for offering her food; he wasn't sure which. She trailed after him and sat on a stool at the tiled counter, tossed her head to settle her long hair down her back.

"Nuked leftovers okay?" He frowned at the clear plastic container he'd pulled from the fridge. "Chicken is my guess."

She came around the counter, took the container from his hand. "How about I earn my keep?" She glanced around the fully appointed kitchen. "I can see we're not exactly roughing it here." She tilted her head and looked up at him. "Which means there must be wine."

"Just red."

"Perfect."

As Mac headed for the wine, his phone rang.

"My cell quit miles back," she said and looked puzzled.

"Satellite. If you have calls to make, feel free." He abandoned the wine project and crossed the room to his phone. "I'll only be a minute."

He was twenty minutes at least, and by the time he hung up, two plates with chicken, salad, and rolls were on the table.

She'd found the wine and was reaching vainly for the wineglasses on the top shelf. He took his gaze from the four inches of bare back her stretch exposed and went to stand behind her, easily picking a pair of wineglasses off the high shelf. This close to her, he couldn't ignore the scent of roses drifting up from her hair, or the rousing pressure where his groin met her buttocks as he'd reached above her head.

He sure as hell couldn't ignore the stir behind his zipper when she turned—almost in his arms—to look up at him, her eyes not quite focused, face delicately flushed, lips parted in perfect invitation.

Pupils dilated.

Mac knew the signs, sensed the vibes, and damned if he didn't get hard thinking about it. About her.

The air between them burned blue-hot.

Could he . . . Could it be this easy?

Their bodies touched, held, exuded heat, one into the other.

Neither stepped away.

Mac raised the empty glasses, looked down at her.

"Need anything else?" he asked, his voice deeper than he intended.

He heard the hitch in her breathing, knew his own followed suit. Then . . . she blinked.

And slid away from him with the speed of a cornered cat.

"No, that's it." She coughed as if to clear her throat. "Let's eat. Then if you'll show me to my room, I plan to sleep for at least twenty-four hours. Oh, and I have to call Hugh, and—" Her words were rushed, anxious, her face still pink.

"That call was Hugh. He's called three times to check on you. I told him you were fine." He stepped back. "The phone's yours if you want to tell him yourself."

"No. That's okay. Thanks." She rubbed her hands down her thighs. "Let's just have dinner, all right?"

He nodded.

They managed a spotty local-news-and-lousy-weather conversation during dinner, but her eyes didn't meet his directly until a half-hour later when he showed her to her room, where she muttered a weary "Thanks, Mac" and a good-night before she closed the door in his face.

Mac went back to the fire, poked at it, and, for the first time since Hugh called and woke him early this morning, smiled.

The smile dropped off his face when he thought about his brother and his feelings for Tommi.

If it weren't for Hugh, he might strap on some emotional armor—and a condom or two—and get in line after all.

For the next few days at least—for once—that line would be damn short. He'd promised Hugh he'd take care of her, keep her safe.

Fucking her was not an option.

* * *

Tommi sat heavily on the edge of the bed. What in heaven had happened down there? And what magic had transformed the skinny, awkward boy who used to be Mac Fleming into a calendar hunk of the month?

She'd always thought Hugh handsome, but Mac had morphed to absolute male-gorgeous. Still grim, still sober as a church pew, but gorgeous all the same.

And when they'd touched . . .

Heat rose, as it had in that moment, warming her throat and face, then scorching down to settle roughly between her thighs, pulsing, promising, wanting.

Agitated, she stood, walked to the window, and stared out into the bleakness of the storm. A rivulet of rain wended its way across the glass, and she traced it with her index finger, followed its shaky path down to the wooden sill. She placed her chilled fingertip on her lower lip, tasted the cold.

Tommi was a sensualist, knew it, and gloried in it. She was tactile, moved by the slither of satin over her skin, cool water pooling in her palm, the sun caressing her shoulders—the hard, strong length of a man buried deep inside her, his breath hot in her ear.

She leaned her forehead against the cold window-pane.

Mac's skin was so clear and tan, his jaw a slash of strong bone and determination, and his mouth was . . .

She stared unseeing into the blackness outside the window, her mind drifting, circling to finish her thought.

. . . his mouth was an unopened gift—and it kissed her without a touch.

I need to stop thinking about him. Now!

A clap of thunder brought her to her senses, and she squinted through the window, certain she'd seen a flash of light in the trees beyond the clearing. She stared for a good five minutes. Nothing.

Great! First I fantasize about Mac, now I'm seeing things.

Exhaustion. That was her problem. Her eyes were playing games with her sleep-deprived mind, making her paranoid.

Assuring herself Reid had no idea she was here, she hugged herself and stepped away from the window.

The Mac thoughts? The lust at first sight? Nothing but a few misfiring synapses—and a not-so-subtle nudge from her under-utilized hormones. She wasn't here to sleep with Hugh's brother. She was here to get away from Reid McNeil and think through what—and how—to tell Paul about what was happening in his company.

But not tonight—she stifled a yawn, headed for the bathroom. Bone-weariness made thinking a waste of time. No doubt she'd conjure another dumb paranoia, as she had on the ferry; she'd been so sure that big man was watching her, until he'd turned the other way when they'd unloaded. No doubt to go home to his wife and six kids!

When she came back from the bathroom, she put one of her bags on the bed, opened it, and pulled out her short blue chenille robe. She draped it across the foot of the bed, stripped, and crawled quickly under the covers. She wondered if this was Mac's bed, then yawned again. If so, she was eternally grateful—even if they'd never be in it together. She snuggled into one pillow, pulled the other close to her naked breasts.

The sheets were flannel, the duvet goose down, the bed a lemon-scented cloud; she was asleep within seconds.

Her dreams were uneven, disturbing, snaking between her running from Reid and running to Mac. And there was a knife, slashing curtains, gouging wood . . . blood. Blood everywhere. A light in the forest. Flickering.

She rolled and tossed, trapped between sleep and wakefulness. Panicking. She shook her head back and forth. *Oh, no!* Reid had the files now, and she was hanging by her fingers at the edge of a bottomless pit. Reid lifted his foot to stomp on her hands . . .

I'm falling, can't stop falling. I'm going to die.

Abruptly she sat up, disoriented, her heart a frightened bird, her chest a cage.

She saw a shadow move—at the foot of the bed.

Rising, it came toward her.

3

Tommi covered her mouth to hold in the scream.

"Easy." A hand offered her a glass of water. "Drink."

"Mac?" Finally her eyes adjusted to the stingy light leaking in through the open bedroom door. "Is that you?" she asked stupidly, needing to be certain, to hear his voice again.

"Yes. It's me." He shoved the glass into her hand. "You okay?"

She saw his eyes, dark and intense, in the shadowed room. "Fine . . . I'm fine. But why are you here?"

His gaze slid down to chest level. "You want questions answered, might be a good idea to cover up."

Tommi yanked the duvet over her bare breasts, a furnace of heat in her neck. "Sorry. I sleep in the nude."

"So I see."

Tommi felt foolish, then angry that she'd apologized. "What are you doing in here, anyway?"

"I was heading to my room." He gestured with his head to the hall. "You called my name."

"I did?"

Mac sat on the edge of the bed, put a hand on the

other side of her legs, and leaned in until his face was close enough for her to see his eyes. "What's going on, Smith? Tell me and I might be able to help."

"I don't need your help."

He stroked her upper arm. "These say you do." He touched her other arm, raised a brow.

She looked where his hand touched. She had bruised, not badly, but considering the dark marks formed a matched set, it was difficult to come up with a plausible explanation.

"Someone did this. Tell me who." His voice was firm, his tone low. "I'm not leaving this bed until you do."

She let out a breath, suddenly and irrationally desperate to tell someone. "I was seeing this man—"

"No surprise there."

"Excuse me?" His interruption caught her off balance, confusing her.

"Forget it. Go on."

"I work with him. A few days ago I discovered he's been stealing from the company. Maybe as much as a million dollars."

Mac whistled softly. "Busy guy. How?"

"False invoices, Internet bank transfers. There's probably more but those I can prove."

"And you told him what you knew."

She looked down, wanted to escape his knowing gaze. "I trusted him . . . cared for him. I thought if I spoke to him, he could find a way to put the money back."

Mac didn't say a word.

"You think that was stupid, don't you?" If he agreed with her, she'd kill him. She'd given herself the required forty lashes for idiot-girl thinking—she didn't need more from him.

"It doesn't matter what I think." His hand grazed her knees as he straightened and rose to stand over her bed.

"The problem is," she went on, "Reid told me there were others involved—"

"That's his name, Reid?"

"Reid McNeil, CPA. Brought in by . . . Hired by Del Designs over a year ago to streamline all the admin and accounting systems."

"And you think he's telling you the truth—about these 'others.' "

"That's just it, I don't know."

"You don't have to."

"What do you mean?"

"Because you only have one option."

"And that is?"

"Call the cops. Turn what you have over to them."

She hesitated.

"You have a problem with that?" He bent to turn on the nightlight on her bedside table, kept his attention fixed on her face.

The low-wattage bulb didn't do much to lighten the room, but it was enough for her to see Mac's skeptical expression, his mouth—so close to the sneer she remembered so well. She wanted to explain her reluctance to go to the police, but was afraid it would sound as dumb as her first mistake, confronting Reid.

When she didn't say anything, he raised a brow, shook his head—definitely disapproving. "If that torch you're carrying for McNeil is still lit, he damn well better be worth it. Because if you don't turn over what you know—and quick—you might find yourself named as a co-conspirator and be responsible for returning your share of the funds."

Tommi felt her eyes widen. "What are you talking about?"

"That's the way it works. So you'd best make up your mind what you like best, your bank account or your boyfriend."

"Boyfriend!" She would have leaped from the bed—if she'd had any clothes on. "Give me my robe!" She pointed to it, her exhaustion replaced by a powerful surge of anger.

Mac tossed it to her, and she shrugged into it, reaching under the covers to pull it down before getting up. For all her precautions, she knew Mac got a generous view of her thighs.

So mad she didn't care, she shot to her feet and poked a finger in his unyielding chest. "First off, Mr. Smug and Self-righteous, Reid is a liar and a thief—not my boyfriend. And second, I didn't go to the police because Del Designs is a family business. Reid is stealing from Paul McNeil, his own father. And if it was my family, I'd want to handle it my way. Paul lost his wife last year. And now, to hear about Reid—" She closed her eyes against her friend's pain. "I've worked with Paul for over six years. He's been good to me. He deserves the chance to deal with his son in his own way."

Mac took her finger from his chest, cocked his head. "So why didn't you go to him?"

"He's in Europe on a buying trip, and I can't bring myself to tell him about this mess over the phone. It would be cruel." She sat heavily on the edge of the bed, shoved her hair back with both hands, held it there, and pressed her palms against her temples. Anger gone, bone-weariness rushed front and center. She refused to cry, refused to give in to the confusion and bottomless fatigue—the fear of what Reid might do. "Oh, God, I don't know . . . maybe I should call him, maybe things will be an even bigger mess by the time he gets back. Especially if Reid didn't lie and there are other people involved."

Mac took her hands from her head, held them between his own. "I doubt there are. Embezzling's generally a loner's game. Probably just his way of scaring the crap out of you." He touched her hair, pushed some wild strands off her forehead and secured them behind her ear. Then he lifted her chin, made her face him. "Get some sleep. It's two in the morning—there's nothing we can do about it now. We'll talk it over when we're both awake."

He pulled her to her feet and threw the covers back on the bed. "Get in," he instructed.

Nearly asleep on her feet, Tommi nodded, started to drop her robe.

"Whoa." He grasped her hands. "A man can only take so much."

His voice seemed muted and distant. "I forgot you were here," she said, not completely sure it was true.

"Thanks for the ego boost." He stuffed his hands in his pockets, glowered at her, then jerked his dark head toward the door. "My room is down the hall. I'll leave the door open. I'm a light sleeper, so I'll hear you if there's a problem."

Under the covers, she shimmied out of the robe and let it slide to the floor. Mac draped it over the foot of the bed.

Her head nestled deep in the soft pillow, her eyelids weighed down with lack of sleep, she said, "Right now the only problem I can think of is how I'm ever going to leave your bed, Mac." Then she promptly fell asleep.

Mac wasn't so lucky. Between the rage of the storm battering his window and a cock that felt as if someone had loaded it with hot steel, he prowled the house for hours.

Close to 9 A.M., the storm took a break. It hovered offshore in a line of black clouds that told him it hadn't finished its dirty work yet. He decided to use the break to check out *Night Waters*, his 35-foot power boat, to see how she weathered the night.

Anything to get out of the house and away from the woman sleeping down the hall.

He rolled his head to ease the growing tension in his body. It didn't work.

Need slammed into him like a well-aimed punch when his sorry excuse for a mind replayed that glimpse of breasts and thighs he'd caught last night; the dark pink areola ringing a jutting nipple begging for his tongue, the long, lean legs leading the way to heaven— or hell, depending on a man's point of view.

But, damn it, right now he'd take either if it meant going in hard and deep—making Tommi climax, come soft and wet under his hand, his mouth . . .

He cursed, sealed his eyes tight.

After last night, if there were justice in this world, he should be anointed for not being all over her. Which he damn well would have been if she'd dropped that skimpy robe of hers.

Convinced it was going to be a long, frustrating few days, he headed for the shower.

A few minutes later, when he passed her door, he stopped and listened. Nothing. He felt a stab of guilt about the unwaveringly carnal direction of his thoughts. He'd bet sex wasn't on Smith's mind. Guessing at the extent of her exhaustion, she'd probably sleep until noon.

Fine with him.

Because if there was one thing he knew for certain, Hugh hadn't sent her up here so Mac could fulfill an adolescent fantasy. She was here for his protection, not sex. Plus, he reminded himself, the lady had a lot on her mind.

The morning was bitter cold, and Mac quickly discovered his visit to *Night Waters* was well timed. One of her lines was free and another frayed.

He had work to do—thank God—and he got right to it.

"McNeil?" Borg had given up on his cell phone and was now crammed into the smallest phone booth in North America in the rattiest, smelliest gas station this side of the Pacific. "You owe me. And I ain't lettin' you forget it."

"Where are you?"

"Close Bay, a godforsaken place on a godforsaken island in a godforsaken rain forest—that's where I am." Borg was pissed, even more pissed when he heard McNeil pause and take a drink of what he imagined was hot, strong coffee. He'd kill for that right now. Hell, he'd kill just to get this damn job over with.

"More to the point, where's Smith?" McNeil asked, his voice slick as a whore's tit. "You didn't lose her, did you?"

"No, I didn't lose her. I slept in my damn car under her damn nose, but I didn't lose her. Rained all night. I'm fuckin' deaf from the sound of it, but I didn't lose her, McNeil, which means you better be ready to flash up that checkbook of yours and write a pile of numbers."

"You'll get your money."

"Yeah, so you keep sayin'." Borg took a pull on his smoke.

"Can you see her now?"

"No, I can't see her now!" he spat into the phone. "I'm in a damn phone booth calling you, because my fuckin' cell phone won't work. This place is in the middle of hell's asshole."

McNeil's voice was lethally low when he said, "You don't want to do this job, Borg, I can find someone who will."

Borg tossed his smoke into the muck outside the booth. He wanted to get in his car and drive back to Seattle, tell him to stuff his damn job, but he knew if he did, McNeil would stiff him for sure. And he needed the green.

As his tire iron-wielding bookie took pains to remind him.

"Look." He kept his voice flat. "There's one road in and one road out—the last eight or ten miles is nothing but a cow trail. I go in there, get stuck, and it's game over. If she leaves she has to travel this road. I'll pick her up then."

"Where the hell is she, anyway?"

"At a private fishing camp. With some guy"—he fumbled in his pocket for the piece of paper he'd written on—"named Mac Fleming. A big shot, the locals tell me. Lots of bucks. Lots of smarts. Owns some TV stations or something. Looks like she's got herself a safe, warm nest and ain't planning to leave anytime soon."

"Shit!"

"You want I should do something?"

Borg sure as hell hoped not, because right now all he wanted was a room in that roach motel he'd spotted down the road. It probably had a twelve-inch TV, soap the size of a cereal flake, and towels you could spit through, but right now it looked five-star to him.

But the silence on the other end of the line made him uneasy. He could damn well hear the bastard's mind clicking.

"I want you to kill her, Borg. You do that and you've got a ten-grand deposit into that empty bank account of yours."

This guy was a wacko. Borg's mouth went dry. "No way. I'll watch her tail from now to neverland, but I don't do spade work. Nope. I ain't no killer."

"Fifteen thousand."

"Same answer."

He heard a long, irritated sigh. "In that case, you useless bastard, give me directions—*specific directions*—to where you are. And go back in there and get me a layout of that camp. I'll need a map. I'll be there tomorrow. Wait for me. And while you're waiting, go do some shopping."

"Shopping? What kind of shopping?"

McNeil laughed, then added in a tone altered for an idiot, "Buy me a rifle, Borg, a great big rifle and lots and lots of pretty bullets. You can do that, can't you?" His voice hardened. "And keep an eye on that bitch. Do not—*I repeat*—do not let her leave there. She moves, you move. Got that? Then you call me. It turns out dear old dad is coming home early and I'm fresh out of time."

It was noon when Mac went back to the house. Plan? Get back to those files he'd brought. As a lust antidote, work was all he had.

When he stepped into the house, the aroma of frying bacon greeted him. Tommi was in the kitchen behind the long counter, fluttering between cupboards and pans. Damned if she wasn't wearing that damn robe. It covered her from his eyes, but not his newly activated imagination. He hung his jacket on a peg, took a breath, and began his monk's journey.

"Hi," she said. "Hungry?"

"I'm a thirty-year-old male, and there's bacon in the air. What's your bet?"

She smiled. "That's good because I've made enough for a logging crew."

He watched her move around the compact cooking area, easy and competent, as if she'd worked in it a thousand times. But that was the thing about Tommi; even as a teenager, she was always so in control. Yet, she had this . . . sexually attainable look. Had to be all that bed-mussed blond hair, those smoky eyes of hers. But looking at her now, tense and vulnerable, Mac wondered for the first time how much of it was a mirage, brought on by wishful male thinking after one look at that centerfold-class body of hers.

Maybe he should ask Hugh. At that thought his stomach rolled. They might be brothers, but banter about sexual conquests wasn't in the relationship mix.

Tommi must have felt his eyes on her because she shot him a look from over her shoulder, and from that point on, her movements in the kitchen were a lot less competent, more along the lines of a major klutz.

When she came close to burning herself pouring coffee, he got off his stool and went to take the coffeepot from her hand.

"Thanks," she said. "But you can sit right back down. Everything's ready." She loaded a plate for him—eggs, bacon and a pile of perfectly browned hash browns, then made a smaller version for herself.

He took both plates to the table.

After a minute or two of silence, she said, "About last night. I've been thinking."

"Uh-huh."

"I don't want to call the police about this thing until I talk to my boss—in person."

"You'd be smart to do that sooner, rather than later."

She stopped eating, put her fork down. He heard her take a deep breath, let it out. "Maybe so, but he'll be back next week. I'm going to wait." She lifted her eyes to his. "The thing is . . . I'd like to stay here until he does—get back, I mean." Her voice went up on the final word, nervous, fearful. "Will that be okay?"

He shoved his plate back and took in her anxious expression. "This Reid guy—he's bad news, isn't he?"

She hesitated, then said, "Yes. I think he might be *very* bad news."

He touched her robe-encased arm where the bruising lay hidden under soft cotton. "He did this."

She nodded.

"Does he have any idea where you are?"

"No. Thanks to Hugh. God, I don't know what I'd have done without him."

Mac narrowed his gaze to her eyes. "And Hugh? What does he think about your being here? With me."

She looked confused. "He was the one who suggested it. I thought you knew that." She got up, took her half-eaten breakfast to the sink, then turned, leaning one hip against the counter and crossing her arms under her breasts. "When I called him for help, I'd hoped he'd lend me his cabin on Whidbey, but Veronica was there with her mother." She grinned, a slight crooked grin that flashed in her eyes. "Making, as Hugh said, 'more endless arrangements.' "

It was Mac's turn to be confused. "What are you talking about? Who's Veronica? And what arrangements?"

"You don't know?"

"Know what?"

"Hugh's getting married to—"

"Someone named Veronica." He shoved a hand through his hair. "I'll be damned."

"You didn't know." She came back to the table and sat down, looked wryly amused. "Men. Amazing what they *don't* talk about." She picked up her coffee mug, held it with both hands, and looked at him over its rim. "Hugh met Veronica in September. It was love at first sight. He proposed to her a couple of weeks ago."

He shook his head. So that was it. During their call yesterday, Hugh hinted he had some news, but said he'd save it until they could get together. Now he knew what the news was—he was happy for Hugh. The guy was programmed for a wife and kids.

"I really can't believe he hasn't told you," she said and raised her brows.

He swept his gaze over the woman across from him; her tumble of golden hair, smoldering blue eyes, the smile playing over her full mouth.

A rush of pure adrenaline jerked his chain, and happy as he was for his brother, he was suddenly even happier for himself.

"I didn't think he'd ever do it," he said.

"Most of you get roped up sooner or later, and Hugh's crazy about Veronica. A trip to the altar makes perfect sense."

"That's not what I meant."

"What did you mean?"

"I didn't think he'd ever get over you."

4

Mac watched a flush creep up Tommi's neck, bloom in her cheeks, and waited for her to deny his brother's feelings, make light of them.

"Hugh and I had that out years ago," she said.

"And?"

"We agreed to be friends. I love your brother. Just . . . not that way. We're friends. Nothing more. And that works for both of us."

"And this Reid character, what do you feel for him?"

She put her coffee down. "Why this sudden interest in my relationships?"

"Answer my question, and I'll answer yours."

"I thought I did answer it. Last night."

"I'd like to hear it again. In daylight." He wanted to be sure, because he never messed with another man's woman.

She knit her brows, gave him a wary look. "Reid's a thief, probably a violent one. The more distance I keep between him and me, the happier I'll be." She tilted her head. "So, why the questions?"

Mac had boxed himself in. He owed her an answer; he just wasn't sure she was ready for it. Hell, he wasn't sure he was. What he did know was that he wasn't going to let his dick—untrustworthy at the best of times—make a fool of him. If he was going to have this woman, it would be on his terms. "Why don't you put on some clothes? We'll take a walk. The rain's let up," he gestured to the gray day outside the kitchen window, "temporarily at least."

"You didn't answer me."

"I'm not sure you're ready."

"Ready for what?"

"To talk about sex . . . with me."

Her eyes widened, but she didn't play the shocked ingénue. She simply rose and walked to the window, looked out for several seconds before she turned to look at him again. "You're to the point, I'll give you that."

He shrugged, tried to look more at ease with this conversation than he was. "We've got some time to kill. And I want you." He paused. "But I guess you've heard that a few hundred times."

"Not with quite the cold-blooded approach you've taken."

Mac went to stand in front of her. With one finger he touched her chin, lifted her face to his, wanting to see the depths of her eyes. "Trust me on this, sweetheart. There's nothing cold-blooded about it." He bent, brushed his mouth over hers. A charge shot through him, a blue-hot, thousand-volt charge—and the damn floor dropped out from under his feet. He pulled back, saw the kiss in her eyes, the dark, expectant hunger of it.

She wanted more.

He wanted more.

But not yet.

"How about that walk?" He ran his knuckles over the cream of her skin, down the line of her throat. "You're tight as a drum." And he knew exactly how to loosen her up.

She blinked, one of those slow, where-am-I kind of blinks, then slipped sideways, pulling the sash on her robe tight. He could span her waist with his hands. "I'll be right back." She headed quick-time to the stairs leading to the second floor. On the landing she stopped, frowned. "My staying here? It isn't dependent on going to bed with you, is it?"

"No." Why he felt insulted she'd ask, he had no idea.

"Good," she said, "because while I've done a few less-than-admirable things in my life, I've never exchanged sex for favors. And I'm not starting now." With that she headed up the stairs and disappeared from view.

Mac stared after her. The woman was no slouch in the straight-talking department herself. He liked that.

If he didn't watch it, he'd start liking her.

Which wouldn't be smart, and if he was anything, he was smart, and careful, and determined to be detached, especially when it came to his current housemate. Getting in deep—on anything but the physical level—with Tommi Smith would be nothing but trouble. When he decided to settle down with a woman, which he would sometime in the distant future, he didn't want to worry about her having one eye on him and the other on the lookout for her next conquest.

Tommi wriggled into her jeans, did up the six fly buttons, and snuggled into a cream-colored sweater. She brushed her hair and pulled it back roughly in a tortoiseshell clip. She frowned at her white sneakers . . . not the best in this weather, but they'd have to do.

When she was done and she'd caught her breath, which had been untrustworthy since she'd closed the bedroom door behind herself less than ten minutes ago, she sat on the chair near the window and stared out at the misty afternoon.

That kiss . . .

She sorted through her ragtag thoughts, stunned she hadn't given Mac a good shin-kick and stormed out like the good and proper girl most mothers raised their daughters to be. Trouble was, she hadn't had a mother, only a father who hadn't had time for her. And she'd never quite considered herself proper, but even if there had been a man or two too many, there hadn't been enough to put her in the running for the Susie-does-Seattle award.

Not even close.

Now here she was, in a lodge at the back end of the world, seriously considering going to bed with Hugh's brother.

Which makes me either crazy or sex-starved.

Damn it, she liked sex. Wouldn't apologize for that. She especially liked sex with talented lovers. Lovers at ease in their bodies, and easy with hers. That lovin' feeling . . . A hard, powerful male body straining for release. Sensations of polished steel over brushed silk. The musky scent. The heat of desire in his eyes when he explored her body, stroked her warming skin . . . rubbed her clitoris with a deft finger. Tasted her.

The rush of coming and coming . . .

She crossed her legs, tight, and inhaled deeply. At least she'd been smart enough not to go to bed with Reid. She'd come close—he'd made all the right moves—but something held her back. Instincts, plain and simple.

Instincts she needed now, more than ever. Closing her eyes, she listened for those subtle whispers to tell her what course to take. But this time they weren't so clear. In one ear they urged her toward Mac's bed, Mac's body. In the other they murmured, *be careful*.

A woman never knew when one more mistake would be one too many.

She decided to heed the be-careful signal, reminding herself she'd come here to be safe, not sorry.

If she was in the market for a fresh load of regret, all she had to do was go to bed with Mac before she'd thought it through.

He shouldn't have kissed her—if you could call the soft meeting of their lips a kiss. She touched her mouth and her breathing stalled. She compressed her thighs against the tiny pulses playing havoc at their apex. If the barest touch of his lips to hers made her body throb—where it had no business throbbing—they'd be lethal applied to more vulnerable body parts.

She wanted that . . . Mac over her, in her, his mouth on her breasts and his hands—

No! She did *not want* to sleep with Mac. It was nothing but a sexual hum, a dark coaxing from a traitorous body. She would not listen. Hugh was her friend and by extension so was Mac—or could be if she played her cards with common sense. Better to gain a friend than a lover. She wasn't about to mess things up to have rash, mindless sex.

She went to the closet and rummaged for a jacket. Too light, but it would have to do. She headed for the door.

A walk was a good idea. It would clear her head. The farther she and Mac stayed from roaring fires, big, comfy sofas, and even more comfy beds, the better off they'd be. Trudging over soggy earth under rain-drenched trees on a freezing November day would definitely put the thought of sex on hold.

Mac waited at the door, wearing the same yellow rain slicker he'd worn when she'd arrived yesterday. He eyed her jacket.

"Here." He handed her a hooded fleece pullover. "Put this on under your jacket. The wind's a killer."

"Thanks." She pulled it on and he helped, opening the neck area wider so she could more easily poke her head through. When the clip holding her hair came loose and fell to the floor, he picked it up, looked at her, and slipped it in his pocket.

He forked his fingers through her long hair, tucked it in the hood. "Leave it down," he instructed.

"You planning on using it to drag me to your bed?" She asked, not sure how she felt about his caveman tactics.

"Would it work?"

"As a first move, I'd say it's a nonstarter."

"Too bad. Those early boys had a good thing going." He came close to smiling.

"Do I detect the glimmer of a sense of humor?"

"Not when it comes to you, Smith. You're serious business."

She let that go, didn't want to ask what he meant by it, because on some level, the idea of being Mac's *serious business* made her uneasy.

Outside, the weather huddled, wraithlike and unpredictable, the clouds heavy and dark, the air salty and ocean-damp. Wind stabbed them with cold, sharp gusts, and mist, low-lying and eerily opaque, drifted among the trees.

Tommi filled her lungs with fresh air and looked around. It was so dark when she arrived last night, until now she had no sense of the property around the lodge. It was beautiful, she thought, so deeply green and mysterious. Two or three cleared acres accommodated the fishing lodge which was settled back from a deep cove protected on both sides by rocky outcroppings. With towering cedars and hemlock ringing three sides, and the broad expanse of the Pacific Ocean forming a moat on the other, the camp was a fortress in the wilderness.

She couldn't see where they'd walk, unless it was in a circle or along the pocked and rutted road she'd come in on.

"This way." Mac said. "I want to show you something."

He pointed to what looked to be an impenetrable wall of trees on the far side of the camp. "Lead on." She fastened the last button on her jacket, already intensely grateful for the fleece Mac gave her.

Closer to the trees she noticed a cave-like opening. Mac went in first, holding back a tangle of bush so she could follow. She stepped onto a narrow, rough path, a gauntlet of puddles, sludge, sodden leaves, and jutting stones. And, if she weren't careful, enough eye-level branches to either smack her stupid or take out an eye.

"It's steep in places, so best you stay behind me. It isn't far."

"What's not far?" she asked.

"You'll see."

Tommi was happy to wait, because in seconds it was all she could do to keep up with him as he strode, sure-footed, along the winding path. She let him do battle with the malicious slapping branches while she watched her white sneakers morph into mud-caked combat boots.

Fifteen minutes in, she smelled the sulfur, saw the

steam. Another five and she saw a pool several feet below them. There were cedar-plank steps leading down to it, but Mac didn't take them, just stood at the top.

"A hot spring!" She stepped up beside him, looked down.

"One spring, three pools."

The enticing waters, bubbling up from the earth's depths, shivered at its surface to catch shadow and daylight with equal ease.

She breathed in the stew of sulfur, cedar, and sea air. The mix was sharp and heady, like some ancient spice wafting ahead to herald a rare and sumptuous meal. "It smells so"—she searched for the word—"exotic."

"There"—he pointed to the upper of three pools—"is the source. About 115 degrees. Too hot to use. The water cools as it meets the air and flows over the rocks. The third pool is formed by a waterfall from the second." He shifted his hand to the last of the three pools. "It's about 85 or 90."

"Amazing."

They started down the cedar-plank steps toward the ocean. "Watch your step," Mac warned. "The stairs get slippery."

The bottom pool, carved deeply into ancient rock and worn smooth by ever-flowing waters, was large enough to take four people with ease. Here, so close to the beach, the pungent sulfur odor gave way to the scent of ocean winds.

It was magical. Every tense and tired muscle in Tommi's body tingled, drawn to the ease and relaxation the waters promised.

Mac started to take off his jacket.

"What are you doing?"

"Going in." He peeled off his shirt to reveal a broad chest, lightly sprinkled with hair, and amply muscled. His hand went to his zipper.

"You're not going to—"

"Take it all off?" He didn't smile, but he did raise a brow. "Only if you want me to." He took off his shoes and socks, then shucked out of his jeans, draping them carelessly over the walkway's two-by-four railing.

What a body! Tommi didn't know whether to be thrilled or alarmed. An image of the young Mac Fleming popped into her head, that skinny, too-tall kid with the glower from hell. Whoever that boy was, he was gone, kidnapped by life and passing years and replaced by a man as physically perfect as she'd ever seen; his body was hard-muscled and tight, his smooth skin taut over angular, strong features, as unambiguously male as . . . the thickness in his briefs.

She watched him ease into the pool, held her breath when the quivering waters reached his muscular thighs and higher, molding those briefs to his heavy sex before he sank into the steaming waters waist-high. He stretched his arms along the rock shelf behind him, put his head back, and closed his eyes.

They were still closed when he said, "Take it off, Smith, and get in here. I won't bite. And I won't touch." He opened his eyes. "But I will look."

Tommi didn't move. Couldn't. Mac was lying. He would touch. If he didn't, she would. Her fingers ached to explore him. She studied the man stretched out in the pool, her throat tight, her heart seeming afloat in her chest, its beat loud and unsteady. It made no sense. Mac didn't like her but he wanted her. He was a stranger to her, a mistake waiting to happen . . . *and she wanted him.*

Risk. It had been a long time, but it wouldn't be the

first time. Still she hesitated. And the first pellets of
rain hit her cheeks.

Mac gave her a speculative look. "You're going to
get wet either way."

"I'm not wearing a bra."

"Good. From that preview I had last night, I'd say
I'm a lucky man." He shifted over, nodded at the stone
bench seating nature had provided. "Unless they don't
stand scrutiny in the cold light of day. Or you think I
can't keep my promise not to touch." He did one of
those almost-smiles of his, the challenge implicit.

"Most men wouldn't."

"I'll bet you know the comeback to that one."

"You're not most men."

He didn't answer but kept his gaze on her, fixed, un-
wavering.

"You're daring me, aren't you?" She shook her
head.

He smiled, patted the rock beside him.

As overconfident males went, Mac was top per-
centile.

"And you won't touch me," she echoed, warming to
the challenge.

"Not an eyelash." He crossed his heart.

Suddenly the waters with a half-naked Mac showcased to full effect became a tantalizing playpen. And
considering she hadn't played for a long time, much
too tempting to pass up.

She had to stop herself from smiling.

It would be fun to see the man suffer. And distracting.

She stroked the tab on her jacket zipper, pulled it
down slowly, maybe eight inches. "Okay then, Fleming—ready or not, here I come."

5

Tommi undressed in a cold, misty rain—and Mac watched her every move, as she knew he would. Ignoring the fact she was damn near freezing, she forced herself to make a show of it. First the outer jacket, then the fleece. When she was down to her sweater, she took off her shoes and started undoing the fly buttons on her jeans, flicking them open slowly, one by one. Finally she shimmied out of what was fast becoming skin-sticking denim.

She met Mac's gaze directly and pulled her sweater over her head. With nothing between them now except heavy rain, wind, and a slice of sheer black silk, she stood, hands on hips, and let him look his fill.

He wasn't going to touch, he said.

She'd see about that.

Mac managed not to swallow his damn tongue, but nothing short of the grim reaper could stop him from getting hard. He memorized every curve as Tommi unveiled it, the line of her hip, the rounds of her firm breasts, the triangle of black covering the territory he most wanted uncovered.

Even her goddamned knees were perfect.

As he'd imagined her. As he'd dreamed her.

She stood over him, rain a silver slick over her straight shoulders. Her nipples pebbled, two strong juts into the wind and rain. She looked like some kind of nature goddess.

Except for that black silk triangle.

And he'd promised not to touch. He was a madman. An egotist who'd taken bull-headed pride to new heights. As penance, he'd probably have this hard-on for life. And he knew damn well she was teasing him. Either that or she was enjoying freezing her butt off.

"If you don't get in," he said, sounding like he felt, frustrated and angry, "you'll get pneumonia. And I'll embarrass myself."

She stepped down into the pool and sat on the stone shelf opposite him. When the water covered her to the shoulders, she closed her eyes. "Oh . . . this is heaven, absolute heaven." She lifted partway out of the water, forked her fingers through her rain-soaked hair. In his sex-fogged brain, her breasts, wet with steam and water and only an arm's length away, seemed luminescent; her eyelashes, when she raised them to meet his gaze, were diamond-tipped and sleek.

"Glad you took the dare?" If he didn't say something, he'd drown in his own juices. God, he hurt.

"Yes." She made a swimming pose with her hands, playfully pushed the water aside, then looked at him from under lowered lids. "Except—"

He waited. "Except what?"

She skimmed her palms over her nipples, cupped her breasts and lifted them. *Offered them.* "It's making me . . . hot." She grinned at him, a grin full of mischief and sexual mayhem, and stood. The water now only to her waist, she waded toward him. "Very hot." Standing over him, she purred, "What about you? Is your temperature rising?" She rested a hand palm-flat on her stomach, ran a finger under the trim of her panties.

Thunder rolled and roared somewhere in the distance. The weather was closing in, as was Tommi. Torturing him with his own promise.

The steam rose from the pool to curl around her like smoke, making her unreal, dreamlike. A sexual feast, just out of reach.

He dropped his gaze. Below the surface of the water he saw the black triangle, the slight rise of her sex. A handful. A perfect handful. And under that—

He cut his thoughts. A promise was a promise. He'd have her, all right, but when he chose the time and place. When he was in control and could make her so hot she'd combust under him. In a primal way he wanted to brand himself on her. So she'd never forget . . . probably never forgive him.

He stretched out his legs on either side of hers, his erection aching—and blatant, and leaned back against the rock. "You're playing me, Smith. It won't work. You can save the 'come fuck me' routine for another time. Right now, all I want is nature's hot tub."

He gave her credit—she didn't flinch, she laughed. "Looking at that"—she eyed the hard length of him visible beneath the clear water and smiled—"I'd say what you want is me."

"Figured that out, did you?"

"Uh-huh. Actually, I passed the Introduction to Male Arousal course sometime in the sixth grade. There were pictures and everything." She looked at him again, more studiously this time. "You'd have made a good model. Long. Straight. *Very* impressive."

"Thanks for the kind words. Now . . . sit." Her eyes

might as well have been her hands on him, stroking—but coming apart in the hot springs wasn't his plan. Tommi knew the sex game, played it well, which both pleased and irritated him.

"I could go on." She looked at him as if she knew he was suffering and she had the cure.

"You planning a second career doing phone sex?" he asked through a locked jaw.

She laughed then, stepped over his leg, and sat beside him. Her arm touched the side of his chest, under his outstretched arm. He turned his head a second, closed his eyes and took in some oxygen, his promise now looking like a marathon of self-control—or a fatal attack of male masochism.

Tommi didn't let up. "I could straddle you right now, take off your briefs, and take you in . . . deep." She ran her tongue over her lower lip. "Or I could just taste you? Which would you like?" She lifted her brows, gave him an innocent look totally at odds with her provocative words. "Of course, that would involve us touching."

His mind stuck on auto-sex. *Tommi . . . tasting him.*

Every testosterone-loaded cell in Mac's body detonated, the din of it deafening him, blotting out reason. He turned his head to look at her, see what was in her eyes. "I'd like both. And you damn well know it. But—" He stopped, the devil on one shoulder telling him to shut up and begin the feast—make her chew on her own taunts—the irritating wingless angel on the other telling him to be honest. If he were honest, his guess was Tommi would be out of the water with the speed of light. *Shit!*

"But?" she said, keeping in the game with her wide eyes and sultry tone.

"That's all I want. To fuck you and forget about it."
The want part was a given, the forget-about-it part?
Not such a sure thing.

She froze in place, the smile slipping from her face.
She looked away briefly. "I guess I should have expected that." Her smile came back, but it was weak and
wobbly, and she kept compressing her lips. "You look
at me and you see a bed, a babe—and sex."

His lungs seized up, tight. "Tommi, I—" He was
going to apologize. *Like hell!*

She held up a hand. "Forget it. You were honest.
That's something." Her wobbly smile held, but the
shadow in her eyes darkened. "I'll admit to a time in
my life when I, uh, looked for love in all the wrong
places, but I'm not the girl who, as some of my so-
called *friends* in high school predicted, was 'the gradu-
ate most likely to suck her way to the governor's
mansion.' "

Silence.

"What kind of *girl* are you?" Mac felt like Jell-O—
at least most of him did. The rest felt like hell.

"For one thing, I'm not a girl, not anymore. I'm a
woman—and like every woman, I work hard, try to do
the right thing—when I can figure out what it is, and—"

"And," he prodded.

She laughed, a thin laugh, soft and regretful. "And I
try to stay away from men who have nothing to offer
but sex in an emotional vacuum." She moved away
from him, settled herself on the rock ledge across from
him, and sank deep into the water.

"Or in a hot spring?"

It was as if she didn't hear him. "Reid McNeil was
the first man I'd dated in two years. And I blew it
again. I don't feel good about that." She looked at him.

"And now I'm here . . . with Hugh's younger brother in hot water again—literally, this time—about to make another mistake by seducing him." She slanted him an odd look. "A younger brother who didn't, maybe still doesn't, like me all that much."

Mac's heart, which had finally slowed to normal, kicked again, but he said nothing. He might need to revisit some faulty thinking, but he wasn't ready to deny her accusation.

"I never slept with Hugh. You should know that." She hesitated. "He wanted to. I didn't."

The weight that lifted from Mac's chest was a semi-load.

"He was—is—too good a friend. Sex would ruin that." She crossed her arms over her breasts, rubbed her shoulders. When her foot brushed his under the water, she pulled it back.

"Sex doesn't ruin things. People do." He moved through the water until he was braced over her. She put her hands on his chest, held him back. He let her.

"You haven't denied it," she whispered, her voice catching.

"Denied what?"

"That you don't like me. Will you tell me why?"

"I'm starting to like you. Is that good enough?" Now wasn't the time to answer her question, and he didn't wait for her answer to his, because he wanted her mouth put to a better use.

Her lips were moist, her mouth welcoming, and her eyes, wide and wary when he lowered his head to hers, closed when their mouths joined. Her hands curled into his chest hair and, finally, his tongue entered to taste her. His sex lay heavy, achingly ready, against her black silk triangle. Before their kiss sapped all his strength, he lifted his head. Ignoring the sear of tension between his thighs, he watched her eyes come open, languid and dazzled.

Good. Dazzling women was what he liked to do best.

He touched a finger to her cheek, then ran it down her throat. When her eyes opened and fully met his, they went from dazzled to guarded. "You're good at it, aren't you?"

"Sex?"

She nodded.

"Very good." He drew a line with his index finger between her breasts, then circled one hard nipple before gently rotating it. "And when the prize is as good as this"—he bent to blow on her damp nipple, watched her breathing stall—"I do my best work."

Instead of giving him a shot about his boast, as he expected, she flattened her palms against his chest and gave a slight push. "I think we should go back."

"Why?"

"Because I'm not going to have sex with you until I think about it."

He kissed her again, this time without pressure. "You're afraid."

"Not of you." She ran a hand under the water, cupped him, took the weight of his balls, ran a finger up his straining erection. "And definitely not of this"—she squeezed him—"this I like. It's that emotional vacuum I mentioned." She took her hand away. "If I'm going to let you . . . use me, I need to be ready for the lack of follow-up."

She squeezed again, then let him go. Hell of an object lesson.

Mac concentrated on dragging in some oxygen and bringing moisture back to his dry mouth. Hell, he'd damn near come in her hand. Tommi wasn't the only one who needed to think. He liked sex—what red-blooded American male didn't?—but so far, he'd managed not to lose himself in it, stay one step removed. Until now it hadn't been all that difficult.

But imagining Tommi thrashing under him, hot and wild, he wondered if holding the line would be possible.

Wondered if he'd want to.

He shifted back, let her get up and out of the pool, then followed. The rain amped up to torrential by the time they'd donned their soggy clothes. He threw his slicker over her shoulders and pulled her face to within an inch or two of his own, kissed her again. "It may be just sex between us, but it will be damn good sex."

She kissed him back, then stepped away. "I've had lots of good sex." She cocked her head, gave him a challenging stare. "If I decide to do this, I'll expect better than good."

"Ah, a woman who raises the bar." He ran a knuckle along her chin. "Then I guess I'd better make sure your time in my bed is as good as it gets."

"Promises, promises." She pointed to the hot spring. "And the way I see it, you've already broken one."

He frowned.

"The touching?" she reminded.

"I was provoked."

"You were randy."

He laughed. "Still am." He raised his face to the rain, let it sluice over him and cool his skin. "But we'd better get going. Mother Nature's getting mean. And it's going to get worse."

They headed for the trail, neither of them certain what was at the end of it.

* * *

Tommi didn't let go of Mac's hand until they reached the porch, and he needed it to open the door. On the trail the wind had come up, and even within the safety of the trees, it shoved at their backs, chilled their wet clothes.

If sex was on her mind when they left the pools, thoughts of pneumonia now replaced it. She was an icicle.

"Go take a warm shower, get into some dry clothes," Mac said. "I'll stoke up the fire, get us something hot to drink."

Tommi didn't need persuading. She bolted for the stairs and in under five minutes was thawing under a cascade of hot water. When the heat of it finally reached her bones, her thoughts turned back to Mac and the sizzle between them . . . the weight of his sex pressing against her in the hot springs.

Get a grip, Smith. You're salivating.

She stepped out of the shower and wrapped herself in a navy blue bath sheet, determined to get dressed and go downstairs with her cool—what there was left of it—intact.

A car backfired! The sound was unmistakable.

Her throat knotted with her own breath, and she ran to the window. Peering through a thick veil of rain, she couldn't see anything except masses of dripping evergreens and above them a dark, ominous sky.

Another backfire.

She flew out of the room, called to Mac over the railing. "Did you hear that?"

He was kneeling, prodding the fire to a full blaze. "Hear what?" He looked up at her, and it registered he hadn't changed yet.

"A car backfire. There's someone out there." She kept the panic from her voice—barely. "I'm sure of it."

She expected him to argue, tell her she was hearing things, overreacting; instead, he shot to his feet. "I'll check it out." He put his yellow slicker over his wet clothes. "Stay here." With that he headed out the door.

Outside it was midstorm dismal, the mist between the trees now a deep gray, half steam, half fog. Mac ignored the rain and shoved the hood back off his head to look around. Nothing but the usual wall of soaring cedars, bush, and endless ocean. The only sound was the flapping of branches beating at the wind and the roar of the surf.

He headed toward the road, which under the onslaught of sky water was now a series of muddy pools, some of them damn near knee-deep—even his four-wheel wouldn't guarantee getting through the sludge. He skirted the worst of the pools and checked through the dense bush on either side of the road. Still nothing.

Then he saw them. About a half-mile out.

Fresh tire marks, on the road and up the bank. Whoever it was had obviously stalled on their way out and had a bitch of a time getting out of the mud.

Maybe that asshole Reid was after Tommi.

His gut tightened, and he clenched his fists at his sides. He stared up the road into the deepening gloom and worked to level off his breathing, temper the blasts of raw anger.

One thing was certain: if Reid was stupid enough to try again, he'd be waiting for him—with a loaded shotgun.

In the meantime, he'd keep his eyes open and his mouth shut.

What he wasn't going to do was tell Tommi what he'd found. There was always the chance it was some schmuck who'd taken a wrong road, and he'd upset her for nothing.

He stared at the gouged-out mud the tires had thrown up to get free, then looked at the black sky. If the second storm came as predicted, they'd be safe enough. Another few inches of water and you'd need a tank to get through on this road.

Had to be the first time Mac, now a Pacific Northwesterner to his bones, prayed for rain—and plenty of it.

6

When he got back to the lodge, Tommi was waiting, her eyes too bright, her movements agitated. "I made some hot chocolate," she said. "And some sandwiches."

"Great."

When he didn't say anything more, she added, "Did you see anything?"

"About a million soggy trees."

"I heard something, Mac. I did." She looked desperate to have him believe her.

"Probably a branch or two snapping off a tree. Distant lightning, maybe. Could have been anything."

She frowned.

"There's nothing out there." The lie rested easy on his conscience. He peeled off his wet shirt, then headed for the stairs—and his rifle. From here on he wanted it ready, willing, and able—and close at hand. "Put a hold on the hot chocolate, will you? I'm going to get out of these clothes." He forced a smile. "Want to help?"

She hesitated, then smiled back. "Tempting. But I think I'll stay here and keep the chocolate warm."

"Chicken."

"Absolutely."

"It's going to happen."

"The 'it' being?" She slanted him a gaze.

"You. Me. Sex."

"You're awfully sure of yourself, Mac Fleming."

He went back to where she stood by the door and lifted her face to his. "Part of me is. Damn sure." He was caught by her eyes, the edge of melancholy in them. His stomach knotted. "Or maybe I want you so bad I can't imagine you don't feel the same." He drew her to him, kissed her with all the restraint he could muster. When neither of them could draw an even breath, he released her.

They looked at each other for what seemed an hour.

Finally, Tommi, her face unreadable, her skin flushed, said, "Can we—" she stopped.

"Go on," he urged.

"Slow down."

He heard the catch in her breath, but couldn't figure out why the air between them now filled his lungs like glue.

She touched her fingers to his lips, looked directly into his eyes. "I'm scared, Mac."

"There's nothing out there," he lied again.

"Not that. I can handle that!" She looked all tensed up again. "It's this *thing* between us . . . I don't want to make another mistake."

"Sex is never a mistake."

"Spoken like a true male." She touched his jaw, ran a finger over the seal of his mouth. "For me, sex has been a mistake most of my life. The best decision I ever made was *not* to sleep with your brother. I got a valuable friend out of that." She looked up at him, her expression thoughtful, remote. "What will I have after I sleep with you, Mac?"

Mac sensed the question was meant more for herself than him—and impossible to answer either way. But he sure as hell liked the positive sound of it. He forked his hands deep into her blond hair, made her look at him. "You think too much." He kissed her deeply, let her go while he still could, and headed for some dry clothes.

When he looked back from the top of the stairs, she was still looking at him. He'd have given his first million to know what she was thinking.

The night closed in on the lodge with a tight fist, windy, black, and wet. If there was a threatening world beyond the walls they were enclosed in, it was safely distant. Mac had built the fire to a hectic, crackling roar, and Tommi, curled in one of his big chairs, tried hard to concentrate on the book she'd taken from his shelves.

Tried even harder to ignore the quiet man in the chair across from hers. A man who didn't seem to be having any trouble at all concentrating on the file he'd opened, while leaving another pile neatly stacked at his feet.

The only light in the room came from the fire and the lamps they were reading by, the only sound the hiss and crackle of the flames and the night wind rapping for entry at the windows.

When Tommi lifted her gaze to look at Mac—for the thousandth time—she gave up her attempts to read and rested the book in her lap.

Since Mac came back down from his bedroom, hours

ago now, his hair damp and curling around his ears, his athletic body clad casually in fresh jeans and an olive-colored cashmere sweater, she'd been mesmerized, rapt in every detail, down to his long feet and white sport socks.

Her mind went to those white cotton briefs he'd worn in the pool this morning, and what she knew was under them—all for her.

If she wanted it.

Oh, yes, she wanted it, wanted Mac. Her body reminded her of that wanting with every stolen glance.

Her imagination set his hands on her breasts, his mouth at suckle . . .

At the graphic images, her breathing shallowed. Heat suffused her, made her limbs and torso limp with want of him. Burn with need for him. Her heart, a stone these past few weeks, lightened in her chest.

She stared into the fire. Maybe she had grown too cautious. Maybe she did, as Mac said, "think too much." Even Hugh told her she'd "elevated picky to an art form."

She shot another glance at Mac. She wanted him. Here in a time out of time, in a place at the back of nowhere.

And she could have him. All she had to do was put aside unreasonable expectations and go for it. Sex for sex's sake, then let it go. Mac was definitely worth it.

She wondered what Hugh would think of his baby brother passing her picky test and smiled at the thought.

"What's funny?" Mac's voice brought her back to the present.

"Nothing. Just something I read." She nodded at the abandoned book.

He craned his neck, strained to look. "*Renaissance Theology*," he read aloud. "Unless they've put in a foreword by Dave Barry, I must have missed something." He got to his feet, walked over, and picked up her wineglass. He raised it and lifted his eyebrows in silent question.

"Sure, although I think I've already had one too many."

"You've had one, period." He filled her glass, handed it back to her, and went to stoke the fire.

"I don't drink much. Too, uh, susceptible." Tommi held the glass up to the dancing flames, then took a drink—not a sip, a drink. It never hurt a girl to have a shot of extra courage. "I've been watching you, you know," she said. "Sneaking peeks at you over the top of my riveting reading." She took another swallow and put the glass on the table beside her chair. Empty.

"I know." His shadowed eyes concentrated on her face. "I've been watching you, too."

"And waiting patiently?"

"Waiting, yes. Patiently? No." The look he gave her had more heat than the roaring fire.

"Then you'll be pleased to know the waiting is over."

He cocked his head, sipped his wine.

"I've decided your idea is a brilliant way to pass the time." She got to her feet, and set about turning off the two lamps. The wild blaze in the grate was light enough. She walked to where Mac stood by the mantel. "And making love—sorry, *having sex*—is a great way to relieve stress." She gave him a sideways gaze. "You okay with being a stress reliever?"

Mac hadn't known what to expect, but it sure as hell wasn't this. Had to be the wine. The fire. The inevitability.

He stuffed his hands in his pockets, eyed her, and, not sure what to make of her, said nothing.

She looked frustrated, then irritated. Maybe because he hadn't jumped her bones the minute she opened her mouth, like any man with half a brain in his dick would have. "What part of yes didn't you understand?" she asked.

Oh, he'd caught her yes message all right, but it didn't sit right. Too easy. "Just like that?" He looked down at her. *So damn close.*

She lifted her chin, and he spotted a tremble around her mouth, an appealing uncertainty. "Are you disappointed?"

"Only that you needed to snort wine to do it."

"I did not snort! That would be much too unladylike."

He clasped her chin to scan her face. Read it. "You sure about this?" His ears had registered her affirmative; now he wanted to see it in her eyes. *Yes. Yes. Yes.*

"No." She pulled her face from his grasp. "When is anyone ever 'sure' about sex?" She took the wineglass from his hand, set it by hers on the table. "But I'm sure of one thing. Biology 101. There's no way you and I are going to spend a week here—alone—and not sleep together."

Mac reached for her. "Why the hell would we want to?"

This time, when he took her in his arms, took her lips, he wasn't going to let go. Not tonight, at least. Tonight, Tommi Smith was his, all his, and he planned to savor every soft, silky inch of her. "God, you taste good." He raised his head to look into her already half-closed eyes. "Your mouth is a damn miracle." His own eyes heavy, his erection a hot ridge of need behind his zipper, he added, "I can't wait for the main course."

She stepped away from him, stripped off her sweater, bared her fantastic breasts and smiled at him. "Your turn."

He grabbed the pillows from the sofa behind her and tossed them haphazardly on the carpet in front of the fireplace; then he went to work on his zipper, with extreme caution. Now was not the time for a sports injury.

When he was done, Tommi dropped to her knees in front of him.

She stroked him through his briefs, pulled them down, and when his erection was free, iron-hard and long against his belly, she stroked him again, softly as if he were made of glass. Then she nuzzled him, planting air-light kisses along the length of him.

Blood thundered, thick and furious, through his veins. Jesus, she was going to do him! Tommi Smith was going to do him.

He closed his eyes, lifted his chin skyward. His neck muscles strained, wire-tight. He held her blond head in his hands, stopped himself from coiling his fingers in her hair—until she drew her tongue along his length.

The breath he let out matched the gale-force winds blowing outside the lodge, and he dragged her to her feet, before he crumpled at hers. No way was he going to shoot off like a goddamned teenager. The smile he tried failed—couldn't make it through the pain. "You trying to kill me here?"

"I've wanted to touch you since the Springs. You're beautiful. Big." Her eyes were dark, her lips glossy, and when she looked down at him—the iron upright between his thighs—she moistened her lips. "And . . . I wanted a preview of what's coming."

"What's coming is me—too damn soon, if you do

something like that again." Even as he said it, he prayed for it. He tackled the sweatpants she was wearing. Elastic at the waist, they were a heap at her feet in a nanosecond. This time the triangle was red lace, deep scarlet red.

Red for *go*. He stripped them off.

Tommi was a natural blond.

When she was naked, he grasped her by the waist, ran his hands along the curves of her hips, and gripped her buttocks to pull her hard against him. Skin to skin, his temperature rose a hundred degrees.

She sighed, stood on tiptoe, and rolled her hips into his. "We're going to be good together. I know it."

"Better than good." Heated by their bodies, flush to one another, he kissed her slow and deep. Her breath was minty, her lipstick—what was left of it—held the faint taste of strawberry. "I probably shouldn't admit this, Smith, but I've wanted you since I was thirteen."

She wrapped her arms around his neck, laughed into his eyes. "I'd love to say the same, but . . ."

"The bony knees and attitude didn't do it for you, huh?" He cocked a brow, ran his hand down to cup her. Molten gold. Slick, plump, and creamy.

"Hmm . . ." She closed her eyes, pushed deeper into his hand. "You're doing it for me now."

He explored her opening, slipped his finger inside, ran it lightly between her velvet folds. Wet. Ready. "Lie down." His voice was low to his ears, and harsh.

She did what she was told, and when she was on her back, she stretched her arms above her head.

He stared down at her, soaked her in. She was a vision in firelight, a vision that locked Mac into place— some kind of time warp.

His body thrummed with need, but he refused it and continued to gaze down at her. Hell, it wasn't every day a man's fantasy lay spread in front of him unashamedly naked, with everything on offer. His breath shortened painfully. Jesus, he'd dreamed of her like this, open and waiting for him. Only him. There'd been more women in his life than one man deserved, but none of them was Tommi. Not even close.

He wanted this image—her lush curves burnished by firelight, her blond hair tumbling across a blue cushion—imprinted on his mind forever.

But a man's patience had its limits.

"Open your legs," he said, his voice ragged. "Wide."

She complied, and he sank to his knees between them. The dew on her pubic hair glistened, beckoned. He touched her once, then pulled back, to brace his hands on her knees, push them farther apart. "I want to look at you."

"I kind of figured that."

"And"—he bent his head, licked her seam—"I want to feast on you."

He saw her breasts heave, her tongue come out to dampen her lips. When she spoke, it was a whisper. "Be my guest." Again she licked her lips, this time with an edge of nervousness. "But it's been a while for me, so be prepared."

Mac had been preparing for Tommi for over half his life, and he knew what he wanted from her, what he wanted to give her.

He separated her folds, already dripping with the slick juices that would pave his way. Stroking her, he watched her eyes close, listened to her uneven, shallow breathing, then moved his gaze to her sex—the heaven he'd imagined as a boy and was about to experience as a man.

He dipped into her, first one finger then two, in . . . out, in . . . out . . . Each entry and withdrawal rhythmic and deeply penetrating.

When she started to thrash under him, he put a hand on her stomach to calm her, and bent his head.

He knew exactly where he was going.

Nestled in her soft folds, her clitoris was stiff and waiting. He drew circles around it with his finger, made it stand alone, then took it in his mouth and tasted her. Sweet, salty, spicy. Exotic.

He damn near exploded!

To stop himself he eased back, took his mouth from her and blew softly on her swollen pubis.

"Oh, God . . . more, Mac, more . . . please."

When she thrust herself upward to his mouth, he went down hard, soft bites, licks and suckles. His cock was a spike, diamond-hard and past ready, but it didn't stop him from the glory under his tongue.

He pulled the nub of her deep into his mouth, let it go, and gave it one long rasp of his tongue.

She purred, moaned, screamed his name, and came apart in his arms.

His breath coming so loud and fast he was deafened by it, he slipped on a condom, lifted her hips, and centered himself.

He rode in deep, the last of her contractions shimmering along his throbbing length. He pulled back, thrust again, his mind a whiteout, his skin too tight for his body. He was in Tommi, he was home, so deep in . . .

He erupted, flamed out, split into a million shards— a planet too close to the sun.

The cedar log in the fireplace crackled and hissed—

like Mac, its last drop of moisture consumed by the flames.

Knowing he was heavy on her, he rolled onto his back, covered his eyes with a forearm.

In the large room the only sound was their breathing—first, short and sharp; then, long and languid.

Tommi rose up and over him, her breasts squashed against his chest. She smoothed the hair back from his damp forehead, brushed her lips over his. "Not bad. Not bad at all." The words were playful, her tone oddly sober, implying she was as shaken as he was.

He opened his eyes to look into hers. He should feel empty, want to sleep. Instead, his gut felt thick and warm, and he was more awake than he'd been in years. He ran his knuckles across her smooth cheek. "I was inspired."

"Yes, you were." She stared at him a long time, her expression turning to one of puzzlement.

"What?" He pulled her face back to his, raising a brow.

"Nothing. I was just thinking I should have taken up no-strings, recreational sex years ago. I could get used to this." She got to her feet. He looked up, past her still-damp mound and flat stomach, to her mouth. A half-smile played there. "And given that your particular form of inspiration caused dehydration"—her smile widened—"I need some water. You?"

He wasn't sure how he felt about being the catalyst for her renewed sex life, but he kept his mouth shut. He didn't want to get in any deeper with her than he already was. And post-fuck conversation was a hell of a lot more dangerous than the sex. So while she got the water, he dealt with the condom and stoked the fire.

He watched her cross the room toward him, two glasses of ice water in her hands. He was impressed with how casual she was being naked. He was impressed by how uninhibited she was making love.

He was impressed. Period.

The million-dollar question was, where the hell did he take it from here?

7

Tommi handed Mac his water and sat down beside him. "That was a first, you know," she said.

"Excuse me?"

"A double orgasm. That's never happened to me before." She turned her dreamy blue eyes full on him. "You knew exactly when to . . ."

He drank some water. For some damned reason, his neck was hot.

"I've embarrassed you."

"You always so talkative after sex?"

"When I have orgasms like that, I am." She tilted her head, looked amused. "I guess I figured inquiring minds would like to know." She paused, frowned. "I'd forgotten how shy you were."

He laughed. Shy, he wasn't. There was just something about Tommi. "That was a long time ago. I was a kid." He set his water glass down and pulled her over to sit between his legs, her back to his chest. Jesus, the second her ass collided with his cock, he sprouted like a goddamn magic beanstalk. It was his turn to smile. Maybe he was still a kid, when it came to Tommi.

"Speaking as a man, I'm delighted to hear about your double orgasm—and envious as hell."

She smiled at that and settled against him, resting her head on his shoulder. His brain damn near melted when the scents of sex and shampoo wafted up his nose. He covered her breasts with his hands, and kissed her hair. Roses, her shampoo smelled like roses. He started to play with her nipples and she sighed, snuggled back into him. A sigh was good. A moan was better. He slipped his hand between her legs, played inside her cleft. In seconds he had his moan.

"I gave you a rose once, did you know that?" he whispered against her ear. *Where in hell had that come from?* Wherever it was, he wanted to shove it back.

She covered his hand with hers, held it still, and turned to look at him, her misty eyes going sharp. "I don't remember."

Hell! "I wouldn't expect you to."

"Tell me."

When she got to her knees and turned to face him, it was his turn to sigh. *Damn big mouth.* "I was fourteen, maybe fifteen." He stopped, twisted his lips. "You came for dinner. It was your birthday. You were leaving the next day."

"When I was nineteen! I remember. It was the day before I moved to Seattle. It was kind of a good-bye for me and . . . Hugh."

"Right." A good-bye that brought Hugh to his knees. That night he'd seen his brother cry. He'd never forgotten it.

"But I don't remember a rose," she said, prodding him to continue.

"It was red. I sneaked in before dinner and left it on your plate." Jesus, his neck was heating up again. What the hell was wrong with him?

She stared at him. Blinked. "That was from you? How—"

"For God's sake, don't say *sweet*."

"It *was* sweet."

He rolled his eyes. "How sweet could it have been? You tossed it in the bathroom trash can."

"I didn't."

"You did."

"I wouldn't do that!"

"I cleaned up the trash."

She started to say something, then covered her mouth.

"You're laughing."

"I'm trying not to, but we're—"

"Fighting over a fifteen-year-old rose," he finished, his own lips turning up in spite of himself.

"I shouldn't have thrown it out."

"No, you shouldn't have." He drew her back into his arms, oddly lighthearted. "What you should have done was kiss me stupid, so I'd have had something to remember you by. That's what I was angling for."

She shifted in his arms, enough to take his face in her hands. "How about I kiss you stupid right now?"

"Sounds good to me."

But she didn't—she hesitated instead, held him away from her. "That night? Saying good-bye to Hugh? It was bad, Mac."

"He followed you to Seattle."

"Yes. It took him some time to, uh, take no for an answer. But in the end he did, and now I value his friendship more than any other in my life."

"You strung him along for years, Tommi. I watched you." *God, watch you was all I did.*

She chewed her lower lip. "Yes, I did. I was vain and selfish. I strung lots of boys along. It was stupid. I was stupid." She touched his chest, ran her fingers through the hair. "I made mistakes. A long line of them."

He clasped her hand in his, watched her eyes. "And this—us—is it another mistake?"

Tommi trembled, the intensity in Mac's eyes cool and unnerving. She wondered what answer he wanted, but she opted for the truth. She leaned and brushed her lips across his. "So far, it doesn't feel like one." She kissed him then, and murmured into his ear. "What feels like a mistake is you not being inside me."

In seconds she was under him, looking into amused eyes. "Now, *that* is a mistake I'm happy to rectify."

Tommi opened for him, and he entered her, slick and easy.

Abruptly, he pulled out. She heard him inhale, then exhale with the force of the wind banging at the window.

"Damn!" he muttered. "No condom."

"Unless you belong in sexual quarantine, it's okay. I'm on the pill." She circled his penis with her hand, ran a thumb over its lush tip, and drew him back to her opening. She wanted him, all of him, as deep inside as she could have him.

"Thank God for science." He slid into her, this time with an easy, unhurried languor—as if he had all the time in the world, as if her body was created to sheath him, only him. She felt him to her soul . . .

Tommi raised her hips, closed her eyes, and gave herself over to the sensation of his rich fullness stroking her tender interior flesh. Mac tipped himself up, braced himself over her, until each luxurious penetration caught and rubbed the head of her erect clitoris.

Making her reach and reach . . .

She bucked, her inner walls clutching him, vibrating around his thickness.

"Oh, Mac"—she thrust up, held herself hard against him—"you feel . . . like heaven." Then a whisper from inside, the first flutter of coming, low in her belly, lower . . . then a quivering, silent rush of release that grayed her mind, numbed her senses.

Limp now, she was a vessel for him, still hot, still wanting, dazed and entrapped by the hard muscles of his body, the plunge and pull of his sex in her sex.

Rock-hard and rooted in the depths of her, Mac reared up and looked down at her with glittering eyes. He reached between them, pressed his thumb on her hot nub and began a slow, lazy game. "One, baby. That was one. Three's the charm." He leaned down and softly bit her distended nipple.

She nearly shot off the carpet as heat pooled and spread to heat her thighs and pubis. She couldn't breathe, couldn't think. Overwhelmed by his length inside, his fingers and mouth outside, she writhed and panted, each breath shorter, harder to draw than the last. To speak, she stifled a yearning moan. "I'm willing to go for a record if you are." She cupped his testicles. "But don't hurry—we've got days."

"And days," he ground out, taking a nipple into his mouth on a strong, suckling pull.

Then he got serious.

Mac opened his eyes to paltry morning light and a hard-on with a hand around it. A hand that had either started the erection process or was determined to finish it. He wouldn't have believed, after last night, she'd have the energy. But he knew a good thing when he felt it.

He turned to face Tommi, and she put a leg over his thigh to give him access. He went into her as if he were made for the purpose, and his lungs constricted at the sweetness of it. If there was a better way to start a day, he couldn't think of it.

But he was having real trouble keeping it slow.

Tommi put her mouth to his ear, whispered, "Don't fuss, lover. Just fuck me." She nipped his earlobe.

Not a man to refuse a gift, he took her hard and fast. When it was over, she gazed at him, her expression soft and satisfied, and ran her hand over his morning stubble.

"Now, that's what I call a good morning," he said when he could hear himself over his pounding heart.

"I figured you'd like that." She smiled at him, a lazy, pleased smile that if he were standing would bring him to his knees.

His insides went quiet, and he shoved her wild hair behind her ears. "You're more than I expected, Smith."

"As in better or worse?"

"You know the answer to that one." He brought a handful of her hair to his nose, took in her scent, then finger-combed it away from her face. "I'm glad you're here."

"And you'll be glad when I go."

Her comment rocked him. "Where did that come from?"

She sat up and pulled the top sheet over her breasts. "I thought we both needed a reminder that our time together will be short."

He couldn't read her. "That's what you want?" He cursed himself, knew his question was leading, that an answer would take him where he hadn't planned to be. In deeper with Tommi.

She stood and wrapped the sheet around her, toga

style. "I have no idea what I want, but you were clear. You wanted to 'fuck me and forget about it.'" She arched a brow, then smiled, one of those weird woman smiles that knotted a man's gut and would take a thousand years to decipher.

He did what any sane man would do under the circumstances—kept his mouth shut.

"I take that to mean," she said, her voice cool as glass, "we won't be exchanging apartment keys anytime soon." It wasn't a question, and she settled those big blues of hers on him as if they were sun rays.

Hell, she was right. He had said that, and even after last night, he meant it. Long term, Tommi wasn't for him. He wouldn't let her be, wouldn't set himself up for a fall. Some women didn't know how to love, didn't know how to be loyal, and in some dark part of himself, Mac figured Tommi was one of them. Last night, he'd had the best sex of his life, but it didn't wipe out history. And it didn't erase distrust.

And they had Reid McNeil to deal with. A thief, maybe a dangerous one, and her latest lover.

Finally, he nodded, then got up. "I apologize for being crass, but, yeah, the sentiment stands."

If his harsh words had an effect, she didn't show it. "Good," she said. "I like a man who keeps his word." She picked up the dragging edge of the sheet and headed for the bathroom. "First a shower, then breakfast. I'm starved. You?" She didn't wait for his answer.

"Tommi?"

She stopped but didn't turn to face him.

Hell! "You're crying."

She spun to face him, tears glittering along her lashes, fire in her eyes. "Of course I'm crying, you idiot. Why wouldn't I cry?" She trundled the sheet and hobbled back to him. "I'm not all about sex, Mac. In here"—she

stabbed a finger at her chest—"there's a heart, an honest-to-God heart. And right now, it's confused as hell."

With a suddenness that stunned him, she dropped
the sheet and raised her arms. "This," she said, leaving
no doubt she meant her lush Guess-girl body, "is not
all that I am. Even though I've yet to meet a man who
can see beyond it." She dropped her hands to her sides.
Her eyes blazed through the sheen of tears. "More fool
me. Last night, for a moment there, I thought—hoped—
you had a brain, that something was going on in your
head as well as your penis. I was wrong."

Before he could speak, not that he knew what the
hell to say, she picked up the sheet, rewrapped herself,
and lifted her chin. "I'm going to have my shower"—
she centered a steely gaze on him—"alone. Then I'm
going to make breakfast. Later today—if you're willing and able, which I'm certain you will be if last night
is any indication of your bedroom stamina—I'd like to
have sex at the hot spring."

Mac's jaw dropped so far it damn near fused with
his chest bone.

God, what a woman!

Reid McNeil arrived at the Close Bay Motel earlier
than expected. He checked out the rifle and ammo
Borg had secured for him, got a detailed description of
the lodge and directions on how to get there. He waited
while Borg checked out of the motel, then bought him
a big country breakfast as a going-away gift.

It was a happy Borg who agreed to drive Reid back
to his car—"parked up the road a way."

It was a dead Borg who was rolled into a deep mud-
and-water-filled ditch along an abandoned logging road.

Reid got back into his powerful black Expedition.

Borg's directions and rough maps, strewn on the seat beside him, were good, but nothing beat a personal reconnaissance, so he decided to spend the early part of the day checking everything out.

With his father due back tomorrow, he didn't have time to make mistakes. Everything had to go like clockwork.

Do the bitch properly—and probably her new boyfriend as well—then get back to Seattle before anyone even knew he was gone.

Tommi stepped out of the shower, made a sarong out of one of Mac's bath sheets, and went back into the bedroom.

He was sitting up, his back against the oak headboard, his chest bare, his lower half covered with the quilt. A forearm rested on one raised knee. With his ragged hair and whisker-shadowed jaw, he was sinfully enticing.

His eyes lit on her like two green crystals, bright but fathomless. "My towel never looked so good."

She made a point of keeping her distance from the bed. "I'm done in there." She jerked her head toward the shower, the gesture as rocky and uncool as she felt.

"Come here." He patted the empty space on the bed beside him.

She studied him, hesitated.

"Talk, Tommi. That's all."

She shook her head again, more firmly this time. "Let's stick to what we're good at, okay?"

"You mean sex." He looked disgusted.

"Exactly." She didn't intend to go into conversational territory with Mac again, because she didn't trust herself not to say something she'd regret. Something like, *It wasn't just sex for me, Mac. Something happened last night, something fabulous and special, and wonderful and crazy and—*

She squeezed her eyes shut, closed down the thought, perilously close to taking the first spiral down in a long and dangerous fall. Falling for Mac would bury her emotionally. Bad enough she'd dated Reid, hope sprouting in her chest—again!—like some evil seed given a thimble full of water. But this . . . sexcapade with Mac, her telling herself she could make love with him and walk away, having no hopes at all, was dumber still. It hurt her heart to admit it, but Mac was right to be cautious, to protect himself from her. Hell, if she couldn't trust herself, why would anyone else?

She headed for the door. Mac's voice stopped her.

"What then? What happens after the lovin'?" His voice was low, oddly distant, as if he were talking to himself more than her.

She may even have caught an edge of regret, but she didn't turn to look at him, couldn't face the temptation. "Odd you're the one asking that question, considering you made the rule going in."

"Maybe, but I'm still asking."

"Okay . . . we say thanks for a great time, and give each other an air kiss," she said, her own voice as soft as his. "And then we get on with our lives. Couldn't be simpler." Her heart in her throat, she put her hand on the doorknob. "I'm going to my room for fresh clothes. I'll see you downstairs."

Mac was already in the kitchen when she got there—forty minutes later. She'd thought about disappearing for a time, taking a long walk, but the dense woods surrounding the lodge made her nervous. Then she'd thought of getting in her car and driving as far from Mac and this place as possible, but knew that would be emotionally cowardly and physically foolish. Reid was still out there, angry and dangerous. She didn't know what he was capable of and didn't want to find out. Waiting until Paul got back was her only option. Just a few days. She could handle it. And she could handle Mac.

And she could more than handle making love with him . . . forever.

She straightened her shoulders, took a seat at the counter, and faced her biggest challenge. Bravado would have to do what her aching soul couldn't.

"Hey," Mac said by way of acknowledgment. He'd made coffee, and what looked like pancake batter lay pooled in a bowl near the stove. He poured her a mug of coffee, set it in front of her, and went back to the stove.

"Thanks." She took a life-affirming drink, and watched him, impressed by the easy, agile way he moved around the kitchen, his every movement fluid and economical. As if this morning-after was like every other morning-after. Tommi's hands tightened around her mug, and she twisted her lips. Mac picked up the bowl and stirred the batter, managing to look irritatingly, excitingly masculine in the process. "Multiple orgasms and he cooks, too. What more could a girl want?"

He glowered at her. "Don't."

"Don't what? Talk about sex on an empty stomach?" She eyed him from over the rim of her mug, ignored the way her stomach fluttered looking at him. His hair still damp from the shower, he wore soft over-worn jeans, and an even softer black cotton sweater. Even with angry lines etched on his forehead, he took her breath away.

"Don't play the hard-nosed harlot. It doesn't suit you."

"Oh? What does suit me, Mac? Other than my birthday suit, of course."

He looked as if he had a mouthful of rivets. He opened his mouth, closed it. He took an obvious deep breath before he said, "You want anything besides pancakes?"

She laughed so she wouldn't cry. "Ah . . . the deft, oh-so-masculine approach to the emotionally charged moment. Change the subject."

He was around the counter in a flash, and she was yanked from her stool in the flash after that. "I am not changing the subject. I just have no idea what to say." He looked away from her, and when he looked back, his eyes were stark. "Because I don't know what the hell I feel. Okay?"

8

Tommi, speechless, could only stare into the frustrated face of the man holding her up against his chest, so close to his face she could smell the peppermint on his breath.

He loosened his grip but still held her, his voice quieter when he said, "And your lousy pretense at playing the wicked witch of the north doesn't help. You got that?" He glanced away, looked as if he wanted to tear out his own tongue.

When her heart found its rhythm, Tommi found her voice. "I got it, Mac. Now can I have my arms back?"

He let go of her arms as if they were electrified, and his eyes met hers, hot, startled. "Jesus, I'm sorry. Did I hurt you?"

"No. Reid did." She rubbed her bruised arms, looked up at him, unsure what her eyes were saying. "I don't think you'd ever do that."

His gaze met hers squarely, and he raised her chin with his knuckles. "No, I wouldn't." He used a thumb to stroke her cheek, fixed his eyes on hers.

She saw the heat settle into his glance, heard his breathing heighten, felt the need emanate from his lean body. Her own body's quivering answer.

No, Mac would never hurt her . . .

Not physically, anyway.

She pulled her face from his grasp, ignored the charged air sizzling between them, the invisible tug of his powerful masculinity.

He stood tall in front of her, a wall of male energy and self-assurance. "We *will* have that talk. But not now. Now we're going to eat. And we're going to keep our hands off each other for the next few hours." He grimaced. "Which, you should know, won't be easy."

She looked down at him, the thickness of his erection evident behind the soft denim.

"Then, when this lousy rain lets up," he went on, "we'll go to the hot spring." He leaned down and brushed a feathery kiss over her mouth. It made water of her knees. "Where I will commence my efforts to surpass all that has gone before." He paused, then added, "After that . . . we talk."

Tommi stared at him, thought about holding her ground, but wasn't sure where it was. "Who put you in charge of the agenda?"

"You don't approve? I could have sworn it was you who wanted sex in the hot spring. I remember your instructions as very specific—and explicit."

He had her there. Still . . . "This is getting confusing, Mac. I don't know if I—"

He shook his head, touched her mouth. "Right now, you don't have to know, and you don't have to think—about anything." He took a step away, put his hands in his pockets, but kept his eyes on her. "We've ended up here with a few days to spend together." He paused, for a moment looked uneasy. "Me? I entered into this arrangement of ours with certain assumptions. Maybe wrong, maybe right. I'm betting you did, too. Now I'm suggesting we use the rest of our time together to test those assumptions."

She eyed him, looking curious but guarded. "That's more words than you've strung together in all the time I've been here. Very . . . boardroomish."

He didn't smile. "I like to approach problems logically."

"Me being the problem?"

He took a moment to mull over her question. "Yes."

"And I should be flattered by that?"

He smiled, ever so softly. "Yes, I think you should." He took the two steps necessary to stand directly in front of her. He didn't touch her. "Can we eat now?"

Food was suddenly the last thing on Tommi's mind, but she nodded.

"After that, if you don't mind—I intend to keep my hands off you by keeping them busy making a couple of phone calls, then going through some files. You okay with that?"

"I think I can last a few hours without you inside me, Mac. You okay with that?" She looked at him from under lowered lids.

"Low blow, sweetheart," he said and grinned. "But given I'm the guy who suggested the downtime, I'll consider that loss as my temporary purgatory. Temporary being the operative word."

Reid inched his way along the deserted, damn near impassable road. Borg hadn't exaggerated; it was one long river of a mud hole, and it got worse the closer he got to the lodge. Reid hadn't intended to drive up to the front door, but he'd sure as hell planned on parking closer than what he guessed was two miles away.

Suddenly the front wheel of the big ATV dropped into a goddamned lake in the middle of the road.

Shit! After several tries he managed to reverse his way out, but there was no doubt this was as far as he could risk going.

Frustrated, he tapped his fingers on the leather-wrapped steering wheel. He'd have to leave the truck here. He backed up to where he could turn it to face the way he'd come, then reversed as deep into the bush on the side of the road as he could. Satisfied the vehicle couldn't be seen from the road, he went back to wipe out the gouges and tire tracks the Expedition had left near the washout and tossed a few cedar boughs over them for good measure.

Back at the truck, he grabbed a backpack from the front seat and retrieved the rifle and ammo from the back.

If he had to walk, he'd better get started. He needed to figure things out, make certain he had plenty of time to get back.

He didn't want any screwups.

He slung the rifle over his shoulder and headed down the path, hoping he wouldn't have trouble getting rid of the new boyfriend along with Smith. No way did he plan on having some rich schmuck live long enough to play the hero and tail him back to the truck.

Around three o'clock the rain stopped, but when Mac looked at the leaden sky, saw the turbulent clouds scudding over the ocean's surface, he knew the break was again temporary. This far-north rain came damn near nonstop this time of year.

He tossed the file he'd been reading onto the pile

beside his chair. With Tommi curled up on the sofa across from him, he'd had a hell of a time keeping his mind on business for more than sixty seconds at a time. When she'd dozed off half an hour ago, her book open in her lap, her golden hair a wild curtain over her eyes, he'd given up, given in to the need to simply look at her and listen to the sound of her quiet breathing, while his own lungs constricted to the point of pain.

He wanted her. He ached with wanting her, and he knew himself well enough to know a few days of her wouldn't be enough. That air-kiss scenario she'd outlined? It wasn't going to happen. Maybe he didn't trust her, but maybe he could live with that. And maybe the Pope was an undercover Hare Krishna.

But maybe, just maybe, he could love her enough for both of them.

The oxygen evacuated his lungs as if attacked. The love word had a way of doing that to a man, showing up like a SWAT unit in riot gear to lay waste to his life and logic.

He rubbed his chest, got to his feet, and turned the L-word over in his mind. There were a thousand reasons why Smith wasn't the woman for him, but right now he couldn't think of one of them. It had to be the sex.

The SWAT thought reminded Mac he had something to do before he and Tommi went to the springs. He'd walked the perimeter of the compound twice today, then walked the road again. Two miles out there was a water-filled crater the size of a semi, with no sign of tire marks on either side. A guy would need a Hummer to get through the mess. Considering even a Hummer was a possibility, he planned to be ready for it.

He padded toward the stairs as quietly as possible, but the movement woke Tommi.

Her eyes still closed, she stretched, a languid stretch that made the tee she was wearing tighten across her unbound breasts. She opened her eyes on Mac, blinked slowly and asked, "Where are you going?"

"You always look so damn good when you wake up?"

She stretched again, smiled a bit, and sat up. "You always answer a question with a question?"

"I'm going to get my rifle." It wasn't as if he could hide the damn thing on the way to the pool.

She straightened, instantly alarmed. "What for?"

He gestured with his chin toward the dark day outside the window. "If we're going to the spring, I thought I'd take it with me. There's always a risk of wild animals." The lie sat on his tongue like sugar. The way he saw it, what she didn't know wouldn't worry her. He didn't like her to worry, and he didn't bother to think why.

"You didn't take it yesterday."

"Forgot. Shouldn't have. I try not to make the same mistake twice." He stopped on the first stair. "I'm also going to get some towels. Unless you've changed your mind." He raised a brow. Waited.

Tommi hesitated. Maybe she should change her mind. Maybe she should stay here with her nose in a book. Then she looked up at Mac, still as a panther on the lower step, his hand on the newel post.

The hot spring.

Pure, warm water surging over naked flesh, erotic, skin-softening steam, and the scent of cedar boughs heavy with rain. The textures, the silkiness of Mac, deep, deep inside her. Four days. She had four days. She'd done her reality check, revisited the rules—all sex, no expectations. She'd be a fool if she didn't take all of Mac Fleming she could get. "No. I haven't changed my mind." She got to her feet. "I'll get a heavier sweater."

A few minutes later they were on the front porch,

Mac with a rifle in his hand, and her with a knapsack strung over her shoulders, full of towels and goodies she'd raided from the kitchen.

When he put his arm around her and leaned to kiss her, she raised her mouth to his, eagerly, avidly, her body already overheated thinking of what they'd be doing in less than half an hour.

Mac scanned the lodge compound, hiked the rifle over his shoulder, and took her hand. They headed for the path.

From the far edge of the clearing, Reid watched them duck into the trees. He couldn't believe his luck. They were out in the open, exactly where he wanted them. He gave them a five-minute head start, then darted across the open compound.

Mac led the way as he had before, this time holding Tommi's hand. They moved along the path in silence, Mac concentrating on missing as many snags and puddles as he could, while Tommi's attention centered on keeping pace with his long strides.

A few minutes in, Mac stopped in the middle of the path, so abruptly she collided with his back. "What—"

"Shh!" He shook his head, put a finger against her mouth, and stared back in the direction they'd come, listening intently.

Tommi's heart pounded, and she put her hand over it. She listened, too, but didn't hear a sound—not even rain.

Suddenly Mac cursed softly. "This way!" He dragged her roughly off the path and into the heavy underbrush. There, he put his hand on her shoulders and forced her to her knees. When she opened her mouth, he shook his head again, whispered, "Stay down and stay quiet."

For interminable minutes, they crouched deep in the bush.

When Tommi saw who came down the path, her lungs seized. She clapped a hand over her mouth, felt the cold air against her fear-widened eyes. Every muscle in her body tensed. When he stopped to look around a few feet from where they'd taken cover, she clamped her teeth together to stop them from chattering.

"Easy," Mac muttered near her ear. "Easy, sweetheart."

Stunned by seeing Reid McNeil in this impossible place, she couldn't take her eyes off him. Couldn't move.

She felt Mac's breath on her ear, then the first drops of rain on her cheeks, sharp as ice pellets. "McNeil?" Mac whispered, his gaze locked on the man on the path.

She managed a nod. Reid turned, rotated slowly, and looked around as if to get his bearings. Her hands clenched on her knees, froze there. "He's got a gun." The words came out on a hiss.

"I know." Mac took her hand. "Let's go. I need to get you to more cover." Still crouching, he pulled her deeper into the bush, his movements low, fluid, and furtive.

Tommi's movements were awkward and stiff. The uneven ground, broken branches, fallen logs, and lethally slippery leaves made it impossible for her to find her stride.

Her foot caught on a fallen branch, and she fell, hard and headfirst into a rotting, moss-covered stump. Her forehead scraped along a protruding branch and blood trickled down beside her ear.

Mac dropped to his knees at her side. "You okay? Can you get up? You have to get up, Tommi."

He grasped her arms, tugged her to her feet.

Too late.

"Well now, isn't this convenient." Reid stepped out from behind a tree, raised the rifle, and leveled it at Tommi. He looked around at the dense bush, amused. "I won't even have to bury the bodies."

Beside her, Mac shifted his weight. Reid immediately swung the rifle barrel toward him. "Drop it. Now." Reid's face was as hard and relentless as the rain now growing in force and dripping in pellet-sized drops from the branches over their heads.

Mac's eyes blazed with a deadly determination. She saw him tighten his grip on his rifle. "I don't think so, McNeil. I prefer the odds with this in my hand."

Reid swung his rifle back toward Tommi.

She sucked in a breath, paralyzed by the sight of the evil black hole at the point of the barrel—the thought of dying. "You don't have any odds." Reid curled his lip. "*Drop it* or you watch the lady chew on a bullet."

Mac, his face taut, dropped the gun.

Reid trained his rifle on Mac. "Actually, while I was walking in here, I decided I'd do you first." He cast a glance at Tommi. "I never did get to fuck this bitch. I figure, out here, why not?" He slanted Mac a filthy look. "Trouble is, I don't think you'd sit still to watch." He lifted the gun barrel, centered it on Mac's chest.

"No!" Tommi went for the gun—Mac's death in Reid's hands. She almost made it . . .

A searing pain shot across her shoulder, and she heard Mac yell, "You son of a bitch!" Then a crunch of bone on bone, before she crumpled to the sodden moss at her feet. She tried to get up, fell again . . . everything colorless, hazy . . . dark.

Have to help Mac.

* * *

She forced her eyes open—seconds later? Minutes later? She tried to pull herself to her knees. Blood dripped onto the moss like red rain. From her . . . face? Shoulder?

"Mac!" She couldn't see through the blood on her face, her eyes. She brushed at it, desperate now. "Mac, where are you?"

"I'm here, Tommi. Right here."

Then his hands were on her, all over her, stroking, probing, holding. "God, if you weren't hurt, I'd kill you myself. That was crazy!" His voice was low, angry and thick with concern. He tore away her jacket sleeve, looked at her arm, and let out a long, harsh breath. "Just a graze—but bleeding like hell." He picked her up, cradled her in his arms.

"Reid?" she croaked, barely finding her voice.

"Out cold. His head collided with my rifle butt. He's belted to a tree." He shifted her to a more comfortable position against his broad chest. "To hell with him. He can rot there, until the cops get here. I'm taking you back to the lodge." He kissed her bloodied forehead. "But you'll have to come clean, sweetheart, about the embezzling. You won't have a choice."

She nodded her still-spinning head. "No choice," she parroted and passed out against his shoulder.

A cop who looked no older than eighteen arrived by boat within the hour—Mac had advised him against attempting the flooded road. Mac led him along the forest path to where he'd left McNeil, propped up and lashed tight to a cedar. The young cop was briskly efficient. With Mac's help, he handcuffed the cursing, threatening McNeil in the stern of his patrol boat, and in minutes was back at the lodge to take Tommi's statement.

"Tommasea Violetta. Interesting name." He closed his notebook. "Never heard it before."

Tommi figured, given his age, there were lots of names he hadn't heard before. Propped up on Mac's bed, a bandage on her forehead and her arm wrapped and resting on her stomach, she smiled at him. "I think they were trying to make up for the Smith."

He nodded, his expression serious. "Doctor Kenning will be along shortly to take a look at that, although it looks as if you were a lucky young lady. Just took a patch of skin off, is all."

Tommi's smile deepened at being called a "lucky young lady" by someone who probably did his first shave a month ago.

A few minutes later, she heard his patrol boat roar away from Mac's dock, presumably with a trussed-up Reid McNeil in the stern.

Tommi put her head back and closed her eyes, gingerly touched the bump under the bandage on her forehead.

A big, warm hand closed over hers. She opened her eyes when Mac's weight settled on the bed beside her. "You'll probably get one hell of a shiner." He propped a knee on the bed and played with the hand he held in his lap.

"Thank God for M.A.C." Her quip didn't make her less afraid to look at him and see what was in his eyes. Their time together was over. With Reid gone, there was no reason to stay. From here on, it was all about good-byes. At that thought her chest seemed to fill with lead.

"Why did you do it? Put yourself at risk like that?" His voice was low, troubled. "What in hell were you thinking? I could have lost you." His eyes were angry, confused, and filled with something she couldn't identify . . . fear?

She glanced aside, looked for the words that so needed to be said. Words harder to give than your body. "I did it because . . . I couldn't imagine waking up in a world without you in it." Her eyes were dry, her chest thick, cluttered with nameless emotions.

Silence.

Mac's throat worked as if he were swallowing stones. Finally, he lifted her hand to his mouth, kissed her knuckles, and said, "About the sex . . ."

Tommi's heart tumbled, and her throat closed. It was always about the sex.

"What's between us has gone past that." His eyes lightened, and he smiled at her in a way he never had before. "Truth is, Smith, I fell for you the second I laid eyes on you. Trouble was, I was thirteen, you were eighteen, and there wasn't a hell of a lot I could do about it."

She held her breath. "And now?"

"Now I can." He let go of her hand and braced himself over her, a hand on each side of her hips. The same position he'd taken when he'd come to her after her bad dream. "I don't want this to end. I don't want *us* to end. I want to take what's between us and build on it. You okay with that?"

Tommi's heart didn't make it to her mouth, but she'd swear it lodged halfway up her throat. She shut her eyes against the tears, the ache of relief. *I'm such a sap for this man.* "I'm very much okay with that."

"There's something else that needs to be said." His expression darkened. "I should have trusted you, Tommi. Should have trusted—what I felt for you." He stopped. "When you stepped in front of me today, my whole goddamn life shut down. I kept thinking, what if I lost you—when I'd just found you."

"Then don't think." She touched his chin. "Just kiss me, Mac. Just kiss me."

He gestured toward her bandaged arm. "I'll hurt you."

She shook her head, used her good arm to pull him toward her. "Hold me, Mac, hold me forever and love me"—she stopped, the words, so long withheld, poised on her tongue—"the way I love you."

Before he could answer, she brought his mouth to hers. He took her in his arms loosely with aching care, deepened the kiss.

Tommi gave herself up to the magic of his mouth, the warmth of his body, while deep inside a smile bloomed.

She had secrets. Precious secrets.

She wondered what Mac would think when she told him he was the first man she'd ever loved—and today was the first time she'd ever said, *I love you.*

DEAL WITH THE DEVIL

Cate Noble

1

Max DeLuca exited the private elevator and stalked across the dimly lit salon of the corporate penthouse in Boston. It was after midnight, but he didn't turn on any additional lights. Ellie was in the guest suite and he didn't want to wake her.

Or did he?

He stopped short, nostrils flaring at the faint, lingering scent of feminine cologne. The simmering irritation that had bedeviled him since leaving Rome twelve hours ago disappeared. In its place was a more primitive sensation: a raw, aching, heat that left him as aroused as he was furious.

Oh, there were a lot of things he wanted to do to his sister-in-law—former sister-in-law—but all demanded her full attention. For now, sleeping beauty was safe.

Scowling, he detoured toward the bar. It was just as well she wasn't awake. He was in a foul mood, had been spoiling for a fight all day, for reasons that weren't completely attributable to Ellie.

Which wasn't to say he didn't have good cause to be pissed right now. When it came to Ellie—

He cut off the thought. The past was like quicksand. Waiting at the first mental misstep, it sucked the weak under. "Do yourself a favor—focus on the business at hand," he muttered.

And the matter at hand was, literally, business. Max wanted Ellie to sign an agreement that would extend the terms of his late half-brother's will. The deal would grant him continued control of her stock holdings in his company. From a purely financial perspective, his proposal was sound. In the three years since Stefan's death, Max's strategic business partnerships had more than doubled the size of DeLuca Shipping International. Ratifying the new contracts was a fairly routine matter that should have been settled months ago.

Unfortunately, nothing between Ellie and him had ever been *routine*. Their respective attorneys had locked horns from the start. Then the press picked up the story, adding a Machiavellian twist. At that point Ellie withdrew from negotiations, remaining virtually incommunicado for weeks.

Until two days ago, that is. Then she'd sent an e-mail to Max's personal account. Her message had been cryptic:

I want to propose a private deal.
A deal that will satisfy both of us.

His curiosity had gone ballistic. So had his libido. He'd been willing to promise anything to get her back to the table, but she eschewed discussing specific details, insisting instead on a private, face-to-face meeting: *just the two of us*.

Because her mind-blowing e-mail had provoked a seemingly relentless hard-on, he had considered sending a surrogate here tonight. Except he worried that move would tick her off and derail discussions permanently.

Funny how all those concerns had faded during his flight. A little dose of fury—a lot, actually—had done the trick. Maybe too well. Before he met with Ellie he needed to chill, think things through.

He dumped his briefcase in a leather chair and reached across the bar. The carved ebony decanter held his favorite anger-management tonic: an exceptionally rare, forty-year-old, single-malt Scotch. He poured two fingers, neat, then made it three. He'd earned it.

Before taking a sip, he mockingly tipped the glass toward the line of ancestral portraits on the wall. Yet another family tradition Max had no intention of continuing.

After six generations of patriarchal excess and legendary debauchery, DeLuca Shipping International had been flirting with bankruptcy when Max unexpectedly inherited the reins seven years ago. He'd single-handedly turned the tides, rebuilding the company from the bottom up. *They* owed *him* a nod. Especially his half-brother.

Max rubbed the scar above his left eye. The guilt he'd carried about Stefan's death had faded during the court battles that had erupted over his brother's estate. Stefan had mimicked their father in all the wrong ways, including literally keeping a different woman in every port—and an unsuspecting wife at home. If Max were in a more generous mood, he'd feel sorry for Ellie. Except it wasn't as if he hadn't tried to warn her. *You're marrying the wrong man . . .*

Feeling restless, he carried his drink out onto the terrace. The high-rise overlooked the twinkling lights of Boston harbor, typically one of his favorite views. But tonight it was the horizon that held his attention.

Fierce lightning backlit mile-high thunderclouds, a glorious preview of the storm still at sea. The sweltering July night, perfect for the building squall, seemed to mirror his mood.

The day had been arduous, his transatlantic flight a marathon of hostile business calls and videoconferences. If something could go wrong, it did. First, there had been the last-minute renegotiations of an important merger that would inject some badly needed capital into Max's coffers. The deal, destined to solidify DSI's top position in the global shipping market, had derailed when Haru Mizuno, the owner of the Japanese shipping conglomerate, had tried to back out, citing a personal crisis.

Some quick digging by Max's staff uncovered Mizuno's so-called crisis: a gambling debt owed to none other than Peter Fourakis, the owner of a rival Greek shipping firm. This wasn't Fourakis's first attempt to undermine Max. It also wasn't the Greek's worst offense.

Fourakis had been circling like a buzzard ever since the news leaked that Ellie McMann DeLuca, dubbed *gorgeous, loaded, and available* by the tabloids, would soon gain full control of her substantial stakes in DSI. A photograph of Ellie and Fourakis dining together had fueled speculation of a romance. It had given Max heartburn. So had the stories that implied Fourakis was the reason she refused to extend her agreement with Max.

Knowing such stories were usually fabricated didn't help. Though immune to seeing his own name in the tabloids, seeing the private details of Ellie's financial holdings splashed across cheap newsprint infuriated Max. Especially in light of the security briefing he'd just received.

He frowned, recalling the details. According to the

report, Ellie had a cyber-stalker, one she'd only recently reported, despite weeks of harassment. Weeks. That bit of information left Max seeing crimson. Part of him wanted to go snatch her up out of bed and shake her for not being more circumspect. The other part of him *thickened*.

Once again, Max's thoughts drifted down the hall, to the guest suite. To what he'd really like to do if he hauled Ellie out of bed.

He drained his Scotch and stared at the cloud-strangled moon. Coming here tonight, in such a dangerous mood, had been a mistake. Not that staying away had been an option. Perhaps he'd change clothes and go downstairs to the gym. Punching a bag, taking a cold shower, would help.

He headed for the master suite. Just outside he halted. The door stood ajar but what stopped him was the scent of cologne. It was stronger here.

Was Ellie in his room?

He shut his eyes against the vision that filled his head: Ellie naked. The thought of her in his bed sent a hot rush of blood to his cock. *Down, boy*. He recalled her message: I want to propose a private deal. So would he. Face-to-face, straight up, inside her. It didn't get more private than that. Maybe it was time Ellie and he had it out—cleared the air, once and for all.

He pushed open the door and stepped inside. A gentleman would knock, but that was the last thing he felt like at the moment. Besides, this was his room, the open door an invitation.

The perfume was stronger inside. And all wrong. Too heavy. He paused, senses alert.

"Hello, Max. Miss me?" The words hissed out from a dark corner, snakelike.

He recognized the woman's voice, knew the reason

for her antagonism. Bridgette St. Regis was the thrice-divorced daughter of oil magnate Arnaud St. Regis. Max had dated her casually, but broke off their affair completely two months ago. The split had not been amicable; they were both control freaks.

What was she doing here? And where was Ellie?

Max pinpointed Bridgette's exact location in the dark before flicking on the light switch. His eyes took in the disheveled bed. Had she been in it?

"How did you get in?" He kept his voice calm.

She stepped out of the shadows, diamonds sparkling at her throat as she shrugged. "The doorman recognized me."

His jaw tightened. "Maybe what I should have asked is why in the hell you're here. Because I'm in no mood to talk."

"That's a relief." She raised a brandy snifter in an exaggerated toast and shifted unsteadily, confirming this wasn't her first drink. "Talking never was our strong point. Let's just move on to making up."

"There's nothing between us, Bridgette."

"Don't say that!" She lowered her voice, feigning contrition. "I know why you're mad. You're right—perhaps I shouldn't have talked with that reporter."

It took Max a moment to figure out what she meant. Then he recalled the interview she'd granted to one of the celebrity rags. "That's old news. Give it a rest."

"How can I? That reporter was an idiot. He twisted everything I said, including the bit about us being engaged. Obviously he read quite a bit into the fact I was defending you."

"I can defend myself."

"Well, I couldn't just stand there while he insinuated *Il Diavolo* had no heart."

The Devil. If she were sober, she'd remember Max

detested the tabloid nickname, detested being in the spotlight. She'd also recall he had ended their affair weeks before she'd dished a few X-rated details to the reporter.

Bridgette stepped closer, invaded his personal space. "I've missed you, darling. And I miss this." Her hand moved to his crotch and tightened. Her dilated eyes widened, gleaming in anticipation. "We can start over. It can be like it was in the beginning. No commitment. No strings. Just sex."

The magazine had a field day with that one. Max's motto: *No commitment. No strings. Just sex.* Suddenly he loathed it, loathed himself. He moved free of her grasp.

"It's over, Bridgette. You need to leave. I have company and—"

She cut him off as she twirled away. "You had company, though I'd hardly call that little tart of Stefan's a guest."

"What do you mean *had*?" His gaze went to the door.

"Look at me! I came here tonight willing to grovel and what do I find? Her—half-naked in your bed, claws extended."

"I doubt that's what—"

Bridgette stamped a foot. "Don't you dare defend that witch! The note she left, oh-so-casually propped against the Tiffany lamp in the foyer—very clichéd, Max, really—made it very clear what she intended."

What she intended: A deal that would satisfy. Heat and outrage slammed through him. "Where's the note?"

"Gone. Same as her."

Max had heard enough. Picking up the bedside phone, he punched in a string of numbers as he spoke curtly over his shoulder. "You can leave on your own,

Bridgette, or with security. Either way, a cab will be waiting by the time you reach the lobby."

"So this is how you're going to play it? Fine, I'll give you a little more time to come to your senses." She laughed coldly, then extended her drink and dumped it out on the Persian rug. "Just don't make me wait too long, Max. You'll regret it."

"I'm the wrong person to threaten. Stay the hell out of my life, Bridgette. Pull another stunt like this and I'll have you arrested."

"We both know you don't really mean that." She strolled from the room. "*Arrivederci.*"

Max watched to make certain she got into the elevator. Then he called the doorman. "Bridgette St. Regis is on her way down. Whoever let her up made a big mistake. If it happens again, someone will be looking for a new job. Do I make myself clear?"

"Yes, sir," he stammered. "But I just came on duty, sir."

"Then make certain the appropriate party gets my message." Max pinched the bridge of his nose. "Also, Ms. DeLuca was here earlier this evening. I need to know when she left and how."

"I'll get right on it, sir!"

After hanging up, Max prowled around the suite. How much of what Bridgette said was true? The idea of Ellie half-naked in his bed, while improbable, drove him crazy. Same with the suggestive note. Clearly something had transpired between the two women. Why else would Ellie have left? She'd been an invited guest whereas Bridgette was a party crasher.

A niggling sense of suspicion slowed his pacing. This was the third time in a week he'd run into Bridgette. Since their first two meetings had been at restaurants in Rome, he'd written it off as coincidence. But this? How had she known he'd be in Boston tonight?

Max had just replaced his corporate security chief following a series of safety breaches. Gerard, the new guy who'd also prepared the report on Ellie, had warned there were a lot of holes. Was this an example?

The phone rang. "Ace Limo picked Ms. DeLuca up about an hour ago," the doorman said. "They took her up the coast, to Rockport."

Max recognized the address the doorman read off. It was the beach house Ellie had inherited from her grandparents. He should have known she'd go there.

"Mr. DeLuca?" The doorman cleared his throat. "Is there anything more I can do?"

"Yes. Have my car brought around. I'll be right down."

He thought about calling Ellie first. But if she'd indeed had a run-in with Bridgette, she'd likely avoid his call. Things hadn't been all wine and roses with them lately. Damn it, he never should have let things get to this point between Ellie and him.

When the elevator arrived, he entered and jabbed the LOBBY button. But just as the doors started to close, he spotted a crumpled ball of pink paper beneath the sofa. Swearing, he hit OPEN. The elevator lurched to a stop. He went back inside.

Had Ellie really left a note? Was that it? He recalled Bridgette's accusation. *"The note she left . . . made it very clear what she intended."*

He grabbed the paper and quickly unfolded it, recognizing Ellie's elegant handwriting.

> *Here's my price to extend our arrangement: One night . . . like it used to be. No commitment, no strings, just sex. Deal?*

2

A noise woke Ellie. She sat up, her mind still trapped in the foggy span between her erotic dream and wakefulness. *Dreamus interruptus*.

The ragged in-out of her own heavy breathing echoed in the room. She shoved a tangle of hair off her face and studied the unfamiliar shadows. Thunder rumbled outside, low and distant. The sense of panic subsided as she realized what woke her and where she was. The beach house. The storm.

She sank back into her pillow and shut her eyes, seeking calm. Immediately, she got sucked back into the dream. Max . . . naked . . . his erection throbbed against her thigh as he moved to plunge up and in—

She groaned. Flipping onto her stomach, she buried her face in the sheets, cheeks burning. How could she even think of him after the disastrous scene at the penthouse?

It had taken such colossal nerve to send Max that e-mail to begin with. "I want to propose a private deal."

They'd been relaying messages through their legal mouthpieces for so long that she hadn't even been certain he'd personally reply. He did. His response had been swift and every bit as provocative as her query.

Name your price. Any time. Any place.

His words had made her feel brave. *I can do this.* She'd played it coy, agreeing only to a time and place. But that hard-won bravado had weakened the moment she heard the penthouse elevator chime. She'd already been in and out of Max's bed a dozen times, second-guessing everything—her choice of lingerie, her motives, her intentions. There had been no turning back then. She had lain in his bed, while nervously imagining him reading the seductive invitation she'd left propped on the bar.

Name your price. She had.

Using his very own words, his motto, she'd offered to sell her soul to the devil for one night in his arms. Long before she'd been Stefan's wife, she'd been Max's lover. And she'd never stopped wondering . . . *what if*? If they had one more night, could she forget him and move on?

She stifled another groan. Good Lord, had she honestly thought that's all it would take to purge him from her system? One night?

Yeah, she had. Hair of the dog, and all that. Once upon a time, she and Max had seemed perfectly suited. Maybe they hadn't been. Maybe she'd let her fairy tale recollection fog reality. It had certainly fogged her judgment. Since Max seemed to avoid being alone with her, she'd decided to use the stock agreement as leverage. A way to force him to meet with her privately.

Huge mistake.

She'd never forget Bridgette St. Regis bursting into

the room, shouting. *What are you doing in Max's bed? How dare you plot to seduce my fiancé! You don't honestly think he would be interested in his little brother's castoffs, do you?*

Mortified, Ellie had fled the penthouse.

Max was engaged. The news had been shocking. How could she have gotten everything so wrong? Sure, the tabloids had linked Bridgette and Max; the insatiable *Il Diavolo* was linked to a different woman every week. But Ellie's source—whom she'd forever doubt now—had assured her that Max wasn't seriously involved with anyone.

Not for the first time, Ellie had misread the cues. The extreme measures Max had taken to resolve the messy court proceedings over Stefan's estate had not been done for her benefit. Just when it seemed there would be no end to the scandals that surfaced following Stefan's death, Max had charged in and bought out all the other claimants. She now had to assume he'd mortgaged his own shares of DSI to do so, in order to settle things prior to his marriage to Bridgette. Which meant his desire to extend their management agreement was simply a means to safeguard his fiscal position.

Ellie covered her eyes with her hands. In the morning, she'd sign Max's agreement, as is. That would be her apology. *Mea culpa.* Then she'd have her attorney work up a stock transfer in Max's favor. That would be her wedding present.

Max deserved to own the company one hundred percent. That had never been an issue. All she'd ever wanted from Stefan's estate was what she'd come into the marriage with: her inheritance from her grandparents and her maiden name. Those would allow her to start over, to revive her once-thriving design business. Unfortunately, she hadn't realized her and Stefan's financial affairs had become so entwined and complicated. Hell, she hadn't realized a lot of things about her marriage.

Unable to sleep, Ellie sat up. The house felt warm. Her arms were damp with perspiration. Thunder rolled again, louder and more ominous. In its wake the house seemed inordinately quiet. A glance at the digital clock confirmed that the power was out.

"Great," she mumbled. What else could go wrong tonight?

Kicking free of the tangled sheets, she piled out of bed. She snatched her robe off the chair and tugged it on over the short nightgown and headed toward the door. As long as she was up, she might as well—

A sound caught her attention. *Glass breaking. Downstairs.*

Instinctively, she grabbed the cordless phone from the nightstand. But without power there was no dial tone. And her cell phone was plugged into the charger downstairs.

Her thoughts flew to the creepy e-mails she'd received over the last few weeks. At first she'd dismissed them, convinced they were pranks orchestrated by an overzealous member of the paparazzi. Then she received a string of photographs of herself shopping, dining, leaving her apartment in Manhattan. The police had labeled the man a cyber-stalker. At the time, the term sounded surreal. Distant.

Right now, though, his latest message came to mind: *I want to watch you dream.*

"Stop it!" she hissed. If she gave in and let him scare her, he'd win. Besides, the cyber-creep had no way of knowing where she was. She'd left New York this afternoon for Boston, and had already fled there.

The house remained quiet, which encouraged her. *Instead of jumping to dire conclusions, think.* A storm front was moving in, remember? The wind could have blown something into the house. The fact the alarm didn't go off was the clincher, though. The system had a battery backup.

"See? Everything's fine." She'd go downstairs, check things out, and maybe grab her laptop. Looping the robe's ties, she went back to the door.

Just as her hand closed around the knob, another sound echoed. Closer, out in the hallway. *There.* This time the sound repeated, distinct and unmistakably identifiable. The creak of the staircase.

Someone was in the house. And headed upstairs.

Panic and terror collided in her mind, producing one thought: Get out! Screw clothes; screw shoes; just go! She crossed the room to the window and raised it.

The old, Sixties-style beach house had a narrow wooden deck that encircled most of the entire second floor. She'd climb down and run to a neighbor's to call for help. She paused long enough to close the window. If someone came into her bedroom, she didn't want to leave an obvious sign.

A three-quarter moon floated free of the clouds, bathing everything in an eerie blue-gray light that seemed to make her white robe glow in the dark. She shifted into the shadows beneath the overhang. A gust of wind blasted sand and grit against her bare legs as she scrambled to the far side of the house and the stairs. She plunged down them. More thunder echoed. Simultaneously, the rain started, the drops fat and heavy.

As her foot touched the ground, she saw movement in her peripheral vision. Before she could react, a hand clamped across her mouth. At the same time, a strong arm snaked around her, beneath her breasts, snapping her back against a solid male frame.

Instantly hysterical, she kicked, struggled, but her attacker had the advantage in size and strength. Fear fouled the air in her lungs as she realized there were two of them. Someone inside and another outside. The thought of what they had in mind made her feel nauseous. Rape. Murder. She had to fight, get away—

"Ellie, it's me."

The voice—the same husky whisper from her dreams—brought relieved tears to her eyes. *Max*. Her body sagged against his. What was he doing here?

"I need you to remain silent," he breathed against her ear. "We're not alone." His grip tightened reassuringly now. "Nod if you understand and I'll let you go."

She nodded. Once he released her, she faced him. He had tugged her back into a corner. As always, she felt affected by his mere presence. The man dominated space, changed the dynamics of gravity. At six-three, he towered over her. His long, dark hair, normally tied back, was loose. Wet from the rain, it was plastered to the side of his face. In the shadowy moonlight, the gleaming scar above his eye gave him a sinister look, like a dark, avenging angel. *Il Diavolo*.

"Are you okay?" he whispered. "Did he hurt you?"

"No."

"Is he still inside?"

She nodded and pointed. "Upstairs."

A volley of thunder and lightning had Max glancing at the sky. He pressed a set of car keys into her palm. "Outside the gate is a black SUV. Lock yourself in. My security people are en route."

She grabbed his forearm. "Where are you going?"

At first she didn't think he'd answer, then he cupped her chin. "I don't want whoever's inside to get away."

"But what if he's armed? Or there's more than one person?"

"I'll handle it." Dropping his arm, he stepped back. "Now, go. This storm's going to get a lot worse."

As if he'd commanded it, the rain intensified. Ellie took a few steps away, then turned back. She had wanted to remind Max to be careful, but he had already disappeared. Clenching the keys in her fist, she started running toward the driveway, her head bowed to keep the rain out of her eyes.

Just as she reached the gate she heard someone shout her name. She slowed, spun around. A tall figure—a man—burst out of the dark and ran straight toward her. Too late, she realized it wasn't Max.

Terrified, she took off. The man cut across the yard and leaped out in front of her. She skidded to a stop. Even in the gloom she could make out that a black ski mask covered his face. She met his eerie gaze and in that brief moment, his teeth flashed white, his lips curving in a macabre smile.

"Not so fast, Ella-baby." He lunged forward, his fingers brushing her shoulder.

She staggered backwards, unable to look away. *Ella-baby* was the nickname her cyber-stalker used.

He made another swipe for her arm. She feinted left, then immediately darted in the opposite direction, focused on getting back to the house. Rain sliced downward, stinging her skin. Barely able to see, she tore diagonally through the flower garden. She shoved a tiered stone birdbath sideways, hoping to slow him. She heard the man swear as he tripped.

She pushed ahead, increasing her lead. Where was Max? Was he still inside? Had he been injured? Her feet slipped in the mud. She flailed her arms and recovered her balance, but the momentary delay allowed her attacker to close in. This time he grabbed the back of her robe.

"Gotcha!" he snarled.

"No!" Frantic, Ellie yanked the tie at her waist. The robe slipped off her shoulders. Free, she sprinted toward the garage. There was no way she could outrun this man. She needed to hide.

Max burst from around the side of the house, nearly colliding with her. "Ellie! I'm here."

Relief had her knees buckling. She glanced over her shoulder, unable to spot her assailant. "He's out there!"

"I'll handle it. Go!" Max gave her a slight shove and disappeared.

Pushing forward, Ellie rounded the side of the garage. A sharp pain shot up her left leg as something sliced into her foot. Biting back a scream, she collapsed against the house, breathing hard. She tried to put weight on her heel, but couldn't. Whatever she'd stepped on was still there.

Jagged prongs of lightning slashed down from the sky, giving her a momentary snapshot of the scene. Her attacker was running down the long expanse of driveway with Max in pursuit. Then darkness swallowed them.

Her heart slammed in her chest. If something happened to Max—She looked around. Overhead was a small garage window. If she could get inside, maybe she could find something to use as a weapon.

She moved behind the bushes to get closer, but still couldn't reach the window. Rainwater poured off the roof and onto her back, shockingly cold. Frustrated, she moved away. Then she heard Max shout her name. She turned back toward the drive.

"Over here," she called, realizing he couldn't see or hear her.

Waving her arms, she took a step and cried out. Even the lightest pressure on her injured foot sent pain up her leg.

Max was beside her in a moment. His hand closed around her upper arm, supporting her. "You're hurt!"

"I don't think it's serious." She balanced on one foot. "A cut. Did you catch him?"

"No. The bastard made it to his car and got away."

Ellie shivered. That meant the man was still out there. Could try again. She hugged her arms in front of her.

"I got a partial plate number," Max went on. He unbuttoned his wet shirt as he talked, then stripped it off.

She watched, distracted by his bare chest. Her mouth opened, shut. She realized he still talked, that he held out his shirt to her. She tried to cover with a joke. "That will hardly keep me dry."

"I was more concerned with keeping you covered." He tipped his head back toward the gate. "I told you, I've got security people out there."

Ellie glanced down and for the second time that night, she felt utterly mortified. Her soaked gown had turned completely transparent. In the dim light her pale skin seemed luminescent. Cold and wet, her nipples jutted out obscenely.

She raised her arms to cover herself. Max moved closer and settled his shirt over her shoulders. Before she could speak, he swept her up into his arms, and cradled her against his chest. In spite of the rain and wind he radiated heat. She shivered, miserable and ashamed.

"Let's get inside and get you dry," he said. "My men will contact the police."

Ellie shook her head. "You've done enough."

"Enough? I haven't even started."

She bristled at his irritated tone. "I can handle this, Max."

"Like you handled Bridgette at the penthouse? I don't think so."

3

The storm unleashed its fury with a triple explosion of lightning. Max crushed Ellie against his bare chest, doing everything possible to shield her as the gale-force winds turned even the tiniest bits of debris into projectiles.

His first instinct had been to take her away from here—but right now they needed shelter from the weather. He also wanted to check her foot.

He crossed the deck and used the same door the perpetrator had broken into. Shards of glass smashed beneath his shoes as he shouldered his way through the open French door. Ellie gasped, as if just realizing that this was how the man had entered.

The near-constant lightning illuminated parts of the interior of the house. Moving slowly, Max negotiated around the living room furniture and headed for the kitchen. While he hadn't been in the house in ages, he doubted he'd ever forget the floor plan.

Ellie squirmed in his arms. "You can put me down now."

"No."

"Please, Max—"

He tightened his grip. Doing so cut off her argument and discouraged further conversation. And right now, the less he said, the better.

The thought of what could have happened eroded what was left of Max's fuse—not that it had been long to begin with. He'd driven here in a foul mood, rehashing the scene with Bridgette, remembering Ellie's note. As soon as he arrived, he'd noticed the parked car across the street, half hidden beneath trees. Something about it had pinged his radar.

He had decided to look around and spotted Ellie climbing out the window. It was a no-brainer that something had spooked her, most likely a break-in. He'd seen a flashlight beam move in the house, but the man slipped out and went after Ellie.

Damn it! What if Max hadn't gotten here when he did? What would have happened to her? His thoughts had zeroed in on the reports of a stalker. Was it the same guy? His desire to beat the crap out of the bastard spiked.

In the kitchen, Max set Ellie on the counter beside the sink. The storm's ferocity continued to swell. Thunder reverberated, a lethal warning of more to come. Rain hammered the glass, sounding more like metal pellets than water.

He shoved the curtains away from the large window in an attempt to let more of the strobe-like lightning fill the dark kitchen. It didn't help.

"Flashlight?" he snapped.

"Uh . . . there's a jar candle in the cabinet to your left."

But the candle wasn't there. He shook his head. Swearing under his breath, Max started opening and slamming drawers until he found it. Then the ancient disposable lighter next to it didn't want to work. It took a few tries, but finally the candle's wick ignited. He set it next to the sink. The glow, while soft, was at least steadier than the lightning.

Moving back to Ellie, he grasped her left foot and angled it toward the candlelight. A thick, triangular-shaped piece of glass was still wedged into her heel.

"How bad does it look?" she asked.

Instead of answering, Max twisted the cold water faucet on full blast. The anger that he'd felt earlier over not catching her assailant flooded through his veins again. Because of that fucking creep, she was hurt. He wanted to—

"Please talk to me, Max." Ellie touched his arm, drawing his attention. "Say *something*."

"This will hurt." He yanked the glass out, then held her foot under the faucet.

He felt her fingers dig into his forearms. He heard her gasp as she sucked in air and just as quickly cut off a cry. He looked up, but she had dropped her head. Pulling away, she reached for one of the hand towels.

Regret swamped him. That he'd hurt her—even under the guise of helping—instantly deflated his temper. Left him feeling like a brute. Before he could apologize, a loud boom resounded. The tree outside took a direct hit. Clusters of lightning seemed to explode inside the kitchen as branches slammed against the window.

Max had already swung Ellie back into his arms. "Let me get you someplace safer." In the living room, he had to pause to let his eyes adjust, then carried her to one of the sofas and set her down. "I'll be right back."

Retracing his steps to the kitchen, he retrieved the

candle and another hand towel. When he returned, he found she had drawn into the corner of the couch.

She had a towel pressed to her foot, but her eyes were shut. She looked exhausted, miserable, and incredibly fragile.

Max felt like a jerk for being insensitive to her anguish. He tried to justify his anger, but couldn't. She had been victimized tonight, not him.

The coffee table had a three-candle centerpiece which Max quickly lit. The additional wicks didn't help that much but still he moved them closer. He knelt on the floor in front of her. "I'm sorry if I hurt you, El." Very gently, he reached for her ankle. "Will you let me?"

Ignoring her resistance, he coaxed her foot up firmly but gently. He peeled back the towel. The wound still bled, though not as bad. With the poor light, it was difficult to assess how bad the cut was. He refolded a different towel into a makeshift bandage, applied compression, and then secured it around her ankle.

"Are you current on tetanus?"

She nodded, still not speaking. Damn it, he hated the silent treatment. Even if he deserved it.

"We'll wait a moment to see if it stops bleeding," Max went on. "Then I'll figure out if it needs stitches."

That got her talking. "I don't think it's that bad." She shifted forward.

"I'll be the judge of that." He reached for her hand, to prevent her from loosening the towel, and found that her fingers were like ice. "Christ, sweetheart, you're freezing."

He looked at her closely, noticing her struggle to hold herself upright. He touched her arm. Her skin felt chilled and she was shaking all over, probably from shock as well as cold. The wet clothes had to go.

He snatched the decorative blanket draped across the back of the couch. Then he sat beside her and pulled her onto his lap. Her lack of protest concerned him.

His shirt still hung on her shoulders, but it had gaped apart, the sheer fabric clinging to full breasts. He saw a hint of delicate-colored areolas. Lower, a shadow of tawny curls suggested she wore no panties, a fact Max had suspected when his hand brushed her bare butt when he'd first picked her up.

"Let's get you dry. Warm." He moderated his voice, cajoling her like he would a child as he stripped his wet shirt from her with quick, efficient moves.

He tossed it to the floor. The wet scrap of gown followed. That seemed to rouse her, but before she could move, Max swirled the blanket around her back. Then he pulled her forward against his chest, holding her in place with one hand while the other tugged the long, wet strands of her hair free of the blanket.

She made a strangled protest at the first press of bare skin to bare skin, but just as quickly she buried her face against his throat, seeking warmth. Her cheeks and nose felt frosty. She shivered violently now.

Max tucked the edges of the blanket in, making soothing noises as he ensured every inch not pressed against his chest was snugly covered. She shifted, huddling closer. Even after being drenched in the rain, he could still smell the soft floral scent of her shampoo. The feel of her pearled nipples digging into his chest made his body react.

Gritting his teeth, Max reminded himself that this wasn't about sex. *Yeah, right.* When it came to Ellie, that's always where his mind went. Even—God help him—when she'd been married to Stefan. Staying away had been Max's only choice.

And being here now, at this house, triggered a lot of old memories, a lot of regrets. He had first met Ellie here seven years ago. They'd made love upstairs. She'd been a virgin, but not for long. His arms tightened possessively around her shoulders, remembering.

At twenty-five, he had thought he'd already seen everything the world could offer, whereas she'd been only nineteen—shy, proper, and bursting with life. She and her college girlfriends had taken over the house while Ellie's grandparents traveled overseas. That summer had been idyllic.

Or had it just been the calm before the storm? Ellie had returned to college. They both made promises. But his father died a few weeks later, forcing Max to move to Italy and assume a role he'd felt ill prepared for. Twelve months later, Ellie's grandparents were tragically killed in a train crash. That's when Stefan had weaseled in and—

Shit. Who was Max trying to kid? No matter how many times he'd replayed the *why* and *how,* the bottom line was the same. Back then he'd been an idiot and let her go.

A particularly loud crash of thunder made her flinch. Max squeezed her tighter. Recriminations about tonight's incident continued to eat at him. As much as he wanted to blame her for not being more cautious, he felt some culpability. If Bridgette hadn't been at the penthouse, Ellie would have stayed. He would have found her note. And they would be discussing—or acting on—the terms of her "deal," not the aftermath of an attack.

How long they sat there, Max didn't know. The storm seemed to end with the same abruptness it had started with. The wind settled outside and suddenly all was quiet.

Ellie stirred, tried to sit up. He countered the movement, purposely tipping her back against him, not ready for the intimacy of the moment to pass.

"Start at the beginning and tell me what happened here tonight," he said.

She cleared her throat. "Something woke me up. The power was out, so I got up. That's when I realized someone was in the house, coming up the stairs. It frightened me so much, I simply bailed out the window."

"Had you set the alarm before going to bed?"

"Of course! But it didn't go off."

Max made a mental note to have the system thoroughly checked. "Look, I know you've had some incidents recently with e-mail."

"How did you know that?"

"We've had some corporate problems. I hired an outside firm to assess risks and vulnerability."

"And I was considered a risk?" She sounded offended.

"They looked at all key personnel and shareholders, Ellie. Routine stuff, including police reports and public records. I know about the stalker. Do you think these incidents are connected?"

For a moment he didn't think she'd respond. Then she nodded. "I recognized something he said tonight, something he'd written in one of his messages."

"What kind of messages does he send?"

"The cyber equivalent of heavy breathing—I'm-thinking-of-you-naked, that type of stuff."

I'll throttle him, Max thought. "When did this start?"

"Three weeks ago." She rubbed her head.

About the same time the tabloids started running stories about her shares, he calculated. "Why did you wait so long to go to the police?"

"I pretty much blew it off until—" Her voice trailed off.

"Until what? You might as well tell me everything."

"He sent a photograph of me, at a coffee shop. I'd been there less than an hour before. His last message said he wanted to watch me sleep." Her shoulders dipped. "He obviously knows I live in New York, but I thought I'd be safe here."

"Who knew you planned to come to Rockport?"

"No one. It was a last-minute decision and it was late when I left the penthouse." She met his gaze now. "So how did you know where I went?"

"The limo service." And it had been surprisingly easy to procure that information. Who else had gotten it?

"But how did you know I needed help?"

"I didn't. To put it bluntly, I came because I was pissed you left Boston." He could feel tension gather in her, but refused to drop the subject. Better they get it all out in the open. "I wasn't happy to find Bridgette at the penthouse tonight. I didn't invite her."

She held up a hand. "I shouldn't have—"

"I found your note, El."

Silence. Pulling the blanket completely around her, she broke skin contact and tried to squirm sideways off his lap. Max stubbornly held her in place.

"Well, this is awkward," she said finally. "My behavior at the penthouse was totally inappropriate, Max. I didn't realize you and Bridgette were engaged."

"Jesus Christ! We're not. We're not even dating, if it matters. Unfortunately, Bridgette's been talking with a reporter. You obviously know what has been printed. You quoted it."

ONE NIGHT. NO COMMITMENT, NO STRINGS, JUST SEX. He hadn't liked having his infamous motto thrown in his face, especially by Ellie. So he'd concen-

trated on the first two words. *One night*. When he and
Ellie had been lovers, their time together had been too
short. Hell, they'd probably only had sex a half-dozen
times that summer. Privacy had conspired against
them, then fate. One night wouldn't begin to make up
for all the years of regret.

He caught her chin, forcing her to look at him. Even
in the diffused light, her expression was easy to read.
The entire topic distressed her, the incident with Bridgette too recent.

He pushed ahead, refusing to let her withdraw. "The
bottom line is this: I accept your proposal with one
caveat. I want a week. Seven days, not one. Deal?"

4

The man looked over the photographs he'd spread across the motel bed. He picked up his favorite, taken a mere eighteen hours ago. *Ella-baby.* He had trailed her from Manhattan to LaGuardia. And while waiting to take the same flight, he'd managed to digitally capture a few unguarded moments.

That's when he'd nailed her allure, her essence. Where others saw blond hair, flashing green eyes, and a fab bod, *he* saw her spirit. Her inner magic. Chicks like her went straight to heaven when they died. It's how angels were made.

Devils were a different story. His hands fisted. He'd been furious when the other man had shown up. And more than a little scared. Holy fuck, DeLuca had been livid.

In the end, however, he had prevailed. He'd gotten away. Lived to fight another day. No harm, no foul . . . yet. But after he finished this job, he'd figure out a way to get back at DeLuca.

He glanced at the clock. If things had gone as planned, he'd still be there with her. *As planned* meant it would have been over by dawn. Now that he'd show-ered, calmed down, he wasn't so sure he wanted it to end that quickly.

He'd touched her tonight, felt her heart beat beneath his gloved hand. Her reaction, her fear, had been better than he'd imagined. And he'd get to do it all again. *Sweet*.

Yeah, the police would be brought in, but he wasn't worried. They hadn't caught him the last three times. He was good at what he did, getting rid of nuisance ex-wives and mistresses. Worth every cent of his fee, too. Though he might have considered doing Ellie for free. His previous marks had all been older, miserable women. He hadn't wanted to do to them the things he planned to do to Ellie.

Picking up the prepaid cell phone he'd purchased the day before, he dialed a number.

The person answered on the first ring. "Yes?"

"You screwed up. My fee just doubled."

"Don't pull that crap on me."

"You were supposed to handle DeLuca."

"There were problems. Tell me what happened."

He summarized the evening's events. "DeLuca ended up looking like a hero."

"Where's Ellie now?"

"With him."

"Did either of them see you? Or anything that can be tied to you?"

"No." He'd left his kit behind, but the items in it were common, untraceable. Wal-Mart probably sold thousands of rolls of duct tape a day.

"Then lay low until I figure something out. She'll prob-ably return to New York, but security will be tightened."

"We both know that's not a problem. Just get DeLuca out of the picture and I'll handle the rest."

5

"Deal?" Ellie wasn't certain she'd heard him correctly. He wanted a week? "Max, I—"

The broken door swung open just then, its squeaking hinge a warning. A uniformed officer pushed into the room, flashlight in one hand, a gun in the other. "Police! Put your hands where I can see them."

Ellie closed her eyes against the blinding light. Her hands were already clutched in front of her, holding onto the blanket for dear life. If that didn't qualify as visible, well . . . he could shoot her. She'd been caught naked enough times tonight.

"This is the owner of the house, Ellie DeLuca." Max had raised his hands, while leaning slightly closer to her.

Another officer and a blond man wearing a suit came in. The civilian pointed to Max. "That's my boss, Max DeLuca."

The first officer nodded, holstered his weapon. "Sorry, ma'am. Are you folks okay?"

"Yes." Ellie hugged the blanket and moved to get up. "But if you'll excuse me, I'm going to get dressed."

Max shifted her back into his arms and stood. "I'll carry you up."

She choked back a protest. No one listened to naked people anyway. She'd have more sway fully dressed.

"Crime scene won't like it," the officer said.

"We probably obliterated the crime scene coming back in here," Max pointed out. "But with the storm, we had no choice."

The officer shrugged. "Try not to touch anything the intruder might have touched."

Ellie suddenly recalled something else about her assailant. "You won't find fingerprints. He wore gloves. Thin, latex ones. Like a doctor or dentist uses."

The officer pulled out a small notebook. "We'll need a full description."

"Give us five minutes and a flashlight," Max said.

The blond man handed his light to Ellie. Max nodded and turned away. "That's Gerard Warhaven, DSI's new chief of security, by the way. I'll introduce you properly when we come back down."

Upstairs, he went straight to Ellie's old room and set her on the bed. Her skin prickled as she swept the beam around the dark room. Had that creep come in here?

Max stepped away.

"Don't leave!" She swung the light toward him.

He was at her side in an instant. His hands closed over hers, squeezing them. "I'm not going anywhere, El. Just tell me what you need."

"My clothes are in my suitcase. By the dresser. And my shoes—"

"Stay put." He swung her suitcase onto the bed. "Don't worry about shoes right now."

After she pulled out underwear, jeans, and a tee, he turned away, giving her privacy. The lump in her throat swelled as she dressed. "All clear," she said a few moments later.

"We need to go back down." Max moved in, but instead of picking her up he cupped her chin. "I know this isn't easy. I'll get us out of here as fast as I can."

Us. Uncertainty—about everything—threatened to overwhelm her. "Did I even remember to thank you?"

He scooped her off the bed. "Not yet. But then, I probably forgot to thank you, too."

She had looped her arms around his neck, grateful he carried the flashlight this time. "For what? Dragging you out in the middle of a stormy night?"

"I'm talking about our deal, El. Thank you for saying yes."

He thought she'd agreed? "A week?"

They were at the top of the staircase now. "We'll talk about it later." Max started down the steps. "Okay?"

Ellie took a deep breath. If she wanted to protest, to preserve her right to renegotiate, now was the time to speak up. *Who was she kidding?* A week with Max? "Deal."

As soon as he set her on the couch, the power came back on. She blinked at the sudden brightness, tried to take in the people milling around.

Gerard Warhaven came over. Max introduced them. "I'd like Gerard to examine your foot, Ellie."

"I was a field medic in the Army," Gerard explained over her halfhearted protests. He cleaned the wound, then used butterfly sutures to close it before he bandaged it. "I'll see if I can find a couple ibuprofen to ease the pain while you talk to the cops."

It didn't take long for Ellie to give her statement. It was sobering to realize the actual incident had occurred in a matter of minutes. The memory, the fear, would stay with her forever. Uncertainty gnawed at her. What would she have done if Max hadn't shown up tonight? Could she have escaped?

She'd like to think so, but listening to the officer's recap of the events had been disturbing. The power to the house had been cut off by throwing the main switch.

"Overriding the burglar alarm was fairly easy because it's an older system," the officer said. "The guy probably bought the tools to do it over the Internet. You should have the system replaced."

She nodded. "Trust me, I'll have everything replaced after this."

"Based on what you've told us, I'd surmise that someone followed you here from New York," the officer went on. "When you get home, you should call the detectives there. Let them know about this."

Max came up then, nodding at the officer before sitting beside her. "How's the foot?"

"Throbbing." Like her head. "Could be worse, though."

"Look, why don't you go back to Boston with Gerard. When the police are finished, I'll secure the house and meet you there."

She started to object, then stopped and looked around. Staying here was no longer an option. And if she were going back to the penthouse, she'd prefer to get there ahead of Max, to have a little time to gather her wits.

"I'll see you there, then."

As soon as she reached the penthouse, Ellie curled up into a ball on the sofa, physically and emotionally exhausted. *I'll just close my eyes and wait for Max,* she told herself.

When she woke, sunlight streamed in through the terrace doors. As she lowered her foot to the floor, a dull ache climbed her leg. A check of the time confirmed it was after ten.

Disappointment rolled over her as she sensed that Max hadn't returned. Had something else gone wrong? Or was he having second thoughts about their deal?

Was she?

No. Not exactly.

Her reasons for wishing Max was present were complex. Tangled. Last night he'd made her feel protected, which she wasn't sure she liked. She lived alone by choice and the experience at the beach house made her realize how much she took her sense of personal freedom and safety for granted. Damn it, she wasn't going to let some creep rob her of that, either!

Then there was the *other* issue. Max wanted a week. At first she'd felt flattered to think one day wasn't enough. But seven were? She frowned.

An indistinct beeping startled her from her reverie. Her cell phone. Where was it? She pushed off the sofa, slowed by her injured foot. By the time she found her phone, she had missed the call.

The screen blinked, indicating she had a voice message.

She checked the caller ID first. It had been Max. She listened to his message. He sounded tired.

"I'm back in New York. An urgent business matter came up and I went straight to the airport. Gerard's got orders not to let you out of his sight. If you've got a problem with that, tell me. Not him. I'll call later." She started to disconnect, but then she heard Max's voice continue. "I'm really looking forward to our week together, El."

Those last words melted the annoyance that had crept in over his high-handedness. She was disappointed he hadn't indicated how long he'd be in New York. Last night he'd promised they would discuss the details of their deal later. She'd assumed he meant this morning, but in the harsh light of day, reality encroached.

They were both business people. There were schedules to be considered. Arrangements to be made. Calendars to be coordinated. More so on Max's end. He ran one of the largest multinational shipping companies in the world. In an interview he'd joked that his office was his private jet. Which meant he could be in New York for breakfast and Rotterdam for dinner.

Since Ellie was just beginning to resume her career, her schedule was wide open. Her successful career as a designer had imploded following the lawsuits that erupted after Stefan's death. No one wanted to risk scandal by association, so she was shunned by most. The one exception was a friend, Peter Fourakis. Peter had even asked her to prepare a proposal for a hotel chain, but that wasn't due for a month.

And even though her schedule wasn't busy, it could be weeks before her agreement with Max was sealed. Viewed like that, their deal now seemed, well, perfunctory. Not exactly what she had in mind.

After showering and changing, Ellie made coffee. Gerard joined her in the kitchen and offered to rebandage her foot. She let him.

"It looks better," he said. "Not as bad as I'd first thought."

"That's good news."

"By the way, Mr. DeLuca's been trying to reach you. He sent an e-mail regarding your itinerary. Have you had a chance to review it?"

Ellie set her cup aside, sloshing coffee as she nearly missed the tabletop. Max had sent an itinerary already? "No, I haven't seen it, but I'll check my laptop now."

Ten minutes later, she logged into her e-mail account. Forty-seven new messages. She paged down, holding her breath, half expecting another threat. Last night she'd given Max her e-mail password so the police could monitor it for new messages. Knowing Big Brother watched didn't make her feel better.

Ignoring the obvious SPAM, she scrolled down looking for Max's message. When she found it, she grew anxious waiting for it to open as her antivirus software twiddled its cyber-thumbs. What if his schedule was virtually impossible? How far out would he propose that they postpone their week together? Weeks? Months?

Max's message, while short, surprised her.

Will meet you at the hangar at three this afternoon.
Pack light. Lots of sunscreen.
Yours,
M

This afternoon? Surely he didn't think their week started today? Slightly panicked, she reread the note.

Pack lightly? *Sunscreen*? Where were they going? Had he not mentioned their destination in an e-mail for security reasons? Her eyes fell on the clock. She had less than five hours.

She hit Reply, intending to list all the reasons she needed more time. Except none of them held water.

She clasped her hands in her lap and stared at her nails. To do as Max bid was wildly impulsive. God, when was the last time she'd done anything impulsive?

Duh. Try yesterday. Coming here, leaving that note. It didn't get much more impulsive than that.

Still, she felt nervous over making love with Max for the first time. She frowned at her word choice. Technically, this would be their seventh time. In seven years.

If it wasn't so pathetic, all the sevens would sound quasi-mystical. The truth was anything but. Seven years ago she'd been an overprotected nineteen-year-old eager to lose her virginity. Losing her heart hadn't been a concern.

Until she met Max DeLuca. Even then, he'd had a reputation. *He comes from a long line of womanizers,* her grandfather had warned. *Stay clear.*

At first, she'd heeded that advice and kept her distance. Max had been larger than life. Young, rich, and privileged, not to mention worldly and drop-dead gorgeous. From the first moment they'd met, he'd seemed determined to pursue her. Eventually she'd succumbed. It had been summer break and she and her girlfriends had taken over the beach house. Max and his pals were ensconced next door. Sex was on everyone's mind back then. When Max learned she was a virgin, he'd backed off. But he hadn't given up. "No pressure," he'd promised. "Your first time should be unforgettable."

And that's exactly what it was. A week before she had to return to campus, she'd given in. Looking back, she realized their first time hadn't been glorious. In fact, it had been awkward. Max had been patient and understanding, promising it would get better with practice. However, privacy with a houseful of party animals had been rare. Sex between them was rushed, secretive.

They'd spent their last night together on the beach. And *that* had been unforgettable. That night she'd finally found the rhythm. She had been eager to learn everything, but time transpired against them. Max had promised there would be endless opportunities to explore all things carnal in the future. They promised to keep in touch, promised to get together in the fall.

It never happened. Fate spun both of them in different directions.

She sighed. Was this her chance to turn back time? Were the sevens an omen? Once before, she'd had seven days with Max, but back then, she hadn't known it would end. Now she did.

That meant making every moment count. She picked up the phone and paged Gerard. "I'd like to leave early. I have a little shopping to do on the way to the airport."

6

A computer glitch at Logan International had flights backed up. As it turned out, it was after five when Max's private jet finally taxied up to the hangar—without Max.

From Gerard, Ellie learned that their destination—Charleston, South Carolina—was temporary. "From Charleston you'll be taken by boat to San Regale," he had told her. "Mr. DeLuca will meet you there."

A riff of excitement played up her spine. San Regale was a private island off the coast of South Carolina; it had been in the DeLuca family for years. Nicknamed "Sensual Isle" by the tabloids, San Regale had its own rumor factory. Several stories purported that exotic orgies were hosted regularly there, with yachts coming and going in the dark of night to preserve the anonymity of the rich and famous.

The island had a public mystique as well since it was the only DeLuca holding that had never been extensively photographed. And while the DeLucas had homes and villas tucked all over the world, mostly for philandering, Stefan had always made it clear that San Regale was off limits.

Ellie's imagination worked overtime during the flight. Was she ready for this? Her original proposal had been for one night, which she felt confident enough to handle. But seven nights alone on an island with Max? Was she insane?

In Charleston there was another delay, this one weather-related. Ultimately, she was ferried to the island by a helicopter. Gerard bid her farewell at the airport. "Mr. DeLuca will be waiting at the island."

They touched down on a wide stretch of beach just as dusk was setting. Her breath caught at the sight of Max. He was dressed casually in worn jeans, a polo shirt, and shabby deck shoes. His dark hair was loose and a five o'clock shadow darkened his jaw. In short, he looked . . . dangerous.

He helped her disembark, pulling her close and bringing her hand to his mouth. He kissed her fingertips, then held her hand, his thumb stroking lightly over her knuckles. She felt electricity zing clear down to her toes.

"How are you?"

"I'm fine," she lied. *Actually, I'm about to jump out of my skin, thanks.*

"I apologize for not meeting you earlier. My flight was already under way by the time I learned you'd been held up."

In a flurry of windblown sand, the helicopter took off, leaving them alone. Max had already loaded her luggage onto a golf cart. Before she could protest, he picked her up and set her on the seat.

"Thank you." Sue her if it was passé, but she liked it when Max held her.

"My pleasure. Didn't Gerard say you should take it easy with the foot for a day or two?"

"It's been a day."

"Humor me."

The vehicle's oversized, knobby tires had no problem in the sand as they zipped along the south side of the island. In the fading light, it was hard to see much. The number of trees surprised her. From what she could tell, the dense pines seemed to shelter much of the grounds.

"The main house is just ahead," Max said. "Straight up from the dock."

The dock had a large powerboat berthed on one side, a sailboat on the other.

"How many houses are on the island?"

"Four. The big one and three smaller ones. Two of those are guest quarters, on the far side. They're empty. We have the place completely to ourselves except for Tyler, our groundskeeper, and his wife, Maria. They live in the third home. Maria keeps house and cooks. You'll rarely see them, though. Our family has employed them for years—I trust them one hundred percent." Max looked at her. "I want you to know you're safe here."

His words and sincerity touched her. *Just don't read anything into it*, she reminded herself.

The main house was a two-story Cape Cod with porches and decks adjoining the ground floor. At Max's insistence, Ellie explored the downstairs while he took care of her luggage. What she saw shocked her. She had expected a tasteless, brothel-type macho-pit, complete with nude sculptures and mirrored walls. Instead the house was, well . . . cozy.

Ferns and fragrant orchids were everywhere. A set of double doors led into a library. That room, a long rectangle, had French doors and a patio on one side. She took in the professional touches—the showpiece rug, the original watercolors.

The view beyond the doors was spectacular. Open water. A large mahogany desk dominated one end of the room. A briefcase and laptop rested on the desk's polished surface. Max's? Just beyond the desk were more glass doors that led to a swimming pool. The work space layout offered simultaneous views of ocean and pool.

The room's interior wall boasted floor-to-ceiling bookshelves. She scanned the titles, a collection of expensive leather-bound classics. Again, not what she anticipated. The gilt spines of the books were pristine. For show, she thought. What a pity.

She moved toward a sloppy-looking shelf closer to the desk. The books here were worn, well used. Well loved. One had dog-eared sheets of paper stuck inside. She read the titles. These were Max's books. *Yacht Design. Outboard Engine Specifications. Powerboats For Racing.*

She smiled, remembered boating with him during that long-ago summer. While their friends sunbathed and partied, Max had pointed out different vessels, talking about hull shapes as if he were describing a lover's body. He'd talked about designing boats— yachts, really—and had showed her some sketches. He'd teased her about decorating what he'd build. "*We'd make a great team.*"

He'd been so wrong.

Hearing footsteps in the hall, she turned just as Max joined her.

"You found my favorite room," he said. "So what do you think of the place?"

Ellie turned and nodded. "Um . . . It's lovely."

"You sound surprised."

She tried to cover her gaffe. "I've heard stories."

"About the orgies?" He chuckled. "My mom's sister started them."

"Why did she do that?"

"To piss off one of my dad's subsequent wives. San Regale was originally my father's fishing retreat. Until my mother came along. My father said she visited the island once and next thing he knew, she was having a house built here. Each successive wife added on, until eventually Dad simply banned females."

"I bet that went over well, given the orgy rumors."

"Exactly." He moved toward a bar tucked in the corner. "I know you had dinner in Charleston, but I thought we'd have a few hors d'oeuvres later. Wine?"

Before she could respond, Max's cell phone started ringing. He tugged it out and glanced at the display. "Sorry. I need to take this."

She nodded. "Actually, I'd like to shower and change. It's been a long day."

He answered his phone with a quick, "I'll call you right back." Snapping it shut, he escorted Ellie to the foyer. "Your things are in the guest suite at the top of the staircase. It's got a private terrace and bath." Once again, he brought her fingers to his lips, but this time he pressed a kiss to her palm, then folded her fingers over it. "Let's meet on the patio in an hour."

When Ellie reached her suite, she shut the door and leaned back against it. They weren't sharing a room. Was she relieved or disappointed?

Her eyes fell on the bed, the physical equivalent of the million-dollar question. *Where would they do it?*

His room? Hers? This bed was queen-sized. Adequate. Until she recalled Max's suite in the penthouse; it had an oversized king. Something suited for sexual Olympics. Pros. Not amateurs.

For the umpteenth time, she wished she were more experienced. More sexually sophisticated. She had this nagging suspicion that *seen one, seen 'em all*, was based on a larger segment of the population.

The dismal truth was, she'd acquired very little hands-on skill during her marriage. Stefan had expressed disappointment the first night of their honeymoon and left her in tears while he went searching for a little more "action." He'd blamed her for not being exciting enough to interest him. Then he'd browbeaten her for kissing Max before their wedding ceremony. Max had been drunk and stumbled into her room while looking for Stefan. He'd taken one look at her and swept her up in his arms. If Stefan hadn't walked in . . .

Where would that kiss have gone?

Nowhere. When Max sobered up, he'd never mentioned it. Probably forgotten it. Stefan, however, had never let her forget, and had practically accused her of infidelity. He'd been a fine one to talk!

She pushed those thoughts away. Her marriage had been a mistake. She'd stayed in it way too long, nursing a tattered pride that in the end amounted to nothing. Pride did go before a fall.

Restless, she explored the room. The soft green walls and natural rattan furnishings suited the island motif. More French doors opened onto a small balcony that overlooked the same view as the library below. The adjoining bathroom repeated the rattan theme. Her case with her toiletries sat on the counter.

Ellie caught a glimpse of herself and grimaced. Her

hair looked flat, her clothes travel-wrinkled. Suddenly an hour didn't feel like nearly enough time. She turned on the shower.

As she blow-dried her hair afterwards, she mentally inventoried her luggage and decided what to wear. In her whirlwind trip to Nordstrom's, she'd found a chic, black sundress with off-the-shoulder sleeves and a low-cut bodice. A strapless, pushup bra would guarantee that Max's attention would be on her, not the dress. If she played her cards right, she wouldn't be wearing either very long.

Back in the bedroom, she paused. A wrapped box sat on the dresser, a note propped beside it. A single red rosebud completed the trio. Max must have slipped in while she was in the shower.

His thoughtfulness made her smile. She brought the rose to her face, delighted in its fragrance. Her heart thumped at the flower's meaning. A red rose.

She picked up the note. Max's handwriting was as bold as his words.

Ellie,
   In my dreams, you're not wearing anything more than this.
Max

She eyed the box. It was small. Whatever outfit it held had to be skimpy. Sexy underwear, perhaps? The idea of Max selecting lingerie for her was titillating. And nerve-wracking.

Her palms grew moist. She picked up the box, found it heavier than she'd have guessed. The wrapping paper and ribbon hit the floor in shreds. Inside the package was a flat leather case emblazoned with an exclusive French jeweler's crest.

Her eyes widened as she opened it. Nestled against white satin was a thick, gold-and-emerald necklace. The heavy piece fit like a choker. Matching drop earrings and two bracelets completed the set, which had no doubt cost a small fortune.

Her smile wavered as she reread the note. *In my dreams* . . . The meaning was clear. He'd thrown down the gauntlet. An emerald-studded gauntlet.

She took the case and crossed to the oval mirror standing in the corner. Then she dropped the towel and looked critically at her body, trying to imagine herself in nothing but emeralds.

Holy God! Could she do it?

7

Max cut across the south lawn. He climbed the steps at the side of the house, two at a time, and then strode across the patio, his mind still picking apart his latest problem. One of his major suppliers had suddenly demanded cash on delivery, citing rumors about DSI having cash flow problems.

This wasn't the first time, and Max stepping in to personally handle the matter had enabled them to resolve it discreetly. But it was only a matter of time until it happened again. Rumors like this were insidious, difficult to trace and stop. Max had faced a similar situation after his father died. This particular pattern of industrial sabotage was especially difficult to prove, too. When he found the person responsible—

He stopped short when he saw the table. Maria, bless her, had taken care of everything. Wine, canapés, candles. Roses. He checked his watch, found he had ten minutes, maybe less. Not enough time to shower and shave.

He stroked the stubble on his chin. If he kissed Ellie

he'd have to be careful. And he damn sure planned to kiss her.

He refilled the glass of wine he'd poured earlier, then paced across the lanai to stare out into the darkness. Tree frogs and cicadas chirped, their music carried on the sea breeze. Typically the night sounds relaxed him.

But not tonight. He was wound up, and with each passing second the tension increased. He prowled along the railing, eyes flitting from shadow to shadow.

His thoughts were chaotic, which was almost humorous, considering Max prided himself on clear thinking. His strategic skills had been honed to a reliable perfection that served him well. In business, he was coldly rational.

The problem was . . . Ellie wasn't business. Not anymore. That line had been crossed and there would be no going back. In the past, he'd managed to keep his distance with Ellie by compartmentalizing, thinking of her in terms of corporate structure.

He'd even told himself the trip to Boston was about maintaining control of her stock shares. A business proposition. Until he'd found her note at the penthouse. ONE NIGHT. Then after the incident at the beach house, he'd told himself it was about her safety. Until he'd held her naked. Then every memory, every fantasy, every regret he'd buried over the years came home to roost.

From the first moment Max had met Ellie, he'd known she was special. Unfortunately, he'd been too dumb to act on it. Given his parents' track record to the altar—they'd had eleven marriages between them at the time—Max hadn't been in any hurry to settle down. His father's demands that he produce an heir— the firstborn son of the firstborn son—fell on deaf ears.

The biggest mistake Max had ever made was telling Stefan how he felt about Ellie. *"If I didn't know better, I'd think love at first sight was true*," Max had admitted.

Sadly, the two men rarely got along. Stefan had later taken perverse pleasure in telling Max that he'd only married Ellie to thwart Max. *"I'm grateful you never told Ellie how you felt about her*," Stefan had laughingly thrown in Max's face. *"You made it easy for me."*

But Max had come close to telling Ellie once, on her wedding day. Another big mistake. The bad blood between the half-brothers had grown worse after that. In fact, the last words they'd exchanged had been heated.

Max had confronted Stefan on his infidelity, had threatened to warn Ellie. The two men were on their way to a board meeting in the Alps. Stefan had been driving . . . and looked away from the road. He had died instantly when the car plummeted off the road. Max had escaped with only cuts and bruises. And enough guilt to keep him away from Ellie.

Until the court battles erupted over Stefan's estate, that is. Max was executor and everything, rightfully, had been left to Ellie, with Max as temporary overseer. But then there had been claims of illegitimate children, which DNA proved false, followed by palimony suits filed by four mistresses. He had previewed their depositions, knew each promised a scandalous trial.

That's when Max pulled the plug. It had taken a gargantuan effort to make it go away, but he did it. Unfortunately, he hadn't acted soon enough to save Ellie's public reputation. The production company that had been publicly wooing Ellie with a lucrative television and designer magazine offer abruptly backed out.

After that it seemed all her clients bailed as well.

She'd quietly closed her offices and started doing work privately under her maiden name.

He pushed the memories away. At some point he and Ellie needed to discuss their past. Their future depended on it. For now, though, he simply wanted to let the week unfold. She'd made the all-important first move. He'd countered. Next move was hers; his balls were in her court . . .

He took a sip of wine, wondered how Ellie had reacted to his gift. He probably shouldn't have mentioned the part about her wearing only the emeralds. After all she'd been through at the beach house yesterday, the last thing he wanted was for her to feel pressured.

In another part of the house, a clock chimed. He counted seconds, waiting, then turned and strode back into the library. He'd find her and apologize—

He found her standing just inside the door.

Wearing the emeralds with a short, white sundress that barely skimmed the tops of her thighs. Her hair was tousled and curled, pinned up to fall down her back, affording him an unimpeded view of her lush curves. The halter top plunged low, nearly to her navel. And no bra . . .

His reaction was sudden. His cock turned to marble and strained against his trousers as he moved toward her.

Her eyes lowered, widening as she took in the bulge at his crotch. She raised her gaze, her cheeks pink.

"Take it as a compliment, Ellie. You look beautiful."

"Thank you. And thank you for these." She touched the emeralds. Then her eyes darted down again. "After reading your note, I worried I'd be overdressed."

We'll fix that shortly. "You're perfect."

Understatement. The dress was clingy in all the right places. Her breasts were magnificent—two large, firm globes. Centered high on each was a small, pink nipple. Tightly drawn and pointed, they strained against the shimmery fabric. He remembered the taste of them, the way Ellie had responded the first time he'd suckled them.

Part of him wanted to pick her up and rush over to the plush sofa on the far side of the room, losing the dress along the way.

Instead, he took her arm and escorted her outside, to the patio. "Let me get you a drink."

Ellie scarcely heard his words. She was still processing the evidence of his erection. Right before her eyes he'd grown hard. Witnessing his reaction had been heady. She sat on one of the cushioned benches and shivered.

"Cold?" Max's gaze raked over her once again.

She decided to play it honest. "No. I'm . . . nervous."

"Don't be." He filled a wineglass and handed it to her before picking up his own. "A toast. To our week ahead."

"Our week." She sipped her wine, grateful to have something to do with her hands.

"The emeralds match your eyes." He sat next to her and stretched an arm along the back of the seat.

"The jewelry is exquisite, Max." She touched the necklace. "You shouldn't have."

"A beautiful woman deserves beautiful baubles."

"That makes it sound like you think I can be bought with shiny rocks."

"Hardly." He moved closer, touching one of her earrings. His fingertips skimmed down her shoulder to her arm.

Butterflies danced in her stomach.

"I want to hold you, Ellie," he said. "Feel you in my arms again."

The butterflies did aerobics now. On crack cocaine . . . She nodded.

He took her wineglass and set it aside before tugging her onto his lap. His gaze missed nothing. Then he lowered his mouth, catching her lips in a kiss that was both tender and demanding.

Her arms circled his neck. She kissed him back, surrendered without a battle. Max could do anything to her. Everything. She felt his fingers at her nape, working the ties that held her bodice. There was a slight tug and then her top fell forward. She felt the fabric puddle at her waist, the night air on her bare skin. His hands pressed at her sides, shifting her slightly toward him. And when his fingers finally closed over her breast, she moaned in pleasure and approval. Wanting more.

She tugged at his shirt, also wanting equal access.

A knock sounded, distant.

Max broke the kiss, pulling her dress back in place as the knock repeated, louder this time. When Ellie was decent, he called out. "Yes!"

A small woman appeared in the door. Max introduced Maria, then frowned as the woman relayed an urgent message.

Ellie listened. She recognized the name. Tony Breeden was DSI's Chief Financial Officer.

"Tell him I'll call right back," Max said.

When they were alone, Ellie retied her top. "So much for first impressions. I can imagine what she thinks."

"Maria is extremely discreet."

"Oh, that makes me feel better. Is she used to finding half-naked women in your arms?"

Max chuckled. "Actually, you're the first woman I've ever brought here."

She gave him a *yeah, right* look.

"I'm serious. San Regale is my personal retreat. I come here to escape," Max continued. "I'm guilty of bringing work with me, but that's it. That's one of the reasons I picked this place for our week together. We can really be alone here, Ellie."

"Without the phones?"

"We'll see. There are a few loose ends I must deal with. Like this one tonight. I might be tied up a while."

She nodded, masking her disappointment. "I'll go upstairs, then. It's been a long day."

"I'll take you up." In one smooth movement, he stood, keeping her in his arms. "Talk to me. I can tell you're upset."

She started to say, *it's nothing, I'm fine*, but she was weary of the false pretenses. Instead she looked him straight in the eye. "You promised me a week. Seven days. And today's already gone."

They had reached her room now. Max slid her down the front of his body, making sure she felt his erection.

"Our week doesn't start until tomorrow, El. Trust me, I wouldn't dream of cheating either of us out of one single day."

8

Exhausted from the lack of rest the night before, when Ellie did fall asleep, she went too far under. Nightmares pulled at her, the sinister images jumbled, frantic.

Disembodied voices screamed for her to get out of Max's bed. To get out of his life. A masked man chased her through rain that had turned to sticky black tar, making it impossible to get away. She was stuck, sinking. She heard macabre laughter. *You're mine now, Ella-baby.*

Then the man grabbed her. She struggled against the hands that tightened on her shoulders.

"Ellie! Wake up!"

A light came on, harsh and sudden. She jerked upright, blinking at the too-bright light. Her heart pounded hard, making breathing difficult. The room felt warm, her gown clingy from perspiration.

Her eyes darted around, trying to take in everything—the rattan room, the wrecked covers, Max sitting beside her. She knew where she was, knew she'd been dreaming. Neither fact helped her shake the insidious sense of fright.

"Easy, sweetheart." Max kept his voice low as he shifted closer and gently pulled her, sheets and all, into his arms.

She practically crawled up his chest. "Oh, Max!"

"It's okay. I've got you." His arms tightened, making her feel safe, secure. He wasn't wearing a shirt, his skin warm. He rocked her, stroking her hair as he made little *shhhh* noises, over and over.

Slowly her pulse evened out. She forced her fingers to relax, hadn't realized they were digging into his arm.

"Want to talk about it?" he asked.

She took a deep breath, trying to dispel the images rattling around inside her head. "No. I don't even want to think about it."

"Then don't. It must have been bad, though. I had a hard time waking you."

She suppressed a shudder, remembering her assailant's laugh. "I haven't had a nightmare like that since I was small and worried the big, bad wolf lived in my closet."

"And here I'd hoped your fantasies would have been of me."

She closed her eyes. She'd started out with those fantasies. Pretty hot ones. But those dreams had nothing on the comforting reality of being held in his arms. She rubbed her cheek against Max's chest, savoring the feel of firm muscle. "I'm sorry if I woke you."

"I'm not." He brushed a kiss to the top of her head, then lifted her back onto the bed. "Move over."

He didn't have to ask twice. She scooted away, tugging and lifting the sheets to make room for him. Her pulse elevated as Max leaned forward to snap off the bedside lamp. But the room didn't go dark. He'd left the bathroom light on, the door slightly ajar, so a soft glow filtered in.

He stood and turned, giving Ellie a clear view of his profile. In the tangle of dreams and bedclothes, she hadn't realized until just that moment that he was naked from the waist down, too.

It was impossible not to stare. His penis jutted out majestically from a nest of dark hair. It was larger than she remembered, long and thick. Semi-erect, it curved slightly away from his body, mesmerizing her.

The mattress dipped as he climbed in and stretched out on his back. He extended his hand, his voice a low and husky invitation. "Come closer."

Nothing could have kept her away. All her worries vanished in the simple need to be in his arms. She moved in next to him and put her head on his shoulder, pressed her belly against his side. His arm stretched down the length of her, pressing along her spine, urging her pelvis into his hip. Then he shifted one leg slightly, forcing her legs apart. She drew her knee up, eased it over his. The sensation of being tucked in close was soothing and erotic at the same time.

He had entwined her fingers with his, his thumb stroking rhythmically back and forth over her knuckles.

"Better?" he asked.

Trick question, she thought. *Better* would mean moving her hand beneath the sheet, to touch him. *Better* would mean both of them naked.

"Yes," she said.

"Good. Can we lose the gown?"

Ellie felt her cheeks grow warm. Had he read her

mind? "I should refuse since you said our week doesn't start till tomorrow." But even as she spoke, she reached for the hem of her gown and started peeling it up.

Max helped. His fingers grazed her sides as he tugged the material. "It's after midnight, so technically it is tomorrow."

Balling up the gown, he sent it sailing to a corner of the room. Then he pulled her across his chest, stretching her out on top of him. His arms crossed over her back, ensuring there wasn't one iota of her that didn't touch him. The textures, the muscles, the heat of a full frontal hug were shocking. Delicious.

Max was a big man. All over. Hard, too. All over. Fully aroused, his erection teased her bottom. They were shoulder to shoulder, which put her pelvis closer to his navel, and still she felt him. Sensual images filled her mind. She wanted to scoot lower, to grind against his sex.

"You feel good," he said. "It's been a long time."

He had no idea how long. She rolled her hips, felt him *there*.

Max's hand went to her hips, holding her still. "We need to discuss safe sex, El. While I still have adequate blood flow to my brain. I've got condoms in my room."

She didn't want him to leave, didn't want the moment to be shattered by mechanics. "I'm on the pill," she said.

"Birth control: check. But I still want you to feel reassured about . . . other things. I've never had sex without a rubber, Ellie." He flexed his erection up against her and groaned. "And I'd kill to be inside of you without one."

The thought that Max wanted her so intimately inflamed her. Even when they'd made love years before, he had worn a condom. He'd joked about being lectured on the subject since grade school. Back then, she'd been grateful that he'd taken care of the matter. Now she was grateful that she had choices.

"Never?" she repeated.

"Ever."

"So I'd be your first?"

He smiled. "Yes." His mouth captured hers in a brief kiss. His teeth dragged gently on her lip before moving down to her neck. He nibbled softly on her earlobe. "But I'll get one if you prefer. Your call, sweetheart."

Need tightened with the power that his request granted. The idea of experiencing all of him sent waves of excitement spiraling to her lower body. Max pulled away. It took her a second to realize he was waiting for her response. His control amazed her. Wasn't it obvious that she wanted him badly *as is*?

"You'd be my first, too," she said at last.

Immediately he drew her closer. "God, I'd hoped you'd say that."

His mouth slanted over hers in a demanding kiss. She opened fully, inviting him in, her tongue dueling with his as her fingers speared through the silky strands of his hair. He smelled fresh, like he'd bathed in a sparkling ocean.

The quiet compliments and encouragement he murmured against her mouth sent her shyness fleeing. She reveled in the feel of his strong hands sliding down and over her. He smoothed the long length of her hair before lifting it and then gently massaging the muscles of her back.

His fingers traced her spine to her tailbone and bracketed her hips briefly before curling around her buttocks. He squeezed, pressing more of his erection into her abdomen. With each touch, each movement, her desire built.

"Max, please . . ."

"Please what?"

"Make love to me. Right now."

He chuckled. "That's what I thought I was doing."

For a wild moment, Ellie wished the room was pitch black, though her cheeks would likely glow red in the dark. "What I meant was—"

"Faster?" His hands tightened on her buttocks, pressing his shaft more fully against her wet nether lips. He groaned. "The way that feels. Just . . . you . . ."

"Just us."

"Flesh to flesh." Max shifted her off of him and onto the mattress. Instead of moving over her, he pushed up on one elbow and gazed down. "This sounds selfish, but I want to remain outside of you as long as I can. Because once I'm in—" He trailed the back of his hand upward along the inside of her arm. "I won't last."

His hand closed over her right breast. She arched into his palm, eager for his touch. His fingers toyed with her nipple, delicately at first. Then he rolled the erect tip between his thumb and forefinger. Her nipple tightened almost painfully in response.

He bent his head and licked the aching peak, teased it with his tongue. Then he caught the tip, lightly grazing her skin with his teeth, tormenting her. She whimpered at the sensation.

He transferred his attention to her other breast, treating it to those same hot kisses, before pulling her nipple fully into his mouth and sucking. Heat arced on invisible lines within her as Max took his time and drove her wild with his mouth.

She tried to speak, but no words came. Only a

moan, a hiss. His mouth was doing sinfully exquisite things, his touch like fire. It felt marvelous, made her crazy for more.

As if sensing her need, he caught one nubin between his teeth, tugging on the swollen, sensitive tip. She protested when he stopped, then pleaded when he changed sides. She eased her hands down his chest, thrilling to the play of his sculpted muscles. She toyed with his nipples, then explored lower. At his hips, she drew her fingers forward and encased his sleek, pulsing penis in her grip. The skin felt hot, taut like it might burst. She measured the length of him with her hands, wondering how he'd fit.

"Squeeze harder, El," he encouraged. "Use your fist."

She closed her fingers and pumped him, felt him move with her, rubbing and pressing himself fully against her hand. "I want you, I want this inside me, Max," she whispered. "Please."

His response was immediate. Once again he caught her lips in a fierce kiss as he levered his body up and moved over hers. He pressed between her knees, opening her. Dominating her. He paused, holding himself still above her as his eyes skimmed down her length. "I forgot how perfect you are."

Her gaze followed his. She looked down between their bodies, taking in her breasts, his pecs. She could see his penis protruding from the dark hair between his legs. Moisture leaked out from the tip, the head swollen and red, like an overripe plum.

She licked her bottom lip, wondering briefly what that plum would taste like. That thought disappeared as Max lowered himself, bringing his erection directly against her wet, sensitive center. Reason melted away, leaving only feeling and sensation in its wake. He moved his hips, stroking the full length of his shaft against her mound.

She felt fevered, rushed. She shuddered as he settled the fat head of his erection at her opening. Rolling her hips eased the ache in a small way, but she knew only one thing would make it better. She raked his sides with her nails, wanting him to hurry.

Max had other ideas. He caught her mouth in a bruising onslaught. Then he captured her hands and stretched them over her head. He was in control.

The increased pressure this position put on their joined hips made her tremble. "This is making me crazy."

"You mean this?" He dipped his mouth to tease the tips of her breasts again. He licked them, then blew a hot breath across her wet skin. Her nerve endings felt as if they'd been jolted by electricity.

"Or did you mean this?" He swiveled his hips, grinding his erection against her clitoris.

She bucked beneath him, wanting to get closer, wanting him to move faster, harder. Nothing was enough.

"I want it all." She arched backwards, offering herself wholly. The tension inside her escalated. It had been too long since she felt anything like this.

His mouth skimmed down her body. He released her hands and her greedy fingers entwined in his hair, cradling his head as he plundered her neck, her breasts.

His fingers stroked down her side, to her hip, then lower, seeking the heat between her thighs. He pressed a finger up inside of her. "You're wet."

"For you," she whispered.

"The magic words." He levered himself up and stared down at her. "You're beautiful, Ellie."

His swollen cock nudged against her labia, parting her. She welcomed him, feeling impatient and shaky at the same time. She bit her lip, concentrating on the marvel of what he made her feel. He pressed into her. His penis felt massive.

He withdrew slightly. "Damn, you're tight."

She panicked. "Don't stop." She clutched at his shoulders. "Please don't stop."

"I couldn't if I tried. Let's try this." He moved his legs, changing positions slightly before pushing into her again. "Raise your knees. Wrap one leg around my waist."

She did as he asked and felt him slowly sink in. For a moment, she felt overwhelmed with sensation; there was too much heat, too much mass.

Max lowered his mouth, spreading kisses lightly across her face. "That's it, sweetheart," he encouraged. "Let me in, El."

That's when she felt it. Him entering her. Inch by inch by inch. The pressure grew irresistible. She felt lost, out of control.

"Look at me, Ellie," he commanded. "Tell me what you want."

She met his gaze. "I want more, Max."

"Hold on, then."

He began thrusting deeply, eyes still fastened on hers. The tempo changed, increased. She blinked, unable to take the intensity of his look as his movements fanned her desire. She strained to meet him thrust for thrust, wanting him closer.

"You got it." He punctuated words with his body. "You've. Got. What. I. Need."

His thrusts grew deeper, longer. More eloquent. Then faster, harder. And more powerful.

Sensations exploded as Max shouted her name. Ellie felt a rush, then climaxed with a passion that matched his.

9

Max had felt the earth shift. It had happened once before, long ago. Both times he'd had his cock buried deep inside Ellie.

He stared down at her. Her eyes were half closed, her glorious golden hair mussed wildly on the pillows. Gathering her into his arms, he rolled onto his back, settling her on his chest. His cock was still hard, still deeply embedded in her tight sheath as the aftershocks of his climax vibrated in his veins. If she noticed that he kept their bodies linked, she didn't protest.

He wanted to take her again, but she had to be exhausted. It was almost three and neither of them had had much sleep the night before. At the moment, though, he felt energized, his body ready to go again. And since he didn't have to replace a condom . . .

His cock swelled. In its happy place, undoubtedly. A very happy place.

The condom issue had always been second nature to him, never optional, but suddenly the thought of wearing one again was objectionable. He couldn't. At least never with Ellie. And the thought of having sex with anyone but her was incomprehensible. Great. *That* warning certainly wasn't printed on the outside of the condom box.

Ellie stirred on top of him. His body reacted, his cock thickening, lengthening. She lifted her head and looked at him with uncertainty. "You're still hard. Did you . . ."

"Come? Oh, yeah. But with you, my dick gets greedy." He pressed a kiss to her forehead and started to withdraw. "I'll pull out."

"I'm okay with it." Her inner muscles clenched tightly, catching the head of his cock.

The sensation was exquisite, almost painful. *Good* painful. Max drew a sharp breath, not daring to move. He was mostly out now. "You sure you can take it again?"

"No. But I'd like to try."

He exhaled and flexed back in with one long, slow push. He paused. "I probably shouldn't ask this, but you're so damn tight, honey. Have you been with anyone since Stefan?"

She closed her eyes and shook her head. "Pretty much not him, either."

"I should apologize for asking, Ellie." He pressed a kiss to each of her eyes, then hugged her close. "And this sounds chauvinistic as hell, but I'm glad you haven't been with anyone."

She didn't say anything, and for a moment, Max worried that he'd stepped over the line. Shit, he'd probably obliterated the line. With Ellie he wanted to talk after sex—deep, heavy conversations. Conversations they should probably continue outside of bed. "Look, El—"

She cut him off by licking one of his nipples. "I

thought we were going to make love again." She nibbled now.

His body responded, going from zero to sixty in a nanosecond. He pumped his hips, jacking his cock into her. Ellie tilted her hips, pressing back to take Max in fully. Then she swiveled her pelvis.

The move had him gritting his teeth. "Keep that up and I won't last three strokes."

"You mean this?" She did it again. "Oops."

"Oops, my ass."

She grinned. "I think I like being on top. Nice to have the upper hand for a change."

"Oh yeah?" He dropped a hand to her hips, holding her in place while his other hand tunneled between their bodies. He speared his fingers through her damp pubic hair, his thumb stroking across her clit, coaxing a shudder from her. Then he eased his fingers lower, to her tender insides where her skin was stretched and swollen around his embedded cock. "The question is, can you keep the upper hand?" He stroked her clit again.

"Max!" She jerked involuntarily, taking him in deeper.

He caught her nipple in his mouth and sucked as he thrust into her again and again. She groaned and pleaded for more. Max was glad to oblige, shifting to her other breast and suckling that nipple every bit as thoroughly.

Ellie was close to climax again. He gently scored her skin with his teeth, then bit softly. She came undone, her body pistoned, ever faster, stroking up and down, rapid-fire.

When it was over, Max withdrew. He was still ready, still wanted more. But staying inside her would cripple him. Blood had to flow to other parts of his anatomy besides his cock.

"I'll be right back." He pressed a kiss to her forehead before climbing out of bed. He went into the bathroom but when he returned with a damp cloth and towel, he found that she'd already drifted off. He debated briefly about going to his own room. They both needed sleep.

But there would be plenty of time to sleep next week.

He washed her as best he could without waking her, then dried her. Then he climbed in beside her and pulled her close.

Late the next morning Ellie showered and put on a two-piece swimsuit. Max had promised to show her the island's waterfall.

She felt sore but satisfied. And wanton. They had made love twice during the night and again at sunrise. Afterwards she'd fallen into an unbelievably deep sleep.

Her nervousness about doing it was gone. In its place was a worry about not doing it. What would she do when their week was over?

Don't think about it. Her time with Max had barely begun. And she didn't want to waste one moment fretting about the future. For now, she'd simply take everything he would give her.

She found him downstairs, on the patio, talking on his cell phone. He disconnected as soon as she walked out, but still she frowned. Out of nowhere came a feeling of possessiveness. This was her week, damn it. Or was it?

She paused, realizing she thought in terms of 24/7. Had she misunderstood the terms? Perhaps Max thought only the nights were for them?

"Do you need to work this morning?" she began.

He climbed to his feet and held out a chair for her. "Yes and no. I'm trying to keep the interruptions to a minimum, but a couple emergencies have popped up. I'll need to keep my cell within reach."

"Emergencies—plural? Sounds serious."

"Urgent. Actually, my staff is handling most of it, which gives me a new appreciation for their capabilities. Coffee? How did you sleep?"

"Fine. And yes to coffee." The way he morphed from talk of business to personal matters amazed her. Or did he view his time with her as just another business transaction? *A deal*? Was zipping from the bedroom to the boardroom part of his everyday routine?

"I noticed you're not limping this morning," he said. "Is the foot better?"

"Yes."

"Good."

He had picked up a carafe and filled her cup. "There are pastries in the basket. Or, if you prefer, I'll whip up an omelet."

"I usually skip breakfast, though an omelet sounds great for lunch."

He refilled his own coffee, then settled opposite her again. "Seeing as it's one o'clock, anything you eat qualifies as lunch."

"I never sleep this late." Of course, she never stayed up half the night making love, either.

Max winked. "I haven't been up that long myself." He grabbed a croissant, slathered it with butter. "By the way, I spoke with Gerard. The door at the beach house was repaired this morning. He hired a private security firm to look after the place until you get back and can review the new alarm system he's recommending."

"Private security? Does he think the guy will return there?"

"I won't take that chance. The intruder was able to override your alarm and its backup system with ease."

Ellie sipped her drink. "I wonder if I'll ever feel secure there again."

"Yes, you will, eventually. You do have to start taking security more seriously. Even after this bastard is caught."

"And do you think the police will catch him?"

"Yes. Allowing them to access your e-mail account will help. Speaking of which, if you send e-mail, or make calls from here, it's important that you don't give your location or mention that we're together. I'm working to keep news of the break-in out of the press, too."

For security reasons? she wanted to ask. Or general publicity? Was Max worried about what others would think of their deal?

She pushed her cup away.

"If you're done," Max said, "I'd like to show you the island."

As it turned out, Ellie only saw half of the island.

"The guest houses are the only things on the far end," Max said.

They were in the golf cart again. He turned off the beach and drove along a neat path that twisted beneath the canopy of trees. He stopped at a small clearing. "This is what I wanted you to see. What do you think?"

Her eyes widened, trying to take it all in. At first glance, the small lagoon looked ethereal. The water was a brilliant aqua green, and a slight waterfall gurgled melodically at the far end. She half expected fairies to

fly by. She spotted the pots of orchids. The area's natural beauty had been enhanced with several types of
flowering plants and trees.

"It's phenomenal," she said. "Someone on the island has a green thumb."

"Tyler." Max helped her out of the cart.

She followed Max to the water's edge and watched as
he spread a blanket in the shade. They hadn't brought a
basket, so the blanket wasn't for a picnic. At least not
one that involved food.

Was sex all she thought about? She turned toward
the water to divert her thoughts. The pool was crystal
clear and looked shallow. "Is it warm enough to
swim?"

"Let's find out." Max peeled off his trunks, freeing
his erection.

Ellie found it impossible not to stare. Maybe she
wasn't the only one with a *thinking* problem.

He moved close and tugged at the string ties of her
swimsuit top. "You saw the sign: No suits allowed."

Her top fell, baring her breasts.

"What sign?"

He tugged her bottoms free. "The one that's going
up tomorrow. Come here."

She stepped closer, taking pleasure in the desire
etched in his expression. The man was like a drug, and
she was an addict. He picked her up and waded into the
water. The center of the pool was deeper than she had
guessed, nearly to Max's chest. They swam the length
twice, the first time in a race. The second time in a
chase.

Max caught her near the waterfall and kissed her.
Excitement and anticipation swelled inside her chest.
They were both panting now, and not just from swim-
ming. Her arms were looped around his neck. Under

water, she pressed her pelvis against his erection. The question wasn't *if* they'd make love. It was when. Where.

Max coaxed her toward the shallow water beside the waterfall. He lifted her, sitting her on the bank, while he remained in the water. He pressed his hands to her knees, opened her.

Ellie felt an instinctive shyness at being displayed in broad daylight, but it quickly disappeared as his fingers stroked her.

"You're wet," he said.

"That happens when you swim."

He laughed, his hand moving more intimately against her. He inserted a finger into her. "Are you going to tell me that swimming makes you hot and horny, too?"

She moaned, wanting more. "No."

"Mmm. But you are hot." His thumb sought her clit, massaging it, lightly at first, then increasing the pressure until she bucked forward and grabbed his shoulders. He slid another finger up inside. Then he leaned in, licked one nipple and pulled away. Purposely holding back. Teasing her. The man was relentless.

"'Fess up, El. If swimming didn't make you hot, what did?"

"You make me hot, Max," she admitted. "Only you."

"Good. Hold on."

10

The man sat outside, on the café's patio, sipping coffee while staring at his laptop's screen. Like all hotels these days, the one he currently stayed at offered Wi-Fi, but he'd come here because it was close to the docks. His gaze swept the crowded café, a favored spot amongst tourists waiting to take one of the day cruises that departed Charleston harbor.

He set his cup aside and scrolled through the latest online version of *Hot Life*. The tabloid promised that its upcoming print edition—hitting newsstands in one week!—would feature an exclusive interview with *Il Diavolo*. The headline hinted the story would set straight all the rumors swirling about him, his former sister-in-law Ellie DeLuca, and socialite Bridgette St. Regis.

There were teaser photographs of Max DeLuca boarding his private jet in Boston, and disembarking from that same jet in New Zealand. He studied the photographs. Neither one was current. An aerial shot of the fabulous DeLuca compound near Auckland had an overlaid sketch indicating where a tent might be erected. *Celebrity Wedding*? the caption read.

Nice trick, he admitted grudgingly. Someone—his client, most likely—had handfed this news to *Hot Life*. As expected, the paparazzi had flocked to Auckland. *Fools*. Only he knew the truth, that Max DeLuca had Ellie sequestered on San Regale.

Once again he wondered about the inside source his client had. He wouldn't have found Ellie this quickly on his own.

A waiter drifted close, offering to refill his coffee. He shook his head, then took one last look at the tabloid's photographs. Time to go.

"Soon, Ella-baby." He closed his laptop and prepared to leave, his mind ticking off items on a mental checklist. He'd already found the perfect place to take her. A quiet cabin, in the middle of nowhere, two hours north. He still had a few supplies to get. Rope. Latex gloves. Food. They'd be there at least a day, until he made certain his final payment hit his account. Then the real fun would begin.

11

Max carried Ellie back to the blanket and gently lowered her. Determined to take his time, he hovered over her and kissed her mouth, long and slow. Then he nuzzled her neck, easing his way toward one of her breasts.

Her fingers were tangled in his hair, stroking, encouraging. They tightened in tactile approval when he started sucking.

After a minute, he switched to her other breast, laving that nipple with his tongue. Ellie writhed beneath him, her thighs squeezing his cock in a tempting, sensual massage, trying to rush him. Except Max refused to be rushed.

He released her nipple. His mouth made wet noises as he pressed kisses along the underside of her breast before trailing down to her navel.

He heard her sharp inhalation as his tongue delved and swirled before he dipped lower still. With teasing bites, he nipped the tender skin of her lower abdomen. His hand cupped her core, parting her, as he moved his body downward. He shifted his hands, reached beneath her buttocks, lifting her. The musky scent of her readiness perfumed the air.

Max blew softly across her damp curls before closing his mouth. His tongue drew over her, lapping at the sweetness. She tasted like heaven.

Ellie bucked, her movements frantic. "Max! Wait, I—"

He paused and looked up, his mouth bare inches from her flesh. "Do you want me to stop?"

She shook her head. "No, I'm just afraid I'll . . . climax too soon."

He started to say, *so come*, then realized the real reason she was nervous. They were having sex outdoors, in broad daylight. He sought to reassure her. "No one can see us." He eased back, but only slightly, and pressed a kiss to the inside of her knee.

"We're safe here, Ellie, okay?" He pressed a kiss lower, to the inside of her mid thigh.

"Okay."

"Relax."

She did. He lowered his mouth and felt her fingers brush his scalp. Her trust humbled him. He took his time. Soon she was thrusting beneath his hands, restless. Raising slightly. Eager for more.

He gave it. He licked, nibbled, feasted. She made sexy little noises and arched herself against his face, her hands holding him in place now. Encouraged, he pressed two fingers up inside her again, probing and stroking while his tongue teased her.

She shuddered, her breathing erratic. "If we keep this up, I'm going to lose it."

He raised his head, looking at her as he eased a third finger inside of her. She squirmed against his hand, seeking pressure, needing relief. Needing an orgasm.

"Then lose it, El. I've got you." He dropped his

mouth back to her and increased the pace, until her body tightened beneath his mouth.

Then he gently bit her, just barely catching her clit between his teeth. She screamed his name as a climax shattered her.

The ringing of a cell phone startled Ellie. She lifted her head and watched as Max pushed up and stalked toward the golf cart.

The thought of taking his cell phone and tossing it in the water was tempting. And judging by the look on his face, she'd guess he might let her. Maybe she'd even suggest it.

She pushed up on her elbows, debating about getting dressed. She studied Max, her eyes drifting lower, to his cock. His erection looked painful, straining straight out from his body. *Damn*. He'd been so focused on her that he hadn't come yet.

She narrowed her eyes, thinking about turning the tables on him for a change. About being more assertive. More aggressive.

She climbed to her feet slowly and walked up to him. He motioned her closer. He spoke in clipped monosyllables, then mouthed the word *sorry* and held up one finger, indicating she should wait.

Oh, I'll wait, she thought. *On you.*

He was distracted again. Until she dropped to her knees. That got his attention. She paused to see if he discouraged her.

He did the opposite, turning slightly toward her and spreading his legs slightly. She took advantage of the moment and cupped his testicles, massaging them gently. They felt heavy. Full. And as she caressed his sac, his cock grew longer.

She glanced up, saw that he watched her through hooded eyes. *If you're going to do it, do it.* Opening her mouth, she closed it over the head, easing in the first two inches. The heat of it surprised her. His body jerked as he drew a sharp breath.

"I've got to go," he said, voice strained.

His reaction emboldened her. She swirled her tongue on the underside of his shaft, tracing the ridge of the head. She tightened her lips, took in another inch. The width of him stretched her mouth. He was so hard, yet the skin so deliciously soft. She closed her eyes, concentrating on the clean taste of him.

His hand slid into her hair, moving the wet mass back off her shoulders. To better see?

"That feels good, sweetheart," he praised.

Encouraged, she pulled back, then pressed forward again, taking in more of him. His wet shaft glided easily over her lips. She quickly found a rhythm that mimicked the in-out of lovemaking. Then she remembered something he did that had her crazy.

When Ellie started sucking, Max's knees locked. His fingers tightened in her hair. Then abruptly he pulled away, completely.

She glanced up. "Did I do something wrong?"

He pulled her to her feet. They stood, both panting. "Hell, no! You're doing everything right. Too right."

"Are you afraid you'll come, then?"

"I know I'll come. I'm afraid I'll be too rough, El."

She smiled, pleased to know she had that effect on him. She touched his penis, felt it lurch in her hand. "We can't leave you like this."

"We're not."

Grasping her waist, Max lifted her straight up. "Wrap your legs around my hips."

As she did, she felt Max press up inside, filling her with a suddenness that stole her breath.

"Hold on. We're going to storm the beach together."

Max woke up on the fourth morning with a hard-on. Ellie was curled into a ball beside him on the bed, exhausted from making love on and off during the night.

The recriminations came out of nowhere, pounding him.

You shouldn't have walked away seven years ago. You should have told her you loved her on her wedding day. You shouldn't have avoided her all these years since Stefan's death.

All true. Damn it, he and Ellie needed to talk. About everything—their feelings, their past, their present. It was their only hope for a future together.

Which meant he needed to come clean about his real reasons for bringing her to the island. The police had made a grisly discovery that night, when Max had stayed behind at the beach house. A rape kit, they'd called it. Her attacker had brought everything he'd needed to subdue and terrorize. And that very same night, the bastard had the balls to send her another e-mail, promising to wait her out, to finish the job. Max had intercepted that message before Ellie saw it, but so far police had little luck tracing it. Her stalker was a pro, and seemed determined to get to her.

In the end, Ellie's proposed *deal* had turned out to be a convenient means to keep her out of sight, and more importantly, out of harm's way while a trap was set for her attacker. That Max hadn't told Ellie any of this made sense at one time. He hadn't wanted to upset her, hadn't wanted to risk her refusal. *Hadn't wanted to pass up the chance of seven days in her arms.*

But how would she react when he told her the truth today? The good news was, they were on an island. She couldn't run far. He debated briefly about waking her, coming clean right now. Except that would ruin some of his other plans.

He had to go to Charleston this morning, for what he hoped was the last renegotiation with Haru Mizuno. Damn it, if anything else came up with this merger, he'd consider pulling the plug. He didn't expect things to be easy, but when this many problems occurred, there was a reason—beyond Murphy's Law.

While in Charleston, Max would also sign off on a new shareholder agreement. Effective today, he was relinquishing his control of her shares. He had resisted before, because he'd wanted to keep her in his life. Now . . .

He still wanted her in his life. But only if it were her choice. Which meant giving her the freedom to walk away. His feelings for Ellie weren't simple. Or neat. Love never was. That self-admission had been difficult.

As expected, there was an outcry of resistance at his corporate headquarters over his decision to release her stock. "What if she sells out?" his attorney, also a good friend, had asked. "You could be saddled with a partner with different goals. Or worse, a hidden agenda."

"I'll deal with it. No matter what, I'll always be the majority shareholder," Max had replied.

What he didn't tell his attorney was that Ellie had given him an envelope last night, containing their original signed agreements. "It's part of our deal," she'd said. *The deal.* Well, he planned to hand those papers back to her today, along with his new ones.

Then he'd offer her a totally different proposal.

Which reminded him: he wanted to leave early and stop by a jeweler, too.

Ellie couldn't stay in bed after Max left. He had woken her the same way every morning, coaxing her up from sleep with his body before driving her crazy.

This morning had been different. Their lovemaking had been so excruciatingly slow and tender, she had gotten tears in her eyes. The tears returned now just thinking about it, making her glad she was alone.

Last night she'd been upset to learn Max had a business meeting scheduled for today. But after he'd explained how important the Japanese merger was, she'd felt bad for, well, pouting. That's when she'd decided to go ahead and give him the stock documents.

She'd gone to her room and returned with a thick envelope. He'd set it aside, unopened, refusing to discuss it before their week was up. She knew he assumed the envelope held the signed copies of the business proposal he'd sent weeks ago. How shocked would he be to learn she'd reworked the papers? That she intended to sign over all her shares of DSI to him?

Their *deal* had nothing to do with it. It's what she'd intended all along. The problem was that now she felt bad using the shares for sexual exploitation. She loved Max. And while that particular self-acknowledgment hadn't been too shocking, admitting it had uncovered a bigger truth. This morning, when Max had made love to her so gently, she'd realized she'd never stopped loving him.

And one day, one week, would never get Max out of her system.

What the hell did she do now?

* * *

Ellie checked her e-mail, relieved to note that the stalker-creep hadn't sent any new missives. Had Max's presence at the beach house that night scared him off for good? She hoped so. Being here had certainly put the incident far from her mind.

Since Max was off working, she decided to follow suit and tried to work on the design proposal for Peter Fourakis's hotel chain. But everything she came up with felt canned, forced. Which was frustrating, considering what a job like this could do for relaunching her career. A nod from a job this large, with Peter's backing, would go a long way toward erasing her social stigma. And guaranteed opportunities like this were rare. This job was in the bag, Peter had told her.

She frowned. That was part of the problem, wasn't it? Peter would accept anything she came up with. And for all the wrong reasons. While he was one of the few people not interested in her wealth, he was interested in her stake in DeLuca Shipping. Max and Peter had been intense rivals since their college days.

Damn it, she was weary of people wanting—and in some cases, not wanting—to do business with her because of the DeLuca name. Couldn't anyone understand that she wanted to make it on her own merit?

Maybe it was time to put her money where her mouth was. Sitting forward, she deleted the proposal. She would send Peter a note of explanation later.

Restless, she changed into a swimsuit and went for a walk on the beach. The weather was perfect, the sun bright. Seagulls marched along the sand, moving in unison as she approached. Then, when she got too near, they'd flap away, landing behind her. If only her problems could be sidestepped as easily.

She bent down to pick up a seashell. The sound of a

boat motor caught her attention. She held a hand above her eyes, and saw the telltale white breakwater of a large powerboat headed to the island. Max! She felt a rush of warmth low in her abdomen and headed to the dock to wait.

Then she had a better idea. He had remarked last night that the only place they hadn't made love yet was in the swimming pool. She intended to fix that.

At the house, she went to her room long enough to brush her hair and grab a towel. She had time, as the boat hadn't docked yet and had to be moored and secured.

On the patio, she angled one of the lounge chairs closer to the library doors, wanting to make certain that if Max went to his office first, he'd spot her. As she spread her towel out, she recalled their lovemaking from this morning. Max had said he couldn't get enough of her. Did he mean that?

She stretched out in the chair, then impulsively stripped off her top. If he came in with business still on his mind, she intended to distract him.

It seemed like hours passed before she heard one of the doors open. She had her eyes closed, and imagined Max looking at her. Her nipples tightened. Unable to stand it any longer, she sat up and smiled.

Then froze.

Bridgette St. Regis stood in the opening, her finger pointed at Ellie. Beside Bridgette was a man with a camera, busily snapping photographs of her. Ellie realized she had left the front door unlocked, thinking of Max walking in.

Furious, she grabbed the towel and covered herself before striding over to them. "What do you think you're doing?" she said to the man with the camera. He ignored her, continuing to take photos almost frantically.

Bridgette gave her a malicious smile. "Have you met Guido? He's under exclusive contract with *Hot Life*. You'll probably make the cover, so I'd smile."

Ellie thrust out her hand to block the lens. "Quit taking my picture," she demanded. Then she turned on Bridgette. "Max won't be happy you're here. I know you are not welcome."

"Don't underestimate my pull with Max," Bridgette said. "We've been lovers a long time."

Ellie started to speak, then stopped. She wasn't about to stand around and discuss Max with this woman. She turned and made her way into the house. She'd call Max herself and—

But just as she stepped inside, she saw Gerard Warhaven sprint through the front door. Her relief at seeing Max's security chief was tangible. "Where's Max?"

"He's not back yet. But there's a marine charter at the dock," he began. "Who came—"

His response confused Ellie. "Wait. If you didn't come with Max . . ." She slapped her forehead. *The guest houses.* Max had avoided showing her those. Now she knew why. "You've been here all along, haven't you?"

Gerard didn't deny it. "Mr. DeLuca will explain later. For now, I need you to go to your room and stay there until I get to the bottom of this." Dismissing her, he moved past her, having spotted Bridgette and the reporter by the pool.

Furious, Ellie went up the stairs and quickly threw on the first clothes she found. She was a fool to think her so-called deal had really captured Max's attention. Gerard's presence was proof that Max had a private agenda, one that he hadn't shared with her.

From the upstairs window she saw that the boat and

its driver were still moored at the dock. Grabbing her briefcase and purse, she made her way down the back staircase. From the hall, she saw Gerard and Bridgette arguing with the photographer.

Silently, Ellie slipped out a side door and hurried to the dock. Right now she wanted to get as far away as possible. The boat driver stood when she approached.

"Where's that other lady?" he asked. "She owes me fare."

Ellie climbed in the boat. "They're staying. And I'll pay double if we can leave right now."

"Money is money." The man shrugged and fired up the engine. In the distance, Ellie heard a shout. She looked up, saw Gerard frantically waving from the house.

"What about him?" the driver asked.

"Get out of here before he makes it to the dock and I'll make it triple."

Bridgette St. Regis watched the boat pull away. Scaring Ellie off had been easy. But now she had to think fast. She'd been told the island's caretaker was old. The young blond dude was a surprise, but she had yet to meet a young blond dude she couldn't handle.

She tugged her décolletage lower as she pulled a tiny cell phone out and punched in a few numbers.

"She just left. Wait at the docks and follow her so no one sees you. And send that boat back out for me!"

12

Max's cell phone rang just as he was leaving the attorney's office in Charleston.

It was Gerard. "We need to talk, boss."

The news that Bridgette had wormed her way onto the island confirmed Max's suspicion about an internal leak at DSI. What the bloody hell was going on here? Only two people knew he was at San Regale this week. His personal assistant, Joanne, and his Chief Financial Officer, Tom Breeden. Both Joanne and Tom had been with him for years and he trusted them explicitly.

"Does Ellie know Bridgette's on the island?"

"Yes. In fact, while I was rounding up the St. Regis woman and the reporter, Ms. DeLuca left," Gerard said. "She slipped out the back door and took off with the boat driver before I could stop her."

Max had just climbed into a taxicab. He paused long enough to give the driver a destination. "I'm on my way to the docks now. I'll try to catch Ellie there."

"The vessel's name is *Solo Run*. It just left minutes ago," Gerard went on. "What do you want me to do with Ms. St. Regis and the reporter? She's demanding that I call another boat for her."

"Put Bridgette on the phone. And throw that damn photographer's camera in the pool."

"Max!" Bridgette sobbed his name. "I came here to apologize and this, this, man is treating me like I'm some common criminal."

"Listen carefully, Bridgette. Because I'm not going to repeat myself. I want to know how you knew Ellie and I were on San Regale. And whom you told. Your answer will determine whether I send another chartered boat for you . . . or the sheriff's department boat."

"You wouldn't dare!"

"I would. Apparently you haven't spoken with your attorney recently. I had a restraining order drawn up, ready to go before a judge. Your counsel had suggested we could work out a more private deal, to save your father—and the world—from knowing what a menace you are."

Bridgette made a strangled sound. "You don't intimidate me, Max. And my father won't believe you over me."

Max's hand tightened on the phone. "Don't count on it. Put Gerard back on." Gerard came back on the line in an instant. "She's hiding something," Max went on. "She didn't even bother protesting her innocence. Call your sources, see what they can dig up fast on Bridgette. Then put some pressure on her, see if you can get any information."

"You got it."

"I'm almost at the waterfront now. Call me if you learn anything."

Max disconnected. He couldn't imagine what Ellie must be thinking right now. First Bridgette shows up again after Max swore the island was safe. Then Gerard waltzes in. That Gerard was just doing his job probably hadn't registered, since Max had led Ellie to believe they were alone on the island.

He thought about the legal documents she'd given him last night. He'd just opened the envelope a short time ago at the attorney's office, so they could void the agreement. He'd been flabbergasted to find that she'd signed over Stefan's shares of DSI. *You've always deserved to own the whole company. Even Stefan said so,* she had written in her note.

Damn it, he should have been honest from the beginning. As soon as he caught up with Ellie, he was going to tell her everything.

The boat driver got Ellie to the mainland in record time. She paid in cash and disembarked. The walkways were crowded. An arts and crafts show was set up, live music filled the air. People were everywhere. Tugging her briefcase strap onto her shoulder, Ellie made a beeline forward and grabbed a cab that had just swung up to unload passengers.

"The Marriott," she said as they pulled away. It was the first place that came to mind, and if they didn't have a room, she'd go elsewhere.

Right now all she wanted was to be alone, to nurse the ache in her heart and to find a place to lick her wounds in private. She'd calmed down a bit on the boat ride. Bridgette's arrival on the island, while a nuisance, wasn't the reason Ellie had left. Seeing Gerard there was.

The fact that Max hadn't told her about Gerard said it all. Their time on the island was just about *the deal.* God, what had made her think things would be different this time around? She hadn't been able to hold

Max's attention seven years ago. And nothing had changed.

To her relief, the Marriott had a room. She handed the desk clerk her credit card.

"Do you need assistance with your bags?" he asked.

"The airline lost my luggage." A small lie that avoided questions.

He nodded sympathetically. "We have a complimentary kit just for such occasions. Toothbrush, hairbrush, that sort of thing. I'll have one sent to your room."

The elevator seemed to take forever to reach the seventh floor. Once inside her room, she left the curtains drawn and stretched out on the bed. Her head ached and a lump the size of Texas was lodged in her throat.

The simple answer was: get over it. Move on. Something she should have done long before.

So be it. But first, she was going to do what she should have done seven years ago: Tell Max off. For then . . . For now . . .

Pushing up, she picked up the phone and punched in his number. There was a delay before it started to ring.

A knocking sounded at her door. She frowned as a voice called out, "Room service." Then she recalled the desk clerk's promise to send up extra toiletries. She quickly hung up the phone. Waiting to call Max when she wasn't so upset was probably wise.

"I'm coming," she called out as the knocking repeated. She grabbed a few bills from her wallet and checked the peephole. The bellman had knelt to tie a shoelace. Beside him on the floor was a paper bag.

She released the safety chain and flipped the dead bolt lock. "Here you go." She opened the door and held out the tip.

The man was wearing a black ski mask now. *He wasn't a bellman.*

"Hello, Ella-baby."

She tried to shove the door shut, but the man had already pushed into the threshold. She opened her mouth to scream, but the man punched the heel of his palm into the center of her chest, knocking her backwards.

Ellie hit the floor, pain splintering up her spine. She tried to roll to her side, to get away, but the man fell on top of her.

"Easy, now. Don't fight me," he said.

"Get off me!" She bucked against his heavier weight and managed to free one arm. She made a fist and hit him as hard as she could in the nose.

He swore, enraged, then hiked his knee up sharply between her legs, catching her pubic bone. She screamed as his fist swung up.

Everything slowed. Her life, her regrets flashed before her eyes as the man's punch exploded solidly against her chin.

Max found the boat, but had already missed Ellie. The boat's driver recalled her getting into a taxicab, making Max wonder if she had gone to the airport. It would make sense that she'd want to leave, to go home. He'd already tried her cell phone, but Gerard answered. She'd left her phone on the island.

Hailing another cab, Max headed to the airport. The Charleston terminal wasn't that big. Chances were good he'd find her there. His cell phone rang, but had stopped by the time he withdrew it. Missed call, the display read.

He quickly checked the call log, and was surprised

to see Marriott. On a hunch, he hit Redial and asked for Ellie DeLuca's room.

"We don't have a guest registered under that name, sir."

He started to disconnect, then stopped. "Wait! Check under Ellie McMann."

There was silence, then, "Hold please. I'll ring that room now."

Relief that he'd located her battled with irritation that she'd left to begin with. The phone rang but Ellie didn't answer. When voice mail picked up, Max disconnected. Maybe she was in the shower. Or had left to get something to eat.

He leaned toward the driver. "There's been a change. I need to go back downtown. To the Marriott."

Max's phone rang again. This time it was Gerard.

"I've located Ellie," Max said. "I'm on my way to her hotel now. How's it going there?"

"I tried the good-guy routine and asked Bridgette who she knows at DeLuca Shipping, besides you. At first she clammed up, then she said she and a fellow named Richard Nolls dated casually. I called Nolls, who—get this—works in Data Processing. As soon as I mentioned Bridgette's name, Nolls cracked. He admitted tapping your secretary's e-mail and giving Bridgette your itinerary."

"I want Nolls arrested."

"It's already in the works. He's agreed to cooperate in hopes of a lighter punishment. He says he thinks Bridgette was relaying the information to someone else. Nolls thought she was selling it to the paparazzi for money."

Bridgette didn't need money. "Have you told Bridgette what Nolls said?"

"Yes. I thought she was going to have a fit—then

she calmed and demanded to talk to her lawyer. Says she won't say another word without him present."

"That's an odd request, seeing as she hasn't been charged with anything. Yet." The cab jerked to a halt just then, in front of the Marriott. "Look, I'm at Ellie's hotel now. Keep at it. I'll call you shortly."

Max stood near the elevator, waiting for the general manager. As was standard at any reputable hotel, guest room numbers were not given out. However, when the desk clerk dialed Ellie's room, she still didn't answer.

The general manager, who recognized the DeLuca name, seemed willing to give Max the benefit of the doubt. "I'll check Ms. McMann's room personally."

Just then the desk clerk rushed over and spoke in hushed tones to the manager. Max heard every word. "We've had a complaint of screams coming from room 713."

Max turned and raced to the elevators. If anything happened to Ellie . . .

"Have security meet us on the seventh floor," the manager said from behind him.

When they arrived, Max sprinted down the hall toward Ellie's room. He pounded on the door, called her name, but there was no response. Then he heard a scream.

"Ellie!" he shouted. "I'm here!"

The manager had his master key card out but was so flustered he fumbled and dropped it. Max scooped it up and swiped it, then shoved the door. It only opened a few inches before the security chain caught.

"Get back!" Max took a step backwards and kicked the door. On the third try the frame splintered and the door swung free.

Max rushed in. Ellie was on the far side of the room, using the broken base of a lamp to hold off a man who wore a mask. Max tackled the man from behind.

They rolled, crashing into the sofa. The man jabbed Max in the ribs, but Max countered, subduing him with a couple of satisfying punches to the jaw.

Two more men had bustled into the room. "Hotel security," one of them shouted. The general manager pointed to the man Max straddled. "Hold him for the police."

Max waited until the security agents had grabbed Ellie's assailant, then he headed straight for Ellie. She had dropped to the floor and was crying as she talked to the manager. Max knelt in front of her, wanted to pull her into his arms. A large bruise had risen on her cheek, making him want to go back and stomp the man into the ground.

He focused on Ellie. "Tell me where you're hurt."

"I'll be okay." She touched her cheek, then grimaced. "I think."

"Hold on." Ignoring her protests, Max carried her to the loveseat in the far corner. The general manager appeared with an ice bucket and towel.

Max grabbed them and made a makeshift ice pack. "This might sting."

"I'll do that." Ellie took the icy towel from him and gingerly pressed it to her cheek. "How did you know I needed help? Wait—you had me followed, right? I should have known Gerard wasn't your only stoolie."

"Look, I know that you're mad, but you don't understand what's been going on."

"You're right. I *don't* understand. And I *am* mad. But at least this guy's been caught. I don't have to worry who's following me now." She looked at him, her eyes distant. "We both got what we wanted. Now, if you'll excuse me." She pushed to her feet.

Max reached to help her, but she avoided his hands. He reminded himself that she had a right to be angry. He and Ellie needed to clear the air about a lot of things. Their past. Her marriage to Stefan. This whole disaster with Bridgette.

But now wasn't the time.

"There's a room across the hall," the general manager offered. "Ms. McMann?"

"We'll talk later," Max promised. When Ellie left, he walked back toward the man who had attacked her. The security agents had him sitting up on the bed, his hands cuffed behind his back. They had removed his mask. Blood trickled from his nose.

Suddenly Max had a hunch who Bridgette was giving information to. "How much did Bridgette pay you to harass Ellie?"

The man gave him a cold stare and shook his head. "I ain't talking with anyone but my lawyer."

"Funny, that's the same thing she said. Just remember: the DA generally cuts a deal with the first one arrested. Bridgette might beat you to the punch." Max glanced at the hotel's security agent. "Make sure the police know this man is wanted in connection with a home invasion and assault in Massachusetts. I want to make damn sure he never gets out of jail."

The police arrived a short time later. Ellie's assailant refused to identify himself and was promptly hauled off to jail.

Max was now in the room down the hall with Ellie, waiting for the police to complete her statement. The hotel's general manager hovered in the background, profusely apologetic.

Gerard showed up and reported that Bridgette and the reporter were being charged with trespassing. "I told the sheriff other charges would be forthcoming. Bridgette was nearly hysterical to learn Ellie's assailant had been captured. She's also insisting that you still care for her, that you won't press charges no matter what she's done."

Max shook his head. Bridgette's possessiveness had been a problem back when they were dating, but he had no idea she would go to these extremes. "Let me know what else you find out."

When Gerard left, the officer who'd been talking with Ellie motioned to Max. Max moved up and sat beside Ellie.

"The man we arrested," the officer said, "has quite a record. He's also wanted for questioning in the disappearance of at least three other women. It appears he works for hire. Do you have any enemies, Ms. DeLuca?"

"Enemies?" Ellie blinked.

"This may be more about my enemies than hers." Max explained what Gerard had shared about Bridgette.

They talked for a while with the officer. By the time they were finally alone, it was dark outside. "Stay as long as you like," the general manager said before leaving. "Just call room service when you're ready for food."

"I'm really not hungry," Ellie said.

"That's understandable," Max said. "It's been a hellacious day."

She nodded. "At least it's over."

"The worst of it's over, yes. However, you and I still need to talk."

Ellie rubbed her forehead. "If it's about the stock, I'll instruct my attorney to cooperate fully with yours."

"You probably won't believe this, but I went to my attorney's today intending to pick up transfer documents relinquishing my control of your shares. Instead, I get there and find that you had signed over yours."

"The shares weren't really mine. They were Stefan's."

"We can argue that point later." He took her hands in his, squeezed them. "The reason I took you to the island was to keep you safe, El. While I tried to set a trap for this creep. Bridgette's involvement blindsided me."

She tried to tug her hands free, but couldn't. "You should have told me about Gerard."

"You're right. I handled it all wrong." He paused, took a deep breath. "Hell, I've handled this wrong for seven years. So I'm just going to cut to the bottom line. I want a new deal, El. A chance to start over."

"Another seven days?" She looked uncertain.

"No. I'm talking seven weeks, seven months. Seven eternities. And not just on an island. I want a chance to make it work everywhere, El." He linked their fingers together. "What do you say?"

She closed her eyes, and when she opened them, she smiled. "It's a deal, Max."

Read on for an excerpt from Rebecca Zanetti's
blazing hot romantic suspense series, The Requisition Force.

THE HIDDEN

*The Requisition Force isn't your typical government unit. Its
targets are personal. Its methods are deadly. And its agents
risk it all . . .*

Pippa Cracker escaped. That's what she tells herself to manage
the panic attacks. Or when she wishes for something beyond
her quiet haven—such as friends, the chance to travel, or even
a lover. She can't imagine feeling safe enough to chase those
dreams. But now she is off the grid, and she has a sweet little
house with plenty of interesting things to watch through the
window. Like her new neighbor, with his startling green eyes,
killer smile, and sexy bad-boy tattoo . . .

Malcolm West wants to be left alone to forget the hell he unleashed in his last assignment as an undercover cop. A back-
woods bungalow sounds like the perfect place to start over.
Until he discovers he's been set up. Somehow, he's moved
right next door to a beautiful, frightened woman with ties to
one of the most powerful homegrown terrorists in America.
She's being hunted, and even smart prey can't stay hidden for
long. If Malcolm doesn't dig deep and let loose the banished
killer inside himself, Pippa's fears could come true faster than
the flip of a bolt ina lock . . .

Praise for the Bestselling Novels of Rebecca Zanetti

**"Fast-paced romance . . . very compelling. Highly
recommended."**
—*Library Journal*

"Hot and fast from beginning to end."
—Kate Douglas on *Fated*

"Sizzling sex scenes and a memorable cast."
—*Publishers Weekly* on *Claimed*

The day he moved in next door, dark clouds covered the sky with the promise of a powerful storm. Pippa watched from her window, the one over the kitchen sink, partially hidden by the cheerful polka dotted curtains. Yellow dots over a crisp white background—what she figured happy people would use.

He moved box after box after box through the two-stall garage, all by himself, cut muscles bunching in his arms.

Angles and shadows made up his face, more shadows than angles. He didn't smile, and although he didn't frown, his expression had settled into harsh lines.

A guy like him, dangerously handsome, should probably have friends helping.

Yet he didn't. His black truck, dusty yet seemingly well kept, sat alone in the driveway containing the boxes.

She swallowed several times, instinctively knowing he wasn't a man to cross, even if she was a person who crossed others. She was not.

For a while she tried to amuse herself with counting the boxes, and then guessing their weight, and then just studying the man. He appeared to be in his early thirties, maybe just a couple of years older than she.

Thick black hair fell to his collar in unruly waves, giving him an unkempt appearance that hinted nobody took care of him. His shoulders were tense and his body language fluid. She couldn't see his eyes.

The damn wondering would keep her up at night.

But no way, and there was absolutely no way, would she venture outside to appease the beast of curiosity.

The new neighbor stood well over six feet tall, his shoulders broad, his long legs encased in worn and frayed jeans. If a man could be hard all over, head to toe, even in movement, then he was.

He was very much alone as well.

A scar curved in a half-moon shape over his left eye, and some sort of tattoo, a crest of something, decorated his muscled left bicep. She tilted her head, reaching for the curtains to push them aside just a little more.

He paused, an overlarge box held easily in his arms, and turned his head, much like an animal rising to attention.

Green. Those eyes, narrow and suspicious, alert and dangerous, focused directly on her.

She gasped. Her heart thundered. She fell to the floor below the counter. Not to the side, not even in a crouch, she fell flat on her ass on the worn tile floor. Her heart ticking, she wrapped her arms around her shins and rested her chin on her knees.

She bit her lip and held her breath, shutting her eyes.

Nothing.

No sound, no hint of an approaching person, no rap on the door.

After about ten minutes of holding perfectly still, she lifted her head. Another five and she released her legs. Then she rolled up onto her knees and reached for the counter, her fingers curling over.

Taking a deep breath, she pulled herself up to stand, angling to the side of the counter.

He stood at the window, facing her, his chest taking up most of the panes.

Her heart exploded. She screamed, turned, and ran. She cleared the kitchen in three steps and plowed through the living room, smashing into an antique table that had sat in the place for more than two decades.

Pain ratcheted up her leg, and she dropped, making panicked grunting noises as she crawled past the sofa and toward her bedroom. Her hands slapped the polished wooden floor, and she sobbed out, reaching the room and slamming the door.

She scrabbled her legs up to her chest again, her back to the door, and reached up to engage the lock. She rocked back and forth just enough to not make a sound.

The doorbell rang.

Her chest tightened, and her vision fuzzed. Tremors started from her shoulders down to her waist and back up. *Not now. Not now. God, not now.* She took several deep breaths and acknowledged the oncoming panic attack much as Dr. Valentine had taught her. Sometimes letting the panic in actually abated it.

Not this time.

The attack took her full force, pricking sweat along her body. Her arms shook, and her legs went numb. Her breathing panted out, her vision fuzzed, and her heart blasted into motion.

Maybe it really was a heart attack this time.

No. It was only a panic attack.

But it could be. Maybe the doctors had missed

something in her tests, and it really was a heart attack. Or maybe a stroke.

She couldn't make it to the phone to dial for help.

Her heart hurt. Her chest really ached. Glancing up at the lock, a flimsy golden thing, she inched away from the door to the bed table on her hands and knees. Jerking open the drawer, she fumbled for a Xanax.

She popped the pill beneath her tongue, letting it quickly absorb. The bitter chalkiness made her gag, but she didn't move until it had dissolved.

A hard rapping sound echoed from the living room.

Shit. He was knocking on the door. Was it locked? Of course it was locked. She always kept it locked. But would a lock, even a really good one, keep a guy like that out?

Hell, no.

She'd been watching him, and he knew it. Maybe he wasn't a guy who wanted to be watched, which was why he was moving his stuff all alone. Worse yet, had he been sent to find her? He had looked so furious. Was he angry?

If so, what could she do?

The online martial arts lessons she'd taken lately ran through her head, but once again, she wondered if one could really learn self-defense by watching videos. Something told her that all the self-defense lessons in the world wouldn't help against that guy.

Oh, why had Mrs. Melonci moved to Florida? Sure, the elderly lady wanted to be closer to her grandchildren, but Cottage Grove was a much better place to live.

The house had sold in less than a week.

Pippa had hoped to watch young children play and frolic in the large treed back yard, but this guy didn't seem to have a family.

Perhaps he'd bring one in, yet there was something chillingly solitary about him.

Of course, she hadn't set foot outside her house for nearly five years, so maybe family men had changed.

Probably not, though.

He knocked again, the sound somehow stronger and more insistent this time.

She opened the bedroom door and peered around the corner. The front door was visible above the sofa.

He knocked again. "Lady?" Deep and rich, his voice easily carried into her home.

She might have squawked.

"Listen, lady. I, ah, saw you fall and just wanna make sure you're all right. You don't have to answer the door." His tone didn't rise and remained perfectly calm.

She sucked in a deep breath and tried to answer him, but only air came out. Man, she was pathetic. She tapped her head against the doorframe in a sad attempt to self-soothe.

"Um, are you okay?" he asked, hidden by the big door. "I can call for help."

No. Oh, no. She swallowed several times. "I'm all right." Finally, her voice worked. "Honest. It's okay. Don't call for anybody." If she didn't let them in, the authorities would probably break down the door, right? She couldn't have that.

Silence came from the front porch, but no steps echoed. He remained in place.

Her heart continued to thunder against her ribs. She wiped her sweaty palms down her yoga pants. Why wasn't he leaving? "Okay?" she whispered.

"You sure you don't need help?" he called.

Her throat began to close. "I'm sure." *Go away.* Please, he had to go away.

"Okay." Heavy bootsteps clomped across her front porch, and then silence. He was gone.

Malcolm West knew the sound of terror, and he knew it well. The woman, whoever she was, had been beyond frightened at seeing him in the window. Damn it. What the hell had he been thinking to approach her house like that?

A fence enclosed their backyards together, and he'd wondered why. Had a family shared the two homes?

He grabbed another box of shit from the truck and hefted it toward the house. Maybe this had been a mistake. He'd purchased the little one story home sight unseen because of the white clapboard siding, the blue shutters, and the damn name of the town—Cottage Grove. It sounded peaceful.

He'd never truly see peace again, and he knew it.

All of the homes the real estate company had emailed him about had been sad and run down . . . until this one. It had been on the market only a few days, and the agent had insisted it wouldn't be for long. After six months of searching desperately for a place to call home, he'd jumped on the sale.

It had been so convenient as to have been fate.

If he believed in fate, which he did not.

He walked through the simple one story home and dropped the box in the kitchen, looking out at the pine trees beyond the wooden fence. The area had been subdivided into twenty-acre lots, with tons and tons of trees, so he'd figured he wouldn't see any other houses, which had suited him just fine.

Yet his house was next to another, and one fence enclosed their backyards together.

No other homes were even visible.

He sighed and started to turn for the living room when a sound caught his attention. His body automatically went on full alert, and he reached for the Sig nestled at his waist. Had they found him?

"Detective West? Don't shoot. I'm a friendly," came a deep male voice.

Malcolm pulled the gun free, the weight of it in his hand more familiar than his own voice. "Friendlies don't show up uninvited," he said calmly, eyeing the two main exits from the room in case he needed to run.

A guy strode toward him, hands loose at his sides. Probably in his thirties, he had bloodshot brown eyes, short brown hair, and graceful movements. His gaze showed he'd seen some shit, and there was a slight tremble in his right arm. Trying to kick a habit, was he?

Malcolm pointed the weapon at the guy's head. "Two seconds."

The man looked at the few boxes set around the room, not seeming to notice the gun. Even with the tremor, he moved like he could fight. "There's nowhere to sit."

"You're not staying." Malcolm could get to the vehicle hidden a mile away within minutes and then take off again. The pretty cottage was a useless dream, and he'd known it the second he'd signed the papers. "I'd hate to ruin the yellow wallpaper." It had flowers on it, and he'd planned to change it anyway.

"Then don't." The guy leaned against the wall and shook out his arm.

"What are you kicking?" Malcolm asked, his voice going low.

The guy winced. "I'm losing some friends."

"Jack, Jose, and Bud?" Mal guessed easily.

"Mainly Jack." Now he eyed the weapon. "Mind putting that down?"

Mal didn't flinch. "Who are you?"

Broad shoulders heaved in an exaggerated sigh. "My name is Angus Force, and I'm here to offer you an opportunity."

"Is that a fact? I don't need a new toaster." Mal slid the gun back into place. "Go away."

"Detective—"

"I'm not a detective any longer, asshole. Get out of my house." Mal could use a good fight, and he was about to give himself what he needed.

"Whoa." Force held up a hand. "Just hear me out. I'm part of a new unit with, ah, the federal government, and we need a guy with your skills."

Heat rushed up Mal's chest. His main skill these days was keeping himself from going ballistic on assholes, and he was about to fail in that. "I'm not interested, Force. Now get the fuck out of my house."

Force shook his head. "I understand you're struggling with the aftereffects of a difficult assignment, but you won. You got the bad guy."

Yeah, but how many people had died In front of him? Mal's vision started to narrow. "You don't want to be here any longer, Force."

"You think you're the only one with PTSD, dickhead?" Force spat, losing his casual façade.

"No, but I ain't lookin' to bond over it." Sweat rolled down Mal's back. "How'd you find me, anyway?"

Force visibly settled himself. "It's not exactly a coincidence that you bought this house. The only one that came close to what you were looking for." He looked around the old-lady cheerful kitchen. "Though it is sweet."

Mal's fingers closed into a fist. "You set me up."

"Yeah, we did. We need you here." Force gestured around.

Mal's lungs compressed. "Why?"

"Because you're the best undercover cop we've ever seen, and we need that right now. Bad." Mal ran a shaking hand through his hair.

"Why?" Mal asked, already fearing the answer.

"The shut-in next door. She's the key to one of the biggest homegrown threats to our entire country. And here you are." Force's eyes gleamed with the hit.

Well, fuck.

Connect with

Visit us online at
KensingtonBooks.com
to read more from your favorite authors, see books
by series, view reading group guides, and more.

for sneak peeks, chances to win books and prize packs,
and to share your thoughts with other readers.

facebook.com/kensingtonpublishing
twitter.com/kensingtonbooks

Tell us what you think!

To share your thoughts, submit a review,
or sign up for our eNewsletters, please visit:
KensingtonBooks.com/TellUs.